HUCKLEBERRY SUMMER

JENNIFER BECKSTRAND

KENNEBEC LARGE PRINT
A part of Gale, Cengage Learning

GALE
CENGAGE Learning·

Farmington Hills, Mich • San Francisco • New York • Waterville, Maine
Meriden, Conn • Mason, Ohio • Chicago

GALE
CENGAGE Learning·

LIBRARY OF CONGRESS CATALOGING-IN-PUBLICATION DATA

Beckstrand, Jennifer.
    Huckleberry summer / by Jennifer Beckstrand. — Large print edition.
      pages ; cm. — (The matchmakers of huckleberry hill) (Kennebec Large
Print superior collection)
    ISBN 978-1-4104-7368-4 (softcover) — ISBN 1-4104-7368-6 (softcover)
    1. Large type books. I. Title.
PS3602.E3323H835 2015
813'.6—dc23
                                      2014037863

Published in 2015 by arrangement with Zebra Books, an imprint of
Kensington Publishing Corp.

HUCKLEBERRY SUMMER

CHAPTER ONE

Felty Helmuth took a hearty bite of the mushy concoction in his bowl. "Why, Annie Banannie. This soup is fit for a king. Is this another recipe from that new book of yours?"

Anna smiled and pushed her thick, round glasses over the bridge of her nose. "How kind of you to notice, dear. It's called Indonesian beef stew."

"It's so tender, I can't tell the beef from the potatoes."

"There is no beef. It's a vegetarian dish."

Felty winked at his wife of sixty-two years. "The name ain't quite right, don't you think?"

"Well, the recipe calls for beef, but I didn't add any beef, and I don't think it's my place to change the name of the recipe."

"Right you are, Annie. Was they out of roast at the market yesterday?"

"No, I am learning to cook vegetarian.

Aden is a vegetarian, and I don't want him to starve."

"Aden our grandson?"

Anna nodded and looked at Felty as if he were finally in on the secret.

"Banannie, Aden lives in Ohio. He don't eat your cooking more than once a year or so, but I'm sure he'd be pleased to know you are thinking of him."

"Now, Felty," Anna said. "I want Aden to come and live with us, and he's got to eat."

"Us? Why would Aden want to live with us?"

"He's going through a rough patch."

Felty reached over and patted Anna's wrinkled hand. "Don't worry yourself. All boys his age go through a rough patch."

"*Jah,* but most boys don't get arrested three times."

"He can get arrested just as easy in Wisconsin as Ohio."

Anna pursed her lips and scolded Felty with her eyes. "Boys like Aden need a wife to settle them down. A girl like little Lily Eicher."

Felty sputtered and coughed, and Anna stood up and thumped him on the back until he motioned for her to stop. "Not another one of your matchmaking schemes, Annie. I don't think my weak heart can stand it."

"Felty, your heart is fit as a fiddle. Your knees will give out long before your heart ever does."

"Not these knees. They're titanium alloy. The doctor said so." Felty stood and waltzed around the table to prove his point.

"Now, Felty. Sit and finish your supper." Anna served him another heaping helping of Indonesian beef stew, vegetarian style. "I was right about Moses and Lia, wasn't I? Moses is so happy, he's like to float off the ground. That does your heart good, doesn't it?"

"I suppose so, but what it took to get him and Lia together almost gave me an ulcer."

"Our grandchildren deserve our very best efforts. How will they ever find suitable mates if we don't help them?"

Felty plopped into his chair and kissed his wife on the cheek. "Our grandchildren will get along fine without any help from us."

"Of course they won't. Look at Moses. If we hadn't introduced him to Lia, he would still be pining over that Gingerich girl. And Aden can't seem to stay out of jail long enough to court anyone. He needs to meet Lily." Anna stuck a pat of butter on the top of a cornbread muffin and placed it on Felty's plate. "He's got to come to Huckle-

9

berry Hill, Felty."

Felty propped his elbow on the table and rested his chin in his hand. "Little Lily Eicher probably doesn't know how to cook vegetarian."

"I can teach her."

He sighed. "No doubt about that, Banannie. You are the best cook in Bonduel, Wisconsin."

CHAPTER TWO

Aden clutched the seat belt strapped across his chest and tried to breathe normally. If there was one thing that made him edgy, it was going anywhere in a car with Jamal. Well, not edgy exactly — more like terrified out of his wits. The feel of the wind whipping through his hair and the sight of telephone poles whizzing past was only fun when you didn't think you were going to die.

The whole breathing thing wasn't working. Why couldn't he maintain his calm in Jamal's car? He was Aden Helmuth, after all — the Amish guy who had no fear of chaining himself to a tree or staging a sit-in outside the mayor's office. Aden was the person brave enough for anything.

Well, almost anything. Racing down the road with Jamal, hell-bent for destruction, seemed more like foolishness than courage.

Aden didn't take his eyes from the road,

just in case his steady gaze would keep the car from crashing. "Jamal, slow down."

Jamal liked to look people in the eye when he talked to them, which was a bad thing when he drove. "Chill, man. I've driven this road hundreds of times. If we get there in time, we might get some pictures of them dumping stuff into the lake."

Aden felt his stomach lurch as Jamal took a curve about a hundred miles an hour too fast. "I'd like to get there alive."

Jamal smiled and again took his eyes off the road to look at Aden — a movement that set Aden's heart racing. "You're such a baby."

"Go ahead," Aden said, gripping the door handle until he couldn't feel his fingers, "pretend I'm the one with the problem here."

"Pilot likes the way I drive."

Aden glanced into the backseat where Pilot, his golden doodle, was thoroughly enjoying the terrifying ordeal. He poked his head out the window so far that it seemed like he'd taken half his body with him. His ears flapped in the wind and his tongue hung out of his mouth as if he were trying to catch passing insects. Pilot didn't seem to care in the least that his master would have to pry himself off the seat when they got to the lake.

Traitor.

Aden should have known better than to go anywhere with Jamal. Most of the time Jamal didn't even use his hands to drive. He liked to steer with his knee. At this point, Aden didn't care if they were on the verge of catching the idiots who'd been dumping chemicals into the lake. He'd rather be home mucking out the barn than in this car, taking his life into his own hands, or rather, putting his life in Jamal's hands.

Big mistake.

The rain announced itself like a dump truck dropping a load of gravel on top of the car. Water pelted the windshield, and Jamal flipped on the wipers to their fastest speed. It didn't matter. Neither of them could see a thing out of the windshield in the muted light of late afternoon. Even Jamal wouldn't drive blind. He slowed down and placed both hands on the steering wheel.

Aden said a prayer of thanks for rain.

Pilot pulled his head inside the car, and with what Aden could swear was a grin, shook himself hard, catapulting water droplets in every direction.

With a groan, Jamal wiped the back of his neck. "I just treated these leather seats, you stupid dog."

"At least he doesn't complain about your driving."

Jamal pushed the button and rolled up Pilot's window. Pilot responded by balancing on the edge of the backseat and sticking his head between Jamal and Aden.

Jamal grimaced. "Ya gotta love the smell of wet dog."

"Jamal, they're not going to be up there when it's pouring like this. Let's turn around."

"They probably think this is the best time to dump stuff in the lake. No one up there to catch them."

Aden tried one more time, even though he knew it was beating a dead horse. "The roads are bad."

"Pilot's not complaining."

Aden closed his mouth and held on to the door handle. Better shut up and not divert Jamal's attention. The guy needed to concentrate on driving.

He negotiated a sharp curve, and they both gasped as an elk with an enormous rack of antlers appeared in the middle of the road. He stood as if he were carved from stone and certainly wasn't going to be the one to move.

Jamal swerved hard to the right. The car

14

lost traction on the wet road and slid out of control. Aden felt as if he were living the next few seconds in slow motion. His insides lurched as the car careened down a shallow embankment and splashed into the lake.

Aden's seat belt snapped tight, and it felt like someone had smacked him in the chest with a two-by-four. "Pilot!" he yelled.

In the immediate calm after the crash, Aden took a labored breath and turned to find his dog. Pilot lay on the floor in the back and lifted his head as if Aden had awakened him from a long nap. Aden reached over with a trembling hand and patted Pilot's head. "You okay, buddy?"

To Aden's horror, the car made a sickening creak, tilted forward, and began to sink.

Jamal looked even more dazed than Aden felt. His hands still gripped the steering wheel as his eyes grew wide with every movement of the car. "We're sinking."

The lake in late April was icy cold. Aden felt the water seep into his boots. Biting pain crawled up his legs. "We've got to get out of here."

Jamal jiggled the latch of his seat belt. "It's stuck." He panted and groaned and strained at the latch. Aden, always calm in an emergency, quickly released both of their latches as the water rose to the level of his seat.

"Come on, buddy." Aden got a firm hold of the collar around Pilot's neck while lifting the door handle and pushing hard with his elbow. When the door wouldn't budge, he put his whole back into it. He couldn't open it. The frigid water bubbling at his waist matched the raw terror crawling up his spine. They would be underwater in a matter of seconds.

Jamal pounded on his door and screamed in panic. "It won't open."

"The water is pushing against it," Aden yelled over the deafening roar of rushing water and shrinking air.

Jamal shoved his fists against the windshield. "We're going to die, Aden. We're going to die!"

Pilot struggled onto the backseat, keeping his head above the rising water, and barked as if that would keep the lake at bay.

As the water poured in, Aden propped his feet on the seat and crouched with his head against the ceiling. Jamal did the same. "Help us, Lord," Aden cried. He took in great gulps of air with each breath in case they would be his last. His heart hammered against his chest as he repeated his desperate prayer over and over in his mind.

Aden, thou art careful and troubled about

16

many things, but one thing is needful.

He was surely dying. Random scripture didn't usually leap to his mind.

Probably a foot of air remained in the car.

Jamal became incoherent with fear. "We're going to die. We're going to die."

Pilot whined and bumped his nose against the ceiling. Aden's heart nearly broke. Pilot was an innocent victim of Jamal's reckless-ness. "Please, Lord, could you save my dog?"

Open the door.

Open the door? It wouldn't budge.

Lean not to thine own understanding. Open the door.

Even with his mind racing in terror, Aden was smart enough to recognize the source of that inaudible voice.

"Jamal, don't let go," he said. He grabbed Jamal's hand, took a deep breath, and plunged beneath the water. Jamal struggled briefly as he probably wondered why Aden was pulling him to his death. Then his grip tightened, and he let Aden pull him down.

It was almost too dark to see, but Aden felt his way to the latch. He pulled it up while pushing on the door with both his feet. The door swung open so easily that he barely had to exert effort at all.

Using the open door as leverage, he pulled

himself out of the car with his free hand and tugged Jamal out with him. His lungs burned with the need for air, but how far under the water were they?

Reaching his hand to the sky, he cried out silently for God.

But it was too much. He felt completely spent. He hadn't the strength to get them to the surface, no matter how close it might be.

Just as Aden thought his lungs might explode, someone from above grabbed his hand and forcefully pulled him upward. He and Jamal were on the surface in a matter of seconds. He let go of Jamal's hand so they could both tread water. The air tasted better than anything Aden had ever experienced. He filled his lungs with the sweet flavor and thought he would never want for another thing in his whole life.

Aden whipped his head around and looked for his rescuer. Not a soul to be seen either in the water or on the shore. They were alone. The rain beat a lonely cadence against the surface of the lake.

Someone had pulled them up. Aden had felt the touch of a warm hand as plainly as he had felt Jamal's fingers in his grasp. He gasped for breath as pure astonishment overtook him. Who had saved him, and why

18

was he worth such a miracle?

Jamal flailed about until Aden pulled Jamal's arm around his neck and paddled to shore. Jamal, panting with exhaustion, crawled out of the water and lay down on the jagged rocks. Anything was more comfortable than a watery grave.

Aden turned and swam away from shore.

"Where are you going?" Jamal called.

"I've gotta get my dog."

Jamal sat up and pointed a shaky finger. "Look."

Pilot's nose bobbed to the surface, and Aden watched in relief as his dog paddled to shore with those giant paws of his. Aden followed him out of the water and threw his arms around his best friend. Warm tears coursed down his icy cheeks as he buried his face in Pilot's waterlogged fur. "Good boy, smart boy. Good, good boy." A sob tore from his lips. "Thank you, Lord."

Pilot wagged his tail, but otherwise stood at attention while Aden blubbered out his feelings.

It was still rainy and cold, but the temperature did nothing to calm Aden's racing heart. It might as well have been a hundred degrees outside.

He brushed his hand along Pilot's fur as he willed his breathing to slow down. What had just happened? He'd heard a voice. There was no doubt in his mind where that voice came from. The question now was, what was he going to do about the message he'd received?

Bowing his head, Aden breathed out a silent prayer of immense gratitude and longing. His life had been on one path, and he sensed God trying to make some adjustments. The accident was his wake-up call. But what did the Lord want him to awaken to?

One thing is needful. Open the door.

He released Pilot, and the dog immediately began running up and down the shoreline exploring interesting smells as if nothing traumatic had happened.

Aden looked at Jamal, who sat on a boulder with his arms wrapped around his knees.

"You okay?" Aden asked.

Jamal stared at the spot underneath the surface where his car was buried. "I'm sure glad I spent three hours oiling the leather seats."

"They're vinyl."

"I know, but still, it was nice vinyl."

After their terrible ordeal, the relief was palpable, almost euphoric. They burst into laughter.

"At least you didn't hit the elk. You never

20

would have forgiven yourself," Aden said.

"But technically, I have polluted the lake."

Aden chuckled. "On the bright side, you don't have a car anymore, so I never have to ride with you again. Walking is a much safer form of transportation."

"Cars are plenty safe."

"Said the guy who almost killed me."

Jamal grinned and nudged Aden with his elbow. "You're such a baby."

"Said the guy who almost killed me."

"Said the guy who saved my life."

Aden shrugged off the mention of it. He knew who really saved Jamal's life today, and it wasn't Aden Helmuth. "I'm never riding in a car again."

"That could be a real problem for you, seeing as it's a long way back and we'll freeze to death if we have to walk all the way. It would be better to flag down a ride."

"After tonight, I'm never riding in a car again."

"Said the Amish guy," Jamal added.

"How appropriate."

CHAPTER THREE

Lily Eicher held tightly to the reins and carefully guided the horse up the steep drive of Huckleberry Hill. Her family's buggy wasn't as new as it used to be, and she didn't want to risk a mishap. She didn't come up to Huckleberry Hill often, only on the few Sundays a year when the Helmuths hosted *gmay,* or church, at their house, but Lily thought that Huckleberry Hill was the most beautiful spot in Bonduel, especially this time of year. It was mid June, and thick stands of maples and a variety of other trees stood at attention on the hill sporting brilliant leaves of every imaginable shade of green. In autumn, the plentiful huckleberry bushes glowed flaming red, almost hurting Lily's eyes to look at.

She crested the hill and brought her buggy to a stop in front of Anna and Felty Helmuth's house. The white railing that enclosed their porch had been painted recently, and a tidy row of purple petunias bordered the foundation. The dirt looked freshly turned. They must have planted this week.

Lily set the brake and picked up the plate of sugar cookies for the Helmuths. She'd used a heart-shaped cutter and decorated them with pink frosting and red sprinkles. They looked quite charming on her white plate.

Holding the plate with both hands, Lily tiptoed across the grass, which still felt a bit soggy from last night's rain. She heard a dog bark and frowned at how her heart jumped into her throat. No need to panic. The Helmuths' dog, Sparky, was a little white poodle that wouldn't even nip at her heels.

Hearing the barking again, she glanced behind her and thought she might faint. An enormous tan bear loped toward her, barking enthusiastically. She gasped and threw caution to the wind. Balancing her plate in one hand, she picked up her skirts and scaled the porch steps in a single bound.

But it was too late. She turned to face her attacker as the bear jumped. Since she wasn't tall, the animal easily planted his front paws on her shoulders, knocking the cookies out of her hand and pinning her

23

back against the Helmuths' front door. She cried out in alarm and tried to shield her face from those razor-sharp teeth as the beast opened his mouth. Her heart pounded in her throat.

The animal licked her face and nudged her cheek with his moist nose. Not a bear. It wasn't a bear.

It was a dog. A big, humongous, slobbery dog.

It might not be a bear, but she was still going to die.

"Pilot, get down!" A young man jogged across the yard and stomped up the porch steps. He grabbed the animal firmly by the collar and yanked him away from Lily. Smiling as if he were about to burst into laughter, he vigorously scratched the dog's head. "Sorry. He's a real frisky dog. Wants to be friends with everybody."

Lily put her hand to her throat and tried to catch her breath. She swallowed hard, pushing the tears back with every breath. No need to cry.

The young man seemed unconcerned about Lily's distress even though she'd probably have nightmares for weeks. Not only did she have dog slobber all over her face, but wispy strands of her hair had escaped from her *kapp* and tickled the nape of her neck.

To add to her embarrassment, the young man fell silent and stared at her as if she were a sweet roll in a bakery. What exactly did he think he was doing? Could he see the trembling she tried so hard to subdue?

Lily lowered her eyes self-consciously. Her cookies lay in a pathetic heap on the porch floor.

The dog lunged for a cookie, but the young man held him back. "No, Pilot. Those aren't yours." The young man pointed to the floor. "Sit. Sit." The dog immediately sat on his haunches, cocked his head to one side, and studied Lily's face as if waiting for her approval.

Or deciding whether to give his.

The young man bent down, gathered up Lily's cookies, and arranged them on the plate. He stood and handed her the sorry-looking baked goods. The frosting was smashed every which way and most of the sprinkles had stayed behind on the porch. Bits of dirt and leaf fragments clung tenaciously to the frosting. She wanted to cry.

"I'm really, really sorry about that. Sometimes Pilot doesn't realize how big he is. He probably terrifies someone as petite as you."

She would not melt into a puddle of quivering nerves right there on the porch.

Would not.

Holding tightly to her plate, Lily willed her hands to stop shaking.

The young man's striking green eyes momentarily distracted her. They were the color of maple leaves at the height of summertime. Green eyes and a light dusting of freckles across his nose — a fascinating combination on his face. A jagged scar cut a path through his left eyebrow, succeeding in making him look more rugged. And handsome.

Too handsome. How did he expect a girl to keep her wits about her?

His imposing height didn't help. He stood well over six feet. His height made him seem powerful, like a man in charge of his own life.

Lily shook her head to clear her thoughts. Her near-death experience with that bear-dog must have addled her brain.

How long had she been staring?

The corners of the young man's lips turned down. "I'm really sorry. But please don't be mad at my dog. He's just a puppy at heart, and he would never bite anyone."

Trying to salvage what was left of her pride, Lily cleared her throat and straightened her apron.

The young man's face relaxed into a

26

smile. "Go ahead. You can pet him. He won't bite."

The last thing Lily wanted to do was pet that beast, but the young man seemed so eager, she couldn't refuse. She held her breath as the dog sniffed her hand and then licked it with his germy tongue. Where was the hand sanitizer when she needed it? Keeping her plate of ruined cookies out of reach of that mouth, she patted the dog exactly three times on the head before pulling her hand back to the safety of her apron pocket.

The young man looked a little disappointed at her obvious lack of affection for his dog, but he soon returned to his good humor. He reached past Lily and opened the front door for her. "My name's Aden. Don't be mad, okay?" The dog twitched his ears. "Stay out here, Pilot."

The Helmuths' front door opened into their kitchen and great room. The kitchen smelled of cinnamon and some exotic spice Lily couldn't begin to identify. She stepped into the room with Aden right behind her. The dog stayed on the porch as if the thought of misbehaving was the furthest thing from his mind.

Sparky, the Helmuths' dog, rose from a rug in the great room and waddled to Aden.

Aden cooed and scratched behind Sparky's ears before Sparky padded out the door, sat down next to Pilot, and stared into the house. Lily cocked an eyebrow. It looked as if she were protesting Pilot's banishment.

Although she didn't see him, Lily could hear Felty Helmuth's booming singing voice floating in the air.

"I need no mansions here below for Jesus said that I could go to a home beyond the sky not made with hands."

"Dawdi," Aden called.

Dawdi? Felty was Aden's grandfather? That explained the height. The Helmuths had always been a tall family.

The singing stopped, and Felty shuffled down the hall. He flashed Lily a bright smile. "Well, my goodness, Aden. What a beautiful young lady you have brought for us!"

"I think she's here to see *Mammi,* but I don't know. She doesn't say much."

To her dismay, Lily realized she hadn't said a word since she had set foot on Huckleberry Hill.

"Pilot scared her."

Her profound embarrassment gave her a voice. "Anna asked me to stop by." Lily cringed when the words came out of her mouth. Squeaking was not her usual mode

28

of communication.

Aden seemed to want to help her out. "She brought cookies."

Felty took a good look at the smashed cookies, picked one off the plate, and bit into it.

"Oh," Lily managed to say before the entire cookie disappeared into Felty's mouth. That one had a dead ant half-buried in the frosting.

Felty licked his fingers and smacked his lips. "Delicious. The president of Hawaii never ate a cookie that good. And the ants give it extra protein."

He winked and teased a smile onto Lily's lips.

"Look who's here."

Lily turned to see Anna Helmuth enter the kitchen like a fresh spring breeze. Anna, who moved like someone much younger than eighty-one, had a perpetual twinkle in her eye, as if she would burst into laughter at the slightest provocation. She threw out her arms and gave Lily a sort of sideways hug so that she didn't disturb the plate of cookies still in Lily's hand.

"How nice of you to come today," Anna said, looking at Aden and nodding. "Have you met our grandson?"

"She's only met Pilot," Aden said. "He

made an impression on her."

Anna waved her hand in the direction of the open door. Pilot still sat on the front porch, twitching his tail, probably hoping to be invited in. "Oh, that dog. He is a bit of a handful, but I know you will fall in love with him, by and by." Anna grinned as if she weren't saying what she truly meant.

It seemed Aden felt bad about the cookies after all. "She brought cookies."

Lily held out the plate for Anna to see. "I dropped them."

"Pilot knocked them out of her hand," Aden said.

Anna shook her finger at Pilot in mock scolding. "That dog is a troublemaker, to be sure, but he has a heart of gold. You'll never, ever know a better dog."

"Uh-huh," Lily murmured, unconvinced. The Helmuths could adore that dog if they wanted to, but Lily would be perfectly content to never lay eyes on it again.

Anna took the plate from Lily and set it on the table. "*Cum,* sit down," she said, motioning to a chair at the table. "Let's have a talk." Anna closed the door. Lily felt almost sorry for the dogs. They looked so lonely.

Aden leaned over and kissed his mammi on the cheek. "I'd better get busy on those poles or you won't have any beans this year."

"*Nae,* Aden, sit down. You work too hard, and we won't be but a minute. Cum, Felty. You can sit next to me."

Aden shrugged good-naturedly and sauntered around the table.

Felty pulled the chair out for Anna to sit. Lily was surprised when Aden did the same for her. Amish men weren't usually so accommodating. It appeared Aden had learned a few things from his grandfather.

After Felty sat down, he took Anna's hand and squeezed it. Lily glanced at Aden and folded her arms tightly around her waist. She wasn't taking any chances.

Anna leaned forward and smiled sweetly. "Now, dear, as you might have guessed, Felty and I are not getting any younger. We need a girl like you to help us around the house and pick tomatoes and such. I can't tend to vegetables like I used to. Would you like to work for us this summer? Three days a week."

Lily gave Anna a half smile. She knew she should be grateful for such an offer, but her nerves always seemed to get the better of her. She wasn't used to venturing out of her comfort zone, even in something so small as a job away from home. Of course it was a good thing. Of course Dat would want her to be brave. She sat up straight and tried to look plucky.

"Oh, I think that would be nice," Lily said. "But I don't know how you like things done. What if I don't do a *gute* job?"

Anna didn't seem discouraged. "You will do fine. Your mother says you are a hard worker, and I remember the day of Bielers' barn raising. You stuck with the dishes after everyone else had done, and you picked up nails and construction trash until it got too dark to see."

Lily shook her head. "I didn't want anyone who drove by to get a flat tire, and garbage should never be left on the ground."

Aden hadn't taken his gaze from her face since they sat down at the table. His staring proved the most uncomfortable thing of all.

"And you've befriended Schrock's special daughter too. Such a thoughtful girl," Anna said, reaching over the table and taking Lily's hand. "I know you are the best girl for this job, and I'm never mistaken about such things."

Lily's uneasiness grew as she worried that Anna's expectations were too high. "I don't know if I can be the best girl for the job, but I promise to do my best."

"You will do just fine, dear."

"I do need money for my wedding."

Anna's eyes danced with amusement. "Your wedding? Any boy in particular?"

Lily felt herself blush. "Oh, I mean, in general. Every girl should have money saved up for her wedding, don't you think?"

"Jah," Anna said. "You will want to save up for your wedding, and Aden will be here the rest of the summer. You will both be a big help to us."

Lily cleared her throat. The question had to be asked. "Will the . . . will the dog be staying too?"

Aden leaned back, crossed his arms over his chest, and glanced at Anna. "I'll do my best to keep him away from you."

"And there will be lots of fancy cooking to do," Anna said.

"You're the best cook in the world, Banannie," Felty said.

"Now, Felty."

"Fancy cooking?" Lily said. "For the dog?"

Anna giggled, reached over, and patted Aden's arm. "Aden is a vegetarian."

"Mammi, you don't need to make anything special for me," Aden said. "*Mamm* doesn't cook vegetarian at home."

Lily furrowed her brow. "What is a vegetarian?"

"Aden doesn't eat meat," Felty said.

Dumbfounded, Lily stared at Aden. He

didn't seem like an odd young man, but maybe she had misjudged him. "Why don't you eat meat?" She tried not to sound distrustful.

He gave her a crooked smile, as if he'd been forced to explain himself a thousand times already. "Save the planet," he said.

Save the planet? She had no idea what he was talking about.

"Um, I don't know if I can cook vegetarian," Lily stuttered.

"We can learn together," Anna said. "I just bought a new cookbook called *The Happy Herbivore.* Doesn't it sound fun?"

Aden shifted in his chair. "Mammi, I hate to be a nuisance. I'll get by. Really."

Anna pursed her lips and shook her head. "I won't allow anyone to go hungry in this house. Right, Felty?"

"I've never gone hungry for one day since I married you, Annie."

"What could go wrong when we've got *The Happy Herbivore* as our guide?"

Felty shook his head and smiled affectionately at his wife. "Nothing. It's a wonderful plan, Annie."

"I will have to ask my dat's permission," Lily said, "but I think I should be able to start next week."

"Okay, then. Tell your dat he won't regret

it," Anna said.

"I will tell him."

They stood in unison. Anna came around to Lily's side of the table. She hooked one arm around Lily's waist and the other around Aden's and pulled both of them close to her.

Lily's heart thumped in her chest. She stood within two feet of Anna's good-looking grandson. He was tall and muscular, and up this close, he smelled really good. Could this moment be any more awkward?

Neither Aden nor Anna seemed uncomfortable at all. Aden swung his arm around his mammi's shoulders.

"Aden, this is Lily Eicher, one of our closest neighbors. Lily, this is Aden Helmuth, one of our favorite grandsons."

"Nice to meet you," Lily said breathlessly. Fresh-cut grass. He smelled like fresh-cut grass and cedar.

Aden flashed a smile that brightened the whole kitchen. "Nice to know you have a name."

They stood like that for a few uneasy moments until Lily pulled away. "I will see you on Monday, then."

"Okay," Anna said. "You can help Aden grow vegetables. We are going to need a lot of vegetables. And he tells me he's got some grand plans for our farm."

Aden nodded.

A vegetarian? She hoped they didn't chop down all the trees to plant something awful like parsnips. Lily hated parsnips.

"Wait," Anna said as she opened a tall closet. She handed Lily three knitted pot holders, one green, one sunny yellow, and one with brown and blue stripes. "Give these to your mother and tell her I send my love."

"Denki," Lily said. Anna handed out pot holders like most mammis handed out cookies. "These are so nice."

Lily opened the front door. Pilot and Sparky waited patiently for someone to release them from exile. She hesitated, not relishing the thought of a repeat of her earlier ordeal.

"I'll walk you to the buggy," Aden said.

Lily quickly weighed her options. She'd rather not spend more uncomfortable moments with Anna's handsome-but-strange grandson. What other weird habits did he have? "No need," she said. "Will you just make sure the dog doesn't follow me?"

"Jah. I'm sorry about your cookies. Pilot wouldn't hurt a fly."

Aden watched from the porch as Lily drove

36

her buggy down the hill. "Go play, you two rascals," he said. Pilot and Sparky came to life, bounded off the porch, and chased each other around the yard. "And don't bother the chickens," he added. Pilot still didn't comprehend why the chickens should not be eaten. Aden had to keep a sharp eye on them.

He walked into the house where Mammi and Dawdi waited for a report. They'd told him yesterday what they were up to. They wanted to match him up with a girl in the district and see him "happily settled" — meaning they thought it was time he stopped getting arrested. Well, maybe a change of location would help. Mammi's letter had been the chance for a new start, or a way to hit the reset button, as Jamal would say. Since Mammi's invitation had come three days after the accident at the lake, Aden had taken it as a sign that this was the door Heavenly Father wanted him to walk through.

Choose the good part. Open the door.

Aden still had no idea what that message meant, but Huckleberry Hill seemed a good place to start. Besides, at home, his mamm harangued him every time he walked through the door. A stay at Mammi and Dawdi's would at least give his ears a much-needed rest, although he'd probably get eyestrain from reading all Mamm's letters of chastisement. Mamm wrote notoriously long letters.

Aden didn't regret one thing he'd done, but the good Lord had saved his life, and maybe it was time to include God in his plans. Or rather, time to let God include Aden in *His* plans.

Aden didn't mind if Mammi and Dawdi wanted to find him a wife, but he didn't hold much hope for it working out. If it hadn't already, his reputation would catch up with him, even from as far away as Ohio. And no good Amish *fater* would approve of Aden Helmuth marrying his daughter.

Unless he assumed a new identity and moved to Mexico, his grandparents' scheme wasn't going to work. He went along with it because it made Mammi and Dawdi happy to meddle in his life. Old people, especially old ladies, were like that. They saw a single young man and couldn't resist pairing him with every eligible girl they knew.

Mammi laced her fingers together and lifted her hands as if she were praying. "So, what did you think? She's a very nice girl."

"She's very nice, Mammi."

"And pretty," Dawdi added, although Aden sensed that Dawdi only went along with the plan because it meant so much to Mammi.

"She's the prettiest girl I've ever laid eyes on." Aden didn't say that to humor his grandparents. He had a preference for hazel eyes.

Mammi clapped her hands. "I knew this would work out."

"Gute," said Dawdi, as if that settled everything. "Have a cookie. They're tasty."

"I don't think this girl will work out," Aden said.

Mammi's lips twitched downward. "Lily Eicher is the girl I chose specifically for you. She's cautious and obedient. Your perfect opposite."

Aden couldn't help but grin. "Meaning I'm reckless and rebellious."

"Of course. Lily is your match. There isn't anyone else."

Aden massaged the back of his neck as he felt a headache coming on. "I hate to be picky, Mammi, but could you find me a wife who doesn't think I'm strange?"

"You *are* strange, dear. That isn't a bad thing."

"Being a vegetarian is not strange. In some places, it's trendy. All the cool people are vegetarians."

Mammi frowned. "I don't think Lily

39

knows that. Do you think we should tell her?"

"Maybe you could match me with a different girl."

"I'll do no such thing, young man. I'm not giving up that easily."

Aden shut his mouth and nodded politely. He shouldn't have dared hope.

CHAPTER FOUR

"Ouch!" Lily's older sister, Estee, pulled her hand back from the cutting board.

"Oh, Estee," Mama said, abandoning her pot of stew on the gas stove to examine Estee's injury. "I forgot to tell you I sharpened the knives this morning."

A few drops of blood trickled down Estee's finger. "It's not bad, but it is a bit annoying."

Lily took a look at Estee's finger and retrieved the bandages from the cupboard. "Here, Estee. I will fix you up right quick."

"And I will cut the bread," Mama said.

Estee held her finger as if she were pointing at someone as she sat at the table. "Index finger. It's going to be a nuisance for days."

Lily dampened a paper towel and smeared some soap onto it. She carefully washed Estee's finger, dried it so the bandage would stick, and squeezed ointment onto the cut.

"Tell me if it's too tight," she said as she wrapped the bandage snugly around Estee's finger.

"That's gute. Denki, Lily."

Lily threw the paper towel and bandage wrapping away. "Is Floyd taking you to the gathering tonight?"

"Jah, but you can ride with us. Floyd doesn't mind."

"I don't want to be the third wheel," Lily said. "I can walk."

"Don't be silly. You're not going to walk when there is a perfectly good ride coming by at seven. Besides, Dat wouldn't want you to walk."

Mama put the basket of sliced bread on the table. "It's better if you go with them, Lily. Two lovebirds had best not be left alone."

Estee flexed her finger and smiled. "Maybe you won't have to ride home with us, though. Tyler Yoder likes to drive you."

Mama raised an eyebrow. "He is a very nice boy, Lily."

"Oh, jah," Estee chimed in. "A veeery nice boy."

"I have noticed," Lily assured them, "even though he hardly ever smiles."

Mama clucked her tongue. "He is of a solemn disposition, to be sure, but that

42

means he is steady and reliable. He would make a fine husband."

Lily giggled. "One wedding in the family is enough this year, don't you think?"

Estee flushed with excitement. "Floyd hasn't asked yet, so don't be saying such things in front of him."

"As if it will surprise any of us."

Estee twirled gracefully around the kitchen with the butter as her partner. "Oh, he is the wonderfullest man alive. I want to make a robin's-egg blue dress for my wedding. That's Floyd's favorite color. And Floyd thinks we should marry in November. That way we can be back from our honeymoon trip before Christmas."

Lily shot a teasing look at her sister. "Floyd wants to marry in November? And you still say I shouldn't mention a wedding in front of him?"

Estee set plates and cups on the table. "I want him to think he's surprised all of you. It would make him so happy."

Dat walked in the back door at precisely five o'clock, as he had every day for as long as Lily could remember. He went to the sink and washed up to his elbows. After drying his hands, he gave Mama a peck on the cheek and then wrapped one arm around Estee and the other around Lily. "How are my gute girls today? What gute daughters you are."

Without further ado, the four of them sat at the table and bowed their heads for silent grace. Lily always seemed to finish before Dat did, so she squinted to see when he lifted his head. Were her prayers getting shorter or were Dat's getting longer? That would never do. Tomorrow, she would think of at least four more things to be grateful for. That should make her prayers suitably long.

Once they finished grace, Mama served the soup. With a smile of affection, she gave Dat the biggest helping. Mama took gute care of Dat. Lily wanted that for her own marriage. She wanted to take gute care of a man so that he would adore her the way Dat adored Mama. Lily loved the way her dat looked at Mama, like she was the only good woman in the whole world.

"Dat," Lily said, "Anna Helmuth wants me to work for her this summer. Three days a week. What do you think?"

Dat spread a thick pat of butter over his bread and looked doubtfully at Lily. "That is a generous offer, but I know how you like to be at home."

"Jah, but I want to earn some money. I've never had a job before."

44

"She's so timid, Dat," Estee said. "It would do her good to have a job."

A worry line made a furrow between Dat's eyebrows. "And she'd be working for one of the Plain people. It's too easy to get pulled to the world working out for an *Englischer.*"

"I work out," Estee protested.

Dat reached over and pinched Estee's cheek. "It's only Mrs. Deforest, and I keep a close eye on you."

"Oh, Dat, you do not."

Dat studied Lily's face. "Estee is right. It would be good for you. Can you spare her here at home, Mary? Estee is already gone so much working full-time."

"Jah, it is only three days a week. We can do the canning and cleaning the other days."

"Can you be home every night for suppertime?" Dat asked.

"I think so," said Lily. "Anna wants me to help cook fancy meals, but she didn't say anything about eating supper with them."

"You have my permission," Dat said. "You will do a gute job for them. This is delicious, Mary."

Estee blew on her stew. "Why does Anna want fancy meals? I wouldn't know where to begin to cook a fancy meal."

Lily didn't know why her face suddenly got warm. "They have to fix special food for

45

their grandson Aden. He is staying with them over the summer, and he only eats vegetables."

"Does he have a disease?" Mama asked.

"Nae. I think he doesn't like meat."

Mama buttered a slice of bread. "Is he a special child, like Treva Schrock? You have such a way with special children, Lily. Maybe that is why the Helmuths want your help."

"No, he isn't special."

"Then he must be an odd young man not to like meat," Mama said.

"You don't know the half of it," Estee volunteered. "He's been in jail before."

The other three stopped eating and stared at Estee. "How do you know that?" Dat asked.

"Floyd has a cousin."

"We all have a cousin."

Estee laid her fork on the table and leaned closer to her family to prepare them for the shocking details. "Floyd's cousin, Arty, lives in Sugarcreek, Ohio. He's in the same district as the new boy."

"Aden Helmuth," Lily said.

Estee nodded. "He's been in jail dozens of times, Floyd's cousin says. He came to live with his grandparents because his folks are beside themselves."

Lily caught her breath. Aden, with those irresistible green eyes, had been in jail? "I would die if I got arrested."

"You aren't even brave enough to cross the street without being in the crosswalk," Estee said.

"There's nothing wrong with that," Lily said. "I don't like getting in trouble."

"I thank the Lord that you are an obedient child," Dat said.

Of course she was. Lily would never, ever want to disappoint her father.

"And I'm not obedient?" Estee said in mock indignation. Lily giggled. Estee didn't mind that Lily was the compliant child. According to Estee, Lily was afraid to have any fun.

Lily wasn't afraid, exactly. Just cautious. If Estee participated in too many footraces with the boys, she was sure to twist an ankle.

Estee had more news. "They say the new boy chained himself to a tree once."

Dat reacted as if he'd bitten into a sour pickle. "Chained himself to a tree? Why would anyone chain himself to a tree? Are you sure he's not special?"

Lily didn't know why, but she felt the need to defend Aden even though she barely knew him. "He seems a very nice young man." Her heart did a little skip when she

47

remembered his good looks. "He has a scar on his eyebrow and a dog as big as a bear and he wants to save the planet for . . . something. That's all I know."

Dat chewed slowly and thought for a minute. "He must not be right in the head."

Mama clasped her hands together and looked exceedingly worried. "Maybe you shouldn't work for them, Lily. Being so near the grandson all day is sure to make you nervous."

Estee shook her head. "It will be a great adventure. This boy is one of God's children. We shouldn't shun him simply because he's different."

Lily frowned. "I see the way people avoid Treva, and it breaks my heart. Because she's not as smart as everyone else, people don't see her beautiful spirit. They won't look past her handicaps."

"You always had a soft spot for the downtrodden," Mama said.

Dat buttered another slice of bread. "But you say Aden is not handicapped."

Lily looked to her father, the last word on everything. "I'll do whatever you want me to do, Dat."

Dat leaned back in his chair. "If he has come to Bonduel to mend his ways, we shouldn't let his past hold us back from do-

48

ing our Christian duty."

"So I should take the job?"

Dat took another bite of stew and nodded thoughtfully. "You may work at Helmuths', but stay away from the young man. He isn't right in the head, and I don't want you bringing strange notions into our home. Who knows where they could lead?"

CHAPTER FIVE

Lily trudged up Huckleberry Hill, panting all the way. She'd get some good exercise working this job. In the past, Lily's dat would have driven her all the way to the top of the hill out of concern for her safety and health, but he had told her that he had decided to quit being so anxious and let her spread her wings a little.

Halfway up the hill, she found a stick, about four feet long, that she could use to fight off any dogs that decided to attack her. She didn't plan on hitting the beast, only on using the stick to keep it at arm's length, or stick's length, as the case may be.

She walked up to the porch, keeping a sharp eye out for dogs slinking in the shadows. She breathed a sigh of profound relief. Maybe Aden had remembered she was coming and locked his dog in the barn. She leaned her stick against the porch railing. She'd probably need it if she came

50

outside to do chores.

When Lily got no answer from knocking, she decided to walk in. The Helmuths expected her, and they were probably too old to hear her knock.

To her horror, that dog stood inside the door waiting for her. She caught her breath.

He smiled.

Dogs couldn't smile.

Well, he looked positively cheerful in a dog sort of way. He barked once, jumped up, and plunked his paws on her shoulders. This time, Lily had nothing to prop her up. Grunting in surprise and fright, she toppled to the ground and landed on her backside. That dog still had his paws firmly planted on her shoulders as he leaned in to lick her face. Resisting the urge to burst into tears, she balled her hands into fists to keep from trembling.

"No!" Lily squealed. "Don't you dare lick me."

The dog immediately backed away and cocked his head to one side.

Lily laced her voice with authority. "Sit, Piecrust, sit."

To her relief, the stupid dog took two steps backward and sat down. He gave her a little whine of contrition and looked at her like a naughty schoolboy caught doing

51

mischief.

"And stay there."

Now Aden decided to show himself. He ran down the hall and into the kitchen. "Pilot," he growled, but he didn't sound mad at all as he gave the dog's head a quick pat. "What did you do, Pilot?"

He bent down, gave Lily his hand, and pulled her to her feet as if she weighed no more than a feather. "I'm real sorry about that. He wouldn't hurt a fly, really. I brought him in the house so he wouldn't scare you when you got here. I had no idea you'd just walk in."

Lily huffed her displeasure to cover her distress. "If you taught him some manners, he wouldn't attack innocent people."

Aden had the nerve to grin. "Sorry."

She didn't for one minute believe he felt any remorse at all.

Once on her feet, Lily smoothed the hair under her kapp and reattached a few pins. Her black bonnet had slipped off her head and hung around her neck like a bib. She quickly untied it.

The best course of action, instead of lecturing Aden about his dog's behavior, would be to pretend that nothing had happened. Then she might be able to retain her dignity. She squeezed past the dog, who sat in the doorway behaving himself. "Where are Anna and Felty?"

"In the back. I helped Dawdi fix the toilet. He was trying to do it with duct tape."

Lily stood in the middle of the kitchen, unsure what to do next. Dat had told her to stay away from Aden as best she could, but Aden didn't seem inclined to go anywhere, and she didn't know what Anna wanted her to clean first.

The great room appeared tidy, except for an odd little pile of socks on the floor next to the rocking chair. The table was cleared, but the breakfast dishes sat in the sink. Lily hung her bonnet on a hook and rolled up her sleeves. She'd start on the dishes. If she ignored Aden, maybe he'd get the hint and go somewhere else.

She went to the sink and started filling it with water. That giant of a dog followed and stood next to her like a sentry. His gaze reached above the level of the counter so he could watch intently as Lily poured the soap, picked up a sponge, and started washing.

He twitched his ears and cocked his head to one side and then the other as if trying to figure out how she washed dishes. She looked up to see Aden staring at her. "He likes you," Aden said.

Lily took a damp towel and wiped the paw-shaped dust prints from the shoulders of her navy blue dress. "I'm not sure I return his affection."

"No doubt about that."

Anna appeared just as Lily was about to ask Aden to quit staring at her. Anna's little white dog followed close behind. Sparky padded into the kitchen and stationed herself next to Aden's dog, which still stood guard faithfully by Lily's side. Sparky gazed up at Aden's dog as if looking for her next set of instructions.

"Lily," Anna said, "how nice to see you. Don't worry about the dishes, dear. I want you and Aden to go milk the cow. Together."

"I already milked, Mammi," Aden said.

"Then go out and stake the raspberries. The raspberries need staking, don't they, Aden?"

Aden seemed almost reluctant. "I could always use a second pair of hands."

"I think I should . . . my fater . . ." Lily glanced at Aden. She couldn't very well tell him what her fater had said, but how could she work here and be obedient to Dat's wishes at the same time? She might have to speak with Anna privately about keeping Aden out of her way.

Anna came around to Lily's left side

where there were no dogs and plunged her hands into the dishwater. "Go now. Go. Those raspberries aren't growing any shorter."

Lily didn't have a choice. Anna was her employer, after all. She could still be a faithful employee and avoid Aden. They didn't have to say a word to each other to stake raspberries. She dried her hands and walked past Aden to retrieve her bonnet. Aden's dog followed close behind and stared up longingly at her while she tied the bonnet under her chin. Did he want food?

"Would you like a scarf?" Anna asked. "I knitted one last week."

A scarf in the third week of June would be toasty, but Lily could pretend she was cold and wrap it around her face. A perfect excuse not to talk to Aden.

"Jah, I would love a scarf."

Anna burst with delight. After drying her hands, she bustled to her hall closet and pulled out a deep purple scarf and a green one exactly the color of Aden's eyes. Anna handed the purple scarf to Lily. It felt fuzzy and oh so soft.

"Oh, my. This is beautiful," Lily said.

Anna gave Aden the green scarf. He took it without complaint, though Lily knew they would both be sweating within minutes.

Aden shrugged and curled his lips into a good-natured smile. "Come on, Pilot."

The dog tore his gaze from Lily's face and eagerly followed Aden out the door. Lily wrapped the scarf around her neck and then covered her nose and mouth. Perfect.

She ambled behind the barn to the raspberry patch, which probably covered an eighth of an acre. Stakes were already in the ground with three levels of wire strung between them.

Aden emerged from the barn with the dog trotting cheerily behind him. He took one look at Lily with her ridiculous scarf-mask and his eyes danced. Twitching his lips as if he were trying to hold back a laugh, he said, "Lips cold?"

Lily was glad for the scarf covering half her face since she was certain her cheeks had bloomed bright red.

Aden's scarf hung casually around his neck, lending added brilliance to his eyes. Their depth only strengthened Lily's resolve to stay away from him. She could lose herself in those eyes.

Getting lost was dangerous.

He handed Lily some shears and a ball of twine. "Some of the canes are tall enough to stake to the second wire."

Lily nodded. He laughed.

56

After cutting herself a piece of twine, she sat in the dirt next to the first raspberry plant, picked a cane, and tied it to the wire. Aden sat in the dirt on the opposite side of the row and started tying his own canes.

She got along fine until that mutton-headed dog sauntered toward her. Standing over her like that, he could lick her whole head if he wanted to. Why in the world couldn't Aden babysit his own dog?

Ignoring the butterflies that fluttered in her stomach when she came near a dog, she held up her hand as if stopping traffic and spoke in a loud, authoritative voice so she could be heard through the scarf. "No, Pie Man. Get away."

The dog halted in his tracks, tilted his head, and let out a little whine. All that dog needed was a firm hand and a little discipline. He stared at her pathetically for a moment, then lay down with his paws resting in front of him.

"Good. Stay."

She looked at Aden, who seemed intent on tying his bushes, but a hint of a smile played at the corners of his mouth. Didn't he feel even a smidgeon guilty that he should have been the one disciplining his dog?

Lily tied another cane before glancing at

the dog to make sure he still behaved himself. She was a bit startled to discover that he lay in the same position but that his front paws were mere inches from her foot. How had he managed that?

While tying the next cane, Lily watched Aden's dog out of the corner of her eye. He scooted toward her, quarter inch by quarter inch, until his massive front paws touched her foot. Swallowing her fear, she narrowed her eyes and scowled at him, which probably didn't look too fearsome with a scarf over her face.

The dog lowered his head and pretended to settle in for a nap.

When she looked away again, she heard him scoot closer and felt him lay his snout on top of her shoe. She didn't want to hurt him so couldn't very well kick him away. There was probably no harm in letting him stay there. Her shoes had been exposed to lots worse germs, and he didn't seem inclined to bite.

"He likes you," Aden said.

Lily merely nodded. Why couldn't Aden and his dog leave her alone?

Aden slid toward her to reach the next raspberry plant. "You must have heard some truly horrible things about me."

"What?"

"The way you're acting, you've probably been cautioned to stay far away from me, and it's kind of hard when you work on my grandparents' farm."

Confusion overtook her. She was so embarrassed she wanted to wrap her entire face in the scarf and run to the safety of the house. But with her eyes covered, she'd probably trip over her own feet, fall to the ground, and get licked to death by the dog.

"What . . . what do you mean?"

Aden stood up and walked to where she sat. He squatted down, facing her. The sneaky dog crawled forward and laid his head in her lap. An attack from both sides. Lily didn't move a muscle.

"You're a nice enough girl, but you don't like my dog, and I already told Mammi that's the end of it."

Lily couldn't make heads or tails of what he said. Jah, he was an odd young man.

"Look," he said. "I'm not out to corrupt you or drag you down with my sinful ways. I'm not in Wisconsin recruiting for the devil's team. I'm here to help Mammi and Dawdi and hopefully find a place where people won't judge me harshly." He massaged the side of his face. "Mammi is determined to put us together, and I'd rather not spend the entire summer in silence because you're afraid of me. Can we call a truce and be friends?"

"I'm not afraid of you," Lily said, wishing for a subtle way to lose the scarf.

"Jah, you are."

"My dat . . ."

"What about your dat?"

"He told me to stay away from you."

Aden snorted his displeasure.

"I don't want to be rude, but I must obey my father's wishes."

Aden shook his head. "Did he forbid you to talk to me?"

"Yes. Nae. Not exactly."

A ghost of a grin played at his lips. Lily hadn't expected that. "But he said you have to cover your mouth when I'm around?"

Lily whipped off the scarf and hurled it to the ground. "Nae."

Aden drummed his fingers on his jaw as if deep in thought. "So how far do you need to stay from me to be obedient to your fater?" He scooted two feet away from her. "This far?"

She didn't know how to answer.

He scooted back farther. "This far?"

Lily lowered her eyes to look at the dog in her lap. She scratched his head, if only to have something to do with her hands. "Maybe that would be okay."

"So, as long as I keep a distance of four or five feet, your fater will be satisfied?"

Lily felt herself blushing again. Why did she feel so transparent? "I don't know."

"I wouldn't ask you to go against your dat. You must be comfortable with the distance. How far back do you want me to stay?"

Lily laced her fingers through the curly fur on the dog's head. "You are right. It is a little silly."

"Not silly at all. I don't want to go against your fater."

The dog licked the back of her hand, and she sighed in surrender. "Four . . . four feet is enough."

"Gute, because I think that is the diameter of Mammi's table. At least we can eat dinner together."

He flashed that nice smile, and Lily's heart beat an uneven rhythm in her chest. For such an odd young man, he was certainly charming, even if he was making fun of her.

Aden pointed to his dog, who had rolled onto his back as if wanting Lily to rub his tummy. "And what about Pilot? Should I make him stay away too?"

"He wouldn't listen. He is the most disobedient dog I've ever seen."

Aden scooted back to his original spot and

picked up his shears. "I've been in jail three times."

"What?"

"Only three. Not seventeen times, like I heard yesterday."

Or dozens, as Estee had told her. The plainly boastful glint in his eye put Lily on the defensive. "Three is a lot."

"Three times more than you've been in jail, I bet."

Lily scratched the dog's stomach vigorously as her agitation grew. "I would never think of getting arrested. It's irresponsible."

Aden didn't seem offended by her subtle reprimand. "Do you want to know why I went to jail? The truth is probably less dramatic than your imagination."

"It's none of my business. I should not let your past keep me from doing my Christian duty."

His lips twitched upward. "Sounds like something an Amish fater would say."

This young man was infuriatingly perceptive. "What's wrong with that?"

"Nothing. I heard a lot of talk like that in Ohio, and yet people still avoided me."

Lily smoothed her hand along the dog's neck. His fur felt especially soft there. "We're not like that here in Bonduel."

"Your fater told you to stay away from me.

It sounds like you're exactly like that in Bonduel." He pinned her with that brilliant gaze. "Or maybe it's just you, Lily Eicher."

Lily's face felt like she stood right next to a blazing-hot cookstove. "Don't blame me for your choices. You did something bad enough to be arrested. I would be *deerich,* foolish, not to be cautious around you."

Her words didn't seem to anger him, but they hit their mark. He slumped his shoulders in resignation. "You are right. Of course you are right. For all you know, I could be a murderer." Then the bitterness crept into his voice. "Four feet isn't near far enough from someone like me." He picked up his twine and scissors and stood up. "I'll go weed tomatoes."

Lily felt a little hitch in her throat as she watched him tromp away. She'd been hurtful when all she'd wanted to be was right. A sense of shame washed over her. She had always tried to befriend the ones that everybody picked on, not alienate them.

The dog rolled and lifted his head. Lily pulled her hands away. She'd been petting Aden's dog. How had that happened? The dog stood up, gave Lily a yip of disapproval, and turned away from her. He followed Aden to the vegetable patch without looking back.

It seemed she was unworthy of even the dog.

Well, good, because he was a dirty, bothersome brute. She pulled a small bottle of sanitizer out of her pocket and slathered it all over her hands, but she still felt germy and unclean. There wasn't a bottle of hand sanitizer big enough to sterilize her nagging conscience.

Aden trudged into the house for a drink.

Mammi, it seemed, had been watching for him. She greeted him at the door with a plate of gingersnaps. "How are you two coming along out there?"

"The tomatoes are weeded, but the raspberries are going slow." Aden grabbed a cookie and bit into it. Or tried to. He'd forgotten about Mammi's rock-hard gingersnaps. The cookie scraped against his teeth like a pebble. "Delicious, Mammi," he said, slipping the cookie into his pocket to be eaten when he could soak the thing in a glass of milk.

"What about Lily? Isn't she wonderful?"

"We've decided to stay away from each other."

Mammi threw her hands up in the air, which was a bad thing because the cookies on her plate flew in several directions. One bounced on the table and leveled the salt shaker. "My goodness," she said, "look what trouble I'm in."

Aden motioned for his mammi to stay put, got on his hands and knees, and gathered the scattered cookies.

Mammi bent over so she could look Aden in the eye while he crawled around. "You young people are so uncooperative! I feel like I have to do all the work myself."

Aden remembered how much he loved his mammi and tried not to sound frustrated. "She's not interested."

"Nonsense. She barely knows you. If you stay away from her, she'll never get to know you, and then how, might I ask, will she fall in love?"

Aden found all the cookies he could, stood up, and deposited them on the plate Mammi held out to him. "Mammi, I know you mean well, and I'm happy to let you find me a wife. I don't want to sound picky, but do you think you could find me a girl whose fater doesn't hate me?"

Mammi looked puzzled for a moment. "David Eicher just needs to get to know you. He smothers that girl so she can't hardly breathe. Things will get better. Have another cookie. They're my special recipe."

Aden sighed inwardly and grabbed two

cookies off the plate. They might as well have been golf balls.

Mammi would never give up.

He lost all hope.

CHAPTER SIX

Aden listened as the preacher droned on and on about Matthew 5:9. *Blessed are the peacemakers.* Even though this was his first time at gmay, Aden had a sneaking suspicion that the sermon was meant specifically for him. He didn't intend to take the message lightly, but he found his mind wandering. Contrary to what the people in his new district might believe, Aden had spent his whole life trying to be a man of peace. He just seemed to stir up a lot of trouble at the same time.

Aden shifted on his bench. Some men, no matter how righteous, were not meant to preach sermons. This particular preacher might as well have been reading the phone book.

Aden peered across the room at Lily. She sat with her arm around a Down syndrome girl who looked about the same age as Lily. Lily, in rapt attention, nodded at all the appropriate moments in the sermon. Well-behaved. Lily Eicher was well-behaved. He found that particular quality quite endearing. Aden always desired in his heart of hearts to be well-behaved. He admired people who could actually do it.

She glanced at him and caught him staring, quickly looked away, and turned bright red. *Oy anyhow,* how she must hate him. It was his own fault. He'd put her on the defensive the other day and no doubt hurt her feelings. The poor girl wanted to be obedient to her father. He couldn't blame her for that.

She was, after all, well-behaved.

In hopes of finding a more suitable marriage candidate, Aden let his gaze travel over the girls sitting on the same bench as Lily. She was prettier than any of them by a country mile, but good looks weren't the only important thing in a wife. Maybe he should hold interviews after services.

Do you like big, unruly dogs?

Can you cook vegetarian?

Will your fater allow you to date a young man with a police record?

One of the girls sitting on Lily's bench held a baby, probably a little brother. He fussed while she patted his back in quiet rhythm. He coughed and then spewed the

68

milk from his stomach onto the girl's white apron. She gasped and passed the baby to her mother, who sat on the row in front of her. The front of her apron was soaked through to her dress.

The preacher took no notice. "When the righteous die, they enter into peace. There is no peace for the wicked."

A younger girl in the back row tittered softly. Ladies on the bench in front of the wet girl passed burp rags and tissues to clean her off with. She took the offerings and wiped her apron as her eyes filled with tears. No flimsy tissue would dry her.

With a minimum of fuss, Lily reached across two other girls and took the drenched girl's hand. She gave the girl a reassuring smile, pulled her from between the row of benches, and led her down the hall to a bathroom.

Aden slid off his bench as the preacher called for a prayer. Once the prayer ended, everyone got back on the benches and pulled out their *Ausbund* hymnals. The *Vorsinger,* or lead hymn singer, sang the beginning of each new line and everyone chimed in after him. Halfway through the hymn, Lily and the other girl reappeared.

The girl had removed her soaking apron and wore what must have been Lily's apron over her wet dress. Her eyes were red with crying, but she only sniffed twice before Lily led her back to her seat. Lily, wearing the wet apron, took her place next to the special girl, who smiled brightly at Lily's return. In her blue dress, Lily looked like a patch of sky peeking out from behind the clouds.

Not that she needed anything to make her stand out. Her golden-yellow hair and full, pink lips succeeded in doing that just fine. Was she aware of her beauty? Probably not. Such things were not discussed among the Plain people. A well-behaved, humble girl would not want to attract attention.

Once services ended and Aden had helped the other men move benches and stack them into tables, Aden found a spot between two strangers for the noon meal. They were both boys about his age.

The boy on his left had a pleasant face, straight dark hair, and unusually long eyelashes. Aden sat down, and the boy immediately turned to him and stuck out his hand. "Tyler Yoder." He had a firm handshake and a confident, serious air about him.

Aden smiled. "Aden Helmuth."

Tyler looked at the peanut butter sandwich on Aden's plate. "I hear you only eat vegetables."

Aden chuckled. "Nae, I don't eat meat. But I eat most everything else."

"Peanut butter?"

"Jah."

Tyler studied Aden's face and nodded. "You have a heart for the animals."

Aden almost dropped his jaw. Tyler was the first Amish person Aden had encountered who didn't act like he thought being a vegetarian was strange. Tyler seemed to understand or at least refrained from passing judgment on Aden's choices.

"There are a lot of reasons to be a vegetarian," Aden said. "But yes, I'd rather not see any living thing die for my eating pleasure."

"You take after your dawdi," Tyler said. "Felty has been known to catch spiders in his house and set them free in the woods."

"Jah. I am very like my dawdi, bless his heart."

"Are you an environmentalist?" Tyler asked.

Again, Aden couldn't hide his surprise. "I didn't think any Plain people knew what that meant."

Tyler's eyes seemed to smile although his lips stayed put. "I dabble in stuff like that."

"Really?"

"My dat and I have an organic dairy. Organic milk sells for almost twice what you

71

can get for regular milk."

Aden's heart swelled at the thought of someone he might be able to relate to. "I'm hoping to have my own organic farm someday if I can find a gute piece of property."

Tyler lifted his eyebrows. "No joking? My dat will want to meet you. We've read some books, but I don't wonder if you know some things we haven't thought of."

"Probably not, but I'd love to hear all about your dairy."

Tyler put a hand on Aden's shoulder. "We can help each other. I know I could learn a lot from an environmentalist."

Aden grinned. "I'm more of a conservationist than an environmentalist. Environmentalists seem to want to pick fights. I don't want to quarrel with anybody."

"Are you coming to the gathering next week? It's at my house. We can talk more then."

"I wasn't going to. I'm not one of those boys that everybody likes to have around."

"Now I know you're joking." Tyler, still excessively somber, pointed to a group of girls huddled in the corner, whispering and giggling as only teenagers could. "The girls have talked about no one else since you've been here. They think you're handsome."

"Have they heard about my wicked past?"

"You mean about getting chained to a tree?" Tyler asked.

Aden raised an eyebrow.

"Lily told me. That's how I knew you were an environmentalist, or, I mean, conservationist. You were trying to save the tree, weren't you?"

Aden nodded.

Tyler raised an eyebrow. "It doesn't seem to bother those girls over there."

"It's their faters who have issues with me."

Lily, with her blue dress and flaxen hair, passed their table with an armload of paper plates. The special girl followed close behind, as if Lily carried the sun in her pocket. Lily glanced in Aden's direction but otherwise took no notice of him. "And Lily Eicher. She is bothered by my police record."

"Jah, that kind of thing would spook Lily. But don't despair. Once she decides to be friends with you, there is no one more loyal or more kind."

"It doesn't matter. Her fater has ordered her to stay away from me."

Tyler coughed as he swallowed a bite of pickle too fast. "David Eicher is a gute fater. He lost his brother several years ago, and the experience made him doubly protective of his daughters. But he has a gute heart,

73

and Lily would do anything to please him. I like that about her. She's not one to kick against the pricks."

Jah, Lily held strictly to the letter of the law, and Aden could imagine that there were no *i*'s undotted and no *t*'s uncrossed in her behavior.

It was going to be a very long summer.

As if reading his thoughts, Tyler said, "I will talk to David. He must know how hard it will be for Lily to work on Huckleberry Hill and stay away from you at the same time."

"We agreed on a four feet distance."

Tyler cracked a smile at that. "That sounds like something Lily would do. But it's impractical, just the same. Like as not, David thinks you shot somebody or stole a car. I'll tell him you were in jail to save the life of a tree. He won't understand, but I might persuade him to be less rigid when it comes to Lily."

"Denki. It is uncomfortable working alongside someone who won't even talk to me without checking with her fater first."

Tyler stood. "Don't take this the wrong way, but I would like to talk to Lily, and since you can't come within four feet of her, I am leaving you. But you will come to the gathering? The Wednesday night after next?"

"Jah, I will come." Aden studied his new friend closely as Tyler sidled next to Lily. Tyler was seemingly content to stand by Lily without saying much. Lily acted friendly but didn't gush. A girl who gushed was a girl in love. Aden wasn't sure how Lily felt about Tyler, but she didn't gush.

Aden turned away. Lily's preference in boys was none of his business. But Mammi might want to know if Aden's intended bride loved somebody else.

Mammi's plans for Aden's wedding weren't going to work out. There were too many other boys to contend with. Aden didn't have a chance.

Why were his palms sweating?

CHAPTER SEVEN

Lily wasn't particularly comfortable with children.

Of course, she loved their cherubic faces and their simple faith, but truth be told, children terrified her.

Children were the heritage of the Amish culture. The Plain people cherished little ones instead of seeing them as a burden. But Lily was the youngest in her family, and Estee was the only other child. Lily had no younger siblings and no nieces or nephews to practice on. She had befriended Treva Schrock, but Treva wasn't a child. She was simply childlike. There was a huge difference.

The thought of caring for a child made Lily's throat dry up and her heart race. She had no idea how to quiet a crying baby or change a diaper. And a job as a school-teacher was definitely out. What if a scholar were to break his arm or choke on his lunch?

Today, she thought she might be sick with anxiety.

"I hope you don't mind, Lily," Anna said as she buttoned up her chocolate brown sweater. No matter how hot it was outside, Lily had never seen Anna go on an outing without a sweater — always one she had knitted herself and always a different color than the traditional black. "We might be gone all day."

Lily glanced at the five young faces regarding her doubtfully. She hoped they didn't recognize the panic in her eyes.

Anna's daughter Ruth ruffled her oldest son's hair. "Junior is almost eleven. He will be a gute help."

Lily hoped Junior knew how to change diapers. The youngest little girl bouncing on Junior's hip couldn't have been much older than two.

"They're running tests on Matthias today, and I didn't want to sit alone in the hospital."

Lily swallowed the lump in her throat. "Of course you want to be with your husband."

Felty patted his bulging pocket. "I've got quarters for the vending machines. We'll eat like kings while we're there." He propped his hands on his knees and bent to look at his grandchildren. "I'll bring each of you a

77

candy bar if you don't give Lily no trouble today."

The other boy, who looked to be about six or seven, nodded eagerly. "Can I have a Twix, Dawdi?"

Ruth patted the littlest girl's cheek. "Keep an eye on Amanda. She is very busy and likes to wander off."

Lily tried to catch her breath. "What . . . what do I feed them for lunch?"

"Oh, whatever you want to fix. Sandwiches are fine."

"Can they eat peanuts?" Lily had heard of children dying from eating peanuts. And wheat. Should she ask about wheat?

Ruth gave Lily a reassuring smile. "They can eat most everything. But be sure to cut Amanda's food into small pieces for her. We don't want her to choke."

Lily's heart did a flip-flop. "How small of pieces? Do you want me to feed her one bite at a time? What should I do if she chokes?"

Ruth's smile faded. "We'll hurry back as soon as Matthias's tests are over, won't we, Mamm?"

"Not to worry," Anna said. "Aden will be here."

Aden. The boy who had a bear for a pet and who had practically ignored Lily for two weeks. They'd have to speak to each other if one of the children broke an arm and had to be taken to the hospital.

Lily breathed a sigh of relief. At least Aden would be here. He had younger siblings. She hoped he was as capable as he was handsome.

He walked in the door just as she thought about him.

Jah, very handsome.

"Aden!" Junior put little Amanda on her feet, and he and the other boy threw themselves into Aden's outstretched arms.

Aden stumbled backward and flashed that nice smile that Lily hadn't seen for days. "I almost didn't recognize you," Aden said. "How tall are you now, Uriah?"

The younger boy, Uriah, raised his hand to the top of his head. "About four feet."

"Four feet? Oy anyhow."

Aden's dog bounded into the house and tackled Junior to the ground. Like Aden, Junior didn't seem to have a problem with giant dogs knocking people over and licking their faces with that sticky, wet tongue. Uriah giggled with glee and nuzzled his face into the dog's fur. Ruth's three daughters broke ranks and gathered around the dog, petting him and cooing as if he were the most wonderful animal in the world.

The dog wagged his tail and smiled at all the attention.

Lily looked again. Dogs didn't smile.

"Does he still eat socks?" Uriah asked while scratching the dog's fur.

"He doesn't eat them," Aden said, pointing to a small pile of stockings near the sofa. "He collects them."

Anna gave her daughter a decisive pat on the arm as if Aden's presence solved everything. "He'll be here to help Lily if she has questions, won't you, Aden?"

Aden studied Lily's face for a moment before wrapping his arm around Uriah's neck and digging his knuckles into the top of Uriah's head.

"Hey!" Uriah protested as he struggled to free himself from Aden's grasp.

"The boys can help me work on a new chicken coop," Aden said, as if it were the most exciting news all morning. Lily bit her bottom lip. Uriah looked so small. What if he smashed his thumb with the hammer?

Ruth's oldest daughter pulled a ball of cheery yellow yarn from a small fabric bag she held. "I brought my knitting."

"Gute," Anna said. "You can show me your progress when I get back." She and Ruth gave each of the children a kiss.

"The driver's here," Felty said, patting his

80

pants pocket. "I've got my notebook in case we see any good license plates."

Ruth smiled. "Oh, Dat. Are you still playing that license plate game?"

"Every year." Felty beamed. "I found Alabama last week." Felty took the bulging bag of hospital necessities from Anna. Anna had packed it with sandwiches, knitting supplies, baby booties, and a board game — because you never knew what you were going to need at the hospital, she had said.

Ruth gave Lily one last doubtful look as she shuffled out the door. Aden and the two boys followed close behind, leaving Lily alone and helpless with the three little girls. At least Aden had taken that dog with him. Lily would truly be beside herself if the dog ate one of the children.

The three girls, even the tiny one, stood like statues and stared at Lily until the littlest one began to cry. Lily didn't blame her. She'd cry too if she had herself for a babysitter.

The oldest girl, probably eight, gathered the little one in her arms. "It's okay, Amanda. Mamm will be home soon."

"You're pretty," the middle girl said.

"Oh, uh, thank you." Lily got on her knees to be at eye level with the children. "Tell me your names and how old you are."

81

The eldest bounced the small one on her hip. "I am Rose, and I am nine years old. This is Amanda. She is two and a half, and be careful because when she has to go to the bathroom, you have to take her fast or she will have an accident."

Lily didn't let her smile fade. "Denki for the warning."

"I'm Evie," said the middle girl. Her chestnut hair was pulled back into a bob, like the other two girls', and she had long, dark eyelashes that accentuated her expressive blue eyes. "I am almost five. My birthday is in one month."

"How nice," Lily said. "I love birthdays."

Amanda kept fussing, and Rose handed her to Lily. Rose must have thought Lily would have better luck calming her down.

If only she knew.

Lily stood and started bobbing up and down and humming the song about the railroad that Felty always sang. Amanda seemed unimpressed. Her fussy whining gave way to distressed tears that looked like they were about to turn into full-fledged screaming.

"You can give her some juice," Rose said. "Sometimes she likes juice."

Instead, Lily trilled her tongue and made a high-pitched noise. Amanda stopped crying out of sheer surprise. Then Lily made loud popping noises with her mouth that sounded like water dripping into a sink — a trick that Estee's boyfriend Floyd had taught her. Amanda giggled. Lily made the noise again. Amanda placed her little hands on Lily's cheeks and studied her mouth. The other girls watched her with undisguised curiosity. Apparently, Lily was fascinating.

Lily kept popping until Amanda forgot why she was crying. "Would you like a story?" she asked the toddler.

Amanda stuck her finger in her mouth and nodded. Lily took Amanda to the sofa. She seemed to remember seeing a box of picture books tucked between the sofa and the small end table. The other girls followed, and one sat on each side of her. Rose pulled out her knitting.

Lily reached into the box and found a book about a family of bears that lived in a tree house. She felt a little better. Telling stories was something Lily did well. She liked making all the different voices and giving excitement to the story by raising and lowering her voice.

"Five little bears lived in a tree . . ."

By the second book, Rose had abandoned her knitting and hooked her arm around

Lily's elbow as she listened to the story. Evie had managed to crawl onto Lily's lap. Lily balanced Evie on one leg while Amanda sat on the other. The three little girls listened in rapt attention as Lily recounted the story of Little Red Riding Hood's journey into the scary woods.

"Grandma, what big eyes you have."

Aden came into the house.

Lily's heart did a small hop, and not just out of concern for the children. "Are the boys okay?"

"Keep reading, Lily," Evie said.

Aden stood just inside the door, glued into place as if he had come into the house for no other reason than to stand there. "Jah, of course. The boys are fine."

Lily nodded as relief gave way to puzzlement. He was probably still out of sorts with her about what had happened between them two weeks ago. She really should apologize for hurting his feelings, but at the moment, three little girls surrounded her. "Anything else?"

"You looked a little concerned earlier. I wanted to make sure you were getting along all right."

"Oh, thank you. I . . . I sometimes get anxious over nothing."

"Don't feel bad — it's only normal when

you aren't used to children."

"Lily, keep going," Evie said in breathless anticipation.

Lily trained her eyes on the open book and started reading. Aden stayed put. "Grandma, what big teeth you have."

His bad habit of staring at her made her feel embarrassed and giddy at the same time. Those green eyes shone with an unreadable expression and made her blush.

"The better to eat you with, my dear."

Evie gasped as the wolf jumped from the bed and chased Little Red Riding Hood around the room, but as usual, the huntsman arrived just in time to kill the wolf with an ax.

"Read another one," Rose said, as Lily closed the book.

Aden stood there as if he had nothing better to do. Lily, along with the three little girls, turned their eyes to him. He finally took the hint. "Okay, I will go now."

"The girls and I will have dinner ready at noon," Lily said, as if she already had a plan. Aden seemed like the type who would appreciate a capable girl, one who could adapt to the little upsets of life.

"That would be wonderful gute."

As if it were painful to tear his gaze from her face, he backed away from her, found the doorknob by touch, and opened the door, all without averting his eyes. Then he turned stiffly and vanished out the door.

What an odd young man.

Why hadn't anybody told Lily that children were this much fun?

It had been Rose's idea to make cookies — snickerdoodles — a recipe Lily knew by heart. Lily had propped little Amanda on her hip while instructing Evie and Rose on how to mix the dough. At first, Lily had thought it might be too much trouble, but when she saw how much fun the girls had measuring and sifting and stirring, she knew it was worth the bother. Aden and the boys would be pleased.

She let Amanda sit on the counter, with Lily's arms loosely around her, and plop dollops of dough onto the cookie sheet with the other girls. Nobody's balls of dough were very round or of any uniform size, but the girls had made the cookies themselves and because of that, they were the best cookies money couldn't buy.

Lily insisted on putting the cookies into the cookstove. She would never forgive herself if one of the girls burned her hand on the hot surface. Most of the Amish homes in Bonduel had gas powered stoves, which were much safer, but Anna and Felty hadn't modernized their stove yet.

While the cookies baked, they set the table. Evie put a slice of cucumber on each plate and arranged thin carrot slices around each cucumber. They looked like cheery green suns with orange sunbeams.

Amanda, with Lily holding tightly to her hand, toddled carefully down the stairs to the cellar to fetch two bottles of chicken from the shelf. Rose mixed the chicken with mayonnaise and pickle juice, and they made seven and a half sandwiches — the half being for Amanda.

Aden and the boys appeared promptly at noon.

Uriah looked at the plates on the table. "Look at the suns, Aden."

"I made those," said Evie, beaming brightly.

"And we have a surprise for you," Rose said.

"What is it?" Junior asked.

Rose covered her mouth and tittered. "You'll see."

Aden smiled in amusement and looked at the carefully arranged vegetables next to his sandwich. His expression drooped. "This looks delicious, girls. I can tell you worked very hard on a gute dinner for us."

The boys washed up, and they all crammed around the table. Amanda sat on an upside-down pot as a booster seat next to Lily. Lily kept a hand on Amanda's leg to make sure that Amanda would not topple over while she ate. That arrangement would make eating difficult for Lily.

Aden, still frowning, made a point to sit directly across from Lily — as far away from her as possible at Anna's round table. Even though he had agreed to the distance, Aden's avoidance pricked her heart. And instead of his distance being something they could both laugh about, Lily had seen to it that it was a sore spot between them.

It wasn't until her head was bowed for silent grace that Lily realized what had dampened Aden's mood. He couldn't eat the sandwiches. How could she have forgotten?

Lily groaned inwardly. Evie and Rose's feelings would be hurt when Aden didn't eat their carefully made sandwich. It didn't even matter if he tried to explain himself. The word "vegetarian" meant nothing to a nine-year-old. Lily didn't understand it well herself.

As soon as they all lifted their heads, Lily scooped Amanda up in one arm — she couldn't very well risk a fall — and grabbed the pitcher of milk with her free hand. "Milk, Aden?"

She reached across the table. With Amanda in her arms, it proved quite a feat. "Yilly, put down," Amanda complained as she reached futilely for her dinner.

Aden barely had time to say, "Nae, thank you," before Lily made a show of aiming for Aden's glass. She bumped it with the pitcher and proceeded to pour milk all over his plate, soaking his sandwich and rendering it inedible.

"Oh no!" exclaimed Rose. She jumped from the table and ran to the sink. "I'll get a towel."

Aden sat mute while Lily caught his eye with a sly look and poured a few extra drops on his soggy bread for good measure. He gave her the most brilliant, breathtaking smile Lily had ever seen. Her heart galloped like a horse, and she felt as if she could jump into the air and fly away. She'd never experienced anything quite like that sensation before.

Slightly dazed, Lily placed the pitcher of milk back on the table, sank to her chair, and deposited Amanda back on her pot.

Evie examined Aden's plate and a look of sympathy overspread her face. "Your sandwich is ruined, Aden."

Aden made a show of profound disappointment. "That was probably the best sandwich I would have ever eaten."

"I am extra clumsy today. I'm so sorry," Lily said, which when she looked at Aden meant, *You're welcome.*

Junior held out his sandwich to Aden. It had one bite taken out of it. "Here. You can have mine."

Aden shook his head. "You are a growing boy, and you worked hard this morning. You need that whole sandwich."

"You can eat mine," Rose said, as she came back to the table and handed Aden a towel. "I haven't touched it."

Aden stood and carefully picked up his plate, making sure the milk didn't slosh everywhere. "Uriah, will you open the door for me?"

Uriah jumped to do Aden's bidding, and Aden slowly walked out the door with his brimming plate. He returned empty handed. "Pilot loves turkey sandwiches smothered in milk. It's like a piece of birthday cake to him."

"They were chicken," Rose said.

"What are you going to eat?" Uriah wanted to know.

"I will make him peanut butter and huckleberry jelly," Lily said. "Rose, keep a hand

90

on Amanda, please." She looked to Aden for confirmation that peanut butter and jelly were acceptable dinner items. He winked and nodded.

Boys should not wink at girls. It left them short of breath.

After dinner and the best cookies Aden said he had ever tasted in his whole life, everyone pitched in with the dishes. Before they got back to work, Aden suggested a game of Frisbee on the lawn, which consisted of Aden throwing the Frisbee and the children, including Amanda, and the dogs trying to catch it. Aden's dog wanted to catch every throw, and he knocked children out from under him in an attempt to do it. The children thought it was great fun to be plowed over by an eighty-pound dog, so Lily didn't scold him even though she wanted to.

The first few times the dog came near Amanda, Lily held her breath. Amanda was no match for those giant paws. But Lily soon relaxed when she saw that the dog seemed to have a sense of Amanda's whereabouts at all times. He never knocked her over, but he would occasionally bend down and let her pull his ears.

Not eager to be trampled by the dog, Lily was content to watch the game from her perch on the porch steps.

"Lily, come on," Aden called and motioned for her to join them. "I'll bet you're as good with a Frisbee as you are with a pitcher of milk."

Lily grinned and tentatively stepped off the porch. She'd probably stub her toe or jam her finger, but they looked like they were having so much fun.

She stood at the opposite end of the yard from Aden, and he floated the Frisbee to her with a gentle toss. She caught it with ease, and Aden and the children cheered.

"I knew you'd be a natural," Aden called.

Aden's dog trotted toward her, no doubt in an attempt to kidnap her Frisbee. She held up her hand as she had done before. "No, Pie Dog. Stay." The dog obediently halted a few inches from her and sat down. "Good dog," she said as she scratched behind his ears, but she quickly pulled back her hand as he stuck out his tongue and tried to lick her fingers.

The dog stationed himself next to her as she threw the Frisbee to Aden. It sliced through the air and veered several feet to Aden's left. He sprinted and dove and made an amazing catch. Lily laughed and clapped her hands. "You are truly an expert."

He chuckled and threw the Frisbee back

to her. This time it sailed over her head and landed in a tree at the edge of the yard. The children groaned and cheered and giggled all at the same time.

"I can get a broom, if you need it," Junior said.

Lily assessed the height of the tree. She was entirely too puny to retrieve the Frisbee, but Aden could reach it. He probably wouldn't even have to stand on his tippy-toes. Grinning widely, he jogged to Lily. His smile, coupled with his bright green eyes, prompted more heart gallops. "Sorry," he said. "I don't know my own strength."

They stared at each other for a moment before Lily gathered her wits about her. She trained her eyes on the dog and cleared her throat. "Don't apologize. You're the one who has to get it."

As she predicted, Aden didn't have to stand on his tippy-toes to retrieve the Frisbee. He pulled the Frisbee from the tree and tossed it to the dog, who caught it in his mouth and ran full speed around the yard while the children chased him.

Lily and Aden stood together and laughed as the Frisbee fell out of Pie Dog's mouth when he barked at Junior. Their eyes met, and then Aden took four steps away from her. "Four feet," he said with a tease in his voice.

Lily felt her face get warm. "I'm sorry about what I said. Only he who is without sin should cast the first stone."

"Please don't let it trouble you. I would think less of your fater if he weren't concerned about you spending time with me. He has no idea what kind of person I am. He only knows I've spent some time in jail — not a boy good enough to associate with his daughter. It's okay to be careful."

"I do want to understand. You seem like a godly man. What did you do that got you into so much trouble?"

Aden laughed as the dog snatched the hat off Uriah's head and ran away with it. "My mamm calls me a busybody. I stick my nose into other people's business when I shouldn't." The smile faded from his lips. "But I can't stand by and watch an animal suffer."

"What happened?"

"I used to ride my bike by my Englisch neighbor's house every day after work. He kept this old horse in a tiny little fenced area, with no room to run, and didn't feed the poor animal a thing."

"Oh," Lily said, "That's too bad."

"That horse got thinner and thinner. I

know it isn't the Amish way, but I called the Animal Control people to report him. I thought they would at least make the man feed his horse. Three weeks went by with no sign of Animal Control, so I started sneaking onto the Englischer's property every night to feed the horse. I brought a little hay and sometimes a bucket of oats when I could afford it. My neighbor caught me one night and had me arrested for trespassing. But with my arrest, the police got onto the man's property and found three starving horses. He got fined for animal cruelty, and the horses were taken away from him."

"Were you in jail long?"

"One night. A local reporter heard about it and wrote a story for the paper. The judge couldn't very well sentence me to jail after the whole town called me a hero."

"That was brave. Just thinking about sneaking onto someone's property makes me feel like I am going to have a heart attack."

"Jamal Drake contacted me after that. He works for an environmental group, and he thought it would be fly to have an Amish guy helping out."

"Fly?"

"It means wonderful gute."

95

"You shouldn't have been arrested for that."

"I only spent one night in jail, and all charges were dropped, but my bishop had words for me. Good Amish men do not get involved in other people's business. He thought my behavior was not in keeping with *Gelassenheit,* or the yielding to a higher authority."

"I would have been too frightened to do it, even if I'd seen the need."

Aden gave her a half smile. "There are some things worth taking the risk for. You can be brave when it's important enough."

Could she? She didn't know. She always felt so comfortable in her own little world. It was the way she had been raised, always encouraged to be content with where God had placed her.

The dog leveled Junior to the ground, and Junior gave him a squeeze. "The children adore Pilot," Aden said. "I look at him and think, *what's not to love?*" His lips twitched into a teasing grin. "But you barely tolerate him. Is it because he ruined your cookies?"

Lily coughed as if a bee had flown down her throat. "I like him."

"Don't be so polite. You practically bathe in hand sanitizer after you touch him."

Lily didn't know what to say. A confession

might send Aden running in the opposite direction. She slumped her shoulders. "Don't hate me, but I don't especially love dogs."

"Are you afraid of them? I saw how shaken you were on that first day. I guess I just assumed you were angry."

She stared at the ground. "I know. I'm a big chicken. Estee is always reminding me."

Aden risked standing closer and laid a hand on her arm. It felt warm and strong. "It's nothing to be ashamed of. Lots of people are afraid of dogs, especially Pilot. He's kind of intimidating."

"Kind of?"

"But I can work with that." Aden's eyes danced with excitement. "You just need to get to know Pilot. You won't be so afraid anymore."

Lily couldn't match his enthusiasm. "I guess so." If she truly wanted Aden to stay away from her, this would be the perfect time to tell him the whole truth. He'd run away as fast as he could if he knew she was responsible for the death of a dog.

Aden grinned sheepishly and took two steps back. "Sorry. Four feet."

Lily felt a little silly at his strict adherence to Dat's directions. She turned her face away and watched as the children found themselves in a pileup with the dog. "Where is Amanda?"

Aden looked to the children and then swept his gaze around the yard. "I don't see her. Junior," he called, "where's Amanda?"

Junior and Rose stopped wrestling with the dog and stood up. "She was right here," Junior said, sweeping his gaze around the yard.

Aden furrowed his brow. "Go check behind the barn. Rose, go around the other side of the house. And be careful. There are some thorny bushes over there."

Aden and Lily called Amanda's name and looked behind every tree and bush in the front yard. She had disappeared.

Junior came running from the barn at the same time that Rose came around the other side of the house. "She's not over there," Junior said. "And not inside the barn either."

Rose shook her head. "I didn't find her."

Lily's heart hammered inside her chest and panic rose like bile in her throat. "She was here two minutes ago. Where could she have gone?"

Aden took her by the shoulders. "It's going to be okay. Take Uriah and the girls and go check the house."

"She couldn't have gone in there without

any of us seeing," Lily said, half talking, half sobbing.

Aden pinned her with a look insisting she calm down. "Go look, Lily."

Lily grabbed Evie's and Uriah's hands as if they might disappear if she didn't take them with her. With Rose, they ran into the house and the four of them went through every room calling Amanda's name. Lily checked the cellar even though Amanda wasn't tall enough to reach the doorknob to open the cellar door.

All Lily's worst fears about babysitting were coming true. What if they never found Amanda? What if she had an accident and died?

The children stood in the kitchen when she came up from the cellar. "Stay here," she said, not wanting to risk losing any of the other ones. She ran outside where Aden waited for her. "She's not there, Aden."

Aden pressed his lips into a hard line. "You stay here and keep an eye out for her. I'll take Junior down the path into the woods. Maybe she wandered off that way." He snapped his fingers. "Come here, Pilot."

The dog bounded toward Aden as if ready to play a game of tag.

Aden took Pilot's face in his hands. "Pilot, go find Amanda. Go find her."

Pilot took off like a shot, crossed the gravel driveway, and dove into a thick stand of bushes on the edge of the woods. He wasn't going to find her in that direction. Amanda wouldn't have been able to push through the thick undergrowth.

"Amanda!" Aden called as he and Junior took the path that led to the other side of Huckleberry Hill and disappeared into the woods.

Lily's legs shook violently. She went to the porch steps, sat down, and promptly burst into tears. She buried her face in her hands and started praying.

Rose, Uriah, and Evie startled her from her solitude when they came out onto the porch and started banging wooden spoons on metal pots from Anna's kitchen.

"What are you doing?" Lily said, raising her voice above the din.

"If Amanda is in the woods," Rose said, "she might not know which way to go. If we make noise, maybe she will come to the noise."

Lily ran up the steps and flung her arms around Rose. "What a wonderful-gute idea. Surely that will help Amanda find us." She surveyed the yard. It wouldn't hurt to look everywhere twice. Besides, she found it impossible to remain still. "Don't any of you move from the porch. I'm going to look in the barn again."

After ten minutes, the pot banging grew less energetic. Lily scoured the barn and garden and house again, but still no sign of Amanda. Lily had never felt so helpless or so frightened in her whole life. She wanted to run into the woods herself, but she didn't dare leave the other children alone.

Where was Aden? Why hadn't he found Amanda yet?

Aden and Junior reappeared on the path they had taken ten minutes ago. One look at Aden's face told her it was bad news. She held her breath anyway as he came to her and laid a gentle hand on her arm.

"I think we better call the police," Aden said, his voice heavy with worry.

Lily couldn't find her voice. She nodded.

"I will take the horse and ride down to the Van de Graffs'. They have a phone."

They looked across the driveway as the sound of rustling leaves caught their attention. Pilot padded out of the woods with his head hung low, carrying Amanda on his back as if he were a horse. Her little arms were wrapped around his neck, and she cried as if her heart would break.

Aden bolted to his dog, and Lily, light-headed with relief, followed close behind.

She lifted Amanda into her arms and hugged her close. Amanda was soaking wet. "Oh, Amanda. Why did you run off?" Aden wrapped his strong arms around Lily and Amanda in a three-way embrace. His warmth made Lily feel as if she'd be safe forever and always.

Amanda wouldn't stop crying.

"Is she hurt? Can you tell if she's hurt?"

Aden withdrew his arms and smoothed the wet tendrils of hair from Amanda's face. "Are you okay, Amanda?"

"I fell," Amanda wailed. "Pi-yot bite me."

Lily caught her breath. "Pilot bit you?"

Aden shook his head. "Pilot doesn't bite, Lily." He examined the hem of Amanda's dress. "Did he use his teeth to pull you out of the water?"

Amanda nodded. "I fell."

A pit formed in Lily's stomach. Amanda must have fallen into a puddle deep enough to soak her from head to toe. If that dog hadn't been there . . .

She nudged Aden's elbow and handed Amanda to him. Then she knelt down and threw her arms around Pilot's neck. "Good boy. Good, good dog."

He stuck out his tongue and licked her ear. She caressed his head as he yipped his pleasure and tried to lick her hand. "Oh, you beautiful, beautiful dog."

Aden smiled at her and kissed Amanda's cheek. By this time, Amanda had stopped crying, and she watched as Pilot, obviously pleased with himself, wagged his mammoth tail and ran circles around Lily, who kept trying to pet him.

"Pi-yot!" Amanda yelled, caught up in the jubilation.

Rose, Evie, and Uriah bounded down the steps and tried to give their own hugs to Pilot, but he hopped around the yard like an eighty-pound bunny rabbit as the three children and Lily chased him.

Lily felt like a schoolgirl again and found it impossible to stop giggling. Pilot would rather run around than be congratulated. She finally gave up chasing the silly dog and went to Aden's side. "Let's get her in the house and into something dry," she said.

Aden gave Amanda's arm a squeeze and nodded.

As soon as Lily stood still, Pilot came to her. He sat on his haunches next to her, as he had done before, like he was standing guard by her side. She reached out and petted the curly fur on top of his head. "Good boy. Good boy." Then she leaned over, scratched under his chin, and whispered in his ear, "I'll love you forever, you stupid, wonderful dog."

His wet nose nudged against her fingers.
Hand sanitizer did not cross her mind
once.

CHAPTER EIGHT

Lily had smiled at him today. A lot. But that didn't mean she liked him. That didn't mean they were going to get married or anything.

She was pretty, all right. He could hardly turn his attention from her when she was near, but that didn't mean she was his perfect match.

She had hugged Pilot, but that didn't mean she would ever really be fond of eighty-pound dogs with unruly fur.

Even though small children seemed to scare her, she had warmed up to them today. He loved the way her eyes sparkled just so when she read the children a book, as if she were living in the story instead of simply telling it.

Aden immediately caught a glimpse of her when he walked up the stairs into Yoders' living room for the gathering. She wore a burgundy dress that accentuated the golden highlights in her hair.

One thing was certain. He had to quit staring. A boy his age was too old to moon over a girl like a teenager.

Her face lit up like a sunrise when he caught her eye. She was happy to see him? That was unexpected.

Maybe not totally unexpected. He might have been a jailbird, but his dog had saved Amanda today.

"You came," she said, coming close enough that he could see the green and blue facets of her eyes. Much closer than four feet.

Quit staring. And don't think about how soft and sweet she felt in your arms today.

"Both you and Tyler Yoder invited me," Aden said. "Do you know Tyler Yoder?"

Was it his imagination or did she turn one shade redder?

"Jah. I know Tyler. He is in our district. His dat is the bishop."

Now he felt stupid. Of course she knew Tyler. Aden had watched Tyler make googly eyes at Lily for a full ten minutes two Sundays ago. Since when could he not even talk to her without tripping over his words?

He faked a cough and tore his gaze from her face. "How can I satisfy your dat when you insist on standing too close?" He took two steps back.

Lily shook her head. "That is all forgotten. My dat has given me permission to be your friend." She turned redder. "Tyler talked to him. I am not required to stay away from you anymore."

"In other words, you are instructed to show this misguided young man Christian charity."

She looked down at her hands. "My dat is a wise and gute man."

Aden's heart sank. She wasn't used to his sense of humor. He shouldn't be so flippant with such a straitlaced girl. "I didn't mean to offend you. I'm just teasing." He bent over so his eyes met hers. "Pilot will be happy to know that the *bann* is lifted."

She seemed to snap out of her embarrassment as her lips curled upward. "As if he ever obeyed it in the first place — not that I'm complaining." A shadow passed across Lily's face. "I owe that dog a lot."

"I thought you might have had a heart attack this afternoon."

"I feel terrible. To think Amanda walked away, and I didn't even notice. I'm never babysitting ever again."

"Those things happen. My mamm used to say that she had so many children that she did her best and trusted the rest to God.

She said Heavenly Father assigned an angel to each of us to keep us safe. I know I've got one."

"If that's true, then Pilot was Amanda's angel today. I get goose bumps thinking of what might have been."

"Don't think about that. Think about how everything turned out. That's a much happier ending," Aden said.

Lily glanced toward the entryway of the Yoders' split-level house. "There's somebody I want you to meet." She skipped down the stairs and took the hand of the special girl Aden had seen her with at gmay. She led the girl up the stairs to Aden. "This is Treva Schrock, one of my best friends."

Treva smiled and lifted her hand in a bashful wave but didn't meet Aden's eye.

"Nice to meet you, Treva."

Treva giggled and hooked her arm around Lily's elbow. Aden might have had a heart for animals, but Lily obviously had a big heart for this special girl.

A girl, taller than Lily but with the same hazel eyes, handed Aden, Lily, and Treva warm pretzels cradled in napkins. "They're better right out of the oven."

"Denki," Aden said.

"I'm Estelle, Lily's sister. Everybody calls me Estee." She reached over and tugged the sleeve of a young man behind Aden. The young man stumbled toward Estee, cheerfully letting her pull him into their little circle. "And this is Floyd Miller."

"Hullo," Floyd said. "We've heard a lot about you." He pursed his lips as the color traveled up his neck. "We weren't gossiping. I mean, we weren't trying to spread rumors or . . ." His voice trailed off. He must have decided to quit before he dug a deeper hole for himself.

Estee didn't have the same qualms. "So, you've been in prison. What was it like?"

Lily's face glowed. "Estee, hush!"

"Floyd's cousin says you chained yourself to a tree," Estee said. "Arty Weaver. Do you know him?"

"Jah, he lives in my district in Sugarcreek. Did he write and warn you I was coming?"

The blush continued its ascent of Floyd's face like a rising thermometer. "He wrote to us, but if I'd known he wanted to spread gossip, I wouldn't have read his letter. I should have burned it . . ."

Aden folded his arms and pinched his upper arm to keep from laughing. Poor Floyd.

Around the room, three other girls and several boys fell silent and gravitated closer to Aden. The juiciest gossip came straight from the horse's mouth. Only Lily and

109

Floyd seemed the least bit distressed.

Aden studied the eager faces surrounding him. "It was a beautiful old tree. I didn't want them to cut it down."

"It wouldn't be that hard to cut down a tree with somebody chained to it," Estee insisted, as two or three of the boys nodded. "They could have chopped the branches first."

"Or taken some bolt cutters and cut him loose," volunteered one of the boys.

"Yeah, they thought of that eventually." Aden rubbed the stubble on his chin — might as well announce his transgressions to the whole world and end the speculation. Maybe they'd decide he wasn't such a wicked man. Or maybe not. "There was this oak tree, probably two hundred years old, and some developers wanted to get rid of it to make room for a parking lot. It didn't seem right, this big old tree that was home to probably dozens of birds would be cut down. You can't replace something like that. The city wouldn't listen to our petition, so on the day they were supposed to chop it down, my friend Jamal and I and six other people chained ourselves around the tree. We made it into the newspapers."

"And they arrested you?" Estee asked.

"Once they cut the chains off." Aden

pointed at the boy who'd spoken up. "With bolt cutters. But with all the bad publicity, the developer had a change of heart and built the parking lot around the tree. There's a nice little park where the tree stands, maybe fifty feet by fifty feet, but at least we saved it. I spent three days in jail and one night in the hospital."

Worry traveled across Lily's face. Aden found the emotion particularly endearing. "The hospital? Were you hurt?"

Aden brushed his finger along the scar on his eyebrow. "I caught the butt of the property owner's rifle and got a wonderful-gute concussion."

"Oy anyhow," mumbled one of the boys.

Lily looked around the room, where it appeared that every eye stared at Aden. "He once got in trouble for trespassing because he fed a man's starving horse."

Aden couldn't deny the warmth tingling from his chest to the tips of his fingers. Lily was defending him?

Tyler Yoder seemed to appear out of nowhere. "No animal should suffer at the hands of man."

Everyone nodded.

"I went to jail one other time," Aden said, wanting to confess everything so people like Floyd would not feel guilty about spreading gossip. "A group of us sat in the mayor's office and wouldn't leave. We were protesting a new road that didn't need to be built. We lost that one." The failure still stung. A pond along a geese migration route had been destroyed.

The boy who'd suggested bolt cutters spoke up. "Plain folk should stay out of the affairs of men."

"Jah," Aden said ruefully. "My bishop thought so too."

Tyler broke the silence when he lifted his half-eaten pretzel in the air. "Everybody get a pretzel while they're hot, and we'll go play volleyball."

A woman who must have been Tyler's mamm stood at the bottom of the stairs with a tray of golden-brown pretzels. The young people turned their attention from Aden, marched down the stairs, and filed out the door. Lily whispered something to Treva, and Treva followed the others outside. Besides Aden, only Estee, Floyd, Lily, and Tyler remained.

Apparently, Estee's curiosity was not satisfied. "Did they put you under the bann?"

Lily growled, grabbed her sister's hand, and dragged her down the stairs. "Stop it, Estee."

Aden smiled. These questions didn't

bother him. He wasn't ashamed of what he had done. "If you've heard from Floyd's cousin, you already know the answer to that."

Floyd nearly jumped out of his skin and followed Lily and Estee out the door. Aden mentally smacked himself upside the head. He had to stop being so cheeky. Neither Floyd nor Lily could begin to guess he was only teasing.

Tyler frowned — or at least seemed to frown. His face mostly held one expression. "You know Floyd will feel guilty for days."

"I'll apologize," Aden said as he bounded down the stairs.

"Miss everything he sends your way in volleyball. That will make him feel better."

"I can do that, although he might feel guilty for being a better player than I am."

Tyler's mamm still stood at the door with her tray of pretzels. "Could you boys carry the lemonade and cups out to the backyard?"

"Mamm," Tyler said, "this is Aden Helmuth. He is staying with Anna and Felty for the summer."

His mother's round face bloomed into a smile. "We have heard so much about you, Aden. Floyd's cousin is in your district."

Nobody would want Aden on his team after today. He stood on the other side of the net from Lily and had the hardest time concentrating on volleyball. He didn't need to pretend to play poorly. Every ball Floyd Miller or anyone else hit to Aden came in too fast or had an awkward spin. He'd never played so dreadfully. But Lily kept smiling at him, so his clumsiness didn't matter.

After volleyball, the large group of young people sat under the trees in the backyard and sang songs. While harmony wasn't used at church, the songs at gatherings were rich with layers of sound.

Aden made a point of sitting next to Floyd and Estee during the singing. He leaned in to whisper to Floyd when the voices were the loudest. "You know I was teasing you about your cousin, jah?"

Floyd sat with his forearms propped on his knees. "I shouldn't have listened to gossip."

"It doesn't matter."

"But I spread the rumors. I told Estee."

"I don't want you to feel uncomfortable about it. You didn't do anything wrong."

Floyd twitched his lips upward. "I appreci-

114

ate that. But I've learned my lesson. Gossiping is wicked."

"I don't mind if you get your news from your cousin. He knows me pretty well."

Floyd snapped his head around to look at Aden. "He didn't tell us if you were shunned or not." Aden started to speak, and Floyd held up his hand to stop him. "I don't want to know."

"You'll want to know this. I wasn't shunned. The bann is rare in Sugarcreek."

Floyd's eyes grew wide, and he nudged Estee. "Did you hear that, Estee? That's why Arty didn't tell us."

Aden stifled a chuckle.

They sang for an hour, and then Tyler's mamm and dat lugged out a big orange jug. Everybody lined up for a drink. Aden stood by no one in particular watching all the different youth of Mammi and Dawdi's district as well as the other district in Bonduel. Estee and Floyd were obviously enamored with each other — probably a wedding in store this fall.

Lily came toward him, smiling again, and handed him a cup of root beer. "It's delicious. I didn't want you to miss out."

Their fingers brushed as Aden took the cup. "Denki. That's very kind."

"You looked like you worked up a thirst

115

playing ball."

"I ran after the ball a lot."

Lily's smile faded. "I'm sorry about Estee. She is overbearing at times."

"Not at all. I appreciate that she would come straight to me. Most people circulate rumors without ever trying to find out the truth."

"I can't believe someone struck you with his gun."

Aden fingered the scar embedded in his eyebrow. "I didn't feel much. It knocked me out."

"But the scar is attractive," Lily said, and then her lips twisted sheepishly as an appealing blush tinted her cheeks. "I mean, it looks interesting and . . . never mind."

Aden pretended to look at a distant tree so she could gather her wits. "Denki. I'll be sure to send a thank-you note to the plastic surgeon."

Tyler came toward them with the bishop, his dat, by his side. Tyler in his stiff and formal manner stationed himself next to Lily. "Aden, I want you to meet my dat, Monroe Yoder."

Aden shook hands with the bishop. "We met at gmay."

Tyler was definitely his father's son even though his dat was twice as large as Tyler.

They shared the same thin nose and the same dark eyebrows, but his dat's round belly bulged over his trousers like a muffin escaping its paper.

"Talk to my dat about organic farming. We are thinking about growing vegetables to supplement the dairy."

"I don't want to drench the soil with poisons like so many farmers do," said Monroe.

"We're expanding our herd," Tyler said, becoming more animated than Aden had seen him. His eyes danced with excitement, and he actually relaxed his arm enough to make a gesture. "We're going to buy a methane digester for all the manure and sell electricity."

"Tyler's idea," Monroe said, smiling at his son.

Aden couldn't help but be impressed. "Biogas recovery? That's wonderful gute. It reduces pollution."

"By a lot," said Tyler, nodding vigorously. "And some dairies make more money selling electricity than they do selling milk."

The bishop thumbed his suspenders. "Tyler's got all sorts of ideas."

Tyler shook his head. "They are all from other people. I met a man from Hillsboro who has an organic farm. He's built a

117

chicken coop he can pick up and move from pasture to pasture. The cows keep the grass down and then he moves the chickens in. Two types of fertilizer." Tyler subdued his enthusiasm and cleared his throat. "All this talk of manure and chicken coops is probably boring you, Lily."

"Of course not," Lily said. "A portable chicken coop would be a sight to see. We won't ever be able to move ours. I helped my dat build a sturdy fence around it to keep the foxes away. And we still have to use steel traps in the winter."

Aden's heart flipped over. "You use steel traps?"

Lily nodded. "A fence doesn't stop all of the pests."

He knew before the words came out of his mouth that he shouldn't have said them. "Lily, does your dat know how cruel steel traps are?"

Lily's cheeks lost their color. "Foxes kill our chickens. We count on those chickens to feed our family."

Aden tried to subdue his indignation. That little voice inside his head told him it was none of his business how David Eicher disposed of scavengers on his farm. Unfortunately, Aden seldom heeded that voice. That's why he had a police record. "Those

118

traps have teeth that gouge into the flesh and cause great suffering to the animal. Sometimes animals will chew off their own foot to escape. Or there's the terror of waiting for the farmer to come out in the morning and bludgeon them to death."

Lily's eyes sparkled with tears. Aden clamped his mouth shut and chastised himself for being so stupid. Lily wouldn't dare step one foot out of line, and he'd accused her of torturing animals.

Tyler, obviously more sensitive than foot-in-his-mouth Aden, gazed at Lily with concern. "I'm sure Lily's dat doesn't mean to be cruel. Many people use steel traps."

Aden took off his hat and shoved his fingers through his hair. "I'm sorry, Lily. I get worked up, and then there's no stopping my mouth."

Lily wouldn't meet his eye. Instead, she gathered everyone's empty root beer cups and took them to the garbage can on the other side of the yard — as far away from Aden as she could go.

The bishop glanced doubtfully at Aden. "I'll go see to our supply of cups," he said before walking away.

Only Tyler stuck with him.

"I'm such an idiot," Aden growled. "I didn't mean to hurt her feelings."

Tyler flowed with sympathy. "It's just that Lily never does anything wrong. She's careful about following the rules, and she's very sensitive about animals in particular. You made her doubt herself."

"I wish I didn't get so riled up. Lots of Amish use steel traps. My dat used to use steel traps."

The corner of Tyler's mouth quirked up. He must have been extremely amused. "Until you talked him out of it?"

"Jah. Until I bit his head off."

Tyler smiled while Aden laughed.

"How many more heads do you plan on biting off tonight? Should I stay close?" Tyler said.

"None. I will never bite another head off again. Meekness and persuasion influence more people than coercion ever will."

Tyler raised an eyebrow. "Big words. I don't even know what you said."

"It means I'm going to try asking nicely next time."

"Gute plan. You don't want to lose any more friendships."

He hadn't lost Lily's friendship over something so minor, had he? A painful emptiness unexpectedly filled Aden's chest. It didn't feel so minor after all.

■ ■ ■ ■

The gathering of young people dispersed shortly after Aden had made a fool of himself. Lily didn't venture near him again, and he spent the rest of the evening standing by other people with his gaze fixed in Lily's direction.

She moved and spoke and gestured with a simple grace that captivated Aden so he couldn't think on anything else. With a knot in his stomach, he watched as Tyler slowly, cleverly edged close to her and asked her something. She nodded with a half smile on her lips, and they walked out of the yard together. Tyler had offered to drive Lily home, that much was plain.

The uncomfortable, heavy feeling took Aden by surprise. Why should he be jealous? He already knew he wasn't going to marry Lily. She was a short, little thing who didn't like his dog.

In his mind, he saw Lily, as she had looked earlier today, when she threw her arms around Pilot and hugged him tight.

Aden shook his head to clear it. That didn't mean she liked his dog, and it certainly didn't mean he was ever going to marry her.

When Aden got home, Mammi sat knitting in her rocker while Dawdi dozed in his overstuffed recliner. Aden thought they would have gone to bed by now.

"How was the gathering?" Mammi said as Aden came through the door.

"Fine."

Mammi held up her knitting needles looped with green yarn. "I am making Pilot a sweater. He and Sparky will match."

Aden smiled wearily. "He'll like that."

"Did you make more friends tonight?" Mammi asked.

Aden hung his hat on a hook. "I told them the story of chaining myself to the tree. They liked it."

"That one always busts me up laughing," said Dawdi without opening his eyes.

"Did you see Lily?"

"Jah, she was there."

"Did you ask to drive her home, like I told you?"

Aden sat on the sofa and propped his forearms on his knees. That way he could look Mammi straight in the eye, and she would know he was serious. "Mammi, you have been so gute to me, and I can't begin to thank you for letting me stay here. You've even taken on the chore of finding me a wife. I don't want to sound ungrateful, but

122

could you find me a wife who doesn't already have a boyfriend?"

Closing her eyes, Lily let the cool breeze tease wisps of hair around her face. She loved being in a courting buggy. Riding in the open air at night always made her feel like she could reach to heaven and touch the stars with her fingers.

Tyler kept the horse at a nice steady speed. He knew Lily didn't like to go fast. She feared she might fall out or the buggy would overturn if the pace were too hurried.

Lily glanced at Tyler out of the corner of her eye. He seemed content to ride in silence. Guilt tugged at her. Her interest in Tyler had waned in the last few weeks. Maybe she shouldn't have agreed to let him drive her home. He was nice enough and so steady — a gute candidate for a husband — but lately, she hadn't found him all that interesting.

But Dat encouraged the relationship. He thought the world of Tyler, and who was Lily to disagree? She trusted her father's judgment more than her own. It was a painful lesson the last time she had disregarded his warnings.

So she would persist. Falling in love didn't

always come with bells and whistles. Sometimes it sneaked up on you, like a sunrise. Neither she nor Tyler needed to force anything. Marriage was not in her plans this year. One wedding in the family would be quite enough.

Tyler broke the silence. "Are you feeling better?"

"Oh, of course. Aden did not mean to insult my dat. He has some strange ideas, that's all."

"He is passionate about the treatment of God's creatures, as we all should be. God does not look kindly on a man who makes animals suffer."

"My dat would never purposely be cruel to an animal. He wants to protect our chickens."

"Of course. I'm sure Aden knows that. But Aden is the kind of person who has the courage to speak up for what he feels is right, even at the risk of offending everybody."

"Or getting arrested," Lily said.

"Jah, although our way is not to meddle in other men's affairs. God will make all things right. Aden will learn."

"I know he was mad tonight, but I also know he wouldn't hurt a fly. He has a gentle spirit."

"No doubt," Tyler said.

They turned up Lily's lane and the gravel crunched under the buggy wheels as they slowly rolled to a stop. Tyler jumped down and helped Lily from the buggy.

"Denki, Tyler, for the lovely ride."

"Will I see you at the *singeon* on Sunday?"

"Lord willing."

A wall of heat accosted Lily as she walked into her house. In the summertime, Mama kept the windows open as wide as they would go, but the house always felt stifling hot until late into the evening.

Lily made her way into the kitchen where Mama and Dat sat looking at a pile of receipts.

"How was the gathering?" Mama asked.

"Fun. They had root beer. We played volleyball. Aden Helmuth told everybody how he got the scar on his eyebrow. Tyler's mamm made pretzels."

Dat wrinkled his forehead and regarded Lily with a stern countenance. "Aden Helmuth was there?"

"There is no good reason for him to stay away."

"I suppose not."

"How did Aden get that scar on his eyebrow? Did it happen in prison?" Mama asked.

"He was trying to protect a tree, and somebody cracked him with the butt of a rifle."

Dat grunted his disapproval. "What kind of odd boy tries to protect a tree? Trees can take care of themselves."

Lily didn't attempt to explain. Dat would never understand Aden's passion for living things like Lily did. "We had pretzels."

Dat stroked his beard. "Lily, I know I told you we must show Aden Helmuth Christian kindness and Tyler reassured me that Aden is a gute boy, but take care. Don't get caught in any of his schemes. It is too easy for young people to get caught in schemes."

"As far as I know, he doesn't have any schemes."

"That's what I thought about Zeke's friends. When I learned the truth, it was too late." Hurt flashed in Dat's eyes as it always did when he spoke of *Onkel* Zeke. He didn't need to say more.

"Is Estee with you?" Mama said.

"Nae. Floyd drove her home."

Mama grinned. "And who drove you home?"

Lily cracked a smile, amused with her mama's delight. Mama and Dat liked Tyler Yoder. "Who do you think, Mama?"

Mama clapped her hands. Dat looked at

her as if he knew everything and waited for her to spill the beans.

"A certain bishop's son?" Mama said, gushing with glee.

Lily nodded.

Dat shook his finger at Lily. "Stick with Tyler Yoder. He will make a fine husband, and he doesn't have any schemes."

"Okay, Dat."

Lily sat next to her parents and watched as Mama wrote numbers in the family budget notebook. She nibbled on her bottom lip as she formulated her request. Leaning close so Dat would know she was serious, she said, "Dat, do you think we could throw away our steel traps?"

CHAPTER NINE

Lily hadn't laid eyes on Aden all morning. If he'd wanted to see her, he could have easily breezed into the house and said hello. But no, for two weeks the incorrigible Aden Helmuth had made himself as scarce as hen's teeth, when all Lily wanted to do was practice her Christian charity on him.

And catch a glimpse of those irresistible eyes.

But mostly practice charity.

Her gaze strayed to the window more than once. Maybe he was still mad at her for using steel traps. Well, maybe she was still mad at him for being mad at her.

She wanted to see him, but she couldn't very well abandon the chicken or the nasty tofu frying in the skillet. The coleslaw and biscuits were done and as soon as the chicken cooked, they were off to Cobbler Pond for a picnic.

Lily glanced at the small pile of stockings

near the door. Pilot collected socks like other dogs collected bones. He often presented her with a dirty sock as a going-away present after work. She hadn't seen him today. Even though she always tried to resist that wet tongue, she was getting used to his daily attacks.

Anna and Felty ambled into the great room with Felty singing one of his many melodies. He never sang the same lyrics twice. *"I need no mansions here below, for Jesus said that I will grow, a happy tree in the sky not made with hands."*

Felty carried a pile of blankets, and Anna held the picnic basket. "Almost ready for our picnic?" Anna asked, as if she'd never done anything quite so exciting in her entire life.

Lily turned a piece of chicken in the frying pan. "We could go out here on the grass, Anna, if you don't want to lug everything to Cobbler Pond. It's a half-hour drive."

"Oh, we must go to Cobbler Pond," Anna said. "The trees are lovely."

Felty laid his bundle of blankets on the sofa and walked to the cookstove to inspect the chicken. "We ain't seen any progress for weeks. Anna is redoubling her efforts," he said.

Lily had no idea what that meant.

"Cobbler Pond is quite a romantic spot," Anna said. "The sunsets are beautiful."

Lily decided not to mention that their picnic would be long done before the sun even thought about setting over Cobbler Pond. "The chicken is almost cooked, but I'm not sure I did this tofu right."

Anna bustled to the cookstove and joined Felty in gazing into Lily's pan of fried white mush. "If you made it, Aden will love it," Anna said, patting her on the arm. "You are becoming an expert vegetarian cook."

Expert? Peanut butter and jelly and tofu hardly constituted mastery.

She heard Aden stomping up the porch steps, and her heart somersaulted in her chest. Would he be happy to see her or give her a lecture on the evils of eating bacon?

The door opened, and Aden's dog bounded into the great room wearing a bright green sweater with a lovely blue stripe around the middle. Pilot saw Lily and barreled toward her like a runaway freight train. Lily stood her ground and held up her hand in warning. "Stop, Pilot." Pilot obediently halted and cocked his head to look at Lily the way he always did. "Just because you saved Amanda's life doesn't mean you have permission to jump all over me."

She knew Aden stared at her, but when

she met his eye, he looked away. But he was smiling.

Aden didn't say much as he drove the buggy to Cobbler Pond. Pilot and Felty sat up front with him, and Anna and Lily sat in back. Pilot took up more than his share of the front seat sitting between Aden and Felty, but neither of them seemed to mind. Felty scratched Pilot's head almost the entire trip and periodically gave the dog a hearty pat.

In the backseat, Anna wanted to talk about Aden and her latest knitting projects. "Aden has built us a compost bin," she said. "It's a very clever design. We put apple and cucumber peelings and such inside and then a lever lets us turn it around and around to stir it. Aden says it will turn into gute soil for the garden."

"Would you look at that," Felty exclaimed as a truck and camper passed the buggy. "New York."

Barely a hundred yards wide and probably ten feet deep at its deepest point, Cobbler Pond sat off the road in a nice little hollow east of Bonduel. Lily didn't come here often because she didn't know how to swim and didn't particularly enjoy the water, but the trees were lovely and wildflowers grew in thick clumps amidst the

131

grass surrounding the pond. The water looked murky, and patches of algae floated on the surface near the far bank.

With a firm grip and a strong arm, Aden helped Anna from the back of the buggy as easy as you please. He took Lily's hand as she descended and sent a tingling sensation traveling up her arm, but he released her as soon as she had alighted.

Lily reached into the backseat and retrieved the picnic basket.

"I'll carry it," Aden said, taking it from her hand and gracing her with a half smile. He reached around her and snatched up the blankets too.

His reaching brought him heart-stoppingly close to Lily, and he surprised her when he whispered, "It's been exactly fifteen days, seventeen hours, and twenty minutes. Are you still mad at me?"

The whispering knocked her off-kilter. Why did he get even more handsome when he lowered his voice?

He bent his head toward her so she had a perfect view of his mouth. It was a very nice mouth.

Mustn't stare at the mouth.

Couldn't he sense that this closeness made her nervous? Lily stepped back and away from him but the buggy stood behind her, and she couldn't go far. "I'm . . . are you still mad at *me*?"

He didn't pull away. "I'm not mad. You didn't do anything wrong. I, on the other hand, have been wondering how long I should give it before you forget the whole incident. Do you need a few more days to mull it over?"

"I . . . I am fine." With her heart pounding a wild cadence, she scooted around him and put herself at a more comfortable distance.

Aden slumped his shoulders. "I can't see you getting mad at anybody. It's not in your nature to fight back. I bulldozed you, and I'm sorry."

The dog barreled toward Lily, and it was Aden's fault that she didn't completely have her wits about her. She turned as Pilot, who had been playing in the water, jumped and planted his wet paws on her shoulders. Aden dropped the blankets and the picnic basket and caught her from behind so she didn't tumble to the ground. "Pilot, get off," she commanded.

Pilot, ever the innocent bystander, got down, backed away, and whined contritely.

Lily was acutely aware when Aden released his firm grip on her. She took a tissue from her pocket and made a futile attempt to

133

wipe the mud from her apron. "You did hurt my feelings," she said, "but you didn't mean any harm. Tyler thinks you are brave to speak up."

A shadow passed across Aden's face.

Lily didn't like his cloudy expression. "I will overlook your transgression this once because your dog is a hero."

Aden's mouth quirked into a grin, and he tousled the fur on Pilot's head. "Then I hope Pilot stays in your good graces."

Lily gave up wiping her apron. "He won't."

"Lily!"

Lily turned to see Treva Schrock and her parents trudging up the shore to Helmuths' buggy. Lily threw her arms wide, and Treva catapulted herself into Lily's embrace.

"What are you doing here?" Lily asked.

Few people could understand Treva when she spoke, even when she formed her words with great care. But Lily spent enough time around her to always know what she was trying to say. "Came eat lunch," Treva said, keeping her grip tightly around Lily's waist.

"We're having a picnic today too," Lily said.

Treva's father, a thick, sturdy man with unruly eyebrows, followed his daughter up to the buggy and shook Aden's hand.

"Hello. I am Nathan Schrock," he said. "This is my wife Margaret. Lily is Treva's best friend."

"It's lovely to see you," Anna said.

"I saw squirrel," Treva said.

"A squirrel? Did he want to eat your food?"

Treva wanted to tell Lily all about her picnic, and Lily listened enthusiastically while the others waited. She tried to ignore the tenderness that gathered around Aden's eyes the longer they stood there. He was becoming a large distraction.

"Treva, tell Lily good-bye," said her dat. "There is laundry to do at home yet."

Treva reached up and gave Lily a loud kiss on the cheek. "Bye, Lily. See at gmay."

Holding onto her mother's hand, Treva looked over her shoulder and waved until she ducked into her buggy and her dat drove away.

"I've never seen that girl without a smile," Anna said. "What a treasure."

Aden stared at Lily until she thought she might burst with giddy agitation. "Aden," she finally said, "will you stop that?"

"Stop what?"

"Oh . . . just stop."

He shrugged and flashed her a cocky grin. "How can I know what to stop if I don't

135

know I'm doing it?"

"You know well enough."

His eyes glowed as he studied her face. "You have a gute heart, Lily."

"Nae. None is gute but God."

Anna and Felty, arm in arm, were already halfway to the pond. Aden picked up the basket and the blankets and shrugged Lily's hand away when she tried to take something from him. "There is a nice spot under that tree where we can lay a blanket."

Anna pointed to a weathered wooden jetty that stretched ten feet into the water. "That is where Aden's dat asked Aden's mamm to marry him. Isn't that romantic, Lily?"

"It doesn't look safe to walk on," Lily said, "with no railing like that."

Did Aden suppress a smile? "I'm sure my dat held tight to my mamm so she wouldn't fall." Without warning, he laid his armful on the ground and sprinted to the jetty.

Lily caught her breath as he jogged to the end of the jetty. With each step, the ancient wood creaked under his feet. She thought he might jump into the water. Instead, he shot Lily a mischievous grin and did a cartwheel that took the length of the small dock. He was quite limber for someone so tall.

Lily almost couldn't watch. "Aden Helmuth! You're going to fall in."

"Such a fine young man," Anna said.

"But thick in the head," Felty added.

"Now, Felty. Lily doesn't think he's thick. Do you, Lily?"

Still showing off, Aden did a little jig backward and stood at the edge of the jetty with his back to the water. He raised his arms in victory as Lily's nerves pulled taut. "Look at me, Lily. Not falling," he called, taunting her with that irresistible grin. "Perfectly safe."

Pilot, who never wanted to be left out of the frolicking, stampeded up the jetty at full speed. The look of surprise on Aden's face was priceless right before Pilot crashed into him. They both flew into the water with a giant splash.

Lily let out a cry of dismay, and her heart stopped until Aden's head bobbed to the surface. He spat out a stream of water and burst into infectious laughter.

"It's gute he knows how to swim," Felty said.

Pilot paddled around Aden as they both splashed and made an extravagant fuss. Aden pointed to his hat that floated out of his reach, and Pilot swam to it, captured it in his teeth, and made his way toward shore. Aden followed him with long, steady

137

strokes, and soon they emerged from the water, bringing a good portion of the pond with them.

Aden stretched out his arms. "Want a hug, Mammi?"

Anna squeaked in alarm and waved him away. "Now, Aden, don't try anything tricky."

Lily pulled one of the blankets from the pile. "Here, put this around your shoulders so you don't catch your death."

Aden reached out, but instead of taking the blanket, he grabbed Lily's hand and tugged her toward the pond. "The water's fine. Would you like to try?"

Lily attempted to pull away from him as she pushed down that panicked feeling she always got when she contemplated doing something scary.

Aden kept hold of her hand and chuckled. "Sorry. Just teasing. I would never be reckless with you." He squeezed her fingers and rubbed his thumb along the back of her hand. Time paused as they both studied their clasped hands before Aden curled his lips sheepishly and released her.

Clearing her throat, Lily unfurled the blanket, reached up, and wrapped it around Aden's shoulders.

His gaze pierced her skull. "Denki."

Pilot decided he wanted to share his bath. He shook himself from head to toe, sending water droplets flying over everyone. Anna and Felty both shielded their faces but didn't seem to mind the extra shower.

"Pilot!" Lily shouted. "Get away."

Pilot trotted back to the shoreline and shook himself again. Aden's unruly dog was surprisingly obedient.

"Aden, you're going to catch your death of cold in those wet clothes," Anna said.

"Mammi, it's July twenty-fourth, and it can't be less than ninety degrees out here. I think I'll be fine."

Lily didn't know how Anna managed to be so prepared. She shook her head and pulled a gray knitted scarf from the picnic basket. "Bend over," she said to Aden.

He obediently leaned toward his mammi, and she wrapped the extra-long scarf around his neck three times. "There," she said, patting his chest. "Much better."

Aden grinned and winked at Lily. That boy was completely inappropriate. She turned her face away, sure she didn't fool anyone. Her ears were probably blushing too.

Lily spread the largest blanket over the grass, taking care not to crush any wildflowers. It would make Aden unhappy if she

139

crushed any wildflowers.

Grunting and groaning, Anna and Felty both lowered themselves to the blanket.

"Are you okay, Mammi?"

"Jah, but you will have to help me when it's time to go. I couldn't get up by myself to save my life."

"Me either," said Felty. "I hope neither of us has to go to the bathroom."

Aden set the picnic basket on the blanket. Lily knelt next to the basket and pulled the food from inside. Aden hesitated, glanced at his mammi, and sat down next to Lily, a move that sent a tingle of pleasure down her spine. She immediately sat up straight and banished that tingle straight out of her head.

"I promise not to get you wet," he said.

She merely nodded and scooted a good three inches away from him. Dat would not approve of Aden sitting so close. And neither did Lily. She did not want to get pulled into one of his schemes, whatever they were.

"This food looks fit for a king," Felty said.

Lily assembled a plate of food for everybody, and they ate as they watched two Amish boys on the other side of the pond try to launch their canoe into the water.

They had their horse hooked to a wide,

low cart with the canoe secured on top. They tried to back the horse with the cart into the water, but the horse didn't want to cooperate. Walking backward into the water must have spooked him, because he whinnied and snorted and shook his head in protest as the boys tried to guide him.

Aden turned to stone beside her. The muscles of his jaw tightened as he balled his hands into fists.

He caught her staring and seemed to relax in an instant. Smiling reassuringly, he stood up and left his blanket behind. "I think I'll go help those boys launch their canoe."

He marched around the edge of the pond in purposeful strides with Pilot loping alongside.

Should she go help, or was this one of those schemes Dat warned her about? Lily took a deep breath because she suddenly couldn't get enough air. Remaining safely on the blanket seemed a very good option.

Before Aden could reach them, the horse and cart lurched backward. The cart glided into the water, pulling the horse with it. The horse protested as he lost footing and went into the water with the cart.

Lily flinched. She had no idea the pond was so deep at that spot.

The two boys called out in alarm, and

141

Aden exploded into a full sprint.

Felty, looking as spry as a seventy-year-old, leaped from the blanket. "We've got to help," he said. He held out his hand to pull Anna from the ground.

She waved him away. "Go. You two go. I'll only slow you down."

Lily's heart beat so fast, her chest ached. She'd much rather stay comfortably on the blanket with Anna. But as eager as Felty was, she could still get to the other side of the pond ten times faster than he could.

Sure enough, when she stood and took a step toward him, he said, "Don't wait for me. I'll be along."

With the dread rising in her throat, she turned and ran as fast as she could toward Aden and the horse.

Lily kept her eyes on the far side of the pond. The canoe floated off the cart, and the cart, still attached to the horse, began to sink. With the bottom half of his body already submerged, the horse bellowed as his front hooves tried to find purchase on the muddy shore. One of the boys grabbed the harness at the horse's neck and strained to pull him out of the water. The other boy worked to unfasten the straps that secured the cart to the horse, but the horse thrashed about so violently that the boy couldn't get a good grip.

As soon as Aden reached them, he immediately set to work loosening the straps. He and the other boy labored on opposite sides of the horse. The horse seemed to lose footing with every attempt he made to climb out of the pond. The water soon rose to his withers, and still he sank.

Finally, Aden and the other boy managed to release the straps that bound the horse to the cart. The horse, now with only head and neck above water, stopped sinking, but didn't jump out of the water like Lily thought he would.

She finally reached them. One boy still had his hands firmly around the reins, straining to pull his horse from the water, but the horse didn't budge.

"How deep is the water right there?" Aden asked, breathing heavily.

"He should be standing on bottom," one of the boys said. "I don't understand why he won't come out."

Aden sat down and took off his boots and stockings. "I think he's stuck." He tossed his boots onto the grass while Pilot took care of his socks by scooping them up with his teeth and piling them in the sand.

Lily stared at Aden in disbelief. "You're not going in there?"

"Jah," he said. "I think his hoof might be caught on something."

"He could kick you in the head and kill you," Lily said, the panic growing inside her. "What if you drown?"

Although concern clouded his expression, he flashed a smile. "Some things are worth taking the risk for, Lily."

She laid a hand on his arm as if to stop him.

He winked. "I am a gute swimmer."

Why did he have to wink? The gesture muddled her thinking, and before she could formulate a convincing argument for his staying onshore, he splashed into the water and disappeared beneath the surface. Pilot followed him with a running leap. The dog's head bobbed above the water as he swam in a wide circle around the horse's dangerous hind parts.

"Take care of him, Pilot," she yelled.

Pilot looked her way and nodded.

Dogs didn't nod. She must be going batty.

Lily held her breath as if she were the one swimming in the dark depths of the murky pond. Would Aden be able to see anything under there? She dreaded pulling his lifeless body from the water after the horse had kicked him senseless.

Lily's legs couldn't support her weight.

She stumbled to the edge of the water and sat down, looking for something she feared she wouldn't find.

The horse kept at his frantic struggle, flailing his legs and bobbing his head up and down. He whinnied and groaned as the boys kept a tight hold on his reins.

Aden had been under there too long. Lily's mouth felt full of sawdust. What should she do? Should they find a phone and call the police?

Felty finally made it around the pond and stood next to Lily as she stared into the water, willing Aden to appear.

"He can hold his breath a long time," Felty said. "He's got the Helmuth lungs."

Lily was not comforted. What did she know of the legendary Helmuth lungs? She forced herself to breathe and tried to think clearly. What could she do?

The horse made great waves as he suddenly shifted to his left, found a gentle incline, and climbed out of the water as easy as you please. Pilot, unmindful of his charge to take care of Aden, followed on the horse's heels.

"Where's Aden? Where's Aden?" Lily screamed. Wild with fear, she leaped to her feet and scanned the water. She almost gave in to the urge to jump in herself, though she couldn't swim and Dat would sorely chastise her if she drowned. Her eyes stung with tears.

Where was he?

Finally, blessedly, praise the Lord, Aden splashed to the surface. He took a deep, gasping breath and then sputtered and coughed as he paddled his way to shore. He didn't have to swim far before his feet found bottom, and he trudged through the muck toward her with a handful of gray yarn in his fist.

The light-headedness threatened to make Lily sink to her knees. If Aden ever tried to kill himself again, she would have to remember to keep breathing while she panicked.

Aden wore a delighted smile even though blood trickled from his nose. Coming to shore, he shoved the pile of yarn that used to be Anna's scarf into his pocket.

Lily's overwhelming relief soon gave way to indignation. How dare he get hurt! She charged at him and pounded on his hard chest. "Don't you ever do that again."

He grabbed her wrists before she could do any permanent damage — to her hands — and widened that aggravating grin.

"It's bad enough that you don't have the courtesy to come up for air, then you have the nerve to get hurt." Her voice cracked, and she stifled the sob that wanted to escape her lips.

Aden was soaking wet, but he wrapped his arms around her in a surprisingly warm hug. She could feel his heart pounding against her cheek. "It's okay," he said soothingly. "I'm okay."

Lily let herself melt into his embrace and drew comfort from his strength. Why was she so upset? A boy this strong would never drown. A boy this strong could do anything. After a few seconds of bliss, she realized how soggy she was becoming and pulled away.

Her face blazed with heat. Had she just let Aden Helmuth hug her?

His eyes sparkled as he looked at her, still smiling. His stare unnerved her, as it always did. Averting her eyes, she reached into her soggy apron pocket and pulled out an equally soggy handkerchief. He took it and wiped the blood from his nose.

Anna had somehow managed to make it to their side of the pond. Felty took her hand, and they both looked at Aden as if his standing there dripping and bleeding were an everyday occurrence.

"The horse's rear hoof caught on a piece of wire. He kept pulling forward and the wire was looped around the front of his hoof. When I got down there I realized I still had the scarf around my neck, praise the Lord. I wrapped it around his hoof and pulled back on it while moving the wire as best I could. It's good the scarf was so long. He almost conked me in the head three or four times."

Lily caught her breath just thinking about it.

"Once he was free of the wire, he jumped right out." Aden pulled the yarn from his pocket. "Sorry about your scarf, Mammi."

Anna took what used to be her scarf from Aden and fingered the strands of yarn. "It looks like someone got carried away frogging, but my knitting has never saved someone's life before. It's a miracle."

"It's a good thing you knitted it so well," Felty added. "A lesser scarf might have unraveled instantly."

Anna nodded in awe. "I give all the glory to the good Lord."

Aden dabbed at his nose while he took up his disconcerting habit of staring at Lily. "You still look pale."

"I thought you were drowned when the horse came out and you didn't."

He grinned. "I explored the bottom of the pond before coming up for air. The horse caught his foot on a tangle of baling wire.

148

And there's an old car down there."

Anna worked the fuzzy, soggy yarn between her fingers to determine if any of it was salvageable. "I'll start on a replacement scarf today."

Aden finally quit staring at her when one of the boys drew his attention. They had led the horse away from the shore and tethered him to a tree, where the two boys squatted to examine the horse's leg. Lily saw a minor smear of blood above the horse's hoof where the wire must have cut into his hide.

One boy stood and shook Aden's hand, and Lily could hear him thank Aden profusely for his help. He *should* be grateful. Aden could have been seriously hurt. The boy pointed to the middle of the pond where his canoe bobbed lazily.

Aden turned to Lily, shrugged, and flashed her an apologetic look. Her heart resumed its forceful cadence. "What?" she said.

Aden came back to Lily and his grandparents and spoke directly to Felty, although Lily knew his message was for her. "Neither John or his brother Crist knows how to swim. I'm going to help them get their trailer and their boat."

"No, you're not," Lily said, not caring how bossy she sounded.

"Oh, dear," Anna said, furrowing her

149

brow. "I don't have any more scarves."

Aden finally met Lily's eyes. "I know how to swim."

Lily folded her arms across her chest in a show that she wouldn't budge. "You're not risking your life for their canoe. It will float to shore eventually."

Aden didn't take her concerns seriously. The corner of his mouth twitched upward. "I promise to keep my head above water at all times."

Lily gestured to Felty and Anna, hoping that including them would add weight to her plea. "And leave us here to die of anxiety?"

Aden chuckled. "I'm not in any danger. And they need their canoe. Turn around and close your eyes. I'll be back by your side before you know it."

She opened her mouth to give him the tongue-lashing he deserved when, without warning, he shrugged his suspenders off his shoulders.

Mortified, she quickly turned her back on him. "What are you doing?"

"I warned you to close your eyes," he said, his voice bouncing with amusement.

"It's not funny," Lily protested.

"Keep your eyes closed. These trousers are as heavy as a bag of rocks. I don't think

I should go in again with them on."

Anna turned her back and stood next to Lily. "Such a dear boy."

Lily sorely wanted to contradict her. Aden was not a dear boy. He was a reckless, impudent troublemaker who took too many risks. Her nerves were stretched so thin she thought they might snap if she didn't die of embarrassment first. Was Aden really only five feet away from her stripping down to his drawers?

Terror, indignation, and mortification warred inside her. She was beside herself that Aden would put himself in such danger, but she couldn't very well scold him about it while her back was turned and her face glowed red with mortification.

She heard the splash indicating that Aden had entered the water followed by a massive splash that could only mean Pilot had followed him in.

"Lily," she heard Aden call. The sound of his voice almost prompted her to turn around. She thought better of it and stood like a stone with her eyes squeezed shut. "Lily, I am now swimming to the middle of the pond. My head is above water, and that's why you can hear me yelling."

He tempted her to crack a smile, but just in time she remembered her annoyance with him and folded her arms in protest. Let him yell all he wanted. She didn't care.

"I am now dragging the boat to shore, where I will hand the towrope to John. You will notice that my head is still above water."

Lily stomped her foot. He was the most insufferable tease.

Anna patted Lily's arm. Lily's eyes were still closed, so she couldn't see Anna's expression. No doubt her face glowed with admiration. "Such a delightful boy."

Lily didn't even grunt her disapproval.

"Now I am going to tie a rope around the trailer bar so John and Crist can pull it out of the water. I might have to stick my head under a little to reach the bar."

Birdsong filled the silence for what must have been less than fifteen seconds, and then Lily heard another splash followed by Aden's low, soothing voice. "I am now out of the water. That wasn't so bad, was it?"

She wouldn't give him the satisfaction of an answer.

"I am now attempting to don my trousers, but it is slow going. They are soaked. Now my shirt. It's a little easier, although it's always difficult to stretch a shirt over my massive chest."

It seemed that she would not be able to get him to shut up. A giggle tripped from her lips involuntarily.

Oh, blast it all!

She had been trying so hard to stay ferociously mad at him.

With her eyes still closed, she covered her mouth with her hand to stifle any more outbursts. He sidled up behind her. She could feel his warmth before he touched her. Laying his hands on her arms, he leaned close and whispered, "Are you thoroughly embarrassed yet or should I keep talking?"

His breath tickled her neck, and she trembled until she remembered to be mad. Deciding it would be safe to open her eyes, she whirled around and propped her hands on her hips. "Stop that."

"Stop what?"

"That mysterious whispering thing you do. It's improper."

He raised his scarred eyebrow. "Mysterious? I've never been called mysterious." Except for his boots and stockings, he was fully dressed, looking unnaturally handsome with his untidy wet hair.

She was tempted to reach up and tousle that hair. Instead, she shoved her hand into her apron pocket and made a fist until the tingling subsided. "Maybe we should do something safer, like eat our fried chicken."

153

Aden brushed his fingers through his hair. "You might be brave enough to risk it, but I am terrified of eating fried chicken."

"Oh, I forgot. You get to eat that tofu stuff. After risking your life in the pond, I hope you don't die of food poisoning."

Felty handed Aden his boots. "Good work, Aden. That horse was plenty scared."

Aden frowned and shook his head. "They weren't thinking real hard."

The two boys had pulled their small trailer several feet from the pond and were getting ready to launch their canoe into the water, with them in it this time. Aden beckoned the two boys over. They pulled their boat far enough out of the water that it wouldn't float away and came to Aden.

"Denki, again," John, the shorter of the two, said. "In truth, we would have been sunk without you."

Aden waved his hand around and shrugged off John's thanks. "Will you make me a promise?"

John wrinkled his brow in puzzlement. "Jah, of course, anything for you."

"Will you make sure a vet sees your horse today? I don't want that cut to get infected."

"Okay, we will."

"I am organizing a pond-cleaning frolic. I'd like to pull that rusty car and all that old wire out of the water. In a couple of weeks should be good. How about Saturday the ninth at nine in the morning? Will you come?"

"Jah," Crist said. "We will bring our three brothers."

"And your horse and trailer, okay?"

Both boys nodded and returned to their boat.

Lily stared at Aden. "Since when are you having a frolic?"

"Since just now," he said. "Don't you think it's a gute idea?"

Felty clapped his hands. "A wonderful-gute idea. People throw trash in this pond like a garbage dump, and they've done it for years."

"The water used to be so clear," Anna said.

Aden's eyes lit up. "And we're going to make it that beautiful again, Mammi. Can you help me spread the word? With a dozen people or so, we could make it look a lot better. We might convince the waterfowl to come back."

Lily frowned. "Are you planning on diving in for that car?"

He merely flashed that noncommittal grin. Lily blew out a puff of air. She'd rather stay home from the frolic than stand on the shore wondering if Aden would come up for air. She didn't even try a disapproving expression. If a sharp look from her could convince Aden of anything, it would have worked before now.

Anna took Felty's arm as the four of them hiked back to the other side of the pond. "How many people do you think are coming to the frolic? I want to be sure to make enough scarves for everyone," Anna said.

"They will come in handy when we want to drag things from the bottom of the lake," Aden said.

"I'm not coming," Lily announced. "It will make me too nervous."

Aden opened his mouth in mock indignation. "And miss all the fun? Who will fry tofu for the workers when we get hungry?"

Lily nudged Aden lightly with her arm. "You'll have to find somebody else to do it. I'm not touching that stuff ever again."

CHAPTER TEN

Aden tromped through the mud to the white barn that housed Monroe Yoder's dairy operation. Surrounded by acres of lush green pastures, the barn was indeed an impressive building. It looked to be almost two hundred feet long and three stories tall with a loft at the top. Earth mounded two sides of the first level of the barn tucked into an incline on Yoder's property. Next to the barn, two imposing silos stood sentinel, ready to be crammed with silage for the winter. Aden walked up the small hill and opened one of the doors to the second floor.

Letting his eyes adjust to the dimness, he breathed in the moist, pungent air of the inside of a cattle barn. Tyler, in a pair of rubber boots that went up to his knees, sprayed the cement floor as his dat cleaned the milking equipment. Milking time was over. The cleanup, no doubt, took almost as long as the actual milking.

Aden's heart tripped over itself as he thought of Lily. Would she like working here, helping Tyler and his dat milk the cows and clean out the manure? If she didn't like dogs, could she learn to tolerate cows? Aden tried not to think of Lily as Tyler's wife. For some reason, the thought drained him of energy and made him feel excessively tired.

Maybe Lily wasn't all that interested in Tyler. Would she ever fry Tyler a slab of tofu? Would she ever wrap a blanket around Tyler's shoulders in an unnecessary effort to keep him warm? Would she ever show Tyler that fire in her eyes when he made her angry?

Would Tyler — steady, faithful Tyler — ever make Lily angry?

Tyler was too smart for that. And Lily would never fall for someone who teased her and never did what she wanted him to do. Aden was a lost cause with Lily. That much was certain.

He swallowed the lump in his throat and shook off his sudden languid mood. "Tyler," Aden yelled over the din of the spraying water. "Tyler."

The bishop yelled something to Tyler, and Tyler yelled back, but neither of them made any indication that they had heard Aden.

Aden put his fingers to his mouth and

blew the ear-piercing whistle his dat had taught him. Tyler jerked his head around, and Aden could see bright orange earplugs protruding from each ear. He raised his eyebrows, which meant he was happy to see Aden, and twisted the nozzle on the end of the hose until the water slowed to a trickle.

Tyler's earplugs were connected to each other by a thin orange string. He pulled them from his ears and let them dangle around his neck. "Hullo, Aden. You finally came."

"Jah, I wanted to see."

Tyler motioned toward the door. "Like as not, we can hear better outside."

They walked out of the barn, and Tyler removed his heavy rubber gloves. His face glowed with sweat as he wiped his brow with the back of his hand. "Do you want me to show you around?"

"Jah, of course."

Tyler tromped clumsily down the incline in his big boots. He probably wore them all day long. "We have seventy-two head this year. That's about all we can manage with the four of us."

"The four of you?"

"My dat and mamm, my younger brother Joe, and me. And it's a gute day's work — sunup to sundown. We have to be more watchful of the animals because it's harder to cure them if they get sick. Mamm checks every hoof every morning, except the Sabbath."

"How much land do you have?"

"We've got two hundred acres, so we can take on more cattle if we want. There's plenty of room to grow forage for summer and winter. The cattle graze in the pastures all summer and most of the fall. They like it better than being cooped up in the barn."

Aden surveyed the nearest pasture where dappled Holsteins and caramel brown Jerseys grazed to their hearts' content. "This is how man was meant to farm. I think the Amish are the original environmentalists."

Tyler curled one side of his mouth. "The original Amish might roll over in their graves to hear you say that. I don't think Plain farmers would like to be thought of that way."

"I would."

Tyler curled up the other corner of his mouth. "I know you would." He shook his head with an indulgent smirk. "You are not quite normal, as far as the Amish go."

Aden laughed. "Thanks for noticing."

"But I like you. And I think even Lily is warming up to you."

Aden cleared his throat. That lump lodged

160

there again. "Do you think?"

"Jah. The other night she told me you have a gentle spirit."

A gentle spirit? She must have been thinking of someone else. Aden massaged the back of his neck and resolved to quit teasing her so much. A boy with a gentle spirit didn't take delight in watching Lily Eicher turn red.

But she did have a very attractive blush.

He coughed really hard as his throat got even tighter. "I also came by today because I want to invite you to a pond-cleaning frolic."

"I've never heard of one of those."

"Cobbler Pond is full of all sorts of trash. Since it's close by, I thought you might want to help clean it up."

Tyler rubbed his chin. "The west end of that pond is grown over with algae. The runoff from the surrounding farms brings in all that leftover fertilizer. Maybe that will get better now that our dairy is organic." He studied Aden's face. "Some men ask for help raising a barn or planting crops. You want to do something for a pond that isn't even yours?"

"Will you come?"

"Of course I will come. Is Lily going to be there?"

161

Aden tried to ignore the fact that the lump in his throat moved to form a knot in his stomach. He shrugged off the feeling and gave Tyler a teasing grin. "Why should you care if Lily is going to be there?"

Tyler's neck bloomed bright red and he looked down at his clunky boots, but his lips quirked into a half smile. "No use hiding it. You know I like her."

Aden couldn't help himself. "I like her too."

Tyler snapped his head up and his gaze bored into Aden's skull. "Don't joke about such things."

Aden forced a lighthearted laugh. "I like her a lot. She won't touch my dog without sanitizing her hands afterward, and she thinks I'm weird, but I like her. I made her so mad the other day that she actually socked me in the chest."

"She did?"

"I think she would have tried for the mouth, but I'm too tall. And her dat has nightmares about me, and I have nightmares about him."

Tyler's expression softened.

Aden shoved his hands in his pockets and nudged Tyler with his elbow. "Do you think her dat would like me for a son-in-law? I don't eat meat. I'm cheap to feed."

162

"To own the truth, you would not be David's choice to marry his daughter."

Aden pretended Tyler's words didn't sting. Tyler certainly hadn't meant them to. "But she is really cute the way she carries hand sanitizer with her everywhere. Maybe I should try harder with her dat."

Tyler slapped his gloves against his leg. His eyes danced as he looked at Aden. "She has four different flavors."

"Of hand sanitizer?"

"Vanilla is my favorite."

Strawberry was Aden's favorite. But he didn't say so. Tyler would be alarmed that he'd noticed. Every time Aden caught a whiff of Lily's strawberry hand sanitizer, he imagined running through the meadow with her, holding hands and chasing butterflies. The smell made him want to bury his face in her hair and breathe her in.

Tyler would probably have a heart attack if he knew what thoughts traveled through Aden's mind.

Yep. He'd keep his mouth shut.

"Lily says she's not coming because she doesn't want to worry about someone drowning," Aden said.

"I don't wonder that she would." Tyler considered the problem for a moment and nodded. "I will talk to her."

163

Aden didn't want to frown, but he did. Tyler seemed so sure of himself. Why did he think a word from him would convince Lily when she had flatly refused Aden's invitation?

He knew the answer. He just didn't want to hear it.

Tyler put a hand on Aden's shoulder. "Cum, I will show you where we are going to put the methane digester."

How appropriate. What better activity than to survey the manure supply, when Aden felt like he was swimming in it.

"Lead the way," Aden said. With Tyler walking ahead, he wouldn't catch Aden frowning.

CHAPTER ELEVEN

A flatbed wagon was much less comfortable than a courting buggy. Lily tried to prop herself on her hands as best she could so her arms could absorb some of the shock to her backside bouncing around on the wagon seat. Tyler had come in the wagon this morning because he said he needed to haul something to the pond for Aden. Whatever he hauled sat in the wagon bed covered with a tarp. Something in the shape of a large toolbox sat under the tarp, but there were other lumps that Lily couldn't begin to guess at. She was definitely curious.

Lily counted seventeen buggies parked alongside the road next to Cobbler Pond. Had that many people really come to help Aden clean his pond? Lily couldn't believe it. She thought Aden was the only one who cared about the condition of the Bonduel environment.

Well, Aden and her. Before Aden arrived

165

in Bonduel, she hadn't really thought about it, but she cared very much how clean the water in the pond was. If it was good for the birds and the wildlife, then it was good for everybody. Aden would finally get the pond cleaned, and that would make him very happy. Aden's smile was one of the nicest sights in the whole world.

Tyler pulled up his team and set the brake on the wagon. He must have been excited. He leaped from the wagon like a little boy jumping into a pile of leaves. He offered his hand to Lily so she could climb down. The wagon seat was at least six feet from the ground.

"Let's go find Aden," Tyler said.

Lily had no objections. She'd like to see for herself that Aden was not dead at the bottom of the pond. That thought sent her heart racing. He'd better be safe on dry land or she would give him a good talking-to. Sometimes she thought he did reckless things just to annoy her.

Tyler fell behind as he encountered someone who wanted to talk to him, but Lily didn't wait. What if Aden was drowning at this very minute, and everyone was too busy to notice?

The banks of the pond crawled with people, Englisch and Amish alike. Bright garbage bags dotted the landscape like a field of giant orange flowers. A few of the men were in the water but none looked to be farther than knee-deep. Lily spotted Anna and Felty under the shade of a tree passing out scarves and coffee even though it must have already been eighty degrees outside.

He stood near the shore with slightly damp hair and a sunny yellow scarf around his neck, barking directions to two boys guiding a team of horses. The four horses were harnessed side by side and two deep, hitched to four thick ropes that stretched down to the water and disappeared below the surface of the pond. These were sturdy workhorses with hooves the size of dinner plates and long hair growing at their feet. They strained as the boys guided them away from the pond. Lily's gaze marked each yard as the horses made progress up the gentle slope.

To Lily's astonishment, the curved hood of a car appeared from beneath the surface of the pond, and then the entire front half emerged. The car had no tires and no glass in the windows, and Lily couldn't begin to guess how old it was because there didn't look to be a spot of paint on it — just the bare, tarnished metal.

The water protested loudly as the old car finally made it onto shore. Waves splashed against the back bumper and heaved themselves past the normal bounds of the bank before settling down and giving up the fight.

A young man with chocolate-brown skin and a lime-green T-shirt stood at the road motioning to Aden. "Can they pull it clear up here?"

Aden nodded and called to the boys guiding the horses. Lily recognized them as the ones Aden had helped here at the pond over two weeks ago.

The shorter one, John, waved his reply and led the horses toward the road. Now that the car was out of the water, they had an easier time pulling it, even though it didn't have tires. It had probably been stuck but good in the mud at the bottom.

Lily breathed a sigh of relief. Aden would not need to go into the water to fetch the car. It was already out, leaving Lily blissfully ignorant as to how they had managed to secure the towropes around it.

Aden watched the car's progress up the slope before glancing her way. When he caught sight of her, he flashed a brilliant smile that left the sun in shadow. He appeared at her side before she had time to calm her heart banging against her chest.

She grinned stupidly.

"I thought you weren't going to come," Aden said.

"Tyler talked me into it."

The brilliant smile faded, although it didn't disappear. "You'll have to tell me how he does that. I can't seem to be able to talk you into anything."

Lily shot a quick look over her shoulder. She didn't see Tyler, but she couldn't seem to muster any enthusiasm to find him. "A lot of people came."

Aden's eyes seemed to dance with an inner light. "I wouldn't have believed that so many people cared."

"Of course they care. We want to be gute stewards of the Earth."

He looked at her as if he were trying to find the meaning of life in her eyes. "Do you?"

Lily nodded, unable to muster a coherent reply while he looked at her like that.

Aden fell silent and did that staring thing again. Would he notice how breathless she had become?

How long would they have stood like that? Lily couldn't begin to guess because the young man in the lime-green shirt marched over to them and crashed his shoulder into Aden. Aden stepped back to keep from los-

169

ing his balance and laughed as if getting plowed into was the most fun activity in the world.

The other young man had a bright smile and a deep dimple in his cheek. "When I agreed to help you, I didn't realize you lived quite so far out in the sticks. Do you know how hard it is to find a good cup of coffee in Shawano? Are you really that far from civilization that you don't know what a Starbucks is?"

Aden laughed and winked at Lily. "Lily, do you know what Starbucks is?"

Lily curled up one corner of her mouth. "It's a coffee store."

"A coffee store?" the young man teased. "Nobody calls it a coffee store. You people might as well be Amish for as primitive as you are."

"What do you think?" Aden asked.

"I think this pond is going to look great by the time I'm finished with it," the young man said.

"Do you think you can keep your truck out of the pond?"

The young man slapped Aden on the shoulder and grinned at Lily. "This guy is always giving me grief about my driving."

"Everybody complains about your driving, Jamal. You're terrible."

Jamal rolled his eyes. "You should try it if you think it's so easy."

Aden pointed a thumb in Jamal's direction. "He's totaled two cars."

"Now I have a truck. Stuff just bounces off my bumpers."

Aden chuckled. "Stuff? Like Volkswagens and small children?"

Jamal shoved Aden playfully before taking a step toward Lily and sticking out his hand. "You look pretty enough to be Lily, at least by how Aden described you."

Aden had "described" her to this young man?

Lily had never shaken hands with a black man before. When it happened, it was quite uneventful.

He looked at her expression and smirked. "Please don't tell me I'm the first African American you've ever seen or I'll drive straight home so I don't get sucked into this spooky time-warp thing you've got going."

Aden put an arm around Lily's shoulders but didn't lose his playful smile. "Come on, Jamal, lay off. Your charming personality is better taken in small doses."

Lily studied Jamal closely. He didn't look like the type of person who would chain himself to a tree. He had a dimple, for heaven's sake.

Jamal pointed to Aden. "This guy saved my life, so I'm compelled to obey him, even if it means I have to stop flirting with a pretty girl."

"He saved your life?"

"Jamal drove us into a lake," Aden said, chuckling. "The police really should take his license away."

Jamal raised his voice in protest. "One lousy accident and you want to get the police involved?"

They laughed together. "No," Aden said, "I'd rather not get the police involved."

Jamal shoved a thumb in Aden's direction. "You know what he did? We were both half-drowned, and he dove back in the water to get that stupid dog."

As if he knew they were talking about him, Pilot darted wildly among them and almost knocked Lily over. Jamal and Aden were both too solid to be toppled by a giant horse-dog.

Lily's heart felt like a brick when she thought of Aden nearly drowning. It seemed to be a common occurrence in his life. "Aden is always doing stuff like that," she said, trying to infuse her tone with a light-hearted lilt.

"I know," Jamal said. He looked from Aden to Lily with a knowing grin on his face. "So, are you two — ?"

Aden extended his arm and shoved Jamal three feet away. Jamal merely chuckled and shoved Aden back.

Jamal cleared his throat and started walking backward. "I'm gonna pull the truck closer. Tell everyone they can load the garbage, and I'll make a trip to the dump."

Aden watched Jamal walk to the road, backward all the way. "Jamal is one of the greatest guys you'll ever meet."

Lily loved how his eyes gleamed when he talked of something he felt passionate about. It made him even more handsome, if that were possible. He turned his head and stared at her again. Was he purposely trying to fluster her?

Tyler finally caught up to Lily and knocked her out of her stupor.

"I want to show you something," Tyler said.

Aden pried his gaze from Lily's face. "Um, Tyler. Um, what did you say?"

Tyler, unaware that Lily had been struck by lightning, looked at her as if she were in on his secret. "It's a surprise, Aden, and you're going to love it. It's in my wagon. Come on, Lily, let's show him."

Aden's eyes darted between Lily and Tyler, and he briefly looked unsure of himself.

Then his lips curled. "Lead the way."

Lily didn't relish time alone with Tyler and Aden together, especially when she couldn't take any credit for whatever sat in the back of Tyler's wagon. She obediently followed them as Tyler launched into some story about a man in Green Bay who did such and such. She couldn't really pay attention.

". . . and he said I could borrow it for a few months. It won't be permanent, but at least it's something."

They approached the wagon, and Tyler pulled back the tarp to reveal a flat glassy panel with several shiny squares embedded in it plus a long, black hose and a tan box the size of a large birdhouse. Lily had absolutely no idea what it was. But Aden acted as if all the animals in all the zoos in the world had been set free from their cages.

"*Oh sis yuscht,* Tyler! How did you ever?" He yanked Tyler by the shoulders and pulled him in for a bone-crushing bear hug. Lily's curiosity grew as she stood watching them. They were so different and yet such good friends.

"Do you want to tell me why you're so excited about a hose and birdhouse?" Lily said. She couldn't keep from smiling. All this goodwill was infectious.

Both boys turned to face her, but Aden

174

kept a brotherly arm clapped around Tyler's shoulders. "It's a pond aerator," Tyler said.

Lily folded her arms and tilted her head just so. "Well, that explains everything."

"You can tell when a pond is sick," Aden said, "because too much algae grows on it. It means there's not enough oxygen at the bottom for fish and good bacteria." Aden reached into the wagon and touched the shiny glass plate. "This little machine puts oxygen back on the bottom of the pond."

"And it's powered by the sun," Tyler said.

"Is it okay with the bishop?" Lily asked. It looked like a very fancy machine for an Amish community.

Tyler nodded. "My dat says it's okay — to bring the pond back to its natural state."

Aden walked around the wagon for a look at the other side of the pond thingamajig. "This is wonderful gute, Tyler. I've never known anyone as mindful of other people as you are."

Tyler kicked the dirt at his feet. "But we've only got it for two months. It might not help much."

"A bucket of water is made of a million tiny drops," Aden said. "Let's set it up."

"We'll need many hands."

In his excitement, Aden practically jogged toward the pond. "Okay. I'll get my cousin

Moses. He can put a puzzle together with his eyes closed. And Jamal probably knows a thing or two."

Lily followed after him, walking quickly but trying not to run. Why did he have to have such long legs? "Aden, what do you want me to do?"

Aden stopped and looked back as if he'd forgotten Lily's presence. But he smiled, and made her feel tingly all over. "Cum, I will show you."

He led her to a roll of garbage bags sitting on the ground. "Take one of these. Do you have gloves?"

Lily pulled her garden gloves from her pocket. Of course she had gloves. She wouldn't touch garbage with her bare hands.

"Walk around the pond and pick up trash. If you find any metal, keep it separate, and we'll sell it for scrap. Some of the neighbors are wading into the water to find stuff, but you don't need to do that. If you see something floating in the water, ask someone to wade in and get it for you."

He pointed to Erla Glick, with her hair tied up in a scarf and her feet and legs bare. She looked as if she was doing more playing than working as she waved an empty garbage bag over her head and splashed in the knee-deep water.

"Erla's not afraid of the water. She's been a big help already this morning."

A big help. Ha! Lily had overheard Erla at the gathering talking to some of the other girls about "handsome Aden Helmuth." Jah, Lily just bet Erla was a big help.

"I will be fine," Lily said.

"You don't want to drown," Aden said, flashing her a playful smile.

"I wouldn't think of it," Lily said. "It's too bad you're not as cautious as I am. Then I wouldn't have to constantly scold you."

"I like it when you scold me."

"You do not."

"Jah, I do." He held out the garbage bag to her and when she reached to take it, he seized her fingers and squeezed them.

His skin felt rough with callouses like a favorite, timeworn saddle. She snatched her hand away. What a tease!

She glanced at Erla Glick one more time. "Will you fetch me if I fall in?"

His eyes held a deep green forest. "Oh, yes."

"Well, I'm not going to fall in, so don't get your hopes up."

Aden laughed. "Thanks for coming today."

He walked away, leaving Lily gathering her scattered wits in his wake, and made a beeline for Erla. Erla graced him with a

177

smile that showed off her straight teeth.

Erla had a reputation for being fearless and a little wild. Lily had heard that Erla went cliff diving in Mexico last year, and Erla had two little yippy dogs and a tabby cat as pets — a real animal lover, the sort of girl Aden would be attracted to. Lily narrowed her eyes as she watched Aden and Erla together. Just Aden's type.

Lily couldn't hear what Aden said to Erla, but he pointed toward Lily while Erla nodded vigorously. They seemed perfectly happy to shoot the breeze while everyone else slaved in the hot sun. Aden said something, and Erla's laugh tinkled delicately over the trees.

Lily felt her face get hot. She refused to let Erla pick up one piece of her trash, even if it meant Lily must dive clear to the bottom of the pond for a gum wrapper.

With purposeful steps, she marched to the other side of the pond as far from Erla as she could get and found a nicely littered spot. There was enough trash to pick up here that she wouldn't need to venture near the water. Erla could get her toes all wet and wrinkly if she wanted. Lily was fond of her dry feet.

Across the way, Estee waved to Lily and then must have decided that waving was an

178

insufficient greeting. She grabbed Floyd's hand and dragged him to Lily's side of the pond. They both wore sky-blue scarves tied loosely around their necks. "Floyd found a watch," Estee announced.

Floyd pulled it out of his pocket. "It still works."

"It's like a treasure hunt. Floyd's going to write his cousin Arty about this pond-cleanup frolic. The folks in Ohio need to know what a gute boy Aden is."

Floyd put the watch to his ear. "Oh. I think it stopped. What do you think, Estee? I can't hear it ticking."

"I didn't see your buggy, Floyd," Lily said.

Estee shook her head. "Floyd picked me up on his bike. Aden says bikes are eco-friendly. It's a new word he taught us."

"It means it doesn't pollute the air to ride a bike," Lily said.

"That's right," Estee said. "Aden's so smart." She looked toward the road. "Is Dat coming?"

"Nae. He called it one of Aden Helmuth's crazy schemes, but he gave me permission to come."

Estee laid a hand on Lily's arm. "You should have seen him."

"Who?"

"Aden." Estee's eyes got wide. "He

wouldn't let anyone else go in. He must have gone down there twenty times to get those ropes around that car so they could pull it out."

Lily caught her breath.

"Two times he was down there so long, I was sure he got stuck. I told Floyd to go in after him."

Floyd shook the watch and tapped on its face. "But he came up before I had a chance to jump in, praise the Lord." He furrowed his brow. "I mean, not 'praise the Lord' because I didn't have to jump in, but 'praise the Lord' because he came back up."

Lily reminded herself to breathe. He'd made it out safely, and she hadn't had to watch it. No harm done — except for her near heart attack at hearing Estee talk about it.

"He asked about you," Estee said.

"Who?"

Estee rolled her eyes, willing Lily to keep up with her galloping thoughts. "Aden. First thing, he wanted to know if you were coming. Then he asked what time. He wanted to get that car out before you got here, though I don't know why."

"Come over by us," Floyd said. "We found a fire pit with about a hundred beer cans. Aden says we can get money for them."

180

Lily looked across the pond to where Estee and Floyd had been working. Erla Glick lingered there, playing with the braid that cascaded from beneath her scarf in between picking up cans. "Nae. I have plenty to do on this side."

Estee took Floyd's arm and dragged him away. He didn't take his eyes from that watch.

Out of the corner of her eye, she watched as Tyler and Aden and four others carried the pieces of that contraption to a part of the pond that would get plenty of sunlight but be mostly hidden from view. Aden might have stunning green eyes, but he was still an odd young man. Who ever heard of giving a pond air like a patient in the hospital?

Lily was glad that Tyler was predictable and steady and had a good future ahead of him. Dat thought very highly of Tyler, and Dat's opinion was good enough for Lily. Dat's wisdom, gained from years of experience, was certainly more reliable than the whims of a naïve girl who could easily be swayed by a pair of green eyes.

Her search for trash took her closer to the water, and she spied a Styrofoam cup floating not three feet from shore. She glanced about her. Erla had somehow managed to

181

make her way around the pond and gathered trash in the shallow water no less than twenty feet from where Lily stood. That was quick.

She gritted her teeth. Lily wasn't about to ask Erla for help. She found a long stick and leaned out over the water to snag the cup. Some people didn't need to get wet to get the job done.

Lily heard him charging through the grass mere moments before he attacked. Before she could pull back and get out of his way, Pilot smashed into her and sent her flying into the pond.

Gasping as the cool water washed over her, Lily lost her bearings and thrashed about in panic before her foot found the muddy bottom. As she righted herself, her heart resumed something akin to a normal pace. Although Pilot had given her a good dunking, she stood in less than three feet of water. It didn't even come up to her waist. She swiped the water from her eyes. Pilot swam around her as if playing a game of tag and she was now "it."

Lily growled. "You stupid dog."

She heard a splash and turned to see Aden sloshing his way to her. His look of concern cut deep lines around his eyes and mouth. She had never seen him like that before.

182

Without a word, he promptly scooped her into his arms. She gasped and clasped her hands around his neck so she wouldn't topple into the water again. Surprise rendered Lily mute. What did Aden think he was doing?

With ease, he carried her to shore and gently set her on a flat-topped boulder. She shivered. Whether from the cold or from shock, she could not tell. Aden took the cheery yellow scarf from around his neck and wrapped it awkwardly around her shoulders while she peeled off her soaked gloves. Then he knelt next to her and took her hand. Suddenly, she didn't feel so cold anymore.

But she still felt shivery. All over.

Pilot had the nerve to follow them to shore. He shook the water out of his fur, spraying both Aden and Lily with water droplets. She didn't protest. She couldn't get much wetter. Then Pilot sat on his haunches and innocently studied Lily as if he had no part in her current predicament.

"It's okay," Aden said, his voice filled with compassion, giving her words of comfort she didn't need. "I'm sorry about Pilot. Are you okay? I'm so sorry. I feel terrible."

Lily couldn't believe it. He was truly distressed, when she felt nothing worse than annoyance at that dog.

Aden studied her face and stroked the back of her hand with his thumb. "Are you hurt? I promise I will never ask you to come here again."

How fragile did he think she was?

Judging by his reaction, china-doll fragile. He reached up and nudged a lock of wet hair from her cheek with his fingers. Her skin tingled where he touched her, and those brilliant green eyes pierced her skull.

He hadn't let go of her hand. For some strange reason, she didn't really want him to. Could they sit like this indefinitely?

Shivery. She felt very shivery.

Even in her flustered state, her brain registered that she should have been indignant — indignant that he believed her to be a delicate female who couldn't hold her own against a mouthful of pond scum. But her irritation melted at the thought that Aden was truly anxious about her feelings. She hadn't displayed a lot of fortitude before, so why should he think she possessed any courage today?

Aden's lips drooped as he studied her face. "Please say something."

Lily took a deep breath to clear her head and raised her voice as if she were making an announcement. "That dog is officially out of my good graces."

The look of surprise on Aden's face was priceless. He must have liked what he saw in her expression. He threw back his head and laughed. Lily smiled to herself.

"You're not mad?" he said.

"Mad?" She pulled her hand out of his, if only to gain clarity of thought. "I'm furious." She glowered at Pilot. "Come here."

Pilot crept furtively to her. She put her hands on either side of his head and fluffed his soggy ears while looking him sternly in the eye. "Do you think you are a football player, is that what you think?" She tickled the fur at his jaw, and he wagged his tail hard enough to fan a breeze. "It's a gute thing you saved Amanda, or you would be off to obedience school this very afternoon. As it is, you will get no leftover bread pudding tonight."

Pilot cocked his head to one side.

"Nae, do not try that trick on me. No bread pudding, and that is final."

He stuck out his tongue and licked her arm. She pulled back and lifted an eyebrow at Aden. He stared at her, as usual.

"You're being unusually lenient," he said.

"It is a blessing the water wasn't deeper."

Pilot barked his agreement and trotted away, probably in search of someone else to

185

send into the water.

"I thought you'd be frightened out of your wits."

"I'm not afraid of the water, Aden. I'd just rather not see people drown in it."

"I'm glad to know you're concerned for my well-being."

She rubbed her arms to wipe away the chill. "Thank you for worrying about me."

"I worry about you all the time."

Lily had no idea what that meant, but the way he looked at her made her feel shy and uncomfortable. She searched for a change of subject when she sensed a wet clump of hair sagging at her neck. As she put her hand to her head to assess the damage, her wet hair tumbled from its bun and cascaded over her shoulders. "My kapp," she said. "What happened to my kapp?"

Aden's eyes strayed to her hair, and he reached out his hand to . . . touch it? Instead, he pursed his lips and pulled away.

Breathing heavily, Erla approached Lily's rock dragging her garbage bag behind her. "Are you okay, Lily?"

Aden stood up.

Erla glued her eyes to his face. "I would have gone into the water for her," she said, opting to talk about Lily instead of to her. "I saw her reaching for something and then she fell in."

Lily managed to smile, even though Erla wasn't as concerned about Lily's mishap as she was about making googly eyes at Aden.

"Denki, Erla. I am gute," Lily said, as she plucked a piece of dark green slime from her hair. Nothing that a long bath and a quart of hand sanitizer couldn't fix.

Erla twirled her braid in her fingers and playfully tilted her head to one side. "I found some sort of metal pipe half-buried over there. Can you help me get it out?"

Aden glanced doubtfully at Lily. "Will you be okay?"

He was leaving her? That thought summoned more disappointment than she would have imagined. Now she was being ridiculous. She didn't expect him to carry her around the pond, did she? Although that would have been very nice.

She shook her head a few times to clear her brain.

"No?" he said.

Lily bobbed her head up and down. "I am fine." She most definitely needed a drink. "I will get some coffee from your mammi."

Aden walked away with Swivel-Hips Erla and left Lily sitting by herself on the rock. She felt like a forlorn, waterlogged kitten.

She watched as Aden and Erla got on their

hands and knees and started digging in the dirt like a pair of children in the sandbox. They laughed together as if they were old friends and as if Lily had not nearly died in a tragic pond accident.

The banks of the pond hummed with activity. Some boys pulled long strands of wire and wood from the water. An old fence? That must have been what the horse caught himself on the other day. Two women planted something on the banks near the algae. Tyler still worked on his machine while Anna sat under a tree, knitting. No doubt she was trying to keep up with the demand for pond-cleaning scarves.

Pilot emerged from the water near Lily with something in his mouth. Maybe it was the elusive Styrofoam cup. He jogged to her and dropped his catch at her feet. Lily bent over and picked up the muddy lump of fabric.

Pilot smiled at her.

Her kapp.

She wrung it dry and shook it out. Slimy leaves and twigs clung to it like cockleburs. She couldn't very well put it on. She'd have to soak it in bleach for hours at home. Lily turned it over in her hand. Might as well make a new one.

She put her arms around Pilot's neck. He

tried to lick her ear. "Denki, you stupid dog."

Lily combed through the strands of her hair with her fingers. She had lost her pins and elastic bands in the water and wouldn't be able to fashion her bun back into place, let alone modestly cover her head. Should she let it be? No one would think worse of her knowing she'd lost her kapp in the water.

That didn't matter to Lily. She hadn't stepped one toe out of line during *rumschpringe*. She had never worn Englisch clothes, never gone a day without her kapp pinned securely into place. Her dat would have been severely disappointed if she had.

Her head must be covered with something other than this dirty rag that used to be her kapp.

With regret, she realized she had to go home immediately. Propriety called for it. The Ordnung demanded it.

Her face got hot. Loose like this, her hair looked like an unruly pile of hay or a wild forsythia bush in springtime. Dat said girls who wore their hair down were showing off. She didn't want to be accused of pride, even for a minute.

Lily made her way to Aden and Erla. Aden watched her walk the whole twenty-foot distance. He smiled and held up a dirt-encrusted muffler for her to see. "Look what we found. I think if we search hard enough, we'll be able to find all the parts to that car."

Erla propped her hands on her hips. "Do you want to take it to the scrap pile for us, Lily?"

Aden couldn't seem to take his eyes off Lily's hair. That was exactly why she needed to go home. Her improper appearance probably shocked Aden to the core. She smoothed her hand over her hair self-consciously.

"I'm sorry. I have to go," she said.

He frowned. "Are you cold?"

She showed him her kapp. "It's ruined. Look at my hair."

"I'm looking," he murmured.

Erla waved off her concerns. "You look fine. Technically, you don't need to cover your head unless you're praying. Technically."

Aden looked at Erla. "Lily is more of a letter-of-the-law kind of girl. She's not comfortable unless she is strictly obedient."

Lily studied Aden's face. Was he laughing at her? No, he seemed sincere. Maybe he knew her better than she thought.

With a mild expression, he took his scarf from around her neck, draped it over her

190

head, and tied it loosely around her chin. "Cum," he said. He nudged her forward and walked along beside her while carrying the muffler. "I don't want you to leave."

Lily felt better with something covering her head, even if she did look a little strange with a scarf over her ears in the middle of the hot summer. They walked to Anna and Felty's tree where Anna kept faithfully to her knitting, and Felty lay with his eyes closed and his hands propped under his head, softly humming "I Need No Mansions."

Anna saw them coming. "Lily, are you all right? I saw you fall into the water."

"My kapp is ruined."

"That scarf looks so lovely. It matches your golden hair."

"Mammi," Aden said, "can I borrow a strand of yarn?"

"Of course, dear." She took a skein from her bag and cut a foot-long length of yarn.

"Here," Aden said, placing the muffler on the ground. He surprised Lily when he slipped the scarf from her head and gathered her hair into three equal parts. She willed herself to breathe normally as his fingers brushed against her neck in an attempt to capture all the errant wisps. A boy should never touch a girl's neck. It sent a spark of

191

electricity all the way to her toes.

Should she protest at his closeness? Her mind raced through the eighteen articles of the Confession of Faith. She couldn't remember a thing about boys fixing girls' hair.

She cleared her throat. Two times. "You know how to braid hair?"

He cleared his throat. Three times. "I have many secret talents, and three little sisters."

His touch was gentle, as if he ran his fingers through other people's hair all the time. Once he'd fashioned the braid, he tied Anna's yarn around the end of Lily's hair.

"Do you have those one kind of fasteners, Mammi?" Aden asked. "You know, the ones that look like small tongs."

"Bobby pins?" Anna said.

"Jah."

"Every mammi worth her salt carries at least five bobby pins wherever she goes."

With great effort, Anna rose from her perch on the ground.

"No need to get up, Mammi."

"This is no time to sit," she said. She produced a medication bottle from her bag, but instead of pills, it contained an ample supply of bobby pins. "The bobby pins are in the thyroid bottle."

She handed Aden some bobby pins, but

Lily held out her hand. "I can do it," she said.

Aden grinned. "I can do it."

Lily felt like a baby doll in the care of an attentive six-year-old. He wrapped her braid around itself and secured it into a bun with the bobby pins.

"Very gute," Anna said, as she began pulling pins from her kapp. "You can wear my kapp."

"You don't have to do that," Lily said.

"Stuff and nonsense," Anna said. "Aden wants you here with him instead of at home for want of a kapp."

Lily had already blushed beyond her capacity to blush any redder.

Anna removed her kapp. After such a gesture of kindness, what could Lily do? She gratefully took Anna's kapp and pinned it into place.

Anna rummaged through her bag and pulled out what looked like a knitted white doll blanket with strings. "This is my experiment with knitting kapps," she said. She draped it over her head and tied the strings under her chin. She looked like she was wearing a floppy doily.

Lily felt compelled to return Anna's kapp. Anna couldn't possibly walk around Cobbler Pond wearing a doily on her head.

Lily pulled a pin out of her hair. "No, Anna. You take the kapp. I will go home."

Anna pulled her covering farther down her forehead. "Nae, nae. This is the perfect kapp for a day at the pond. What do you think, Felty?"

Felty cracked one eye open and spied his wife. "Annie Banannie, you look like an angel from heaven."

Lily peered doubtfully at Aden, who sported a crooked smile. "You both look beautiful."

Lily didn't know whether to be flattered or distressed. Did they look beautiful in the same kind of awkward, peculiar way?

Aden took her hand and pulled her out of the shade. "Come into the sun to dry off." Why was he holding her hand? He shouldn't be holding her hand. What did the Ordnung say about hand-holding?

He quickly released her once he'd dragged her into the sun. "Is everything all better now?"

All better?

Let's see. He had risked his life for a car, flirted with Erla Glick, and held Lily's hand. Twice. She had picked up four pieces of trash, fallen into the water, and worn a yellow scarf on her head, all while mentally reviewing the Confession of Faith from

194

memory. He had braided her hair, carried her in his arms, and looked at her with those green eyes until her knees had turned to jelly.

"Jah," she said. "All better."

"Lily."

Both she and Aden turned to see Tyler jogging along the shore. He reached out and took her hands in his. "Are you okay? I heard you fell in. Did you get hurt?"

Aden's face became a cloudy day. He took a step back and folded his arms across his chest.

Lily studied her hands in Tyler's. Something didn't feel quite right. No sparks. "I am gute. Aden's dog pushed me in, and Aden pulled me out."

Tyler kept hold of Lily's hands and regarded Aden with concern. "Your dog must learn to behave," he said. "Lily has told me before how aggressive he is."

The clouds on Aden's face darkened. "I know. I'm sorry."

Lily would have done anything to make that look in Aden's eyes disappear. "Pilot is just a puppy at heart," she said, nudging her hands from Tyler's grasp and stuffing them into her apron pockets. "He wants to be friends with everybody." She looked at Aden. "He probably thought I was playing."

195

"You could have been seriously hurt," Tyler said.

Lily shook her head. "No harm done. Pilot is unruly, but he's also the bravest, smartest, most lovable dog you will ever see. Do not say a bad word against him."

Aden's expression brightened considerably. Lily's heart beat a glad cadence. She hated to see Aden unhappy when he had done so much for her. He should be enjoying the success of pond-cleaning day.

Tyler looked doubtful and then nodded. "If you say so, I'll not disagree." He held out his hands to her again. She hesitantly surrendered the safety of her pockets. "Do you want to see the aerator? It is almost put together." He grasped her hands and pulled her forward as he walked backward. She had no choice but to follow.

She looked over her shoulder at Aden. He stood like a mighty oak tree, tall and immovable.

"Do you want to come?" she asked.

"Nae," he said. The clouds returned to his face.

CHAPTER TWELVE

Lily and Aden strode together through the woods. Aden had insisted on carrying both of the buckets even though they were empty and didn't weigh a thing. Lily wondered if she would feel the same sparks she did that day at the pond if Aden decided to hold her hand. No one was watching. It would be the perfect opportunity if he wanted to take it.

She took a deep breath and attempted to think clearly. Why did she have such day-dreams when her thoughts should be squarely centered on Tyler Yoder? That's whom Dat expected her to marry.

Besides, Aden wouldn't think of holding her hand when he had been avoiding her all week. Today Anna had insisted that Aden take Lily to the other side of Huckleberry Hill to see if the huckleberries were ready to pick.

Huckleberries won't be ready for three more

weeks, Mammi, Aden had said.

But Anna had insisted that Aden hike to the other side of the hill to check on the berries and to take Lily with him. Aden couldn't have refused without seeming rude, but Lily sensed that he had agreed reluctantly. Had he tired of her company, or did other people dominate his thoughts? Other people like Erla Glick?

After Saturday, it seemed natural that Aden's thoughts would stray to Erla Glick. Aden probably thought Erla's bare feet and flirtatious smile were attractive, and he couldn't help but adore the fact that she wasn't afraid to get into the water and search for trash. Erla Glick wouldn't have stayed onshore and wrung her hands while Aden risked his life to save a horse. Erla would have dived into the water and helped him. Lily must have seemed dull in comparison.

Pilot romped among the trees and through the bushes and around Aden and Lily as if there was too much to explore and not enough time to explore it.

Lily didn't like the uncomfortable silence between them. "The pond looks so gute. You must be very happy."

Aden kept up a steady pace, one that with his long legs, Lily struggled to keep up with.

198

"After you left with Tyler, they came to collect the scrap metal. We got two hundred dollars for that old car."

"Two hundred dollars? What are you going to do with the money?"

"I might save it as a down payment on my own pond aerator. They aren't cheap, and we can't use Tyler's forever."

"The pond has to have an aerator forever?"

Aden slowed down slightly when he saw how breathless Lily became while trying to keep up. "Maybe not. It depends on how farmers around the pond use their land."

Lily tried unsuccessfully to grab the dog as he ran by her. "Pilot, come here."

He obediently loped over, jumped up, and planted his paws on her shoulders.

"Get down, right now." Lily pushed Pilot off her while sliding an arm around his furry neck. She did her best to hold the dog while she gently pried a burr from his floppy ear. "It's a wonder he doesn't come home every night with all sorts of plants and animals matted in his fur. He gets into everything." She almost had the nasty seed dislodged from his fur, but Pilot wasn't one to remain calm for long. "Hold still, you stupid dog."

"Stupid?" Aden said with mock indignation. "You told Tyler not to say a bad word against my dog."

As soon as she released him, Pilot bounded farther into the woods, only to return moments later and run a circle around Aden.

"I asked Tyler to speak kindly of Pilot," Lily said. "I never said I would."

Aden grinned.

"That's the first time you've smiled at me for a week. I thought your face was broken."

For a split second, disquiet registered in his eyes, then he turned around and resumed his breakneck speed to the huckleberry patch. "I smile all the time." To prove his point, he flashed her a painful grimace while picking up his pace.

She used all her energy to keep up with him. Who could have a meaningful conversation while saving her breath for a footrace?

At that speed, it didn't take them long to reach the other side of the hill where the huckleberries grew wild. Lily gasped as they came to the clearing and a patch of sunlight illuminated the sea of pinkish berries amidst deep green bushes. She caught up to Aden, who didn't even seem winded, and they stood in silence together, letting their eyes drink in the untamed beauty of the spot. Even Pilot stopped short of diving into the huckleberry patch. Standing at attention next to Lily, he must have sensed that this was a sight not to be disturbed.

Aden set down his buckets and plucked a light red berry from the nearest bush. "Just like I told Mammi. At least two or three weeks before they're ready."

Lily thought of all the delicious treats she could make with a bucketful of huckleberries. Was there such a thing as huckleberry tofu cake?

Aden smirked. "It's gute Mammi had us bring these extra-large buckets."

Pilot turned his attention to catching bees and butterflies in his mouth. Lily knew his location by the occasional cheerful bark and the rustling sounds he made in the bushes.

"Ready to start back?" he said. Obviously, Aden was in no mood to linger in the berry patch.

Lily pointed to a fallen log near the trail. "Do you mind if I check for a pebble in my shoe?"

Aden nodded and followed her to the fallen branch. He set his sights down the trail as if he were in a hurry to be somewhere else. Lily sat on the log and took off her shoe. Would he notice if no pebble fell out when she turned it upside down?

Her heart started galloping. Why did it always betray her? She didn't often risk a conversation like this. It was always safer to not say anything and let trouble blow over. But she sensed that trouble wouldn't blow over this time.

And she had to know if Erla Glick was trouble.

Lily slipped her shoe back on and took her time tightening the laces. "May I ask you a question?"

"Okay."

With all the courage she could muster, she looked him in the eye. "Did your dat tell you to stay away from me?"

That unexpected question caught him off guard. He gaped at her as if she'd just dived into the pond. "My dat? Why would my dat tell me to stay away from you?"

Well, she had his full attention, whether she wanted it or not. "I don't have a contagious disease that I know of, and I've cooked tofu for you three times this week, but when I walk in the house for work, you walk out. If I do chores inside, you do them outside."

He folded his arms across his chest and turned his face from her. "I always have chores."

"If I tend the garden, you find something to fix inside."

"Coincidence."

"Your dat has probably caught wind that I'm a scaredy-cat when I get around ponds and that I have wild yellow hair and I'm bossy."

A ghost of a grin appeared on Aden's lips. "Who would have tattled to my dat about all that?"

"Your dat probably doesn't want you getting mixed up with a girl like me. Has he demanded that you stay at least four feet away from me? Or is it ten? Some dats are quite strict."

"You know how obedient I am."

"Oh, no. It's ten feet, isn't it? I was afraid it would be ten feet."

Aden shook his head. His smile was weak, but she saw his teeth.

Lily felt a thrill pass through her. She had never teased him before. "Have you been given instructions to shun me forever or just for a few weeks? I knew I shouldn't have thrown that plastic bottle on the side of the road. I should have known you'd find out."

Aden chuckled and then sighed as if in surrender. He deposited his buckets on the ground and sat next to her, but she sensed that he did so reluctantly. He propped his forearms on his knees and clasped his hands together. Staring at the ground, he fell silent and Lily, feeling that she'd pushed him too hard already, wasn't inclined to say more.

When he lifted his head to look at her, the pain she saw in his eyes stunned her. "Lily," he whispered, "Tyler is my friend."

"He . . . he's my friend too."

"And I would never betray that friendship."

"Okay."

"Okay then." He hardened his expression, slapped his thighs, and stood up as if that cryptic conversation solved everything. "We should get back."

"That made no sense, Aden."

He frowned and sank back to the log. "Do you like Tyler?"

"Jah. Of course I like Tyler."

He looked devastated, as if she had slapped him across the face. What had she said? He stood up for the second time. "Okay. We should get back."

Lily had never felt so confused or so bold. She reached out and took his hand, pulling him to sit. He sat but withdrew his hand as if she were made of fire. "You are talking nonsense, and I have no patience for nonsense," she said.

He cradled his head in his hands. "You're going to make me say it, aren't you?"

"Say what? Do you have a headache?"

Aden shook his head and looked squarely

into Lily's eyes. "Something happened to me last week. I mean, it's been coming on for a long time, but Saturday was the straw that broke the camel's back." He pulled a weed from the dirt and twisted it in his fingers. "You were trying so hard not to get dirty and you tiptoed around the pond as if avoiding a herd of slithering snakes. I couldn't take my eyes off you. Then you fell in and your hair came undone, and I came undone with it."

That shivery feeling passed up her spine.

"Then Tyler held your hands, and it was like I didn't even exist. And I hated that feeling."

Lily's heart raced with anticipation.

He scooted closer to her on the log. "Lily, do you feel anything for me at all?"

She swallowed hard. "Feel anything?"

"You know what I mean."

"Jah, I do."

"Jah, you know what I mean, or jah, you feel something for me?"

Her hands trembled as she fingered the hem of her apron. Feel anything? How could she entertain such a thought when she tried so hard to resist his green eyes and enticing smile? Warmth tingled through her whole body as she thought of the way Aden had lifted her into his powerful arms

205

and carried her to shore at the pond. She could still feel the brush of his hand on her neck as he braided her hair and deftly tied it with a strand of yarn.

Feel anything? Feelings associated with Aden drenched her. Soaked her through. Submerged her. The sensation felt exhilarating and alarming all at the same time. Was she drowning?

Dat would never approve of her feeling anything for Aden Helmuth. Lily caught her breath and felt an emptiness in her chest the size of a deep cave.

She'd been silent too long. He stared at her with his lips pressed into a hard line. The tension etched on his face made him seem weary.

He slumped his shoulders and sighed. "Say no more, Lily. I understand perfectly." He stood up for the third time and turned his back on her. "We should get back."

Drowning or not, she couldn't stand to see him so unhappy. "One feeling I have about you is that you are a very gute swimmer."

He turned and gazed at her with his brows knit together. "A gute swimmer?"

"And you can throw a Frisbee good."

Aden sank tentatively back onto the log. "Lily, do you like me?"

She couldn't breathe. Of course she liked him — more than she ever thought she would. What she wanted to know was, how much? Apparently, Aden wanted to know the same thing.

Pilot chose that moment to run to her and moisten her cheek with his nose. She growled and nudged him away. "I like you better than I like your hopeless dog."

Aden's lips curled upward slightly, but other than that, he didn't move a muscle. "But you told Pilot you'd love him forever."

Lily lowered her gaze to the ground as her heart beat a strange and unfamiliar rhythm. "I exaggerated. I don't even know if I like him today."

Aden looked hurt. He ran his fingers through his hair. "I should have stayed in Ohio. At least there I didn't know how miserable I was." He stood again, like a yo-yo, bouncing up and down with agitation. "So, Tyler is your choice?"

Lily didn't like it all so plainly laid out for her like that. His words made a marriage to Tyler seem too real. It made her defensive.

"Tyler is a hard worker and a man of God."

Aden frowned. "I know. He's also a gute man, thoughtful and kind. The best of men.

If I had a daughter, I'd want her to marry Tyler."

"Jah, my dat wants me to marry him." Lily felt dull and scrubbed thin.

Aden studied her face. "Do *you* want to marry him?"

"Not . . . yet." Why the bald truth? It was none of Aden's concern who she wanted to marry.

His gaze could have seared a hole through her head.

"Don't stare at me like that," she said. "Green eyes may work on Erla Glick, but I am not so easily impressed."

"Green eyes?" His lips twisted with a hopeful smile, and he leaned closer to her. "You like my eyes?"

"I never said that."

"But you noticed that I have eyes and that I'm gute with a Frisbee."

Lily cleared her throat. "Tyler is the bishop's son, and he can already support a wife with his dairy."

"Do you think Erla Glick likes me?"

Now he was teasing. His eyes twinkled, but Lily couldn't relax. Why was he suddenly fixated on Erla Glick?

"Only because she doesn't know you very well."

"Why don't you want to marry Tyler?"

Aden grew serious again and seemed eager to hear her answer.

"Dat says love will grow with time," Lily said.

"Like a potted plant."

"Like love."

Aden had the nerve to intertwine his fingers with hers. Heaven help her, she loved the feel of his hand. "Potted plants are so predictable," he said. "If one becomes unruly or outgrows its pot, you cut it back. It never grows wild." He squeezed her hand. "Do you like me, Lily? Will you give me some hope, or should I pack up right now and go back to Sugarcreek?"

She couldn't look at him, although she couldn't bring herself to pull her hand away. "My dat doesn't want me getting mixed up in your schemes."

"Of course he doesn't." He nudged her chin with his finger until she looked at him. "But do you like me? Because I am wonderful crazy over you."

She didn't expect the sudden elation that flooded her body, making every finger and toe tingle. She pulled her hand from his grasp and wrapped her arms tightly around her waist to contain the feeling. She couldn't give in to this. Aden was *not* a potted plant. Dat would fall off his chair if he knew what she was doing right now.

"It doesn't matter." Short of throwing herself into his arms, she didn't know what else to say.

"Yes, it does," Aden countered.

"I must honor my father's wishes."

"What of your wishes?"

She managed to look him squarely in the eye. "I never said I liked you in return."

He deflated like a balloon as an uncomfortable and oppressive silence overtook them. He refused to look at her as he stood up for the last time. "We should get back."

What would Dat say about the emptiness inside her?

She heard a rustling in the bushes to her left and expected to see Pilot leap out of the thicket, blissfully unaware of what had passed between Lily and Aden. At least Pilot would be cheerful on the walk home. Lily thought she might never feel cheerful again.

Lily stopped breathing as a black bear bigger than three Pilots lumbered out of the woods and plucked three berries from a bush with his wet, pink tongue.

Every muscle tensed in terror as Lily watched the bear, which was oblivious to her and Aden's presence.

Aden slowly lifted a hand and gave her a signal to stay still. No instructions necessary. Fear paralyzed her.

The bear grunted and snuffled while stripping the bush of its light red huckleberries. Lord willing, it would get its fill and disappear back into the woods without even noticing them. That didn't seem likely with the way Lily's heart pounded like a full orchestra.

Aden reached his hand slowly toward Lily. Did he really think she was composed enough to take his hand, stand up, and walk away while the bear stood not twenty feet away having an afternoon snack? She shook her head slightly so the bear wouldn't notice her. Aden's gaze intensified. "Come on," he seemed to plead with his eyes.

"I can't," she mouthed.

The bear suddenly snapped its head around and caught sight of them. It growled ferociously with a force more savage and threatening than Lily had ever heard. She instinctively clapped her hands over her ears. Aden yanked her hand away from her head, pulled her to her feet, and shoved her behind him.

The bear growled again and rose to its hind legs. Lily gasped. It stood almost as tall as Aden.

"Don't move a muscle," Aden cautioned as he kept his eyes glued to the frightening

211

sight before them.

The bear growled and showed its yellow teeth.

"If he charges," Aden said, his voice barely above a whisper, "run away as fast as you can. Do you understand?"

Lily couldn't so much as nod. She knew her legs would fail her if she tried to run. Aden bent over and picked up a stick, nowhere near big enough to fight off an angry bear. It wouldn't even do as a fetching stick for Pilot.

Lily thought she might die of panic as, without warning, the bear fell back on all fours and came at them at a speed that she would not have believed possible.

Aden lifted his stick. "Run, Lily," he yelled, even as he stood his ground.

Her legs suddenly, unbelievably found their strength. Grabbing his sleeve, she pulled him back. She wasn't about to leave him behind. She might as well have been pulling on an oak tree. Aden had sprouted roots.

As if in answer to a prayer she hadn't had time to utter, Pilot came tearing through the trees, barking ferociously. He took a great leap and landed on the bear's back. The bear whirled in a circle and forced Pilot to the dirt. Pilot regained his feet, bared his teeth, and attacked again. Lily wouldn't have guessed Aden's mischievous dog could look so deadly. The noise between the two animals was deafening. The bear lifted a great paw and swiped at Pilot's nose. Lily stood breathless as Pilot dodged the sharp claws and clamped his jaws at the bear's throat.

She felt pressure on her arm and looked down to see Aden's hand clenched around her wrist. He pulled her but her feet didn't move. He said something, but she couldn't make sense of his words.

"Lily!" His voice finally broke through her stupor. "Lily, we've got to get out of here!"

Almost numb with shock, she nodded and let him half drag, half lead her up the trail to the house. He walked quickly but kept glancing behind him as if expecting the bear to chase them, or Pilot to follow.

The bellowing faded and Pilot's barking traveled away from them. It sounded like the conflict had moved farther into the woods.

Aden picked up his pace until Lily had to run to keep up with him. His grip on her arm was painfully tight, as if he thought she might slip out of his protection if he didn't hold securely.

Finally, the house came into view, and Lily

had never seen a more welcome sight. Aden relaxed his grip but not his pace as they marched up the porch steps and burst into the kitchen. Aden stopped at the threshold, took a deep breath, and put his arm protectively around Lily. "Are you okay?"

"Jah," she said, even as she felt her knees buckle beneath her. "What about Pilot?"

Aden still had that stupid stick in his hand. He laid it on the table before tightening his grip around her shoulders and leading her to the sofa. She sat, and he knelt next to her on the floor. "Can I get you a drink or a Tylenol?"

Lily sank into the soft folds of the puffy sofa. Could he do something for this overwhelming feeling that she was going to faint? "A drink might be gute."

He went to the cupboard for a glass.

Anna and Felty came up from the cellar, giggling like teenagers. "I never agreed to no such thing, Banannie," Felty said. He caught sight of Lily. "Look who's back."

"How were the berries?" Anna said, bustling behind the counter to give Aden a peck on the cheek.

"We left them there," Aden said, filling a glass for Lily. His agitation showed in his every movement.

Anna tilted her head and tried not to

frown. "They weren't ripe?"

Aden hurried to the sofa with Lily's water. "A bear, Mammi. We ran into a bear."

Anna put her hand to her mouth. "Was he picking berries?"

"We saw a bear up there three years ago yet," Felty said. "A black or brown one?"

"Black," Aden said. "Pilot ran him off."

"Probably the same one."

"Are the berries ready to pick?" Anna asked.

Aden sat on the sofa and watched Lily take a few swallows. When he seemed satisfied that she wouldn't melt into a puddle of tears, he jumped up and started rummaging through Anna's cupboards. He pulled out Anna's two large frying pans and without another word headed for the door.

"Where are you going?" Anna and Lily asked at the same time.

"To get my dog," he said, his voice steely with determination.

Lily's heart flipped like a flapjack on the griddle. "Aden, that bear could kill you without even trying."

Aden actually gave her a boyish smile. "You're so cute when you're worried." He opened the door.

Her legs regained their strength, and she bolted to Aden and grabbed his arm. "This isn't funny. I want Pilot to be all right, he just saved my life, but this is too dangerous. You aren't going to be safe armed with two frying pans."

"Black bears hate noise," Aden said, leaning forward, chomping at the bit to be gone. "These are my best weapons."

Lily felt the panic rise like bile in her throat. Her fear at the pond was nothing compared to how she felt at that moment. "At least take Felty's hunting rifle so you're not completely defenseless."

"I don't own a hunting rifle," Felty said.

"I wouldn't ever shoot it anyway," Aden added.

Lily growled in frustration. Blast these do-gooders who wanted to save the planet! Right now, all she cared about was saving Aden. "Then let's call the police."

Aden shook his head. "They'll call Animal Control. Then the bear's as good as dead." He extricated her fingers from his arm. "Lily, you can talk until you're blue in the face — which you kind of are already — but I'm not leaving Pilot out there to fend for himself." He squeezed her hand. "I'm a fast runner."

"And a gute swimmer," Felty said, trying to be helpful.

Lily gave up, even though the terrified part

216

of her wanted to throw herself at his feet and beg him to stay. If that didn't work, she could always grab his ankles and refuse to let go. Fear threatened to overpower her sense, so she decided to fend off the fear with anger. Anger made her feel like she had more control. She scowled at Aden. "You better come back safe or I'm never speaking to you again."

He gave her a reassuring nod. "It is a deal."

He looked ridiculous, ridiculous, running into the woods with a frying pan in each hand. Lily shut the door, too hard, and turned to see Anna and Felty staring at her.

"He'll be right as rain," Anna said.

Felty went so far as to give her arm a pat. "Nobody is better with the animals than Aden. He knows what to do."

At which point, Lily spied Aden's stick on the table and promptly burst into tears.

Lily wished for a cell phone, longed for a cell phone, would have done just about anything for a cell phone at that moment. She didn't care if it was against the Ordnung. This raging anxiety would send her over the edge. Of course, even if she had a cell phone, it wouldn't do her any good unless Aden had a cell phone and they got coverage on Huckleberry Hill, which was a pretty good chance they didn't.

She'd abandoned the house over an hour ago and stood on the porch looking out into the woods in the fading light of dusk. This felt like when Aden went underwater, only a hundred times worse. At least underwater, she knew precisely where he was, and her terror had lasted mere minutes. But now, two hours after Aden had taken to the woods with a set of frying pans, she knew less than nothing. There was no rustle from the leaves, no distant barking, not even the sound of faraway pans being smacked together to give her hope. Had he no consideration for her feelings?

Was this how Dat felt ten years ago when he learned Onkel Zeke was missing? Had he paced the floor, sick with worry for his wayward brother? Had he spent the night in prayer only to learn by morning that Zeke had been killed in a training exercise? Dat had begged Onkel Zeke not to join the Army. Zeke hadn't heeded Dat's voice of warning, just as Aden hadn't heeded hers.

To add to her distress, Lily thought about Pilot and how ungrateful she must be. She prayed hard that when Aden returned, he would bring that troublemaker with him. She couldn't bear the thought that Pilot wouldn't be back.

Anna came outside. "Supper is warm in the oven. Do you want to eat?"

Lily shook her head, not trusting her voice to remain steady.

"That's what I told Felty. 'She won't come in until Aden's back,' I said." Anna smiled in satisfaction. "Felty never believes my plans are going to work out, but I have an extra sense about these things." She wrapped her arms around Lily's waist.

Lily found the gesture immensely comforting. She, in turn, put her arm around Anna's shoulders.

"I have never baked tofu before," Anna said. "Aden stole both my frying pans. So if he doesn't like it, it's his own fault." She smoothed back an errant wisp of hair from Lily's face. "It does my heart good to see how worried you are for my grandson, but let me put your mind at ease. Aden knows how to handle a bear. He's encountered one before, you know."

In surprise, Lily studied Anna's face. "He has?"

"Once he and his dat came upon a mother and her cubs. They both climbed trees until the bear lost interest. He came out with nary a scratch. He will be just fine."

Lily didn't know if this information made

her feel better or not. Aden's life had been in danger before? She felt sick with worry for something that had already happened. But she also felt better knowing that, of all the Amish boys she knew, Aden could best take care of himself.

It gave her a little bit of hope.

Felty stepped onto the porch and stood on the other side of Anna. All three of them stared into the woods. With so many eyes watching for them, Aden and Pilot would surely find their way home.

Felty began to hum a tune. His deep bass voice felt like a warm blanket around Lily's shoulders. *"Pressed down, shaken together, running over, running over. When you give unto the Lord, He will give you more."*

To Lily's surprise, Anna joined Felty on another verse. She improvised a lovely harmony as she blended her voice with his. Lily wondered if they sang together often. Lily didn't mind singing, but she couldn't join in. Her composure felt so fragile, she feared she might break into a million pieces if she opened her mouth.

A movement to her right caught her attention, and she turned her head to see Pilot plodding, not out of the woods, but up the lane on the well-worn path a thousand buggies had traveled before.

"Oh!" Her heart raced with relief and fear as she vaulted off the porch and ran to Aden's dog. He stopped and stood at attention as she knelt down and wrapped her arms around his neck even as she swept her gaze down the lane. The tears trickled down her face. "Pilot, where is Aden?"

Pilot's fur was matted with mud and his ears drooped as if he had no strength left to hold them up. She'd never seen it before, but Pilot did indeed look dog-tired. Keeping her eyes on the lane, she rubbed her hands over Pilot's filthy fur, feeling for dried blood or moist wounds. Nothing that she could tell. A scratch marked his nose but didn't look deep.

Anna came up behind Lily and laid a fleecy soft, white knitted blanket over Pilot. "I was saving this for the next baby in the district, but Pilot deserves it tonight, don't you think?" Anna gazed expectantly down the lane. "Where could Aden have got to?"

"Pilot," Lily said, caressing his ears, "where is Aden?"

"He must be close behind," Anna said. "Pilot would never come home without Aden."

Surely Anna was right. If there were danger, Pilot wouldn't leave Aden for a minute.

Anna patted Pilot's head and led him toward the house. "You have been a very gute dog. I will make something special for you and Sparky for supper tonight." Pilot followed her up the porch steps. "But maybe after a bath yet. Do you like baked tofu?"

Smothering the panic, Lily stood and marched down the lane. Would Pilot find his way home if Aden no longer needed him? Like if he were dead? A quiet sob escaped her lips as her throat constricted, and she quickened her pace.

If he lay dead in the bottom of a river somewhere, she would never forgive herself for letting him leave her. Why, oh why hadn't she clamped her arms around his ankles and held on for dear life?

Her heart stopped beating as she came around the first bend and caught sight of Aden — handsome, wonderful, alive Aden — trudging up the hill. His head was bowed, and he looked as if each step took supreme effort.

"Aden!" she screamed.

He looked at her and gave her the most beautiful smile she had ever seen. Ever.

Losing all sense of restraint, she ran to him and threw her arms around his neck. He caught her in his strong embrace as if he'd been expecting her, as if he wouldn't ever let her go.

Lily wept as relief washed over her. The feeling proved so strong and cleansing that she didn't even try to choke back the great sobs that racked her body. She buried her face in his rock-hard chest and cried as if she had been waiting for a hundred years to release her heart.

He stroked her wet cheek with his thumb. "Hush, sweetheart. I'm back. It's all right. Everything is all right. You're safe. That's the most important thing."

"Don't you ever do that to me again," she sobbed, pounding his chest with her fist. Her voice sounded muffled against his shirt, but she was certain he understood her.

He stood there, letting her cry, until she felt the tension leave her body. She sagged against him. She shouldn't have leaned on him like that. He had been chasing a bear all afternoon.

"If you greet me like this every time I do something dangerous, I will have no motivation to mend my ways."

She growled — a loud, I'm-so-annoyed-with-you growl — and thumped her fist on his chest.

He didn't loosen his grip. "And you're going to give me a bruise, you know."

Lily giggled through her tears. "You'll get

worse if you ever leave me hanging like that again. Get a cell phone if you plan on running off into the woods on a regular basis."

His eyes sparkled as he stared at her and then bent his head to hers and kissed her on the mouth.

Just like that.

No warning. No advance preparation. No indication whatsoever that he was going to lay a feather-soft kiss on her lips and send her floating to the moon. What was he thinking, being so hasty?

A girl would like to be able to prepare herself first.

He pulled away and looked into her eyes. "You are completely irresistible."

"And you are . . . you are not thinking straight when you . . ."

Before she could finish the sentence she had no idea how to finish, he lowered his head and kissed her again. This kiss was as unexpected as the first, but sweeter and longer and more floaty. She must be standing on Mars by now.

He pulled away, gave her a wide smile, and studied her face. "What would your dat say if he knew I kissed you?"

"He wouldn't like it," Lily said. Should she be worried that at this moment she didn't really care what Dat thought?

"What about you?"

"What about me?"

"Did you like it?"

Lily couldn't be anything but honest, especially with her arms clamped tightly around his neck. "I think I liked it."

Aden's lips quirked upward. "Did you like it better than a kiss from Tyler Yoder?"

Lily felt herself blush, but his impertinent question motivated her to pry her arms from around his neck. "Tyler Yoder wouldn't dream of kissing me."

"Oh, believe me, he dreams about it all the time. He just wouldn't be so reckless as to do it before he married you."

"Tyler is anything but reckless."

Aden grimaced and massaged the back of his neck. Lily caught sight of a dark, broad stain on the sleeve of his navy shirt.

Her heart did a somersault. "Is that blood? Aden, are you bleeding?"

He instinctively covered his upper arm with his hand. "I ran headlong into a thicket and a sharp branch caught me. It's nothing."

She pulled his hand away from the wound and got light-headed when it came away soaked in blood. "Aden, this isn't nothing!" She pulled apart the folds of his sleeve and found where the fabric had ripped. Parting the fabric, she pressed her lips together in concern. A deep gash, probably four inches long, curved from his shoulder to his biceps. "This looks awful."

He grinned, and she could tell he wanted to laugh at her response. "It's not bad, really."

"Not bad? You need stitches. I'm taking you to a hospital."

"I don't need a hospital."

"Are you afraid? Is the fearless Aden Helmuth afraid of needles?"

"No," he protested with a chuckle.

Lily wiped her hands on her apron and all but growled at his stubbornness. "You must be in terrible pain."

"You kissed me and made it all better."

Would it be bad to smack an injured man? Maybe not if she hit his good arm. "Let's get back to the house and see what your mammi has to say."

"To tell the truth, after all I've been through, I'm numb."

Unable to stop herself, she took his hand just to reassure herself that he was back and relatively unharmed.

He stared at her hand. "I'm warning you, Lily. If I get this sort of treatment every time I do something dangerous, I'm going to take up skydiving."

226

She rolled her eyes. "Tell me what happened to the bear." She thought for a minute. "And Anna's frying pans."

They trudged slowly up the lane. "I ran for a long time through the woods, following the sound of Pilot's barking. I think I chased that sound for half an hour. At some point I ran into a poorly placed branch and lost a gute chunk out of my arm."

"You need stitches."

"I finally found Pilot stuck in a tangle of green branches. With the way he dives headlong into things, it didn't surprise me."

"Was he hurt? I didn't see any wounds."

"He was limping a bit. I'll take him to the vet tomorrow and have him checked out. I didn't see the bear again. Pilot scared him away. He's probably in Canada by now. Praise the Lord for such a gute and brave dog. We made such a wide circle around the slope of the hill that I thought it would be easier to go down to the road and hike up the lane instead of through the woods. It took a long time but was easier going."

"What about the frying pans?"

Aden chuckled. "I told you I wouldn't need a gun. I didn't even need those frying pans. By the time we got to Mammi and Dawdi's lane, they were so heavy, I left them at the bottom. I'll fetch them in the morning."

"Felty will be happy to know that you didn't have to kill a bear with one of Anna's frying pans."

Aden kept hold of her hand and stopped and stared at her. "My dog saved your life."

"He saved your life too. I will love that dog forever."

"Then, because he is my dog, you owe me something."

Lily narrowed her eyes. "What?"

"An answer." He squeezed her hand. "Do you like me, Lily, or did I just imagine that you kissed me back?"

Lily savored the sensation of her hand in his as they resumed their walk up the lane. Where she tended to lose her head in an emergency, Aden remained calm and sensible. She had already witnessed how kindly he treated everyone and how patient he was with her, even when she acted irrationally. He was tall and muscular and had nice hair, besides which, he took very gute care of his grandparents.

And his lips felt nice on hers. Very nice.

Lily sighed. After today, Tyler Yoder wouldn't be able to measure up.

She swung their hands back and forth and kept her eyes on the Helmuths' barn, which had just come into view. "I like you very, very much." She sighed. "To own the truth, I am quite jealous of Erla Glick."

His eyes danced, and he looked as if he would burst with joy. "You should be jealous. Her dat has never insisted on the four-foot rule."

Lily pulled her hand from his and doubled her speed toward the house.

Aden caught up with her in a matter of seconds — curse those long legs of his. He took her by the shoulders, wincing at the pain in his arm. "Lily, I am not interested in Erla Glick. As I told you, I am interested in you."

To punctuate his point, he kissed her and let his lips linger on hers. When he finally pulled away, Lily was convinced that if something felt this good, it was probably a sin. She should be ashamed of herself. Instead, she eyed his mouth and wondered if he would be shocked if she asked him to kiss her again.

"Now," he said, his lips inches from hers, "how do I get on your dat's good side?"

Aden flexed his newly bandaged arm and arched his stiff back. Every muscle ached for his bed. His mad chase through the woods had not been kind to his body.

Pilot slept on the rug next to the sofa with his pile of socks and Sparky beside him. He hadn't moved a muscle for over an hour. Aden knew the feeling. Any kind of movement took too much effort.

Hearing the crunch of buggy wheels on the gravel, he groaned and stood to look out Mammi's kitchen window.

Dawdi had returned.

Once Lily had tended to Aden's arm, she had helped Mammi give Pilot a bath on the porch. She had insisted, adamantly so, that Aden not lift a finger to help with his dog. Good thing too. His arm throbbed painfully, and he would have been panting in agony by the end of the bath.

They ate supper at almost seven o'clock. Mammi's baked tofu slid down his throat so slowly that he thought he might gag. But he ate it. Mammi's feelings were more important than his discomfort at eating goopy tofu.

After that, Dawdi had driven Lily home. No one wanted her walking in the dark.

Mammi sat knitting in her rocker. "You are going to need stitches, you know."

Aden nodded. "I didn't want Lily to worry. I'll go see the doctor tomorrow when I take Pilot to the vet."

Moving like a man several years older than

230

Dawdi, Aden shuffled out the door to help Dawdi unhitch the buggy. He might have felt like a cripple, but Dawdi wasn't as young as he used to be.

Dawdi saw him coming and held up his hand. "I can do this. Your arm don't look so gute."

"It's a gute dressing," Aden said. "I can help."

Dawdi gazed skeptically at Aden. "I ain't that old yet."

"Nobody said you were."

"You're the one who looks old," Dawdi said, before relenting and guiding the horse into the barn. Aden limped to one side of the horse and unbuckled the straps. Dawdi did the same on the other side.

"The frying pans was a gute idea," Dawdi said as he led the horse out from between the buggy shafts.

They walked together as Aden led the horse to one of the stalls in the barn. "Dawdi, if a boy wanted to gain your approval to court one of your daughters, what would he need to do?"

"Anyone in particular?" Dawdi said, his eyes twinkling in amusement.

"You know there is."

Dawdi took off his hat and slapped it against his leg. "There'll be no stopping your mammi now. She won't rest until she's matched every young person in Bonduel with one of our grandchildren."

Aden found the currycomb and brushed the horse with his good hand to release his growing frustration. He liked Lily a lot, and her dat's approval seemed like a mountain too high to scale.

"What can I do, Dawdi?"

"Think about your own daughter, if you had a daughter. What would a young man need to do to impress you?"

"Organize a neighborhood recycling program?"

The corner of Dawdi's lip curled up. "Okay, maybe we should take a different direction. What do you think would win over a typical Amish father?"

"A boy who has a clean police record."

"Well, stuff and nonsense, Aden. You can't let your past steal your future. The only thing you can do is help David Eicher see you as a gute husband for his daughter."

"I could buy some land and start a farm."

"Do you have the money to buy some land?"

"Jah, enough, I think."

"What else?"

"Maybe I could go to Lily's house and work. Like Jacob did for Rachel."

"You should have a conversation with her dat. Get to know him. Parents don't like boys who stay away because they're too afraid to meet the family."

"Okay, get to know the family. See if they can be tricked into inviting me to dinner."

"And Aden. The most important thing. Every father wants a godly man for his daughter."

"I've been baptized."

"You are careful and troubled about many things, Aden."

Careful and troubled. That's what the voice had told him at the lake. Was it a coincidence that Dawdi used those very words? A thrill pulsed through his veins.

Dawdi studied his face in the shadows of the barn lit by a single propane lantern. "The other boyfriend is a godly man — charitable and devout."

Aden's heart sank to his toes. If even Dawdi thought Tyler was a better man than Aden, his own grandson, then Aden didn't have a chance with Lily's father.

He slumped his shoulders. "I'm never going to measure up to Tyler Yoder."

Dawdi put a firm hand on Aden's shoulder. "I'll measure my grandson against any man in the church."

"But you said —"

233

"I said you've got some thinking to do. You mustn't give up hoping. Anyway, you are not the type to shy away from a challenge."

Aden thought of Lily. He wouldn't even consider shying away. Lily was worth every uncomfortable moment spent trying to win her dat over.

They hobbled out of the barn together. Dawdi hobbled because he was eighty-three years old. Aden hobbled because his legs felt as heavy as lead, and his knees could have been rusty hinges. Not a pretty sight.

"Remember the first day you met Lily? What did you think of her?"

"I wasn't impressed. She didn't like my dog."

Dawdi shook his finger in the air as if Aden had said something brilliant. "The very thing. Nothing is more appealing to a father than a boy who adores his daughter."

Aden smiled. At least he had that going for him.

CHAPTER THIRTEEN

This was going to be awkward. Not the you've-got-broccoli-in-your-teeth kind of awkward, but the I-am-interested-in-your-girlfriend kind of awkward, because that was exactly the conversation he needed to have with Tyler. No man of honor, Amish or otherwise, went behind his friend's back to court a girl his friend had an interest in. Aden would have to come right out in the open about it so Tyler wasn't blindsided.

Aden waited until after the supper hour so that he wouldn't ruin Tyler's day by telling him first thing in the morning. Maybe Tyler would appreciate his thoughtfulness. Maybe he wouldn't.

He knocked on the door. Tyler's mamm answered and the heavenly smell of apples and cinnamon greeted him. "Aden, cum reu. You are just in time for a piece of apple pie."

If she knew what Aden plotted against Tyler, she probably wouldn't be so hospitable.

"Is Tyler here?"

"Just got out of the shower, like as not. Come up and sit at the table, and I will dish you both a piece of pie."

Aden climbed the stairs of Tyler's split-level house and strolled into the warm kitchen. Tyler's brother, Joe, held a piece of pie in his hand like a slice of pizza and took a hearty bite. "Hullo, Aden," he said, with his mouth full.

"Manners, Joe," said his mamm. "Wipe your mouth and go downstairs for Tyler."

Joe took a swig of milk and wiped his mouth with the back of his hand.

"Manners," said his mamm.

Joe popped from his seat and went to the top of the stairs. "Tyler," he yelled.

His mamm jumped. "If I'd a wanted you to yell, Joseph Elmer, I would have done it myself." She pointed down the stairs. "Go fetch your brother like a boy whose mother has taught him some manners."

Joe sighed, glanced at Aden, and clomped down the stairs.

"I'm sorry about that," Tyler's mamm said. "Sometimes that boy acts like he was born in a barn."

She motioned to the table, and Aden sat obediently while she cut two generous slices of pie and put them on two plates. Aden couldn't be comfortable. Tyler was about to get the shock of his life.

Tyler came up the stairs with Joe close behind. Tyler's hair was damp from his shower, and he looked mildly curious at Aden's presence.

Aden stood and shook Tyler's hand. Tyler was still his best friend in Bonduel, at least for another ten minutes or so. "I heard your mamm made pie, and I came to get some."

His mamm laughed. "Oh, nonsense."

"Mamm's pie is the best," Tyler said, sitting next to Aden and picking up his fork. He frowned with concern. "I heard you saw a bear."

"A small black bear. Pilot scared it away."

"Felty told my dat you got stitches."

Aden held out his arm and ran his hand over the spot where the bandage sat under his sleeve. "I got seventeen stitches, plus a tetanus shot and a big bottle of antibiotics."

Tyler's frown deepened. "Dat says Lily was with you. Denki for watching out for her. She would have been frightened out of her wits."

"Pilot saved us."

Tyler nodded. "Even though Lily can't stand that dog, he has helped you out of more than one scrape. I am grateful."

237

Aden pressed his lips into a hard line. Lily didn't still hate Pilot, did she? No, she said she'd love him forever. She also told Aden she liked him more than she liked his dog. He smiled to himself.

Joe sat down next to Aden to finish his pie. "Tyler and I went to the pond yesterday."

"The aerator is still working well," Tyler said.

"How much longer can we have it?" Aden asked. It didn't matter. Tyler would probably yank it from the pond tomorrow once he heard what Aden had to say.

"A couple of months. It's better than nothing."

"It's thanks to you that we've had it at all."

"Lord willing, it will do a year's worth of aerating in only a few weeks."

Aden cleared his throat. The longer he put this off, the harder it would be. He looked at Tyler's mamm. "It wonders me if I could talk to Tyler privately for a few minutes."

Tyler's mamm didn't seem excessively curious. She grabbed a basket from the washroom. "Come on, Joe. Help me take the wash from the line."

Joe groaned and followed his mamm out the back door, dragging his feet all the way.

Tyler regarded him with a serious eye, which wasn't unusual considering Tyler's sober personality. "Something is wrong," he said. "I don't often see you without a smile."

"I have something to tell you, Tyler, and it's going to make you mad."

"I will try not to get angry. He who is angry without cause is in danger of judgment."

Aden attempted a smile. "No problem there, then. I'm about to give you good cause."

Tyler slowly set down his fork and propped his elbows on the table. He stared at Aden as if he were trying to read his mind. "What's the matter? Did the aerator get broken?"

Aden took a fork and flaked the top crust of his pie. "Do you remember the day you told me that you liked Lily?"

Tyler nodded slowly.

"And I told you I liked her too?"

Tyler furrowed his brow.

Aden swallowed the lump in his throat. "I wasn't joking. I really like her."

The lines around Tyler's mouth seemed to deepen, but his face betrayed no other reaction. "Of course you like her. Lily is as bright as the sunshine in January. Who doesn't like sunshine?"

239

"I kissed her."

Tyler remained stone-faced. "You kissed her?"

"Three times."

Tyler stood up so quickly, his chair fell over and crashed to the floor. Running his fingers through his damp hair, he began pacing back and forth in a tight four-foot square.

Was Tyler stoking a fire inside himself or attempting to get his anger under control? Aden watched silently and waited for Tyler to explode.

Tyler stopped pacing and looked at Aden. The explosion was restrained. "I've had my eye on Lily for three years. You think you can come into town for a few months and steal her?"

"I don't want to steal her. I want to win her."

"Sounds like stealing to me."

Aden pushed his plate away. This conversation was too serious for pie. "Our friendship is important to me, but in the end, it would ruin our friendship if I were sneaky about this."

Tyler scowled and folded his arms across his chest. "You destroyed our friendship the minute you kissed her."

"I don't want to court Lily behind your

back. I want to court her in front of your back. No deception, no shame. Because we're friends, I want you to have a chance to put up a fight. It's only fair."

Something seemed to soften around Tyler's eyes. "At least you're honest about it."

"If it were you she'd kissed, I'd want to know so I didn't feel like a fool."

"Thank you," Tyler murmured. He took a deep breath, righted his chair, and sat down. "So, it's a contest?"

"I don't know if Lily would appreciate being considered a prize in a contest."

"You said you wanted to give me a chance to put up a fight. Maybe you're the one who doesn't have a fighting chance."

"Maybe."

An unexpected smile played at the corners of Tyler's mouth. "Her father likes me better. In truth, he doesn't like you at all."

Aden wished the truth didn't bother him so much. "I don't wonder but you have a long list of advantages."

Tyler sat back as he mulled things over. He ran his hand down the side of his face. "Did she kiss you back?"

Since Tyler seemed so confident of Lily's dat's approval, Aden let him squirm a little. "What do you think?"

Tyler cocked an eyebrow. He looked almost cheerful. "You know what I want to do right now? I want to take you out to the far pasture and punch you in the mouth."

His candor took Aden by surprise. The Plain folk never spoke of doing violence, and Tyler, of all men, would never actually consider it. Laughter tore from Aden's throat, and he laughed until his sides ached and his injured arm throbbed with every tremor. Tyler joined him, laughing until tears ran down his cheeks. Aden had never heard Tyler laugh before.

When the laughter subsided, Tyler wiped his eyes and said, "I am trying really hard to hate you, but I can't. It doesn't make sense, but I still want to be your friend."

"It makes perfect sense. I knew the day I met you. You have a gute heart. Anger is not in your nature."

Tyler picked up his fork and pointed it at Aden. "It's a competition, then. May the best man win."

"No," Aden countered. "I don't want the best man to win."

Tyler gave Aden a brotherly pat on the shoulder. "Be forewarned. If Lily chooses you, I'm taking my aerator back."

"No hard feelings," Aden said before popping the last bite of pie into his mouth.

Let the game begin.

CHAPTER FOURTEEN

"When we get there, I'll show you where we saw the bear," Aden said.

"It's a gute thing that pesky dog was with you," Moses said, helping his wife step over a branch that had fallen across the path.

Moses had arrived for the frolic not fifteen minutes ago, and Pilot had already tried to knock Aden's cousin over twice. Fortunately for him, Moses was as tall and as solid as Aden. He had no trouble standing against a giant dog.

Pilot hadn't so much as nudged Moses's wife, Lia. It was almost as if Pilot sensed she was expecting and wouldn't do anything that would risk harm to the baby. Either that, or Moses had given Pilot such a ferocious growl when Pilot ventured near Lia that Pilot guessed it would not be a good idea to mess with Moses's wife.

Lily had seldom seen a more considerate husband than Moses Zimmerman. He carried Lia's bucket and warned her of trail hazards on the hike to the huckleberry patch. And he held her hand while they walked, unconcerned that anyone else might be watching.

It was a wonderful-gute day for a berry-picking frolic. The sun warmed the air to a pleasant temperature. Lily would not feel as if she were baking under her black bonnet as she sometimes did in the heat of summer, and the walk to the other side of the hill would be relatively cool.

Anna and Felty, spry and chipper, led the way to the huckleberry patch leaning on the arms of two of their great-grandsons, Sarah Beachy's boys. Moses and Lia walked down the trail behind them, and Sarah Beachy and her husband Aaron followed with two more sons and two daughters in tow. Sarah was Anna and Felty's oldest grandchild and probably the same age as Lily's mama. Sarah worked as a midwife, and Lia, Moses's wife, served as her assistant.

Lily didn't know Lia well, but her attachment grew the more Lily saw of her. Lia had a quiet, modest way about her that seemed to invite strangers to be her friends.

Lily and Aden took up the rear. Their little band of huckleberry pickers made enough noise to repel any bears moving about. And they had brought Pilot. He knew how to handle unwelcome wildlife, if only he would take his job seriously. He bounded through the trees and bushes, pausing occasionally to smell a rock or harass a squirrel. Lily suspected that Huckleberry Hill was what dog heaven looked like.

Aden was in no hurry today. He ambled beside Lily, holding both their buckets, and let the others outpace them. "Do you know what I'm thinking?" he asked.

"That you should have brought your frying pans?" Lily teased.

"I am imagining how nice it would be to hold your hand on a beautiful September day like this."

So much for not baking under this bonnet. Her face grew hot even as her mouth twitched into a grin. "Your relatives would be shocked."

"Are you saying you wouldn't dare hold hands in front of my grandparents?"

"Of course not. What would they say?"

"Mammi would probably throw a party."

"Either that or fire me."

"My mammi would never fire you. She adores you." He tripped a few steps ahead of her, swinging their buckets in his hands. He turned around and walked backward so he could look into her face. "I've got a few

246

ideas for impressing your fater."

Lily's heartbeat quickened. "I thought you were teasing."

"Does he like pie? I could make him a fresh huckleberry pie."

She giggled. "Do you know how to make huckleberry pie?"

"Nae, but Mammi could help me." He stopped short and thought about what he had said. "Moses's wife Lia could help me. She is an excellent cook. Or I could paint your barn or milk your cow." Aden almost tripped on a tree root but managed to stay on his feet. "Does he hate raking leaves? I could come over and rake your leaves when they drop."

"Estee and I rake the leaves."

"I can rake the leaves for you, then. And I have enough money to buy a small piece of land. Does your dat like boys with land?"

Lily suddenly felt tired. She feared Aden's eagerness would soon be quashed. She slumped her shoulders. "It's hard with my dat. He's wary of outsiders, even other Amish people. I wish I knew what you could do short of changing your name to Tyler Yoder."

Aden lost the bounce to his step as if his entire day were ruined. He stopped walking and let out a long breath. "So that's it?

247

There's no hope?"

"I'm sorry. I didn't mean it like that," she said. "You will have to give my dat time. His brother had a restless spirit and got swept up with a crowd of Englischers who persuaded him to join the Army."

"The Army?"

"Dat was devastated. He'd always watched out for his brother, and then to have Zeke turn his back on everything Dat holds dear — it really hurt. Dat blamed himself, said he should have been a better brother. I'll never forget the day we learned Onkel Zeke had been killed. It's the only time I've seen my fater weep."

"And that's why he keeps a stern eye fixed on you," Aden said.

"I promised myself I would never do anything to give my fater cause to grieve like that."

"You want to do what's right for your fater's sake."

"And mine. My dat and I are both very careful of anything out of the ordinary." She wanted so badly to wipe that frown from Aden's face. Glancing at the trail ahead, she placed her hand over his fingers curled around the bucket handle. "And you are everything out of the ordinary, Aden Helmuth."

Aden surrendered half a smile. "Does he think I will persuade you to sign up for the Navy?"

"Probably."

"But he knows you are smarter than that, Lily. Why doesn't he trust you?"

She dropped her hands to her side and trudged up the trail so she wouldn't have to look him in the eye. "I disobeyed him once, and something very bad happened. He has never forgotten."

Aden matched her determined pace. "What happened?"

"It doesn't matter. My dat just wants what's best for me."

The sadness in his voice gave way to resolve. "So now I have to convince him of my worthiness. It wouldn't hurt to get Tyler married off. Then your dat might be willing to look at other options." He nested one bucket inside the other and took her hand. Lily almost sighed at the warmth of it. She didn't pull away. It felt heavenly, and the others were too far ahead to see.

Everyone else had started picking berries by the time Lily and Aden made it down the trail with Pilot following close behind. Aden had abandoned her hand the minute his relatives came in sight.

Pilot jogged to Sarah Beachy, who cooed

and scratched behind his ears before shooing him away. "Get, Pilot. I've got better things to do than entertain you all day. Go pester one of my boys."

Pilot turned to Lily for some affection. Lily grinned at Aden and pulled a leaf from Pilot's fur. "Go play. I've got to pick huckleberries."

Sarah bent over a low bush. "I'm glad to see you're not so afraid of dogs as you used to be, Lily. A bite like you had would have scared me off dogs altogether."

Aden handed her a bucket and studied her face with those penetrating eyes. "A dog bit you?"

Lily found a bush to pick and turned away so Aden wouldn't discover anything in her face. "It was nothing."

Sarah snorted. "Surgery and twenty stitches ain't nothing. But you've done gute to put it behind you. It's not healthy to be so timid."

Lily quickly scooted away and looked for a faraway bush laden with fruit. With purposeful strides, she put some distance between Aden and her. Lord willing, he would forget all about surgery and twenty stitches. He would hate her if he ever found out, and no matter how happy it would make Dat, she didn't want Aden to hate her.

She knelt down and picked berries in earnest. Despite her efforts, Aden would find out. If she refused to tell him, he would surely ask Sarah the details. She blinked back the stinging tears.

It didn't take Aden long to catch up with her. He tromped through the undergrowth, sat next to her in the dirt, and started plucking berries from the bush.

"Now I'm really sorry Pilot jumped on you that first day. You must have been terrified."

She didn't look at him. The berries required her full attention.

"Do you want to tell me what happened? I promise, I don't think you're a coward."

She should tell him, if only so he would stop looking at her with all that pity, but her throat constricted and she didn't think she could speak coherently.

He stood and brushed off his trousers. "Cum," he said, picking up her bucket and pulling her to her feet. "There are plenty of huckleberries farther in the woods."

With his hand gently resting on the small of her back, he led her down a narrow path, barely visible under the fallen leaves and undergrowth. They were soon out of sight of the others and into thicker woods. But Aden was right. Huckleberry bushes dotted the way.

They heard faint voices, walked a little farther, and came in sight of Moses and Lia. Moses stood with his back against a tree with his arms around Lia's waist. Moses and Lia stared at each other, their expressions overflowing with love, and no doubt whispered sweet nothings that no one else was meant to hear.

Aden and Lily caught Moses's eye. He smiled, but didn't make any move to release Lia. "Can't a man get a little privacy with his wife? If you want to do a little sparking, you'll have to find your own tree."

Aden winked at Lily. "We're just looking for huckleberries, cousin, and you two are shirking. You don't even have your buckets."

Lia looked back at Aden and giggled. Moses smiled and waved them on. "Go away."

Aden and Lily put some distance and some trees between them and Moses. Once they were out of sight of the newly marrieds, Aden found a nice, smooth log to sit on.

"I don't even know which way the huckleberry patch is now," Aden said.

"Are we lost?"

"Pilot will find us. We might have to forage in the woods for a few days, though.

I'm sorry a dog hurt you."

"You're going to hate me," Lily said.

"Not possible."

"I was eight."

Aden enfolded her hand in both of his. "And you think I'm going to hate you for something that happened more than ten years ago?"

Lily pulled her hand away and slid her sleeve up her arm to reveal scars just above her wrist where eight teeth had pierced her skin. She rotated her arm. Five more teeth marks were visible on the underside.

Aden gasped and reached out for her. Up and down, he caressed her skin with his warm, calloused hand while examining the visual reminder of that horrible ordeal. "My Lily," he sighed.

"He clamped on and wouldn't let go. I thought he would bite my hand off."

"He was a big dog, like Pilot."

Lily nodded. "I went with my dat to Schneiders' to buy a plow. He warned me not to wander off. I wasn't so obedient as I am now. I stuck my hand through a barbed-wire fence. The dog latched on to my arm and wouldn't let go. I screamed, and my dat came running. He didn't leave my side for one minute at the hospital, but I could tell he was angry at me for disobeying."

Aden traced his finger down the side of her cheek. "Lily, you didn't do anything wrong."

"And when his brother died two days later, he told me I'd end up just like Onkel Zeke if I didn't learn to obey. I didn't want to end up like Onkel Zeke."

"Oh, Lily." Aden shook his head and leaned toward her as if to say more, but instead he cleared his throat and slowly rubbed his hand along her scars.

The pleasant sensation of his gentle caress traveled up her arm even as her heart felt like a stone. "I never meant for any harm to come to that dog."

Aden pulled his hand away and gazed at her with sudden insight. "They had to put him down, didn't they?"

"Please don't hate me," Lily whispered. "I didn't want him to die."

"It wasn't your fault. They'd have to put down a dangerous dog like that."

"But I know how much you love animals."

Aden stared at her, his eyes full of wonder. "And here I thought you didn't want to tell me because you were ashamed of being afraid, when you thought I'd be mad because of the dog."

"He died because of my disobedience."

"Lily, that dog attacked you, yet you care

254

more about the dog than your arm." He grinned and rubbed his hand along the side of his face. "That sounds like something *I* would worry about."

"But that poor dog —"

In one rapid motion, Aden wrapped his arms around Lily and stopped her lips with a kiss that left her breathless and forgetful. What had they been discussing? It didn't seem all that important anymore.

He kept her close but withdrew his lips. "Denki for caring."

"You're welcome." *You're welcome* for what? Lily couldn't be expected to remember anything with his face so close. He smelled like mint and leather. That was all that mattered.

Without warning, Aden stood and pulled Lily to her feet. "We better join the others before I lose myself entirely out here. Huckleberry picking is more dangerous than I thought."

"Dangerous? I think it's wonderful."

Aden took her hand and pulled her in the direction they had come. "With you, it's both."

CHAPTER FIFTEEN

Lily caught herself doing that thing with her lips again — puckering and unpuckering as if practicing for a kiss. The gesture was almost unconscious every time she thought of Aden. Three weeks ago, he had given her her first, second, and third kisses ever. Four days ago, he had followed up with another kiss. Would life ever be normal again?

Deftly, Lily threaded the wet clothes through the wringer with one hand while turning the crank with the other. Treva Schrock eagerly held out her hands to catch the clothes coming out of the wringer. She put the wet laundry in a basket at her feet, ready to be hung on the line.

"I am glad you came to visit today, Treva," Lily said. "You are a big help with the laundry."

Treva held up a damp purple dress. "I like this."

"That's Estee's. Purple is one of my favorite colors too."

Lily put another shirt through the wringer and puckered her lips again. Had she done it right? How many other girls had Aden kissed before? A boy who'd been arrested three times probably kissed girls every day. Was she a disappointment to a boy with so much experience?

Maybe not. He had kissed her four times. The first one must not have been too bad.

At least it had been enjoyable on her end. Exactly how much puckering should a girl do? She blew a piece of hair out of her face. If she overthought it, fear would paralyze her and she would grow too anxious to kiss Aden ever again.

Did he want to kiss her ever again?

Mama came down the stairs to the cellar. "Lily, the door is for you."

"Who is it?"

Mama grinned and nudged Lily teasingly. "Tyler," she said in a singsong voice. "He's looking handsome this afternoon."

Lily feigned excitement at the prospect of Tyler coming to see her. She had pushed him out of her mind for the last three weeks. Thoughts of Tyler and Aden and her dat made her head spin, and she'd rather not get dizzy. "Okay," she said. "I'll be back, Treva."

Mama plunged her hands into the rinse basin. "Treva and I will finish wringing if you'll help us hang?"

"Jah, sure. I will come right out."

"No hurry," Mama said, still excessively cheerful.

Lily trudged up the stairs and found Tyler standing at the front door, straight-faced as always, holding a drill and a bucket of screws.

She gave him a weak smile.

"I heard your dat mention last week that some of the planks in your barn were coming loose. I came to fix them."

Lily stared at him in puzzlement for a few moments. "Uh . . . okay. That is nice of you, Tyler. Do you know where to find a ladder?"

"Is it still in the toolshed?"

"Jah." Lily didn't know what to do next. Was Tyler using work on the barn as an excuse to see her? Should she keep him company while he worked? His presence felt slightly awkward.

Her heart did a full-twisting backflip when Aden sauntered up her sidewalk with a shovel in one hand and a large plastic bucket in the other. Slightly awkward had just become mortifying. Aden had never been to Lily's house before. His presence was more bizarre than Tyler's.

She felt herself blush. Surely he wouldn't say anything to Tyler about their kisses.

Pilot appeared out of nowhere, bounded past Aden, and ran to Lily as if he planned to bowl her over. She raised her hand as she always did to halt him in his attack, but Tyler beat her to it. He stepped between Lily and Pilot just as the dog leaped into the air. Tyler exclaimed in surprise as Pilot knocked him over like a bowling pin, sending his drill to the ground and scattering his bucket of screws. Pilot planted his paws on Tyler's chest and wagged his tail.

Lily huffed in exasperation. "Pilot, get down right now."

"Good dog," Aden muttered so softly that Lily wasn't really sure she had heard correctly.

Tyler pushed Pilot off his chest and stood with as much dignity as he could rally. "Do you see what I mean, Aden? I don't care about myself, but that dog could hurt Lily someday. Teach him to behave, or I'll have to insist that you keep him away from her."

Aden stiffened as he grabbed Pilot's collar and pulled him back. "Pilot would never hurt Lily."

"He saved me from a bear," she said, hoping to dispel the tension in the air.

Tyler brushed off his trousers and didn't look up. "Jah, I am grateful."

Lily got on her hands and knees and started collecting screws from the porch. Pilot must have taken delight in making people spill whatever they had in their hands.

"No, Lily," Tyler said. "I will do it."

He held out his hand to help Lily up. Aden crossed his arms over his chest when she took Tyler's hand. "Denki," she said.

Aden sank to his knees and gathered screws with Tyler. "That dog is a nuisance," Tyler said.

Aden deposited his handful of screws into the bucket. "Most people would secure that bucket with a lid."

"Only people with naughty dogs."

Tyler and Aden met gazes, and Aden grinned. *"Naughty?* What kind of a word is *naughty?"*

Tyler's features softened. "A perfectly good word."

Lily breathed easier. The icy resistance dissipated somewhat.

Tyler retrieved his drill and stood up. Aden patted Pilot's head and flashed Lily a boyish grin. "You look very pretty today," he said.

"I'm doing some work on the barn for Lily's dat," Tyler said, as if he'd bested Aden in a game of checkers. "He will be glad to see it finished before the cold hits."

Aden lifted his brows and flashed a smug smile. "Somebody plowed into their mailbox three days ago — flattened it. I'm going to dig a nice big hole and cement the post into the ground. Digging holes and pouring cement require a lot of arm strength, so it's gute this is my job instead of yours."

The color traveled up Tyler's face. "You can't lift much with that injured arm. How did you get it again? Colliding with a tree?"

Lily might as well have been a fence post for as much attention as they paid her. Fine with her. She'd rather not get between them.

She studied their faces and her heart sank. Something told her she had already come between them.

"I got this cut chasing a bear," Aden countered. "With my bare hands."

Tyler sprouted a reluctant grin.

Aden chuckled and put a brotherly arm around Tyler's neck. "I chase animals with my bare hands all the time."

"As if you'd ever kill anything," Tyler said. Every ounce of animosity had disappeared from his tone.

They turned and walked down the porch steps together, chatting about bears and muscles and mailboxes as if nothing were amiss. Lily scraped her jaw off the ground. What in the world were they up to?

Aden's job took longer than Tyler's, but Tyler wasn't about to leave before Aden did. Tyler drilled away at the barn while Lily, Treva, and Mama hung laundry. He secured loose boards on the chicken coop, even got up on the roof to check for unsecured shingles. After Treva went home and Lily escaped into the house to help with supper, she could still hear Tyler clomping around on the roof, looking for nonexistent problems.

She couldn't keep herself from checking on Aden's progress too, though in a more furtive way. She stole glances out the window while she dusted blinds in the front room. Blinds took hours to clean properly.

He wasn't exaggerating about needing muscles for a job like that. Digging a deep hole and filling it with two bags of wet cement left him dripping with sweat. She could see the muscles in his arms straining as he dropped the mailbox post into the hole and shoveled cement around it.

She had to tell herself to breathe three

times. Aden looked too handsome to live among people who never sought to attract attention.

She smiled to herself. Was this Aden's plan to win her dat's favor? It might work. A girl texting on her phone had leveled their mailbox a few days ago, and Dat was fit to be tied. A new mailbox secured in cement was sure to please him.

And what was Tyler's plan? He already had his share of Dat's favor. Maybe he was determined not to fall behind.

Lily sighed. She knew what Dat would say about Aden. No daughter of his would ever get caught up in one of *that boy's* schemes.

Aden took off his hat, wiped his brow, and took a swig from his water bottle. He yelled something to Tyler on the roof and then dazzled the afternoon with his smile.

Lily didn't take her eyes from his face.

The blinds had never been so clean.

Estee scored the cucumbers with a fork while Mama arranged the fried chicken on a platter. "They're thinking of putting Mrs. Deforest in a home," Estee said. "I heard her son on the phone before he left for work this morning."

"Does she need to be in a home?" Mama asked.

Lily only listened with one ear as Mama and Estee fretted about Mrs. Deforest. Lily's hands shook slightly as she grated carrots for the salad. She had never been so anxious for Dat to come home. He wouldn't see the new mailbox because he always came in through the back door after parking his bicycle in the barn.

She wasn't sure why she felt so nervous. It was only a mailbox. After supper, she would walk Dat out to the road and show him the beautiful new post anchored into the ground with two whole bags of cement. Dat would nod thoughtfully, stroke his beard, and decide that Aden Helmuth was not such a bad young man after all.

"Neither Floyd or I think I should work after we get married," Estee said, "but I am worried about Mrs. Deforest."

Lily managed to finish the carrots without grating her fingers. "Estee, will you hand me the mailbox — I mean — the mayonnaise?"

Estee retrieved the mayonnaise from the refrigerator. "She's able to get up and down, but she shouldn't be on her own during the day."

Lily must quit fretting about Aden's mailbox, or Mama would know something was amiss, or worse, Lily would end up ruining the salad.

At five o'clock sharp, Dat came through the back door, and Lily's pulse raced. Dat hugged Lily and Estee at the same time. "How are my gute girls today?"

Mama's eyes twinkled as she set the fried chicken on the table. "Lily, go show your dat the improvements in our yard."

So Mama *had* noticed Lily's agitation. Her heart pounded in her throat.

Dat raised an eyebrow. "Improvements?"

Mama laced her fingers together and winked at Estee. "A certain young man has been hard at work today."

Lily's heart wanted to gallop down the road. Mama's support for Aden would go a long way toward securing Dat's approval.

Dat smiled as if he knew the secret. "Shall we go after supper? You don't want the chicken to get cold."

"It's already cold," Mama said. "I made it this morning. We will wait for you."

"Okay," Lily said, suddenly breathless. She so wanted Dat to be pleased. "Cum, Dat. I will show you." She rinsed her hands and headed for the front door.

Mama giggled and pointed the other way. "The barn is that way, dear. My, but you have been *ferhoodled* all afternoon."

Oh. The barn.

Tyler's project.

A pile of stones settled in the pit of her stomach. Of course Mama gushed about Tyler, not Aden. Did Mama even care that Aden worked here today too?

Lily quickly changed course and went out the back door. Dat would see the barn first and then she would show him the new mailbox. It was better this way. Tyler's work was good, but the mailbox would have taken Dat hours to put up.

Dat followed her to the barn. "Tyler fixed the loose planks," she said. And used a fancy drill to ensure they wouldn't come loose again. And walked around on the roof for more than an hour. He'd done a good share of work, but Lily wasn't about to embellish it for Dat.

Dat ran his hand along the barn wall. "How thoughtful of him to use a drill. Nails come loose so easy." Dat ambled all the way around the barn, inspecting Tyler's work closely, wanting to be impressed. He pointed to where the eaves met the wall. "He even knocked down that wasp's nest. That boy thinks of everything."

Lily felt a tinge of guilt that she couldn't muster any enthusiasm for Tyler Yoder, even though her dat burst at the seams with admiration. Tyler had done good work today. The least she could do was show some appreciation. "Jah, he does not do a job halfway."

"That's right," Dat said, putting an arm around her shoulders and leading her toward the house. "He sets himself apart by his good works."

Lily stopped walking. "Wait, Dat. I want to show you something else."

"There's more? Tyler was busy today." Dat smiled. "That is a good sign for you, Lily. Not many boys know how to impress a girl's father."

Lily fidgeted with her apron. "Aden Helmuth also came today."

A shadow crossed Dat's face. "Aden Helmuth? What did he want?"

Lily swallowed past the rock lodged in her throat. "He fixed our mailbox, Dat. With cement."

"Our mailbox?"

Lily felt timid yet proud at the same time. "Come and see. He dug a deep hole and secured the pole with cement. A car couldn't knock it over now."

Dat furrowed his brow and marched to the front yard with Lily doing her best to keep up. He stopped at a few feet from the mailbox, folded his arms, and examined it as if it had fallen from the sky.

Lily clasped her hands together. "He dug so deep, he must have hit bedrock." When Dat didn't laugh, she added, "He worked all afternoon."

Dat placed his hands on his hips and turned to face her. He frowned. "Why didn't you stop him?"

His reaction struck Lily dumb. "I . . . uh . . ."

"The mailbox should be on the other side of the driveway, where it is less likely to be hit. I told you that the day it got knocked over."

"No . . . no, you didn't, Dat."

"Didn't he even think to ask me where I wanted it before he started digging?"

Stunned and confused by Dat's reaction, Lily wasn't quite sure what to say. "He put it back in its original spot."

"So it can get knocked over again," Dat growled.

Lily felt her face get hot. Except for three days ago, the mailbox hadn't been knocked over in all the years they had lived here.

"He didn't even think it might be a gute idea to ask me where I wanted it?"

Surprised by the tears that stung her eyes, Lily stood like a statue as Dat stormed to the toolshed and came back with a crosscut saw. He knelt down and began to saw at the base of the mailbox pole.

She couldn't believe what she was seeing. "Dat, what are you doing?"

"Well, I can't yank it out of the ground now that it's cemented in there. I'll have to cut the whole thing down and start again. A shameful waste of a pole, that's what it is."

"Couldn't you leave it there until it gets knocked down again?"

Dat paused in his back-and-forth motion, but only long enough for him to reject her reasonable idea. "Then no one would learn anything, would they?"

Exactly what did Dat want to teach her by cutting down Aden's mailbox?

Lily slumped her shoulders. Dat's message was for Aden.

Don't try to impress me. You'll only provoke my anger.

"Perhaps Aden doesn't realize he is wasting his efforts. My girls are too smart to get caught up in that boy's schemes. Tyler Yoder is steady and faithful. That other boy can't measure up to Tyler."

She hated to see her dat so irritated. "I didn't know he planned to come today. I'm sorry. I should have told him to go home."

Standing up, Dat nodded and gave her a knowing smile. He patted Lily's cheek. "I don't blame you. You are my gute girl. I know you would never do anything to disappoint me."

"Nae, of course not."

"Aden knows more about the world than you do, Lily. Much more. You must remember that. Do not let him or anyone else lure you into Babylon. It leads to heartache."

Lily thought about Aden's kisses. Was he trying to lure her into Babylon?

Dat caused her to doubt herself, as he always did, being so much wiser than she was. But then again, Dat wasn't the one who had to marry Tyler.

Would Tyler make her pulse race and her face feel flushed after they were married? Would she really have to work so hard at loving someone? Or would it come naturally, flowing to her like water in a brook?

"Cum," Dat said, gazing at her affectionately, "you are my gute girl. You would never act foolishly as some young people do, like your Onkel Zeke."

Lily didn't trust her voice to reply.

Dat took her hand and nudged her gently toward the house. "Let's eat supper, and I will fix this mess later."

"Jah, okay."

His dark mood seemed to lift as soon as he turned his back on the offensive mailbox. "Your mama's fried chicken is my favorite

270

meal. If there are any leftovers, you should take a piece to Tyler as a thank-you for fixing our barn. I can tell he worked hard. He likes you very much." He squeezed her hand and grinned. "I like that about him."

Lily sighed. She would try harder to please her dat.

Before she went to bed tonight, she resolved to make a list of all of Tyler's excellent qualities. The qualities that would make a gute Amish husband. Those qualities certainly did not include owning a slobbery dog, risking his life for that dog, or chasing bears with frying pans.

No matter how handsome, no matter how appealing, she would not let Aden Helmuth drag her to Babylon with his heavenly kisses.

The pathway to hell was paved with good intentions.

CHAPTER SIXTEEN

The propane lamp glowed brightly as Estee shut the book she read and placed it on the nightstand between their beds. "The first thing Floyd wants to buy after we get married is a horse-drawn sleigh. Can you believe that, Lily? He says he wants to take me riding in a one-horse open sleigh, like in the song." Estee giggled and reclined on her pillow, twisting the end of her braid with a faraway look in her eyes. "He's so romantic."

Lily lay in bed, staring at the ceiling in the room she had shared with Estee for nineteen years. This was usually her favorite time of day, just before she and Estee drifted off to sleep. They would share funny stories and giggle like little girls. For the past year, Estee had talked of almost nothing but Floyd, because she adored him and because he seemed to do either something wildly ridiculous or deliriously charming every day.

Floyd was Estee's perfect match. Estee

organized cans of soup in alphabetical order. Floyd would forget his head if it weren't attached to his body. Dat once commented that when Floyd had children of his own, he was likely to misplace them on a regular basis. It was good Floyd had found Estee. She would never lose her own children. Her children would organize their sock drawers according to length and color and walk to church single file in matching dresses and shirts.

Tonight, Lily was on the verge of tears and the last thing she wanted to do was talk about boys, especially about any upcoming nuptials in the family. She feared if she said one word, her voice would crack and Estee would know something was wrong. She'd press Lily for answers that Lily didn't want to give.

Part of her ached to tell Estee about Aden's kisses. Of all people, Estee might understand. On the other hand, Estee might scold Lily for setting foot in Babylon. Lily did not want to be scolded tonight. She felt bad enough already.

Estee scooted farther under the sheets. "Is Tyler romantic? Has he ever tried to hold your hand or anything?"

"Um," was all Lily could muster. Of course he had never tried to hold her hand.

Estee sat up and gazed at Lily. Lily wiped all expression from her face. "He *has* held your hand?" Estee giggled. "Did you like it?"

Estee was talking about Tyler, but all Lily could think about was the way her hand seemed to fit so nicely into Aden's calloused one, like it was made for him. She fluffed her pillow and faced away from her sister. "Of course he hasn't held my hand." She would have to add that to her list of Tyler's good qualities. He would never think of doing something so reckless.

"He came to fix the barn today. That's sort of romantic." Estee sighed. "A boy in love trying to win your father's approval."

Lily felt a pang in her heart. Estee didn't realize how close she'd come to the truth. Except Aden was the boy trying to win Dat's favor, and Tyler was the boy who already had it.

Estee must have taken a nap at Mrs. Deforest's house. She didn't act as if she were anywhere near ready to sleep. Lily held perfectly still. Maybe Estee would think she was asleep and stop prying.

Apparently not. "It was nice of Aden to fix the mailbox today. Too bad he went to all that work for nothing. I haven't seen Dat that irritated since the time the horse threw

274

a shoe on the way to Cousin Perry's wedding. I hope Aden's feelings won't be hurt when he sees what Dat did."

It hadn't occurred to Estee that Aden had fixed the mailbox for the same reason Tyler had secured planks on the barn. Did Estee see a relationship between Lily and Aden so unlikely that she couldn't possibly consider that Aden might be trying to win Dat's approval too?

Lily swallowed hard and fluffed her pillow again. "Dat was mad as a hornet about the horseshoe. Perry is his favorite cousin."

Estee lay down again. "I suppose Aden wanted to do something for us since you have been so gute to his grandparents. He is a nice young man. Floyd is certain he will mend his ways and turn out quite well after all."

Lily's pillow must have developed several lumps in the last twenty-four hours. She sat up and pounded it with her fists before resting her head on it with her back to Estee. "Good night, Estee."

"What do you think?"

"About what?" Lily mumbled, hoping to make Estee think she was mere moments from sleep.

"About Aden. Do you think he'll turn out quite well after all? You see him three days a week. You would know if anybody would."

Lily folded her pillow in half and shoved her elbow into it. Had someone filled it with rocks? She tried her best not to sound bitter. "Aden would turn out very well if people would see fit to give him a chance."

"That's not true. Look how many folks helped clean up the pond. I like him. Floyd likes him."

"Dat doesn't."

Silence for a few seconds, then Lily heard Estee whip off her covers. Lily's bed creaked as Estee must have decided her own bed wasn't good enough. She had the audacity to pull back the sheet and climb into bed with Lily. It was a tight fit. Lily didn't move a muscle.

"I want to know everything."

Lily scooted closer to the wall. "What are you talking about?"

"I feel so foolish that this didn't even cross my mind. Even Dat figured it out before I did," she said, still too cheerful.

Even Dat. Dat was a lot smarter than either of them.

Estee sighed. "That's why he chopped down the mailbox when it was in a perfectly good spot and would have stood for three generations. A team of horses wouldn't have been able to dislodge that thing."

276

Lily waited for the lecture.

Aden is wild. Aden has been in jail. He's got a cottage in Babylon and a dog the size of a pony. Besides which, he's got schemes, dozens and dozens of schemes, with which he is waiting to lure unsuspecting girls.

Estee reached over and grabbed Lily's hand, which wasn't an easy feat since Lily had tucked both hands under her rock-hard pillow. Lily was forced to roll onto her back or risk getting her arm yanked off by her sister. "Ouch. Watch it, Estee."

"Oh, Lily. He is so handsome! And Floyd thinks he's just the smartest. And so nice, what he did for the pond and all."

Lily tilted her head toward her sister. "You . . . you like him?"

"Like him? Of course. It wonders me what I wouldn't like." Estee gasped and squeezed both of Lily's hands. "And he likes you. Oh, how wonderful gute."

"I think he likes me."

"No boy would put that much time into a mailbox just to be nice."

Lily wanted to give her sister a giant hug.

"I don't really need to ask if you like him. Now that the notion has come to me, it's plain enough you're smitten," Estee said.

"Jah, sure. Ten minutes ago you didn't have an inkling."

"Well, then, do you like him?"

Lily cracked a smile. "I like him so much that I can't think about anything else the whole day long."

Estee giggled.

"But I know I shouldn't like him."

"Because Dat likes Tyler Yoder," Estee whispered. She tucked her arm around Lily, and Lily nestled her head on Estee's shoulder. "You don't dare even sneeze without Dat's approval, but you shouldn't marry someone simply because Dat wants you to, even if he's still mourning over Onkel Zeke. It's not right, Lily."

"That's easy for you to say. Dat adores Floyd."

Estee nudged Lily's shoulder. "You're such a scaredy-cat."

"Am not."

"Are too."

They lay next to each other in silence until Lily found some courage. "He kissed me."

Estee almost wrenched Lily's neck when she sat bolt upright. "What?"

"After the bear attack. I think he was relieved to see me."

Estee sat cross-legged and turned to face Lily head on. "You better tell me more than that or I'll never be able to sleep."

Lily hesitated. What would Estee think? "I

278

was terrified he might be dead, and when I saw him coming up the hill, I fell to pieces. I sort of hugged him, and he hugged me back and then he kissed me. Three times. And I liked it. Is that wicked?"

Estee pulled Lily to sit. "Don't tell anybody this, but Floyd kissed me on our first date."

"He did?"

"You know how Floyd sometimes doesn't think before he acts. He claims he already loved me. We were sitting in his buggy talking, and he leaned over and kissed me. I was so surprised I didn't have time to get ready. He kissed my teeth."

Both girls exploded with laughter.

"He didn't try again for several weeks. And then he took my hand and said, 'May I have permission to kiss you?' He wasn't taking any chances with the teeth again."

"So you don't think I'm wicked?"

"Of course not." Estee gave Lily a hug.

"Don't tell Floyd."

"I won't tell Floyd, and I wouldn't tell Dat if I were you."

More laughter, even though a small part of Lily wanted to cry. Dat had chopped down Aden's mailbox. He'd probably burn the post and melt down the metal box if he knew Aden had kissed her.

279

Nope, she wouldn't enlighten Dat anytime soon.

Lily jumped out of her skin when she heard a tap on the window. Estee's eyes grew wide. She took Lily's hand, and they breathlessly tiptoed to the window together. Estee lifted the curtain, and they both caught their breath when they saw Floyd, seemingly standing in midair at the second story.

Estee used both hands to slide open the stubborn window. "Floyd, what are you doing?" she scolded in a loud whisper. "It's almost ten o'clock."

Floyd, who stood on a ladder, looked behind him and then pressed his cheek against the screen. He looked a little silly with half his face flattened against the mesh. "I need your help."

"My help?" Estee said, looking as dumbfounded as Lily felt.

"My bike got stolen today."

"Oh no. How will you get to work?"

Floyd pressed his nose against the screen. "I want you to help me steal it back."

Estee dropped her jaw and stared at Floyd as if he'd sprouted wings on his forehead. "You want me to steal your bike?"

Floyd seemed to be trying to push himself into their room by going through the screen bit by bit. "Randy McCann and his little brother pester me every day after work. They like to knock my hat off and call me 'Amish Boy.' "

"Clever insult," Lily said drily.

"Well, today Randy grabbed my bike as soon as I unlocked it and told me it was his now. He laughed because he said I wouldn't do anything to stop him, which I didn't."

"Randy deserves a gute spanking," Estee said.

"I know he's keeping it in that little workshop garage of his because his dad would make him give it back if he knew."

"You want to take it out of his garage?" Lily felt light-headed at the thought of such danger. "What if you get caught?"

"Can you come help?" Floyd said. "If one of you could stand watch, then two of us could sneak in there and get my bike. It will take three minutes at the most."

"What if it's locked?" Estee said.

"Oh, he never locks that old garage."

"How do you know?" Lily asked. "You might get there and not be able to get in."

"I've stolen back my fishing rod and my hat from Randy before. He always leaves it open."

"Not if he keeps getting robbed," Lily said.

Floyd put his hand to his head and pulled

a bobby pin from his hair. "If it's locked, I can use this. Aden showed me how."

Aden showed him how? What? Did Aden regularly pick locks? Maybe it was a skill they taught him in jail.

"Okay," said Estee, without even consulting Lily.

Floyd thumped his fist on the top step of the ladder. "I'll be right behind you all the way down. You don't have to worry one bit about falling."

Estee glared at him. "Don't be ridiculous. Lily and I will get dressed and come out the front door like normal people."

"You don't want your mamm and dat to hear you."

"I also don't want to break my neck," Estee said.

"Okay, okay," said Floyd. "I'll meet you at the front door."

"Did you carry that ladder all the way from your house?" Estee asked.

"Nae, I took it from your toolshed," Floyd said. "I picked the lock."

Estee's eyes grew wider, and she slammed the window shut. She'd wake Mama and Dat for sure. She let the curtains fall back into place and quickly pulled her nightgown over her head. "That boy," she said. She didn't need to finish her thought.

Lily wrapped her arms around her waist. "Estee, we can't go. What if we get caught? What if they call the police? They'll think we're thieves."

Estee slipped into her dress. "We're getting Floyd's bike back. It's his bike. It's not stealing."

"What if we get caught?"

"We've got to help Floyd. He needs that bike for work."

Lily thought she might be sick. "I can't go."

Estee paused her flurry of activity. "Lily, you've got to come. Floyd needs our help."

"Floyd could go to McCanns' tomorrow and talk to the dad."

Estee went so far as to retrieve Lily's dress from the hook. "Get dressed. You're not getting out of this."

Lily planted herself on her bed and dared Estee to move her. "I'm not going. It's too dangerous."

Estee studied her face for a few moments. "You are the biggest chicken I have ever met," she said, hanging the dress back on the hook.

"I don't want to get in trouble," Lily insisted. "And you shouldn't go either."

Scowling at Lily, Estee snatched her kapp and bonnet from the hook. "I'm not afraid.

Floyd is my fiancé, and he needs me. I'll be back in half an hour." She tied the bonnet under her chin, and without another word to Lily, quietly opened their bedroom door and slipped into the hall.

Lily despised this waiting game.

As soon as Estee left, she had hopped into bed and tried to sleep. Let Estee go out there and risk getting in trouble with the McCanns or the police. Or worse, Mama and Dat. Lily knew she was right to be cautious, but the thought of Estee and Floyd in the clutches of the McCann brothers kept niggling around in her head, and she found it impossible to doze off.

She picked up Estee's book and tried to read it, but after ten minutes, she was still on the same page and couldn't remember a word she'd read. For another half hour, she lay on her bed and listened to the hiss of the propane lantern on the table. That faint hiss was usually a comforting sound, like waves lapping the shore at the lake or fire crackling in the hearth. But tonight the hiss only served to mark the slow passage of time.

She ventured out of her room, slinked down the stairs, and checked the clock on the wall. Eleven.

Where in the world was Estee?

She said she'd be back in half an hour. Had the police picked her up?

Lily's lungs constricted as if a giant snake meant to squeeze her until she suffocated.

Pacing back and forth in the kitchen and checking the clock every thirty seconds did nothing to calm her. She tiptoed back upstairs to her room. The window faced the pasture. Estee wasn't likely to take that route home, but Lily doused the lantern and opened the curtains. Her eyes scanned the darkness for any sign of movement. If Floyd got his bike back, would he ride away and leave Estee to walk home by herself?

If he ever did anything so despicable, Lily would put dead mice in his boots every day for a month. He would deserve worse.

She took a deep breath and stared out the window. Floyd would never leave Estee by herself like that.

When the scene outside hadn't changed for twenty minutes, Lily paced around her room. She counted 193 passes before she gave up and went downstairs to peek at the clock again. Almost midnight.

The panic rose in her throat. Should she wake Mama and Dat? Estee would be in serious trouble. Dat might turn against Floyd just like he had rejected Aden, and forbid Estee from dating him.

Lily thought of never seeing Aden again, and she wanted to cry. The ruination of all Estee's hopes and dreams would not be on her shoulders. She would not alert their parents.

She sank into Dat's favorite chair where she would have a good view of the clock. Walking up and down the stairs to check the time would only risk waking Mama and Dat.

At twelve-thirty, Lily bowed her head and prayed for her sister. She prayed for Floyd and his bike. She prayed that Randy McCann had left the garage unlocked, and she prayed for Floyd's bobby pin. She wanted to be thorough.

Lily started awake and groaned at the nasty crick in her neck. It took her a minute to get her bearings and focus on Mama's clock.

Three A.M.

She jumped to her feet and almost lost her balance. Maybe Estee had sneaked in through the window hours ago. Lily took the stairs as quickly as she could without making any noise and crept into her bedroom. No Estee.

Lily thought she might faint. Estee was certainly in trouble. What could she do?

She thought of the bravest person she knew. The boy who wasn't afraid of going to jail or being reprimanded by the bishop. She could get Aden. Aden wouldn't be afraid of the McCanns. He'd probably jump up and down at a chance to be arrested for stealing Floyd's bike back.

Lily held her breath. If she wanted Aden's help she'd have to saddle up Sandy and ride to Huckleberry Hill in the middle of the night. Not only would it be a terrifying ride, but Dat would be furious if he found out.

She was going to throw up — truly throw up this time.

Before she had time to work herself into a frenzy, she heard the lovely creak of the second porch step. That step whined every time someone walked on it. With heart aflutter, she shuffled quickly to the door and opened it. Estee stood poised to open it from the outside.

Both her bonnet and kapp were missing and tufts of her hair stuck out of her braid like weeds. A thick layer of dirt dusted her navy dress. She limped into the room as if she couldn't hold herself up much longer. Floyd stood just outside the door, his fingers wrapped around the brim of his hat. Weariness and concern seemed to be a permanent part of his face.

Aden stood on the sidewalk behind him, clutching the handlebars of Floyd's bike. Lily's heart pounded so loudly, she thought it might wake her dat. Aden's bright smile was better suited for a day of sunshine and rainbows. He winked at Lily and then turned and sauntered down the sidewalk, rolling Floyd's bike with him.

"What happened?"

Floyd inclined his head in Estee's direction. "See that she gets into bed. We've had a rough night."

He shut the door softly before Lily had time to ask any more questions. Estee had already started ambling up the stairs. Lily caught up and hooked her elbow through Estee's. "Are you okay? I was so worried. I didn't know what to do."

They shuffled into their room, and Lily silently closed the door behind them. She struck a match and lit the lantern. They had been extremely blessed. Mama and Dat would never know.

Lily took Estee's nightclothes from the hook. "Here, let me help you get back into your nightgown."

Estee's legs seemed to give out, and she sank to her bed. "No, thank you."

"You look exhausted. Let me help."

"Oh, *now* you want to help," Estee

288

snapped. She sounded all the angrier because she whispered. "Where were you when I needed your help five hours ago?"

"I'm sorry, Estee. I didn't know. You said you'd be right back."

"We sneaked into the garage but couldn't find Floyd's bike. Then Randy McCann came in, and we hid behind some boxes for an hour while he worked on his car. We didn't even dare to breathe for fear he'd hear us."

"I knew it would be trouble."

"Only because you weren't there to help. He didn't know it, but he locked us in. If you had been keeping watch, you could have helped us get out of there."

Lily's throat constricted with a sharp pang of guilt.

Estee pulled off her shoes and stockings. "Go to bed, Lily. One of us ought to be fresh for morning chores."

"How did you get out? Why was Aden here?"

Estee sighed as if she were losing patience with Lily's curiosity. "I crawled out the tiny garage window. Floyd couldn't make it through." She lifted her dress to reveal an ugly red welt on her thigh.

Lily gasped.

"I scraped the skin all the way down my leg."

"Oh, Estee."

"I couldn't do anything with the padlock, so I ran back here, got Sandy from the barn, and rode to Huckleberry Hill to get Aden. I knew he'd help me."

Lily felt as if she would explode with gratitude. Aden would always come, even if she couldn't find the courage to help her own sister. She sat and put her arms around Estee's shoulders. "I'm so sorry, Estee." Tears of relief mingled with tears of regret ran down her cheeks. "So sorry."

Estee melted and pressed her forehead against Lily's. "I didn't mean to be so harsh with you." She planted a kiss on Lily's wet cheek. "You must have been worried sick. All is well now."

Lily touched the skin surrounding Estee's scrape. "I don't think I have bandage big enough for that."

Estee giggled quietly. "Mama will be suspicious if we use the entire tube of ointment."

"How bad does it hurt?"

"Oy anyhow, something awful."

"I will find some gauze pads. Tomorrow we can buy something bigger at the drugstore."

"A gauze pad the size of a tablecloth," Estee said.

Lily stood. "So you found Floyd's bike. That's good news."

Estee lay back on her pillow. "Do you want to know where it was?"

Lily nodded.

Estee's lips twitched upward. "We found it propped against the wall *outside* the garage. I'm sure glad Floyd brought that bobby pin."

Lily clapped her hand over her mouth to keep from waking her parents with her riotous laughter.

Aden pushed Floyd's bike down the sidewalk until Floyd caught up to him. "Is Estee going to be okay?"

Floyd nodded. "I never should have asked her to come with me. If her dat ever found out, he would grind me up and eat me for supper."

"I'm glad Lily did not come. I would never want to see her hurt."

Floyd's face glowed red in the dim light of the moon. "If I were anybody but me, I would grind me up and eat me for breakfast. I should never have taken a risk with my girl like that."

"Nae, you shouldn't have."

Floyd took the handlebars of his bike from Aden. "I should have come straight to your house. You're always getting into trouble anyway." Floyd coughed. "I mean, not always. I haven't heard that you've gotten into trouble here in Bonduel. I mean, not that anyone is gossiping about you."

"What do people say about me?"

"I don't listen to gossip."

Aden smiled to himself. "I believe you."

"I heard about the bear, but that was only from Estee, and she heard it straight from the horse's mouth because Lily told her — not that I'm comparing Lily to a horse. It's just an expression."

Poor Floyd always talked himself into a corner.

"You'll be happy to know," Aden said, "that I haven't been arrested once since I've been here."

"It's the weather," Floyd said. "It was too hot to make mischief." He coughed again as if the words were escaping his throat without his permission. "But I'm certain that you will not be making mischief now that it's autumn time. I didn't mean that you are bent on troublemaking other times of the year."

"Let me put your mind at ease. I am not bent on making trouble in any season."

292

"Nobody does any carryings-on in the winter. Too cold."

They reached the road. "Do you need help home with your bike?" Aden asked.

"No, denki. It will take ten minutes to ride it home."

Floyd turned east, and Aden turned west.

"Thank you for coming, Aden. I knew you would help us out of that pickle. I told Estee you could pick that lock with your eyes closed. If you ever need a picture of a barn painted on one of your milk cans, I'm your man."

Aden shook Floyd's hand. "And if you ever need help escaping a shed again, I'll be ready."

Floyd gave Aden a halfhearted smile before riding away on his bike.

Aden gazed down the road, arched his back, and massaged a knot at the place where his shoulder met his neck. It must have been four in the morning. He'd be up milking in another half hour. Might as well not go back to bed.

The countryside was always peaceful, but in the early hours of the morning, Aden felt as if he were the only person in the world. Quiet sounds of the darkness crammed his ears — the pleasant hum of chirping crickets, a breeze lightly teasing the trees,

293

and the sound of gravel as it crunched under his boots.

He turned to look at Lily's house. Even that brief glimpse he caught of her at the door tonight was heaven. He loved her hair, especially when it fell carelessly down her back, teasing him to touch it. When he closed his eyes he could feel her presence, as if she had crawled into his bones and taken up residence there.

Had the mailbox pleased her dat?

Aden hadn't even noticed it when they brought Estee home. That's how hopelessly his head was filled with Lily.

Retracing his steps, he looked to the forsythia bush where he had dug the hole. He rubbed his eyes, deciding he must really be tired if he couldn't remember where he had put the mailbox.

No, he was certain . . .

He squatted on the ground to get a closer look in the dim light. A layer of sawdust covered a small mound of dirt. He brushed away the dirt with his fingers and uncovered a stump, flush with the ground, that used to be the mailbox post.

Aden fingered the scar on his eyebrow where an angry man had cracked him with the butt of a rifle. That pain paled in comparison to what he experienced at the destruction of all his hard work.

He'd given every drop of sweat for Lily. For Lily's dat. Jacob worked for seven years for Rachel, but the years seemed only a few days because of his love for her. It was the same with Lily and the mailbox. He would be happy to dig a thousand holes and carry a million tons of cement to please Lily.

But apparently, it didn't please her father.

A groan escaped his lips. Her dat hadn't merely cut down the mailbox. He had sent a clear message.

Aden had been cut down to size and dismissed. Like the mailbox.

At that moment, Aden almost wished he were a mailbox. Mailboxes didn't have feelings. They didn't feel as if their hearts had been ripped out of their chests. They were already empty.

It took him an hour to get home. He wasn't in any hurry. The cows would be waiting for him no matter what time he arrived. Pilot and Sparky sprawled on the porch and didn't even lift an ear when Aden passed.

Mammi had already lit the propane lantern in the kitchen, no doubt making tofu omelets for breakfast. Aden trudged into the house to wash up before milking.

Mammi turned and looked up from her

cooking. Oatmeal. It was a gute day for oatmeal, bland and mushy.

"Aden, you're already up? Felty said you got up earlier than usual, but I didn't believe him. I wanted you to sleep in after working so hard at Lily's house yesterday. Your mamm would be unhappy if you work yourself to death on your dawdi's farm."

Aden hung his hat on the hook by the door. "I'll try to relax after dinner."

"Lily will be here soon."

Aden felt weary to his bones at the sound of her name. "I don't think Lily will be here today. She is not feeling well."

"Oh, that's too bad. Do you think a pair of mittens would cheer her up?"

"Jah, I'm sure they would."

"She is such a gute girl. I'm glad you two are coming along so nicely."

Aden gave his mammi a hug and a kiss. "Mammi, I know you think we are coming along nicely, but truth be told, I wish you had found me a girl who already has a mailbox."

CHAPTER SEVENTEEN

Pilot ran to her as soon as she stepped out of the house after work. That dog seemed to have an extra sense about Lily's location at all times. Even when she saw no sign of him from the kitchen window or he had run off with Aden to do chores, Pilot always reappeared to tell Lily good-bye after work.

Lily took Pilot's face in her hands and then caressed his ears and neck. As always, he tried to lick her fingers, but she didn't mind so much anymore. She kept her hand sanitizer within reach.

Aden walked out of the barn, and she waved to him. He'd been extra somber today, serious and untalkative, but she hadn't minded his mood. Not that she tried to avoid him, but the bike incident still troubled her. And she hadn't told him about the mailbox yet. The truth would make him unhappy. She hated to see him unhappy.

He gave her the first smile she had seen

from him today as he strolled toward her. "Going home?"

"Jah."

"We will see you Monday, then."

She turned away from him but couldn't bear the thought of going three whole days wondering how he felt about her. She changed direction. "You have been awfully quiet today."

"Have I?" He took off his hat and fingered the scar at his eyebrow. "I suppose I have. I've been thinking deep thoughts."

Jah, he was probably thinking he never wanted to kiss a scaredy-cat ever again. "Are you mad at me?"

He bowed his head. "It wasn't your fault."

"Yes, it was. Estee begged me to go. She called me a chicken."

He opened his mouth and closed it again and cocked an eyebrow. "Oh, you're talking about Floyd's bike. Floyd shouldn't have involved you or Estee. I told him to come to me next time. I'm not afraid."

Lily slumped her shoulders. "I'm such a coward."

Aden donned his hat. "You're cautious, that's all."

"That doesn't make me feel better. I should have done it for Estee's sake, like you would do for Pilot."

Taking her hand, he led her to sit on the porch steps. "When it's dire enough, you'll find your courage."

"If I couldn't even find it for Estee, what makes you think I'll find it for anything else?"

"You will. Deep down, there are things you would die for."

"Maybe it's harder to find something to live for," Lily said.

"So true."

Lily savored the feel of his hand comfortably encircling hers. "I have something to tell you."

He looked into her eyes and frowned. "Okay."

"Please don't feel bad about this. He's only doing what he thinks is best, and I love him dearly." If she didn't have it before, she had his undivided attention now. "Dat moved the mailbox."

"Moved it? He chopped it down like a tree."

"Oh, you saw?"

"When we brought Floyd's bike back."

"My dat has his heart set on Tyler Yoder."

Aden let go of her hand and stood up. He shoved his fists into his pockets. "I know. I've been stewing about it all day, trying to decide what to do next."

Lily lowered her gaze and stared at her shaky hands. She didn't want to hear what Aden wanted to do next — he had probably decided to forget her and pursue Erla Glick, whose dat would never chop down a mailbox out of spite.

"Lily, I'm not giving up." Aden bent over and nudged her chin so she would meet his gaze. "Ever."

The way he said "ever" sent a jolt of electricity down her spine. Who could doubt after looking into those eyes?

Her voice trembled like a hummingbird. "Oh, okay. Ever."

He grinned playfully and pulled her to stand on the second step. At this level, she could look him in the eye. He wrapped his arms around her waist and tugged her close, never taking his eyes off her lips. Oh sis yuscht! He was going to kiss her again. She felt giddy and light-headed and completely unprepared. Why didn't he ever give her ample warning?

His lips came within inches when Lily heard the front door open behind her. She abruptly pushed Aden away. He released her and turned as if searching for something in the woods. If it was anything like what she felt, he was searching for his senses.

"Oh, my," Anna said. "The things you

young people do."

Seemingly unembarrassed, she waltzed down the steps carrying two empty buckets.

"What are you doing, Mammi?"

"Getting the rest of the tomatoes off the vines before it freezes."

Aden glanced at Lily and then at his mammi. "I'll help."

Anna had almost reached the barn. "Finish your kissing," she called. "No hurry."

Finish kissing? Not if Lily died of embarrassment first.

Aden chuckled. "Mammi is always so accommodating." Again he wrapped his arms around Lily's waist. "I think we better do as she says."

Lily's heart pitter-pattered with delicious excitement. She was ready this time. Exactly as she had practiced, she puckered slightly as Aden bent his head closer.

To her chagrin, he turned his face away at the last minute to peer down the lane.

She'd been concentrating so hard on being kissed that she hadn't even heard the hum of the truck engine or the crackle of gravel under the rubber tires. Pilot barked and ran around in circles as the truck stopped at the edge of the grass.

Aden's friend Jamal hopped out of the truck and charged at Aden as if he were going to tackle him. Aden charged right back with a big smile on his face. They met and did a strange handshake before hugging while smacking each other on the back.

"I thought I'd gotten rid of you a month ago," Aden said. The happiness in his words nearly overflowed into laughter. "Did you drive by the pond?"

"Yeah, the aerator is working well. That was a great idea, whoever thought of it."

"Tyler," Lily said. "He thinks of everything."

She mentally smacked herself upside the head. Tyler's was probably the last name Aden wanted to hear.

Anna trudged across the lawn with her buckets. Aden and Jamal leaped into action and each offered to carry one. Anna shook her head and kept walking. As she got closer, Lily could see that her buckets were empty.

"It is wonderful gute to see you again, Jamal," Anna said.

"Your gran makes the best yummy-shettly."

Aden raised an eyebrow. "When did you eat Mammi's *yummasetti*?"

"On Tuesday, dear, when you went to fix Lily's mailbox. I knew you would be missing supper, so I made Felty's favorite meat dish. Jamal is not a vegetarian."

Jamal's eyes twinkled. "I came by to see you, but they told me you were out sparking with Lily. I don't know what sparking means, but it sounded important."

Lily reached for Pilot, who stood sentinel by her side, and vigorously rubbed his head so she wouldn't die of embarrassment.

Aden didn't seem embarrassed, but a shadow passed over his features. He wasn't thinking about sparking. He was thinking about that mailbox. "I thought you were going to pick tomatoes, Mammi."

"I decided I need a sweater," Anna said.

Aden took the buckets from her. "I'll hold these while you get one."

"Thank you, dear. You're such a good boy. I tell your mamm, 'Don't worry so much about Aden. He might be going through a rough patch, but he'll turn around all right.'"

Aden smiled sheepishly. "Thanks for your confidence, Mammi."

Anna went into the house, and Aden turned to Jamal. "So, not that I'm not happy to see you, but knowing how much you love Bonduel, why are you in Wisconsin again?"

"I wanted to come back and look at the pond." He paused. "And check things out while I'm in the area."

303

"Looking for environmental transgressions?"

"Pretty much," Jamal said. He cleared his throat, and Lily could see him studying Aden out of the corner of his eye. "I need your help with something."

Aden raised both hands in surrender and backed away. "Oh, no, Jamal. You heard my grandma. I'm going through a rough patch. I don't need to go looking for trouble."

"Oh, come on, Aden. It's just for a couple of hours and no police will be involved, I promise. It's not a big deal."

Lily held her breath. She had an inkling that whatever wasn't a big deal would involve either police officers or deep water.

"You have a specific set of skills," Jamal said.

"Oh really?"

"I need someone Amish."

Aden shook his head as a grin played at his lips. "You can dress up. I'll give you some suspenders and a hat."

"Oh, yeah, like anyone is going to believe an African American Amish guy who can't speak the language."

"You could dress as a Mennonite," Aden said.

Jamal threw up his hands in disgust. "Come on, Aden. This is a big deal."

304

"You just said it wasn't a big deal."

"I meant you won't have to do much, but it's for a really good cause. You like dogs, don't you?"

"I like dogs."

"There's some Amish guys running a puppy mill about an hour outside of Shawano. And I've heard stuff. It's bad in there."

Aden massaged the back of his neck. "Puppy mills are legal, Jamal. We can't do anything to shut them down."

Jamal and Aden seemed to forget their surroundings as they focused on each other, and the fire of indignation smoldered between them.

"But there are animal cruelty laws, Aden, and the authorities can't get in to look without probable cause."

"And you want to give them probable cause."

Jamal laid a hand on Aden's shoulder. "Look, I just want you to knock on their door and distract them while I go around back and take some pictures. I've already scoped the place out, and I can't get in there by myself. There's three or four Amish guys prowling around there all the time."

Aden glanced at Lily. "I don't know. Maybe we should leave well enough alone."

305

"I don't know how to leave well enough alone. Besides, this isn't 'well enough.' Those dogs are starving. They've got skin diseases and rotting teeth. I won't stand by and let that happen. And you shouldn't either."

Lily could tell the moment Aden made his decision. He stood up straight, which at his full height was quite impressive. "How many puppies?"

"Maybe fifty. Plus a dozen adult dogs."

Anna came from the house wearing a deep purple sweater fastened with jumbo hooks at the front. She carried a sizable rust-colored sweater over her arm. "Jamal, I knitted this for you."

She held it out to him, and he took it almost reverently. "Wow, thank you, Mrs. Helmuth." He pulled it over his head and slipped his arms into the sleeves. It fit perfectly and brought out the yellow specks in his brown eyes. The cable pattern on the front wove over and under itself in beautiful symmetry. "No one's ever made me something so nice," Jamal said.

Anna's eyes twinkled. "Ohio autumns can be almost as chilly as Wisconsin."

"Thank you so much. I'll wear it tonight when I'm out with Aden."

Anna took her buckets from Aden. "Where

are you going?"

Aden looked from Lily to Jamal to Anna and back again. "Mammi, there is a puppy mill Jamal wants me to help him photograph. If the police see how badly the puppies are being treated, we might convince them to shut it down."

Anna gasped. "Why would anyone want to hurt a puppy?"

"Do you mind if I go?"

Anna frowned. "Your mamm would write me a stern eight-page letter if she knew."

As if on cue, Pilot nudged Anna's elbow with his nose and whined pathetically, standing in for all the puppies in all the puppy mills in the world.

Anna patted Pilot's head and sighed. "Of course you must help those poor little puppies." She plopped her buckets on the ground and wrapped her arms around Aden's waist. "Don't get arrested. Your mamm would be quite out of sorts with her mother-in-law if you got arrested."

Aden gave his mammi a squeeze. "I will help you pick the tomatoes tomorrow."

Anna waved away his suggestion. "Lily can help me pick. You go save the puppies."

Lily's heart lodged in her throat. Every muscle in her body seemed charged with energy even as she felt the urge to throw up. "I'm going with Aden."

Aden gaped at her as if she'd announced her intention to join the Army.

Jamal furrowed his brow. "We don't really need . . ."

Aden scraped his jaw off the ground and bloomed into a smile. "She's joking. Lily would never go in for this."

Aden had no idea how much his words stung. She would always be a disappointment to him.

Well, not today. Today, she would be the kind of girl Aden could admire.

As long as she didn't throw up all over his boots.

Besides, she refused to play the waiting game again. Storming a puppy mill couldn't be more frightening than staring down the lane wondering if Aden was alive, wishing she had gone with him in the first place so her regrets didn't overwhelm her later.

"I can help," she said.

Jamal rubbed his chin. "I don't mind if you come."

Aden's eyes grew wide. "Of course you're not coming."

"Of course I am coming."

Aden pressed his lips into a rigid line. "This is because of the bike, isn't it?"

"I'm not going to chew my fingernails to

stubs waiting for you to come back."

"Then keep your hands in your pockets. You don't realize how fast these things can get out of hand."

Lily wouldn't budge. "Then you shouldn't go."

"It's not that big a deal," Jamal interjected. "And it's for the puppies."

Anna worried the hem of her apron. "Oh dear, Lily. Your fater would not like it one little bit."

"Dat doesn't have to find out." The guilt flooded over Lily as she said the words.

Aden sighed. He took Lily's hand in plain sight of Jamal and Anna and led her around to the side of the house. "Lily, I am doing my best to get on your dat's good side. He would never let me talk to you again if he knew you came with us."

"It doesn't matter. When it comes to you, Dat doesn't have a good side."

She might as well have kicked his dog for as stricken as he looked. "This would definitely make it worse," he whispered.

"I don't want to be the girl no one can count on."

Aden placed his hands on her arms. "You're cautious, that's all. You work very hard to do what is right. I admire you for that."

"Even Estee says I'm a chicken. You told me one day I'd find out what it is I'm willing to take a risk for. Well, this is it. I want to do this for the puppies."

Aden shook his head. "It is not for the puppies. It's because Estee got mad at you."

"I sat there for five hours worried sick about my sister, and I didn't lift one finger to do anything about it. I was too scared to leave the house. You are the reason things didn't turn out much worse."

"That doesn't mean you should come with us."

"I'm so ashamed of doing nothing."

Compassion filled Aden's eyes, and he pulled her into his embrace. "You have nothing to be ashamed of. I like you just the way you are, Lily, concerned about doing the right thing. I would find you very unappealing if you were one of those girls always looking for a way to break the rules."

"Saving puppies isn't breaking the rules."

"Nae."

"I want to show you I can do it."

Aden fell silent as he held Lily in his arms. He felt so warm, he probably could have melted ice in the dead of winter.

He suddenly let go of her and took two giant steps backward. "Oy anyhow, I should never have kissed you."

310

Lily almost choked on his words. "What?"

"Because I want to do it all the time now."

Lily's heart did a little pirouette. "Don't change the subject."

"What were we talking about?"

"Please let me come."

Aden slumped his shoulders. "Okay, but you're staying in the truck."

Lily gave a little hop for joy. She wasn't about to tell Aden that she had no intention of staying in the truck. He'd find that out soon enough.

They pulled down the deserted country road past the house and parked near the thick bushes off the blacktop. Jamal killed the engine, and they sat in silence for a few moments. Could Jamal and Aden hear Lily's pulse pounding? It seemed to be the loudest thing in the cab of the truck.

For the hundredth time, Lily rethought her decision to come along. Aden had not been exaggerating. Lily had ridden in a lot of cars with a lot of different drivers, but Jamal was the worst driver she had ever seen. He liked to talk and drive, and he looked at the person he talked to instead of watching the road. Lily regretted sitting between Jamal and Aden. Jamal leaned forward to look at Aden when conversing with him, leaving no one to actually mind the steering wheel.

Aden had told Jamal three times to "shut up and drive," but it wasn't until Jamal missed a tree by mere inches that he paid Aden any heed. Lily had not planned on dying in a truck accident. Maybe she and Aden could walk home.

"Okay," Jamal said. "Here's how it's going to go down. First you've got to sort of amble around the barn area and see if there is anybody on the lookout. Figure out a way to round them up and get them into the house."

"Any suggestions on how to do that?" Aden asked.

"You're the brains. You'll think of something. Or let Lily think of something. She looks a lot smarter than you do."

"She's staying in the truck."

"No, I'm not," Lily said, daring Aden to contradict her. "I can help you."

Aden frowned. He didn't look like he wanted her help.

Lily tried a different strategy. "What if a wolverine attacks me in the truck? I'd be safer with you."

"A wolverine can't open doors."

"Nae, but he could gnaw through the metal before you and Jamal got back. You wouldn't want that on your conscience, would you?"

Jamal fiddled with his camera. "She's got a point, Aden."

"Wolverines can't chew through metal."

"No, I mean about being able to help you. You'd be a lot less suspicious with two of you, especially if one of you is a girl."

"I'm not staying in the truck," Lily said. "If you go without me, I'll wait until you leave and sneak out behind you."

Aden rubbed his face and slowly let out a breath. "Okay, but only because I don't want you wandering around this place by yourself. But you've got to promise to stick by my side every minute."

"Cross my heart," she said. That was a promise she would have no trouble keeping. Her legs were already weak with fear, and they hadn't saved one puppy yet.

They got out of Jamal's truck and shut the doors as silently as they could.

Aden pointed into the thicket near the edge of the road. "Jamal, hide over there until you see us go in the house. Hurry and get your pictures, because I'll run out of things to say in about two minutes."

Aden took Lily's hand, and they walked around to the back of the small clapboard house. "Where are we going?" Lily whispered.

"Follow my lead."

She could tell his nerves were tight as a wire as his gaze darted back and forth around the yard.

He squeezed her hand. "I shouldn't have let you talk me into this."

"You won't regret it."

"I already do." He stomped around the backyard. "Is all this excitement making you thirsty?"

Before she could form an answer to his strange question, a dark figure loomed in front of them. Lily bit back an impulsive scream. If she wailed like a baby, she would rouse suspicion if she hadn't already.

A boy, probably a few years younger than Lily, stepped out of the shadows and scowled at Aden, a pretty gutsy expression considering Aden was almost a foot taller than the boy. Even Lily stood taller than the boy did.

What he lacked in height, he made up for in bulk. His arms and legs could have been fashioned out of tree trunks.

Jamal had been mistaken. This boy wasn't Amish. He wore a cowboy hat and blue jeans with a silver belt buckle the size of a large orange.

"What do you want?" the boy said.

Lily clamped her fingers around Aden's hand, likely cutting off his circulation.

"Do you know where Hannah and Marvin Lapp live?" Aden said.

"There ain't no Lapps around here," the boy said.

Aden looked as if he were quite unhappy about this news. "Is this State Road Forty-Five?"

The boy shook his head. "Twenty-Nine."

"Oh, that's too bad." Keeping hold of Lily's hand, Aden turned as if to go. "I'm sorry to bother you, uh . . ."

"Bud. The name's Bud. Forty-Five is south. If you go west until you're almost to Wittenberg, there's an exit to Forty-Five."

"Thanks," Aden said. He put his arm around Lily. "Do you think she could have a drink of water before we go?"

Bud eyed them suspiciously before giving a curt nod. "In the house."

Aden nudged Lily away from him. "You go, Lily. I'll stay out here and have a look around."

Lily thought she might faint. Aden was abandoning her mere minutes after he told her to stick by his side? Should she refuse to go?

"Let's all go in," Bud said. "I'd like a drink

myself."

"I'm not thirsty," Aden replied.

"Come in the house," Bud said. "I won't leave anyone out here alone."

Aden turned to Lily and winked. She managed a shallow breath. Aden had never planned on leaving her alone. He had manipulated Bud into coming with them. His skill impressed her. He'd cleared a path for Jamal and hadn't told one lie.

The screen door slammed shut behind them as they stepped into the house. Lily jumped involuntarily. That slam sounded final, as if they'd never escape.

A lampshade shrouded an electric light-bulb hanging over the kitchen table. Two men sat at the table drinking beer and eating ribs. The older man had to be Bud's father. He had the same tree-trunk arms and the same blond, curly hair, except less of it on top.

Both men looked up and scowled at the same time. That one was definitely Bud's dad. They had identical scowls.

"Who's this?" Bud's dad said.

Bud stood in front of the door as if he were guarding the exit. "They're looking for the Lapps on highway Forty-Five."

Bud's father narrowed his eyes and stood up. "You're Amish."

Aden stretched a smile across his face and extended his hand. "I'm Aden Helmuth from Bonduel."

Bud's father didn't take the offered hand. He turned to the other man still seated at the table. Lily had only seen it once before, but his glassy stare indicated he was drunk, or at least halfway there. "Hey, Reggie," Bud's dad said, "you know any Lapps on Forty-Five?"

Lily kept her eyes to the floor and her hands clasped tightly together. They mustn't see how violently she shook.

Reggie leaned back in his chair. "I don't know, Earl. Is them the folks with the blue silo?"

"No, that's the Jorgensens."

"They want a drink, Dad," Bud said.

Even though she felt like she had a mouthful of dust, Lily couldn't have swallowed a sip of water if her life depended on it. It took all her willpower not to knock Bud aside, dash out the door, and flee into the woods. How much more time would Jamal need?

Bud's dad, Earl, settled into his chair once again. "Glasses are in that cupboard."

She should probably act thirsty and get the water. Forcing one foot in front of the other, she located two glasses and filled

317

them from the squeaky tap that smelled of sulfur.

"Bonduel?" Earl said. "How'd you get all the way out here?"

"We have a driver," Aden said. Lily admired how cool he seemed, as if he were shooting the breeze with Floyd or Jamal.

Earl didn't like that answer. He frowned and scooted his chair out from under the table. "Outside? Bud, go invite their driver in for a drink."

"Oh, he's not thirsty."

Bud let the door slam behind him, and Lily jumped out of her skin at the crack of wood against wood. Water sloshed in the glasses and dribbled onto the floor.

Her legs turned to stone. She stood with the two glasses of water in her hands staring dumbly at Aden as if he could make everything all better.

Aden gave her a slight shake of his head. What did he think she wanted to do? Try to talk her way out of this? Didn't he remember what a coward she was?

"Lily," Aden prompted, "do you want to give me a drink?"

She shuffled to Aden as if she were holding two sticks of dynamite. He didn't break eye contact, which helped calm her nerves significantly. No matter what happened, she was with him, and he would make everything okay.

She handed him both glasses of water and stepped slightly behind him. He chuckled softly and finished off the first glass in four gulps. Lily kept glancing at the door. What was happening out there?

The screen door creaked open, and Jamal walked slowly into the room. Bud followed close behind with Jamal's camera dangling from his fingers. Another boy, taller and thicker than Bud, came last.

Lily held her breath. The last boy had a rifle. He didn't point it at anybody, although that did nothing to calm Lily's galloping heart. He held it slung over his arm as if it were a part of his body instead of a deadly weapon. If she could have moved her feet, she would have bolted for the door and screamed for Jamal and Aden to follow her. Why, oh why had she asked to come?

Bud lifted the camera to show his dad. "He was taking pictures."

Glaring menacingly, Earl stood up and went toe to toe with the bigger boy, probably also his son. Same hair, same build. Only this one looked as if he could break a lamppost across his leg. "And what were you doing, Sammy? Sleeping?"

Sammy pursed his lips like a naughty ten-

319

year-old. "Sorry, Dad."

Earl turned his attention to Jamal and put his nose within three inches of Jamal's face. The older man had to stand on tippy-toes. "What are you trying to pull?"

"Nothing bad," Jamal said.

Lily was amazed that he didn't cower or back down. As Aden had told her, both he and Jamal had plentiful experience in situations like this. They probably enjoyed the thrill. All Lily wanted to do was go home and knit something. She promised herself then and there that she would never, ever do anything so foolish ever again, and she would ask Anna to give her knitting lessons as soon as she got home.

Earl stuck his face closer, forcing Jamal to back away. "You want to shut me down or something?"

Jamal's expression darkened, and he pressed his lips together into a hard line.

Aden stepped in front of Lily and shielded her completely from Earl. "Jamal, don't say anything."

"A man who mistreats animals like you do should be shut down," Jamal spat out, as if he couldn't hold the words inside him.

Earl took his large hand and shoved Jamal against the wall. Jamal's shoulder bumped a picture and sent it crashing to the floor.

Shards of glass exploded everywhere. Earl and Reggie yelled obscenities at Jamal as if he'd thrown a rock through their window.

Aden grabbed Lily's arm. "Lily, get out of here. Go out the front door."

Lily hesitated to leave the relative safety of Aden's side. Her legs wobbled, and she couldn't imagine being able to run to the door. She would be all alone outside. The thought terrified her.

Aden pushed her toward the front of the house. "Lily, get out!"

The harshness in his voice shocked her and spurred her into action. She bolted past Reggie at the table and ran in the likely direction of the front door. Out of the corner of her eye, she saw Aden grab Reggie's arm so he couldn't chase her down. She ran even harder.

Utterly terrified, she didn't stop running until she got to Jamal's truck. Compared to the chaos in the house, the silence outside felt almost eerie. She didn't know what to do. Should she get in the truck and wait? More likely than not, those brutes would find her. Neither Jamal nor Aden would want her back in the house, no matter how badly Aden needed help. Even if she charged back in there, there was nothing she could do to help him.

She was worthless.

A sob started deep in her throat, and she wrapped her arms around her midsection to keep from losing control of her emotions. She couldn't just stand here and wait for those men to drag Aden and Jamal's dead bodies into the road.

Jamal's phone sat on the driver's seat inside the truck. Lily only noticed it because at that moment, it lit up in response to receiving a text. She opened the door and snatched the phone. She'd always wished for a cell phone in a crisis. Now whom should she call?

It took a minute to figure out how to actually make a call on Jamal's phone, and then it took longer to dial because her hand trembled like a leaf in the wind.

"Dispatch. What is your emergency?"

"Please, help my friends. They're killing them. You've got to come now." Her voice rose in pitch with every word until she practically screamed into the phone.

"Did you say your friends are being attacked?"

"Yes, you've got to stop them."

"What is your location, ma'am?"

Lily tried to quell the rising panic. "I'm not sure. I think we are about thirty miles west of Shawano on Highway Twenty-Nine.

322

It's a white house. Please hurry."

"Do you see a house number?"

With the phone plastered to her ear, Lily ran toward the house until she could see the mailbox clearly. "I think it's 435. There's a puppy mill in the back. Do you know where the puppy mill is?"

"Ma'am, try to stay calm. I'm alerting the sheriff now."

Try to stay calm. The four most useless words in the English language. How did one stay calm when Aden and Jamal might be dead?

Almost at the point of hysteria, Lily paced back and forth in front of the truck, crying and groaning and praying for the sheriff to hurry up. She clapped her hands over her ears when she heard faint yelling from the house.

The sheriff announced himself like a soundless exploding firework, and the glare of his bright lights momentarily blinded Lily. She stepped to the edge of the road and waved her hands over her head to get his attention, in case he didn't know exactly where he was going. He pulled up behind Jamal's truck, and she could hear him communicating on his radio.

Two officers got out of the car.

"Are you the one who called in the emergency?" one of them asked.

"Yes," Lily said breathlessly. "Please help them. They're in the house, and one of them has a gun."

Both men suddenly became more alert. They drew their firearms, and Lily had never been so close to passing out in her life. "How many are in there?"

"My two friends and four other men. That's all I saw."

One of the policemen or sheriffs or whatever he was pointed to Jamal's truck. "You stay here until we come to get you. Is that clear?"

Lily nodded.

They disappeared down the road. Lily didn't even see them make it to the front door. Jamal had parked his truck far from the house in the shelter of some tall bushes.

Again she found herself waiting for Aden, sick with worry that he might be injured or dead. She leaned her back against the grille of Jamal's truck and wept until she ran out of tears.

For a brief moment, Aden must have blacked out. He awoke sprawled on the floor, nose stinging, frantic with worry for Lily. He hoped she'd had the good sense to run far into the thicket and hide.

Even though Aden's brain was fuzzy, he remembered Earl nailing him in the face with that burly fist of his. His head throbbed painfully, and he could feel the blood pouring from his nose like a leaky faucet. He managed to sit up.

The yelling had stopped, and Jamal sat next to him on the kitchen floor cradling his head in his hands. Sammy, Bud, and Reggie stood over them, poised for an attack. They hovered but didn't say a word. Aden tried to piece together what was happening. Were they going to shoot them in the kitchen and hide their bodies in the woods?

Nae, Aden didn't fear that. These men weren't that desperate or that evil. Aden hadn't meant to, but he'd provoked a fight when he grabbed Reggie to keep him from catching Lily. Reggie and Sammy had socked him a couple of times, and Earl took a turn with them. Neither Jamal nor Aden had done anything but try to avoid the blows. Early on they had both learned that if they fought back, they could get charged with something big, like a felony.

Aden tried to stanch the bleeding by pinching the bridge of his nose, but even a feather-soft touch sent pain shooting through his teeth. Oy anyhow, his head hurt something wonderful.

Was Lily okay?

A commotion at the front door caught Aden's attention. His heart sank to his toes. Had Lily come back?

"It's the sheriff," Reggie whispered. "Put your rifle on the table, Sammy."

Earl entered the kitchen with two uniformed officers right behind him with their guns drawn.

"You see," said Earl, speaking to the first officer, "they come in here to pick a fight. We was defending ourselves."

The second officer went to the table and retrieved Sammy's gun.

"I wasn't never gonna shoot nobody," Sammy said.

Aden looked at the first officer. "Did you see an Amish girl?"

"Yeah, she's waiting outside."

Aden had never felt such extraordinary relief. It overcame every worry he should have had, like whether he would be arrested yet again. If they took him to jail, he wouldn't be able to tell Floyd that he had kept out of trouble.

Lily was safe. That was all that mattered.

"That girl trespassed on my property," Earl snapped. "Arrest her too."

Aden wouldn't stand for that. It was one

thing for him to go to jail, quite another for Lily to be dragged into that horrible place. "She didn't do anything wrong. She just needed a drink."

Earl shoved a thick finger in Aden's direction. "She was in on your plan all along."

The sheriff holstered his gun and shrugged his shoulders in resignation. "You want to press charges against the girl too?"

"Yes, all of them."

Aden thought he might be sick. Even the experience of riding in a police car would bury Lily in shame. And her dat? Her dat would be completely justified in driving Aden clean out of Bonduel. Aden had exposed David's daughter to things no one should have to see — especially not timid, innocent Lily. Remorse kicked him in the gut.

Jamal stood up.

Grunting, the sheriff bent over, grabbed Aden's elbow, and helped him to his feet. "You got a dish towel or something? I don't want him getting blood on my seats."

Bud handed Aden a paper towel, and he mopped up his nose as best he could even as it continued to drip. He turned to Earl. "Please don't take this out on Lily. She never meant any harm to anyone."

Earl stood his ground. "She can tell the judge."

Jamal knew the drill. He put his hands behind his back, and the second officer clicked a pair of handcuffs on him.

Aden got his own shiny pair of handcuffs, and the sheriff took his elbow and led him out of the house and down the road.

Two police vehicles were parked behind Jamal's truck. Aden searched frantically for a glimpse of Lily. Through the blinding lights, he saw her leaning against the front of the truck. Hearing their footsteps, she turned and screamed his name.

She charged at him and threw her arms around his neck even as the officer did his best to nudge her away. "Aden, I was so scared." She gasped and sobbed at the same time. "You're bleeding. What happened?"

"I'm okay, but listen. Try not to be scared."

"Miss, move away, please."

In bewilderment, Lily stepped back as the officer opened the patrol car door and pushed Aden inside. Her eyes became huge circles as she caught sight of the handcuffs around his wrists. At that moment, every bit of light seeped out of his heart.

He loved Lily Eicher better than his own soul. It didn't matter that she considered his dog a health hazard or that she couldn't cook tofu to save her life. It didn't even matter that her dat hated him. He loved her and he'd face a hundred pairs of handcuffs just to hold her in his arms. He ached with longing.

The officer slammed the door, and Lily pounded on the window with her fists, screaming at the officer to let him go.

Aden watched in horror as the sheriff took her by the wrists in a surprisingly gentle motion and slipped the handcuffs on. Her face twisted wildly with fear as she screamed Aden's name over and over and tried to pull herself away.

He put his face against the window and yelled her name. "Lily, Lily, don't be frightened. I'm right here." She didn't hear a word.

The sheriff dragged her, flailing and screaming, to the front car and shoved her into the backseat.

Aden groaned and clamped his eyes shut, but Lily's terrified expression was seared into his memory forever. He leaned his head against the back of the seat and ignored Jamal beside him as tears poured down his face.

What he wouldn't give to have this day over again.

This was what it felt like to be in the depths of despair.

Jamal lay on a bench, the only thing in the cell, with his knees bent and his feet touching the floor. It was a short bench.

Every nerve in Aden's body seemed to be on fire, and he paced in the jail cell until he should have worn a path in the cement. Two steps this way, two steps the other way. Two steps this way, two steps the other way.

He hadn't seen Lily since they had hauled her away. How was she holding up? She might faint or fall apart before they even took a fingerprint. Aden shuddered. He had to train his thoughts on something else. Worrying about Lily would drive him insane.

When he and Jamal had been thrown in jail before, they usually sat next to each other on the floor of their cell and told jokes until one of their friends came to bail them out.

Jamal, oblivious to Aden's turmoil, was his usual cool self. "Is your nose broken?" he asked as he drummed his fingers on his stomach and stared up at the ceiling. He probably asked to ease the boredom or the tension rather than because he really wanted to know. "You should see how swollen it is."

Aden didn't answer. If he spoke, he'd probably start yelling at the sheriff to let him out *now.*

He was crazy with the need to see Lily.

Jamal kept drumming. "The good news is, I got the memory card out of the camera before he took it. Three pictures is all I got, but it should be enough."

Aden took hold of one of the bars high above him and leaned his forehead against a lower bar. Three pictures. Those three pictures had cost him everything.

Jamal sat up and frowned at Aden. "You okay?"

"No."

"She's gonna be all right, man. I bet they don't even book her. That Earl guy might want to press charges, but she wasn't even in the house when the police came."

"I need to be with her. She's terrified."

"We'll be out of here in another couple of hours, and you can go see her."

"I hate knowing that she's suffering and I'm not there."

"Remind her about the puppies. No girl can resist a puppy."

Aden couldn't stomach his friend's flippant attitude. He moved as far away from Jamal as he could, which in the cell was about five feet.

Emptiness yawned in his chest when he thought about the possibility of losing Lily over this mess.

He immediately lost the ability to breathe.

A pudgy officer appeared with a set of keys in his hand and unlocked their cell. "Sheriff says you're free to go. The Hardys decided not to press charges after all."

"Really?" Jamal said, his mouth turning up into a cautious smile. "Why not?"

The officer raised an eyebrow. "The sheriff told him he'd have to search the place if they wanted to bring up proper charges, and Mr. Hardy wasn't too eager to show the sheriff around his property."

Jamal grew serious. "But they need to see what's in the building behind the house."

"Oh, we're aware of the building behind the house, Mr. Drake. It's been a four-month investigation. We'll have a search warrant served soon enough."

"Did you hear that, Aden? All our work paid off."

This news only served to make Aden feel more despondent. The police already knew. This entire disaster had been for nothing.

"Where is the girl who got arrested with us?"

"She came here to the station and then her father took her home. I'd hate to have to face that man if I were his kid. His glare could have peeled the paint off my Jeep." The officer led them to the front desk. "If you want to save the world, kid, join the Peace Corps. Civilians like you only create problems for us."

Jamal chuckled. "Without people like me, you folks would never have a minute of excitement."

"We got plenty of excitement."

The officer gave each of them a paper to sign and handed Jamal an envelope with his cell phone and keys.

"What about my truck?" Jamal said.

"One of the deputies drove it in. It's parked outside."

"Hey, thanks."

"Don't thank me. He felt charitable to-night. Just stay out of trouble. That's a very nice sweater, by the way. My granny used to knit sweaters like that." The officer took Aden's paper. "Your grandpa's here to pick you up. He drove his buggy all the way from Bonduel. You owe him a steak dinner or something."

Dawdi? How had he found out? Aden had planned on hitchhiking home.

Jamal gave Aden a look of pity. "I guess I won't be driving you, man. You gonna catch it from your grandpa?"

333

Aden shook his head. "If there was ever anyone who didn't have a temper, it's my grandpa. If my mamm were here, everybody in this place would need earplugs."

"I know," Jamal said. "I was with you last time, remember?" He studied Aden's face and gave him a pat on the shoulder. "It's going to be okay. She's probably home safe in bed with her covers tucked around her ears. By next week, you'll be laughing about it."

Not likely. Aden forced a half smile. "See you later, Jamal."

"I think I'll head back to Akron. I'm dying for a good cup of coffee."

Jamal walked through the waiting area where Dawdi sat reading a magazine. Aden watched as Jamal greeted Dawdi, visited with him for a few minutes, and left the building.

Aden took a deep breath. Huckleberry Hill was about an hour from here in Dawdi's buggy. No reason to stall. The sooner he and Dawdi got home, the sooner he could check on Lily.

Aden shuffled into the waiting area. "Hi, Dawdi."

Dawdi examined Aden's face and then gave him a bracing hug. "Broke your nose?"

"Like as not."

"Do you need a doctor? My dermatologist practices at Shawano Medical Center."

"No, I don't think there's much he can do for it."

Dawdi put his arm around Aden and led him out the door. "You'll have a double shiner for sure. I got two shiners once when I stepped on a rake and the handle smacked me right in the nose. My whole head ached for three solid weeks."

If the only thing that ached was Aden's head, he'd consider himself the most blessed man in the world.

CHAPTER EIGHTEEN

The long ride to the police station gave Lily time to compose herself somewhat. It only took her about one full minute of screaming her guts out to realize that it accomplished nothing. The policeman in the front seat didn't pay attention to her, and it wouldn't have been too long before she wore her throat raw. She fell silent and sniffed her tears away as best she could while she tried to make sense of her predicament.

The sheriff wouldn't tell her why she or Aden had been arrested, but it made sense that because she felt horrible about it, she must be guilty of something.

The shame, the terror, the guilt pounded at her like a wall of water, and she found it impossible to come up for air. Making as little noise as possible, she sobbed uncontrollably until her chest ached and her eyes burned and her apron was soaked through with tears.

This was what it felt like to have done something truly wicked, to disregard her fater's guidance and let a boy overrule her sound judgment. Her conscience gnawed at her until she felt raw and unclean. Aden might be immune to the pain, but she was not and hoped she never would be. If ever she considered taking one step from the protection of the community again, she would remember her despair at this moment. Let Aden chip away at his reputation and his life. She was done with living recklessly.

It felt like Aden had abandoned her. Where was he and was he seriously injured? His face had been battered and blood had stained his shirt. Her heart stopped until she remembered that he had been standing on his own two feet when they pushed him into the police car.

He'd been taken to the hospital after the tree incident when he got the cut on his eyebrow. Lily shuddered. He seemed to wear such injuries as a badge of honor, but right now, Lily could find no honor in it. Why would he risk his life for a tree?

It was well after dark when they arrived at the police station. The policeman helped her out of the backseat and took off her handcuffs. Lily immediately reached for the handkerchief in her apron pocket. She must look a mess.

The deputy gestured to the building. "Come in and wait for your family. The Hardys are dropping their complaint. You're free to go."

Lily caught her breath. "I don't have to go to jail?"

"Nope. I just got word from the sheriff."

Lily felt as if the weight of the world had fallen off her shoulders. The relief was palpable.

Thank you, Lord. Praise the Lord.

She numbly followed the deputy into the police station where a woman with a badge sat at the front counter. "You can sit over there, honey, until your dad gets here," she said. "A deputy in Bonduel already notified your family. Your dad is on his way."

The dread of seeing her fater swallowed Lily's relief at being released. Lily sniffled and wiped her nose. Dread or not, she wanted to go home and pretend this never happened. Pretend that she had never met anyone named Aden Helmuth, a boy with a devil-may-care grin and a filthy dog.

She would start pretending she never knew him as soon as she could be assured of his safety. "Where are the two boys who were arrested with me?"

"They're in back. We're letting them think about it for a couple of hours. The both of them made a lot of trouble in Ohio. We don't want them to get the idea they can start here in Wisconsin."

"Are they . . . are they well?"

"The Amish boy's got a broken nose, and the other kid has a fat lip. They'll be fine." The woman at the counter smiled sympathetically. "I don't mind if you want to go see them. A pretty girl like you would cheer them up."

Lily pursed her lips and shook her head as her lungs refused to work properly. She couldn't see Aden without being overpowered with shame and anger. If it weren't for him, she wouldn't be in this horrible place, feeling this unbearable shame, waiting for the wrath of her dat to swoop down upon her.

"I don't need to see them," she said, sitting down and picking up the nearest magazine. It wasn't until the tears cleared from her vision that she noticed the title: *Puppies USA*. She slammed it back on the table and stacked three magazines on top of it.

It couldn't have been ten minutes before Dat came marching through the door like a tornado. He stopped short when he caught

339

sight of her, frowned, and folded his arms across his chest.

The humiliation engulfed her, and Lily jumped up and flung herself into his arms. The weeping began anew in her father's embrace.

His stiffness melted in an instant, and he stroked her back and whispered soothing words. "There, there. That's my gute girl. No need to cry."

"I'm sorry, Dat. I know how much I've disappointed you."

He nudged her away from him and held her at arm's length. "I *am* disappointed, Lily. Disappointed that you would get caught up in this when I warned you against it. Didn't you learn anything from what happened to Onkel Zeke?" Pain flashed in his eyes. "I have tried to protect you from this all your life."

Lily wiped her face. How could she have been so selfish as to put her fater through this?

The memory assaulted her as if it had happened yesterday, even though she had only been eight years old. Dat had been sitting at the kitchen table with his face buried in his hands, sobbing from the depths of his soul. She had her own guilt to carry because she had been discharged from the hospital

340

the day before. With her arm wrapped in a thick, heavy bandage, she had tiptoed near to Dat and laid her good hand on his shoulder. He had scooped her onto his lap and given her a desperate, yearning embrace. "Zeke is dead, Lily, Zeke is dead. Don't you ever do that to me. Don't leave me."

"I promise, Dat. Never," she had told him.

And now, she had broken that promise.

Lily squared her shoulders and looked her dat in the eye. "You won't have to worry about me ever again."

Dat patted her cheek. "There, there. You are a gute girl. I lay the blame squarely at Aden Helmuth's feet. You are an innocent girl who cannot recognize when you are being misled."

A sob escaped Lily's lips. She hadn't recognized it at all.

Her dat slipped his arm around her and led her to the door. "The bishop will hear about this. Such behavior by a man of the church, no matter how young, should not be tolerated. I'll see to it that the leaven of evil is removed from our midst."

She should never have let herself be misled by Aden's schemes. All this time she had been chasing an illusion. That's what Aden was. An illusion.

341

She caught her breath at the thought of him, but quickly pushed his face out of her mind's eye. That feeling when he looked at her or kissed her was so intense, so overpowering, that she had mistaken it for love.

But how could she love someone who was entangled in the ways of the world? How could she love a boy her father disapproved of?

A car and driver sat waiting for them at the curb. They stood outside the car for another minute of privacy.

"There will be changes, Lily. You will no longer work for the Helmuths."

"Jah, that is best," Lily said, with a growing ache in her heart.

"His name will not be mentioned in our home, neither will you speak one word to Aden Helmuth ever again. Do you understand?"

"Yes, Dat." Lily would agree to anything if she could make this awful shame go away.

Dat's lips curled slightly. "Gute. Then it is finished."

He opened the door, and Lily slipped into the backseat. She dabbed at her stinging eyes with her handkerchief and sat back for the short ride home.

So, that was the end of that.

She crossed her arms to subdue the stab-

bing pain in her chest.
She would repent of Aden Helmuth.

Chapter Nineteen

Aden felt like a horse chomping at the bit. If only Dawdi had hired a driver instead of bringing his buggy, Aden would be in Bonduel in minutes. Or if Dawdi weren't there, Aden could have hitched a ride with Jamal. Every second spent trying to get to Lily was agony.

Dawdi seemed to go slower with every step. At this rate, they'd never even make it to the parking lot.

"Do you want me to drive, Dawdi?"

"Nae. Your nose must smart something awful."

Aden sighed inwardly. That would add another twenty minutes to the trip. He tried to quell his frustration. Dawdi had been kind enough to come all the way out here, and he didn't seem angry about Aden's arrest. He should be grateful instead of impatient. Lord willing, he would get home in time to see Lily before it got too late.

Dawdi prodded the horse into a leisurely trot out of the parking lot and onto the road. "I saw New Mexico and Texas on the way here."

"How many more do you have to find?"

"Twelve. But they're the hard ones."

Aden took a deep breath and willed his heart to slow to a normal pace. No amount of anxiety would make this buggy go faster. "Dawdi, how did you know I'd been arrested?" Aden hadn't made the customary phone call when he came to the station. Mammi and Dawdi didn't have a phone, and the only friend who could have helped him had been sitting next to him in the cell.

"David Eicher paid us a visit. He'd been to Shawano to fetch Lily."

"Is she all right?"

"According to David, she'll carry the scars for the rest of her life."

Aden buried his face in his hands. "Oh, no."

Dawdi reached over and patted Aden's knee. "She'll be fine. David just wanted to let off a whole teapot of steam. He came storming up to our house yelling like he'd run into a hornet's nest. I couldn't talk no sense into him."

"I'm sorry, Dawdi."

"He wouldn't listen to me, but he sure

got an earful from your mammi. She looked pretty frightening, waving that wooden spoon around and giving David what for."

Imagining Mammi giving Lily's dat *what for* gave Aden a glimmer of cheer for the first time tonight.

"She told him what you did was for the puppies, and if he couldn't see in his heart to help the puppies, then he might as well go home and cast his heart in stone. At which point, David slammed our door on his way out and Pilot chased him off the lawn." Dawdi sprouted a grin.

Aden groaned and gave up hope of ever winning David Eicher's favor.

But, oh, how he loved that dog!

"I shouldn't have let her come with us. She had no idea what she was getting into."

"Did you?" Dawdi said.

"I always know the risks. I'm willing to take them."

"Trying to do God's job for Him?"

"Of course not. I would be bad at God's job."

"But you don't think He can do His own work."

Aden sighed. Dawdi had tried to tell him this before, and he was just as confused as ever. "I don't understand. I am a tiny speck. God runs the universe."

"But you act as if He has left Bonduel to you."

"I do?"

"Why did you choose baptism, Aden?"

Aden wanted to give a quick answer, but he felt he might be on the verge of something important, so he sat still for a minute and considered the question. "The Amish way of life is gute for the environment. We are true stewards of the earth."

"That is the worst reason to be Amish I've ever heard of."

"I didn't say that was the only reason, or even the best reason."

"What else, then?" Dawdi asked, not even glancing at the road ahead.

"It is the faith of my fathers, what I grew up with."

"That's a bit better."

Aden's eyes filled with tears as he verbalized what he'd never expressed out loud. "I've committed my life to God, Dawdi. I love Jesus. He is everything to me."

Dawdi pointed his finger in the air. "Aha. Now we come to it. Do you remember in the Bible how Mary sat at Jesus's feet, and Martha went cumbered about with much serving?"

Aden remembered. Since the accident at the lake, he'd pretty much committed those verses to memory — not that knowing the whole thing by heart helped him understand how the story applied to him. How did Dawdi know of Aden's struggle with this passage?

"Martha took care of the meal, and Mary just sat there," Aden said. "But Martha got in trouble when all she wanted was some help from her sister."

"Martha didn't accuse Mary. She accused the Lord."

Aden furrowed his brow. He had never thought of it like that.

Dawdi guided the horse farther to the side to let a car pass him. "Martha thought Jesus should have recognized her need. Mary hung on every word from the Lord's mouth. Perhaps Martha thought the Lord wasn't doing His job. She asked Him to tell Mary to come and help."

Aden felt as if he were a bird about to take flight, but he couldn't understand how to use his wings. So close. He was so close he could almost touch understanding. "What did He mean when He said, 'One thing is needful'?"

"Jesus said Mary had chosen the good part. What did Mary do?"

"She sat at Jesus's feet and heard His words."

"Mary trusted in the Lord. Martha fretted that the Lord was not doing enough. It sounds to me like you need to turn your life over to God and then listen when He speaks to you."

Aden's memory traveled back to that night at the lake. God had tried to tell him something, but he hadn't done anything about it. "You think I'm not listening?"

"Have you truly turned your life over to God, or are you just giving Him lip service?"

"Some of the time, I guess. But there is so much injustice in the world."

"And you do not believe God can fix it. So you see people starve puppies or cut down trees, and you take over the job you think God should be doing. This is not our way. Outsiders disagree with us, but we have always believed that we belong to the kingdom of heaven, not the kingdoms of men. It's the reason we don't vote or fight in wars. Puppy mills and new roads are the affairs of men. We concern ourselves with the things of God. We believe in submitting our will to the will of Heavenly Father. Gelassenheit."

"And let evil men go unpunished?"

Dawdi raised a finger to the sky. " 'Vengeance is mine, saith the Lord.' God allows people and animals to suffer at the hands of wicked men so that His judgments will be just at the last day. The wicked will have their reward, even as the righteous will. Do not rob anyone of the reward God has in store for them."

Aden swallowed the lump in his throat. "Dawdi, do you remember when I had that accident at the lake?"

"Your mamm wrote us six pages about it."

"The car filled with water, and we couldn't get out." He ran a hand across his forehead and shivered. He still felt the ice in his bones. "I thought I was going to die. I've never told anyone this before, but someone grabbed my hand and pulled me to the surface."

"An angel?"

"I heard a voice urging me to choose the good part."

Nothing seemed to surprise Dawdi. "That's wonderful gute."

"Not really. I mean, it is wonderful gute that an angel saved my life, but I have been so confused. I feel like God is calling my number, but I can't answer Him because I don't have a phone."

"I've never needed a phone to talk to God," Dawdi said.

"But it would be much easier if I knew exactly what He wants to tell me."

"If God made it easy, we would not grow from the struggle."

"I know."

Dawdi guided the buggy to the side of the road and stopped. He looped the reins around the hook and turned his full attention to Aden. "God pulled you out of that lake. He has a plan for your life."

"So where do I start?"

"Let the police raid the puppy mills."

"No more recycling?" Aden asked.

"I believe the good Lord smiles on your recycling program and things like what you did for Cobbler Pond. We must be good stewards of the earth, and those activities don't force your own will on anyone else. 'Trust in the Lord with all your heart and lean not on your own understanding.' "

Trust in the Lord with all your heart.

Dawdi picked up the reins and got the buggy moving again. "And if the good Lord wants a tree saved, you can call your friend Jamal."

A grin crept onto Aden's lips. He would always be able to count on Jamal. It was time he learned to feel the same way about God.

A car crept up behind them and passed them cautiously. "Oh, look!" Dawdi exclaimed. "Hawaii. I never thought I'd see the day."

CHAPTER TWENTY

Aden's heart felt as heavy as a stone. He passed the spot where the ill-fated mailbox had been and tramped up Lily's sidewalk.

Of course Lily wouldn't be coming back to Huckleberry Hill. Her dat would see to that, and like the obedient child she was, she would comply with his wishes. But a hundred hostile fathers couldn't keep Aden from seeing her and making things right. He knew how she must be suffering from the entire ordeal. He would be able to comfort her and make her feel whole again.

That's what she did for him every time he laid eyes on her.

Even his best hopes of seeing her last night vanished when Dawdi's horse threw a shoe half a mile from Huckleberry Hill. They'd arrived home after ten, and Aden knew he would make matters worse by showing up at her house at that hour.

Sleep had been impossible. He'd spent the

chilly night haunting the tomato patch with a propane lantern, picking the rest of the tomatoes for Mammi, and planning exactly what he would say to Lily. He had forced himself to wait until eight this morning to hurry to her house. Even after yesterday, she'd be awake by eight, wouldn't she?

There were so many things he needed to say to her.

How are you? I'm sorry. I would have come last night. I love you. Jamal went back to Ohio. I promise I'll never raid a puppy mill again. Will you marry me?

Whoa, slow down a minute. His desires galloped far ahead of reality. He'd marry Lily tomorrow if he could, but she probably wasn't ready for that. She'd been through a lot in the last week, and a girl like Lily needed time to sort out her feelings.

Estee answered the door with a sweater draped around her shoulders. Probably on her way to work. She neglected to smile at him, but she didn't seem angry. "You shouldn't be here."

He identified the look in her eyes. She felt sorry for him.

"I need to see Lily."

"That won't do any good for anybody right now. Go home and give them some time to cool down."

354

"I'm desperate to see her, Estee."

She glanced behind her before stepping onto the porch and closing the door after her. "Do you understand what you've done? Dat has forbidden us to say your name."

Aden took off his hat and ran his fingers through his hair. "I know it was terrible for Lily, but if I could talk to her, I know I can make everything right again."

"No, you can't. Lily is not to speak to you. Dat won't yield. Lily says you've taken advantage of her trusting heart, and she never wants to see you again."

Aden felt as if he'd been knocked over by a giant bowling ball. "She . . . she said that?"

Estee huffed out her frustration. "She has an overactive sense of guilt. One word from Dat convinced her that you would drag her to hell yet." She took him by the elbow and whispered, "I wonders me what happened last night. You look like you've been in a brawl."

"We didn't do anything bad. Jamal needed some photos of a puppy mill, and he wanted me to distract the people in the house. Lily begged me to take her along. I didn't want to, but she wouldn't give in."

"She insisted?"

"Jah. When we started snooping around the puppy mill, the people got suspicious and somebody called the police. Next thing I knew, they'd handcuffed all three of us."

Estee glared at him. "You shouldn't have taken her with you."

"Don't you think I know that?" he snapped.

Her expression softened. "Go home. You've made a mess of things."

He felt as if his boots were nailed to the porch. "Please, Estee. Get Lily. I'll not hesitate to barge into your house if I have to."

"That would be foolish."

His voice rose with his agitation. "Desperate people do desperate things. Haven't you heard about Aden Helmuth? He chains himself to trees. He trespasses on other people's property. Your dat already hates me. What do I care how much?"

Estee pressed her lips together and studied his face. She must have decided he was dead serious. "Okay, I will see what I can do. But wipe that scowl off your face or you'll confirm what Dat already believes."

She stepped back into the house and closed the door behind her.

Aden rubbed the scar on his eyebrow. The situation was worse than he feared. His hands trembled and sweat beaded on his forehead. What should he do now?

How long did they keep him standing out there? Five, ten minutes?

He had nearly decided to shoulder his way into the house uninvited when Lily's dat appeared at the door, frowning with every line of his face. Lily stood about three feet behind him with her eyes to the floor and her arms wrapped around her waist. She caught her breath and widened her eyes when she looked at his face. He already sported two nasty black eyes.

David's scowl almost rendered Aden speechless. "I . . . can I talk to Lily?"

"You should have listened to Estee. Nobody in this house wants to talk to you."

"If you have any Christian kindness at all, please let me have my say." It was low to suggest that the Eichers were devoid of Christian love, but he was out-of-his-head crazy to see Lily, and he knew such a declaration would get David's attention.

David clenched his jaw and tilted his head toward Lily. "You have my permission to speak with him. I'll see to it that he won't bother us again."

Lily took precisely one step out of the house while her dat stayed riveted just inside the door. Her red-rimmed eyes testified that she had been crying. Probably all night.

357

He wanted to pull her into his embrace so badly he could almost taste it. "Lily, I'm sorry. It must have been horrible for you. I know how terrified you were. The first time I got arrested it felt like the world had come to an end."

She looked at him with disdain and knocked the wind right out of him. "The first time? I guess it got easier after that."

"I just . . . I know how you are suffering. I feel so bad about what happened."

"But not bad enough to let her be," David said. "Was it a big joke? To drag my daughter to that terrifying place?"

"We couldn't have guessed that the situation would get out of hand like it did." Regret stabbed at Aden again and again. What kind of a boy would put the girl he loved in such danger? His remorse was fitting punishment for trying to do God's job. Aden took Lily's arms above the elbow and nudged her closer to him. She remained stiff as a board.

"Don't," said her dat.

Aden felt his whole world sinking. He dropped his hands. "Lily, please. I love you."

She stared past him as if he weren't even there, but a single tear rolled down her cheek.

"And I think you love me."

"She doesn't love you." Her dat hissed like a snake about to strike. "Girls at her age are attracted to wild boys, but they never want them as husbands. Girls want steady, godly men who will provide for their families. You are no good for my daughter. She sees that now."

Aden bent over and met Lily's gaze. "Does she?"

Lily seemed to crack, and she began to cry in earnest. "I'm so ashamed."

Her dat stepped out of the house and enfolded Lily into his arms. Aden bit his tongue to keep from crying out. He wanted to be the one to hold Lily and wipe away her tears. He wanted to caress those soft lips until she gave up running and kissed him back. Instead, he watched numbly as she took comfort from her father.

She regained her composure enough to speak. "If this is how it feels to be with you, Aden, then I don't want it. I never want to feel like this again. Leave me alone and go corrupt some other girl who doesn't mind being in jail."

David took hold of Lily's hand and turned to face Aden. "I'm going to the bishop later today to recommend your excommunication."

Aden felt as dry and bleak as the desert.

He spread his arms wide in a plea for mercy. "I welcome the shunning. I deserve it."

Lily stopped crying and gazed at him. Perhaps his humility surprised her. Unable to resist, he stroked his finger once down her cheek. She flinched. "I never in a million years meant for you to be hurt."

He felt as if he'd been crying for hours as the pain in his chest gripped him violently. He stepped off the porch and turned back to look at Lily. "It probably doesn't matter to you, but I mean to change things in my life. I will always love you. Never forget."

Aden marched down the sidewalk without looking back. One more look at Lily's tortured face and his heart might cease beating.

Chapter Twenty-One

Aden stared at the fiery red huckleberry patch without really seeing it and reminded himself to breathe. The pain felt so fresh that even filling his lungs took effort. He could only wish that the throbbing in his face where Earl had smacked him was the only discomfort he felt. The pain of a broken nose meant nothing compared to a heart ripped in shreds.

He sat on the same log where he and Lily had rested a month ago when they'd encountered the bear.

The day he'd first kissed her.

The best day of his life.

Aden's heart did a flip-flop as he remembered the way Lily had glared at him when he ran into the woods with those frying pans — as if she cared whether he came back or not.

He leaned his elbows on his knees and contemplated walking back to the house.

He'd been out here for more than an hour, but he couldn't seem to make himself move, even though he needed to head into Bonduel for a load of coal. The nights would be getting mighty chilly right quick, and Dawdi would need to fire up the furnace in the cellar before too long.

Aden felt guilty about leaving Mammi and Dawdi just as winter approached, but he couldn't stay here. Besides his grandparents, not one soul wanted him in Bonduel.

He ached at the thought of Lily's rejection. Even though her adamant dismissal had surprised him, he didn't blame her. He'd deserved it. He really thought she might have loved him, but if her dat spoke the truth, she had merely been fascinated with someone she thought was a "bad" boy.

Well, the look in her eyes this morning made it clear that she was over her fascination, ready to settle down with someone more suitable like Tyler Yoder. They were a better match than she and Aden had ever been. A match made in Amish heaven — well-behaved Lily Eicher and steady Tyler Yoder.

Lily would be happy.

That thought did not bring Aden comfort. He didn't want Lily to be happy with anybody but him.

The sound of dry leaves rustling reminded him that Pilot needed to be fed. He probably tired of frolicking through the woods and now returned to remind Aden of his duty to feed his dog.

Aden stood and turned to see not Pilot, but Tyler Yoder making his way down the trail. His heart sank to his toes. He didn't want to see Tyler today. Or ever. Tyler's presence only served to remind Aden that he would never be good enough for Lily, that Lily deserved someone as good and steady as Tyler and not a hopeless case like Aden Helmuth.

Jah, Tyler was the last person Aden wanted to see.

"Your mammi told me you were out here," Tyler said. "I hope I'm not bothering you."

Yes, you are bothering me something awful. Go away and let me wallow in peace.

"Not at all. What do you need?"

Tyler gazed at Aden as he paused to catch his breath. "Your eyes are black and purple. I've never seen the like. Did you break your nose?"

"I think so."

"I am glad Lily wasn't hurt. I wish she hadn't gone with you."

"So do I."

A deeply solemn frown shaped Tyler's

363

mouth. "My dat is conferring with the ministers right now. I thought you should know."

Aden feigned ignorance. "About what?"

Tyler gave Aden that serious look he reserved for serious matters. "You know very well what. David Eicher practically broke down our door this morning."

Resigned to his fate already, Aden sank back to the log and folded his arms. "Am I going to be excommunicated?"

Aden didn't welcome it, but Tyler sat next to him and placed a hand on his shoulder. "Jah."

Aden averted his gaze and stared at the berry patch. "Good. That is the right decision."

"I disagree."

Aden stood and put some distance between them. He couldn't bear this gesture of friendship from the one person who would eventually destroy all his happiness. "You know what happened. Lily's dat has every cause to be mad."

"It wasn't your fault, Aden."

"It was *only* my fault. You are one of the few people who know what being frightened like that must have done to Lily. I knew the risks, and I still let her come with me."

"Did you force her into the car?"

"She had no idea what she was getting into."

"But Lily wanted to go with you." Tyler's frown deepened. "She must have really liked that mailbox."

Aden recognized Tyler's expression. He wanted to laugh out loud at the irony. He cracked a pained smile.

"What's so funny?" Tyler asked.

"You're worried that Lily likes me?"

Tyler looked away. "Maybe a little."

Aden didn't try to mask the bitterness in his voice. Tyler could handle it. "Let me put your mind at ease. Her dat chopped down my mailbox. There isn't a visible trace of it left. Lily herself ordered me to leave her alone. The way is clear, Tyler. She wouldn't have me if I were the last Amish boy in Wisconsin."

"You may think that makes me happy, but it doesn't. I don't want to win Lily's love just because she thinks you're so wicked in comparison."

"I *am* wicked in comparison, and you are the kind of boy she wants." The words made his eyes sting with regret.

Tyler stood as if he couldn't contain his emotions. "You're my friend, Aden. No matter the reason, it grieves me to see you so miserable. And just because David Eicher

365

demands it doesn't mean you should be excommunicated."

"I deserve the punishment," Aden said. "I'll take whatever the elders want to heap on me as penance for what I've done."

"The bann is not punishment. It is to help the sinner recognize the error of his ways."

"Gute. Let them give me six weeks or eight weeks or however long it is. I'll attend gmay faithfully so everyone in the district can glare at me."

"That's not how it is."

"I want the full weight of it, Tyler. Once you've all shunned me for an acceptable period of time, I'll do a kneeling confession and leave Wisconsin. The whole community will be overjoyed to see me go."

"That's not true. We believe in your gute heart. That's why we helped you clean the pond."

Aden lowered his gaze. "I'm sorry I've disappointed everybody. I really am. The last thing I wanted, ever, was for Lily to get hurt."

"Me too. But the next to last thing I want is for you to believe you don't belong here, or that you don't have a home with us." Tyler peered at Aden, looking for a reaction. "There's a piece of land for sale not far from the dairy. Forty-five acres. You could buy it and start that organic farm you've always wanted, Lord willing."

Aden shook his head.

"I'd sell you all the manure you want."

Aden kept shaking his head. Even if it were the best plot of land in Bonduel, he couldn't settle down here. He wasn't strong enough to be reminded of his loss every time he and Lily crossed paths.

Tyler's offer only served to make him feel worse, another painful reminder of how deserving Tyler was and how unworthy Aden remained.

Pilot finally made an appearance. He bounded out of the thicket, romped to Aden's side, and planted his paws on Aden's chest. Aden ruffled Pilot's ears and nudged him back to the ground. He took a step in the direction of the trail, signaling the end of the conversation. "So when do you think they'll actually do it?"

"The bann? Tomorrow, like as not."

"Then you have less than twenty-four hours to be my friend."

"I will always be your friend."

Aden shrugged off Tyler's declaration. "Come have supper. I'm sure Mammi won't mind."

He and Tyler couldn't be friends ever again. Tyler planned to marry Aden's girl. It kind of put a damper on things.

It was a good possibility that Estee's displeasure had something to do with the announcement of Aden's shunning at church today.

Estee didn't utter a word all the way home. She ignored Lily's pointed questions as if she were deaf and turned her face away from Lily as if she were invisible. Tension between them crackled, making the buggy seem small and cramped. Lily rejoiced when Dat finally pulled into the driveway.

The four of them trudged into the house, and Estee wasted no time in marching up the stairs and slamming the bedroom door behind her.

But why was Estee so upset? Lily was the one who'd been arrested. Lily was the one who'd been humiliated and embarrassed by Aden Helmuth's recklessness. She had forced herself to go to gmay today even though it meant being in Aden's presence while he stared pitifully at her from across the room. Did Estee have no sympathy for what Lily had gone through?

She followed her sister up the stairs, if only to be certain that Estee bore her no ill will. Of course Estee liked Aden, but her first duty should be toward her own flesh and blood.

Lily tiptoed into her room, in case any extra noise would further provoke Estee. Estee stood at the window, looking out at the cows in the pasture. She didn't even turn her head when Lily entered.

"You are extra quiet today," Lily said, sitting on her bed and smoothing the quilt with a casual brush of her hand.

Estee pursed her lips and stared faithfully out the window.

"Floyd had a new hat," Lily persisted. "What happened to his old one?"

Estee remained steadfast, like a scholar with her attention riveted to the teacher.

Lily swallowed hard. She had suffered enough. Couldn't Estee show her a little kindness? "I truly enjoyed the sermon today," she said, unable to think of anything else to draw Estee out and ready to give up trying.

Estee snapped her head around to glare at Lily. "I didn't hear a word of it. The hypocrisy in the room shouted so loudly, I couldn't hear the preacher."

"What hypocrisy?"

"You're oozing with it, Lily."

Lily's mouth dropped open. "You don't think I should have been shunned, do you?

369

It's not my fault I got arrested. Aden lured me in."

"How very convenient to lay all the blame at Aden's feet so Dat wouldn't be cross with you."

"That's not true."

"Did you make it clear to Dat that you demanded that Aden take you with him that night? Aden has been so kind to us, but he got Dat's wrath because you were too chicken to own up to it. It's pathetic, Lily."

Lily fiercely blinked back the tears. "I didn't know the police would come."

"Yes," said Estee, throwing up her hands. "You are innocent of all wrongdoing, and Aden is so wicked."

"You weren't there, Estee. You have no idea what it's like to see your companions attacked, knowing you might be next. Or to escape from the house with nowhere to escape to. There is nothing more terrifying than being yanked into a pair of handcuffs and shoved into a police car." She couldn't keep her voice from shaking. "How dare you judge me?"

Softening her gaze, Estee sat next to Lily on the bed and slowly slid an arm around her shoulders. "It must have been horrible for both of you."

"Don't you care how I feel?"

Estee sighed. "I care. You're my sister. I love you."

"More than you love Aden?"

"Of course."

"Then why do you defend him and attack me?"

"I'm sorry if I hurt your feelings, Lily. I always say what I think, and Aden doesn't deserve to be shunned. If you had made everything clear to Dat, things wouldn't have gone this far."

"I did make everything clear to Dat. Besides, it was the elders' decision to shun him, not Dat's. They saw enough to justify the bann."

Estee slumped her shoulders. "I suppose they did."

Lily's voice cracked into a hundred pieces. "Don't be cross with me, Estee. With everything that's happened, I don't think I can bear your contempt."

Estee wrapped her arms all the way around Lily and patted her back as if she were calming a crying baby. "Don't cry, Lily. What's done is done. I'll not trouble you again by mentioning it. You are still the kindest girl I know and my favorite sister."

"I'm your only sister."

"Dry your eyes, and we'll play Scrabble. You'd like that, wouldn't you?"

Estee must have really felt remorseful for what she had said. She hated Scrabble. Dear Estee. She wouldn't stay mad for long. She was too sensible to hold a grudge.

CHAPTER TWENTY-TWO

Lily carefully tied the strings of her bonnet under her chin before sliding on her coat and stuffing a handkerchief into her pocket. She didn't know why she felt so dull today. She loved auctions. This time, a quilt that she had helped stitch would be up for sale. It would be fun to see how much it sold for.

Really, really fun.

So why did she feel as stale as a loaf of day-old bread?

It could be the change of seasons. She had hoped to avoid an autumn sickness, but maybe she was coming down with something. She cleared her throat to see if she sensed a cold coming on. No symptoms that she could tell. She went to the medicine cabinet in the kitchen just in case. It never hurt to take a vitamin C.

Maybe she needed to go to a gathering. Embarrassed by her arrest, she hadn't been to one in more than three weeks. But Tyler

373

took her driving almost every day or kept her company at home by playing Scrabble or Life on the Farm.

Dat sat at the table reading the paper while Mama made him a sandwich.

"Are you coming to the auction?" Lily asked as she popped a vitamin C into her mouth.

Dat lowered his paper. "Jah, later."

"Do you want us to save you a seat?"

"Nae. We will find a spot." Dat seemed to lose interest in reading. "Tell Tyler thank you for the steaks. They were delicious."

"I will. He'll be happy to know you liked them."

Dat folded his paper and laid it on the table. "You know, Lily, your mama planted plenty of celery this year."

Mama handed Dat his sandwich. "Jah, I did. For Estee, of course, but if there are two weddings, we can buy as much as we need."

Dat nodded. "I know you and Tyler have only been dating for a short while, but we would not object if you wanted to marry on the same day as your sister."

That knot formed in the pit of Lily's stomach where it always did when she thought about getting married. But why should it? She was old enough, and Tyler had a gute income. It would please her parents to see her so happily settled. They wouldn't have to worry about her, and it would save them the trouble of a second wedding a year later. It sounded like a reasonable plan.

She stole a chip from Dat's plate. "The family would like that. They'd only have to come once instead of twice. And the work would certainly be lessened."

"A much better plan than those young people who only think of their own convenience when planning a wedding."

Lily shrank at the thought. She didn't want to be one of those selfish girls who demanded the wedding be her way without regard to anybody else's feelings.

"There is only one problem with your idea, Dat. The boy must do the asking, and he will only do the asking when he is ready." Perhaps Tyler didn't want to get married for another year. Perhaps he didn't want to marry her at all. This thought cheered her considerably.

Maybe she wasn't ready to marry. Maybe thoughts of Aden Helmuth were too fresh in her mind. Maybe she still longed for Babylon and wasn't ready to contemplate marriage to the kind of boy who would be good for her instead of to the kind of boy she shouldn't want.

An unbidden memory sprang to her mind even as she tried to push it down. She thought of Aden's strong arms around her the day she fell into the pond. He had pulled her out of the water and fussed over her until he was satisfied that she would be all right. She had never felt safer than when he had brushed her cheek with his rough fingers and sent sparks traveling through her entire body.

Lily drove those thoughts out of her head by balling her hands into fists and biting her lower lip. She'd certainly been hoodwinked, hadn't she? That dog of his was a health hazard all by himself, not to mention that one time she got arrested. Aden certainly hadn't protected her then.

What would life be like married to such a man? Would she lie awake at night, wondering if her husband sat in jail or had drowned in the river? Would he talk her into chaining herself to a tree while her children went hungry?

No, thank you.

Tyler Yoder was a more-than-satisfactory replacement for Aden Helmuth. She couldn't be happier. And if Dat wanted a wedding this winter, then he would get a wedding. Tyler just needed a little encouragement.

"Tell Tyler to get on the stick," Dat said. "I'm not getting any younger, you know. I want grandchildren."

Lily forced a smile and zipped her coat. "You'll get grandchildren, Dat."

She ambled out the door and stepped onto the porch. A stiff breeze greeted her as she walked across the yard to Tyler's waiting buggy. Good thing the auction took place indoors. They'd all have frostbite if they had to battle the wind. The first week of October, and it was already shaping up to be a chilly winter.

With Tyler's reserved smile greeting her, she climbed into the buggy and snapped the door shut. It did little to block the chill of the breeze.

She remembered Dat's encouragement to get a proposal. "Dat says thanks for the steaks. They were delicious."

Tyler looked satisfied in his serious way. "I am glad you liked them. I will bring more next week. Maybe I will learn how to make cheese and bring your dat some."

"You are smart enough to do anything you set your mind to," she said.

"Denki. I am happy that you think so." They rode without saying much until Tyler took his gaze off the road and lowered his eyes to stare at Lily's hand resting between them on the bench.

Lily saw where he looked and didn't dare move a muscle.

Tyler inched his hand closer until his fingers touched hers. Still she didn't move. Would he gather the courage to actually hold her hand?

Aden seemed to have an abundance of courage when it came to such things. He thought it no trouble to wrap his arms around her and kiss her to heaven. Tenderness and gratitude washed through her. Aden wasn't afraid to risk everything for a kiss. He liked her that much.

Tyler finally wrapped his fingers around hers. She communicated her acceptance by lightly squeezing his hand. His lips curled, and he turned his attention back to the road. Lily sat still as a statue, trying to take pleasure in the feel of his hand. She knit her brows together. There didn't seem to be much of a thrill between them, as when Aden graced her with the slightest touch.

But Tyler's regard was a more steady, predictable kind of thing. Aden was like a flash of lightning. He left her breathless with his very presence.

Lightning was extremely dangerous.

They sat in awkward silence until they

finally arrived at the warehouse where the auction would take place, and by the time he released her hand, her palm was clammy with sweat and her arm felt heavy.

A blush tinted Tyler's cheeks as he helped her down from the buggy. "I liked that," he said.

Lily merely smiled, the only response he seemed to require.

The auctioneer's forceful voice echoed off the high tin ceiling as Tyler and Lily found two empty chairs at the end of a row. "Shall we sit here?" Tyler asked.

Lily nodded, then sat and folded her arms — not that she feared Tyler would try to hold her hand again, because Tyler would never do anything like that in public. But it never hurt to be cautious.

The auction was almost exclusively for quilts. Buyers came from all over the state to purchase quilts for gift shops or fabric stores. One buyer Lily knew of sold quilts on the Internet. The bidding proved exciting, especially when two eager ladies drove up the price for a king-sized Double Wedding Ring quilt. Lily loved seeing how much money the auctions brought in.

She stiffened as she caught site of Aden walking through the crowds that stood to the left and right of the auction block. He stopped to talk to an Englischer Lily didn't recognize. They shook hands, and Aden's whole face glowed with happiness as if the Englischer had offered him a free pond aerator.

It had been three weeks since she had laid eyes on him except at church. Such a long time. The sight of those brilliant green eyes set against his tan face was like seeing her first rainbow. Oh, my, he looked good and so vital, as if life and happiness and love came from him and him alone. Her heart pulled apart as if someone had snatched it like a piece of paper and ripped it over and over until it turned to dust.

She clamped her eyes shut and took a deep breath. She didn't want to doubt her fater when he told her that she didn't love Aden. But if this feeling was an unhealthy fascination with the wrong boy, why did she long for him so? Why could she think on nothing or nobody else?

Hmm, that did sound unhealthy. Staying up late into the night and being too pre-occupied to eat were certainly detrimental to her wellness. She would try to discipline her feelings.

Not daring to turn her head for a better look, she studied Aden in her peripheral vision as he ambled to the third row of folding chairs and sat down. The two Amish men near him looked doubtfully at each other, stood up, and found seats two rows back. Lily wanted to cry.

Was this what it meant to shun someone?

Of course, that was what it meant to Lily's dat. He refused to even utter Aden's name. But was this what it meant to the entire district?

Three Sundays ago, the bishop had made it very clear that the shunning proceeded out of love for the sinner, and that Aden should be treated "carefully" but with kindness. But what did "carefully" mean? Did it mean to refuse to talk to Aden at all? To make him feel isolated from the group while at the same time hoping he would come back?

It didn't make sense. Lily had known only one other person in the district who had been shunned several years ago, and he had immediately left the area so they didn't have to figure out how to treat him.

Every bit of Lily's attention focused on that spot in the warehouse where Aden Helmuth sat, all by himself, watching the auction in isolation as if he were a leper. To her knowledge, Tyler hadn't noticed him.

Two girls behind her giggled and whispered to each other. They weren't very good at keeping their voices down. "Oy anyhow, he is so handsome. He said hi to me every Sunday at gmay."

"And so nice too. He helped my brother milk his cows when my dat got so sick."

"Too bad we can't talk to him now."

"We can talk, Elsie. We just can't go for a ride in his buggy."

"I'd go with him if he asked, even with the bann on him." More giggling.

"Only three more weeks of shunning, and Mandy says he's taking instruction classes with the bishop."

"Could I make him a cake? I could still shun him and make him a cake, couldn't I?"

"Jah, but he only eats vegetables."

"Is rhubarb a vegetable? I could make him a rhubarb pie."

The incessant giggling almost drove Lily to slap her hands over her ears. Resisting the urge, she attempted to focus on the lovely Hole in the Barn Door quilt held up for auction. Or better yet, she should focus on Tyler. She was supposed to be trying to get a proposal from him.

Words failed her as she turned to him. With all this talk of vegetarians and shunnings jumbling her brain, her heart wasn't in it.

Tyler caught her looking and smiled. He placed his hands on his legs, to be in near proximity to her hands if she decided to unfold them. She didn't.

Another quilt sold. Six hundred dollars. Tyler leaned close to her ear. "Do you see your quilt?"

"It's not really my quilt. I just helped with it."

An hour later, every last quilt had sold. Lily's arms were stiff from keeping them folded for so long, and her neck ached with the strain of keeping an eye on Aden without looking at him. Why had he come? He had sat all by himself and hadn't bid on one thing, and the looks and whispers he got from his neighbors would have sent even the most thick-skinned person running for the exit. Of course, Aden wasn't afraid of anything. He probably hadn't even noticed how people were looking at him.

Tyler and Lily stood as men began to put up the chairs, and Lily caught a glimpse of Anna and Felty Helmuth marching purposefully toward her. She hadn't so much as written a note to them since the disaster at the puppy mill. What must they think of her?

Lily comforted herself with the thought that she had nothing to be ashamed of.

Aden deserved the blame for what had happened. He was the one being shunned, after all.

To her surprise, Anna threw her arms around Lily's neck and gave her an affectionate hug. "We've missed you so much. My floors haven't been near as clean since you've been gone. Isn't that right, Felty?"

Lily felt her face get hot, but the reason Lily hadn't been to Huckleberry Hill in three weeks didn't seem important to Anna. Or perhaps she'd forgotten.

"I . . . I hope I didn't leave you in a pickle," Lily said. "I know how hard it is for you to mop."

Felty looked from Tyler to Lily. "Anna is thinking of hiring another little girl. What's her name, Banannie? Erla. Is it Erla Glick?"

Lily's throat went dry at the sound of that name. Erla Glick should mind her own business. Erla Glick was no good for Anna and Felty. She probably didn't even know how to sweep properly.

Anna's eyes twinkled. "Stuff and nonsense, Felty. I wouldn't replace Lily. She's the one I want." She patted Lily's arm. "Don't worry, dear. I'll hold your job for you. And there will be no more talk of hiring Erla Glick."

Lily should have corrected Anna, but she

couldn't bring herself to do it. At least Aden would be safe from Erla, and Anna would eventually realize Lily wouldn't be back to Huckleberry Hill.

Tyler must have recognized Lily's discomfort. "You have been so kind to give Lily a job for the summer, but Lily won't be able to work for you anymore. It might be wise to hire Erla."

Tyler should keep his opinions to himself.

Anna looked as if she were about to burst with the best secret in the whole world. "Of course, dear." She rummaged in the big bag she carried with her everywhere and pulled out two rainbow-colored pot holders. She gave one each to Tyler and Lily. "Give these to your mothers and give them my best, will you?"

"Jah, of course."

Felty took Anna's hand and pulled her toward the concessions. "Come on, Banannie, let's get some hot chocolate."

Anna winked at Lily as she walked away. "Isn't hot chocolate romantic? Warms your heart as well as your bones."

Lily put on her coat and tucked the collar around her neck. Even inside, it felt chilly.

"Do you want some hot chocolate?" Tyler asked.

"No, thank you."

Tyler seemed taken aback by her simple refusal. "Oh, okay." Again, awkwardness prevailed as Tyler's gaze scanned the crowd. Maybe he looked for someone who would accept his offer of hot chocolate. "There's Aden," he said. "We should go say hello."

Lily's heart fluttered involuntarily. She did not, under any circumstances, want to talk to Aden, but she couldn't very well explain her reasons to Tyler. "Let's not. We should be shunning him."

"You know better than that, Lily. People treat him like an outcast even though that's not how the shunning is meant to be. He needs to know that he has some true friends."

She nodded because she suddenly couldn't force enough air out of her lungs to speak. If she looked into those green eyes, she feared she might forget why she ever left him. Her fascination with him was too powerful. She didn't know how strong she could be.

Tyler cupped his hand around her elbow. "Aden is determined to wring every lesson he can out of the bann. My brother says he has shown up to every gathering and sin-geon since the bann. He thinks he deserves to be regarded with contempt. We shouldn't be shunning him. He's hard enough on

386

himself."

Lily couldn't breathe in or out. Did her lungs even work anymore? She didn't want Aden to punish himself. A boy like Aden should be happy all the time.

They walked toward Aden, who busily stacked chairs and didn't acknowledge them. Lily sensed that he was aware of their approach, as if he'd been keeping lookout for them without really looking. He stacked one more load of chairs after Tyler said his name. Then he focused his eyes on Lily, and his intense gaze made it impossible to look away.

Tyler offered his hand. Aden's lips curled downward, and he shook his head. "You shouldn't, Tyler. I don't want you to get in trouble with your dat."

Tyler kept his hand stretched out in front of him. "That is the stupidest thing I've ever heard. Shunning doesn't mean I can't shake your hand."

Aden sprouted a miserable, lopsided smile. "Then I don't want you to get in trouble with Lily's dat."

Aden used a teasing tone, but Lily could not deny the truth. Dat would be furious if he saw his daughter conversing with a boy she had been forbidden to even speak of. She considered making an escape to the nearest exit.

Aden relented and shook hands with Tyler, and then he fell silent and resumed his unnerving habit of staring at Lily. She saw the longing, the pain in his expression as well as another emotion too deep to define.

Aden might want to stare, but Lily had to look away. She bit her bottom lip and lowered her gaze to the ground. It was a gute thing Dat had admonished her never to talk to Aden again. She couldn't think of one word to say.

Tyler was not at a loss for topics. "Johnny Glick told me you painted his barn."

"I want to stay busy."

"Must have been a chilly job."

"I don't mind the cold."

There was no warning of his approach. Before she had time to stop him, Dat appeared, grabbed the cuff of Aden's sleeve, and yanked Aden away from them.

"David," Tyler said in protest, but Dat raised his hand toward Tyler as if stopping traffic.

Aden's face registered shock, but he let himself be led wherever Dat wanted to take him. Dat pulled Aden several feet from Lily, and even though Aden stood six inches taller, Dat waggled a finger in Aden's face as if scolding a ten-year-old. Dat spoke in hushed tones, and Lily couldn't hear what he said, but the rage etched into his face was plain enough. She longed for the floor to open beneath her and swallow her whole.

"Stop him, Tyler," she whispered, when she really wanted to scream.

Tyler's brow furrowed in worry as he stared at Aden and Dat. "I think . . . I think it will be okay."

Okay? An angry rebuke from her dat was not okay. Why didn't Tyler do something? He knew she didn't dare stand up to her dat. No matter what Aden had done, her dat should leave him alone. The shunning should be punishment enough.

Aden did not appear despondent or defeated or even defiant. His expression registered earnest humility as if Dat had a valuable lesson to teach him and Aden was eager to learn it.

Less than two minutes passed before Tyler decided to intervene. Aden's discomfort must have overcome Tyler's desire to impress her dat. "David," he said, loudly enough that the entire warehouse echoed, "I wanted to talk to Aden. Lily never said a word to him, and he didn't say a word to her."

David glowered at Aden. "I told him to stay away from my daughter. He shouldn't have come."

Tyler tried to placate Dat. "Aden didn't know we would be here."

Aden bowed his head. "Nae. David is right, Tyler. I could have steered clear of Lily if I had wanted to. I am sorry."

Without another word, Aden trudged out of the warehouse and didn't look back, not even to see Lily staring at him as if he were her last friend in the world.

Even though Dat dearly wanted Tyler to marry his daughter, he fixed him with a stern glare. "Tyler, I have all confidence that you will keep my daughter away from him from now on. If you want to be Aden Helmuth's friend, I can't stop you, but do not put my daughter in such a situation again."

"I won't," Tyler said, his voice laced with contrition, because ultimately, even though he sympathized with Aden, Lily knew that Tyler wanted Dat's approval. Tyler curled his lips into a sad smile. "I should get Lily home."

Dat placed a firm hand on Tyler's shoulder. "Denki for taking such good care of my daughter."

"I promise I always will, Lord willing."

Dat nodded in satisfaction. "Come for supper. Mary is making potato soup." And just like that, Tyler was forgiven, once again

Dat's favorite future son-in-law.

Lily's heart turned to ice. Both Aden and Tyler had managed to get her off the hook with her fater once again. She should have been grateful, when she only felt weak. Cowardly, helpless, and weak.

And something else occurred to her as she watched Aden slip out the door — she couldn't shake the feeling that she had lost something so dear to her that she would never be whole again.

CHAPTER TWENTY-THREE

Tyler wouldn't have brought her here if he had known that this was where Aden's dat proposed to Aden's mamm. Or that this was the place where Aden had sent a thrill of electricity pulsing through her veins when he'd taken her in his arms and hauled her out of the water. Tyler wouldn't have set foot here ever again if he knew that Lily couldn't think of Cobbler Pond without recalling a thousand splendid memories of Aden Helmuth.

Tyler stopped the buggy a few feet from the tree where she and Aden had picnicked their first time at the pond together.

"Do you need a blanket?" Tyler asked.

Lily zipped her coat and tucked the collar around her chin. "I will be warm enough."

Even though the air felt chilly, Tyler wiped beads of sweat from his upper lip with a shaky hand. "I probably could have picked somewhere warmer, but the pond is so beautiful at sunset," he said, his eyes darting from the pond to Lily as if she might disappear if he looked away for too long.

Lily's heart thudded like a sledgehammer against a slab of cement. She'd seen the proposal coming for days. Tyler had grown increasingly interested in the progress of Estee's wedding plans, and he'd been asking Lily leading questions like would she rather live in a dawdi house or a cottage of her own. The proposal was imminent, and they were both nervous wrecks.

She would tell him yes. Of course she would tell him yes, even though Aden still haunted her dreams. Tyler was a godly man and a fitting husband. She was grateful to him for loving her, and she enjoyed his company. Love would grow in time. Even while feeling disloyal to Tyler, Lily couldn't keep her gaze from skipping across the pond to the boulder where she had sat that day when Aden came to her rescue.

She felt guilty that her thoughts constantly strayed to Aden. Every dog immediately reminded her of dopey, lovable Pilot, who never demanded anything of her but affection. Frying pans and other cooking utensils made her think of Aden chasing bears. Balls and plates prompted thoughts of Frisbees, and seeing people's lips reminded her of

Aden's kisses. Unfortunately, just about everybody in the entire world had lips. The memories were inescapable. Lily wasn't even safe from litter along the road because she knew how unhappy Aden would be if he saw it.

Tyler held out his hand as if he were balancing a tray on it. Was that her invitation to take it? Lily frowned to herself. Why did things seem so unnatural with Tyler? Aden held her hand as if they were made to be together.

"I had to take the aerator back last week, but at least we had it as long as we did."

Lily took his hand and let him lead her down to the shore where they looked out over the pond. "Jah, it is beautiful."

She turned to Tyler and caught him staring at her. "Very beautiful," he said.

She looked away in embarrassment. Tyler didn't need to try so hard.

They ambled along the shore to the wooden jetty where Aden had performed a cartwheel and Pilot had knocked him into the water. A smile came unbidden to Lily's lips. She rarely saw Aden taken by surprise. Leave it to Pilot to take his self-assurance down a notch.

Tyler, who looked as if his collar might be too tight, tugged on her hand and motioned toward the jetty.

"Nae," Lily said. "We'll fall in."

Tyler immediately changed course. "Oh, jah. That's a little too scary for you."

Instead, he chose one of the benches surrounding the fire pit, and they sat down together. "This is a gute view of the sun setting behind the trees over there."

She didn't answer because she didn't want to delay things with idle chitchat. She'd rather get the whole thing over and go home to her warm house.

Tyler cleared his throat three times. "Lily, I'm sure you know what's on my mind. This might seem sudden, but I have been thinking of no one but you for a whole year. Ever since Rosie Schrock coupled us up for her wedding, you're the girl I've wanted to marry. You are kind and generous and a hard worker. And a girl that any parent could have confidence in. Someone a husband can have confidence in." Tyler swallowed hard and spoke breathlessly, as if he'd run a long race. "Lily, I'd be honored if you would marry me."

Dat would be a very happy man. "Yes, I will." Lily's lungs didn't seem to be taking in sufficient air and a lump the size of Jamal's truck formed in the pit of her stomach.

Tyler smiled and wrapped his arms around her. Was he going to kiss her? Or merely give her a hug? And with a smile like that, would she end up kissing his teeth like Estee and Floyd? She didn't want to find out. With Aden's kisses so fresh on her lips, she wasn't ready to be kissed by anybody else.

She turned her head to look over Tyler's shoulder so the possible kiss turned into a friendly hug. Love would grow. She didn't need to force anything.

Tyler didn't seem to notice her resistance. He released his grip and stood up. "Let's go ask your fater."

She let him pull her to her feet. Of course it was proper to ask the father of the bride, but in this case, completely unnecessary. Tyler already had Dat's permission. And blessing. And urging.

No potential bridegroom would ever have it so easy.

They were at Lily's house in less than twenty minutes. A man in love wasn't about to let the horse take a leisurely walk to Eichers' farm.

Dat had watched them drive off with a gleam in his eye, and he greeted them at the door when they returned. "Well, look who's back. I hope you had a pleasant drive." With a smile that would have put the

Cheshire cat to shame, he shook Tyler's hand as if they hadn't seen each other in ages, and he pinched Lily's cheek as if she were four years old.

Dat's eagerness delighted Tyler. His eyes lit up with happiness, and he and Dat wore a matching set of stupid grins. "Is there somewhere we can go to discuss an important matter?" Tyler said.

Dat thumbed his suspenders and laughed. "We can talk out here. I hold all my most important meetings on the porch."

Lily felt a little sheepish at Dat's eagerness. It wasn't as if he felt relief that someone had finally come along to take her off his hands. More likely, he rejoiced that she had not followed a certain young man into Babylon.

"I will go help Mama in the . . . Estee probably needs me to . . ." Lily's voice trailed off. Why did she feel the need to make up an excuse? All three of them knew exactly what went on, and neither Tyler nor Dat paid her any heed.

She slipped into the house and tripped down the hall to the kitchen where Mama and Estee frosted chocolate marshmallow cookies.

Mama glanced up from her work with a knife full of frosting in her fist. "So?" she said, her voice charged with anticipation.

"So."

Mama and Estee both halted what they were doing to watch her, as if her answer would stop time altogether.

"So, as long as Dat says yes, Tyler and I are getting married."

Mama squealed with glee, put down her knife, and pulled Lily in for an affectionate hug. "Oh, this is wonderful-gute news. I will have the two best sons-in-law in the world, and you will both live close. Not like Bertha King's daughter, whose husband carted her off to Ohio."

Ohio. Aden was from Ohio. Good thing she wasn't marrying Aden. She didn't want to be carted off to Ohio.

Estee took her turn hugging Lily, but her enthusiasm was tempered. The corners of her lips curled downward, and her expression darkened. "You are a fortunate girl. Dat adores Tyler."

Why did Estee have to look at her like that? A giant pickup truck already sat in the pit of her stomach.

Mama took both her hands and pulled Lily to sit at the table. "How did he ask you? Was it lovely?"

"It . . . it all happened so fast," Lily stuttered. One minute she was trying hard not to think of Aden Helmuth, and the next minute she was engaged.

Estee handed Lily a cookie from the cooling rack and sat down next to Mama. "We made your favorite."

"Do you know when Tyler wants to get married?" Mama asked.

"We're not sure yet. We could do it the same day as Estee and Floyd. It would be less work if we combined the two weddings."

"How practical and unselfish," Estee said.

Lily looked at Estee doubtfully. "Dat suggested the two weddings together. I don't want to take anything away from your special day, Estee. We could get married in January. I don't even mind if we wait a year."

"Wait a year?" Mama interjected. "What a thought! Tyler won't want to wait, and your dat won't think it wise. But I only have two daughters. I am happy to give each of you your own wedding day."

"I don't mind a double wedding," Estee said. "The real question is, what do you want, Lily?" She pinned Lily with a piercing gaze. "What do you really want?"

Lily had a suspicion that there was more to Estee's question than just what day she wanted to get married. She lowered her eyes and picked up her cookie. She wouldn't have to answer any of Estee's probing questions with her mouth full.

Because her stomach felt as if it were filled with lead, she took a small bite and pretended she couldn't talk anymore.

She heard the front door open and Dat and Tyler laughing as they came down the hall. Tyler never laughed. He must be ecstatic.

Mama leaped from the table and threw her arms around Tyler. "Congratulations. I am the happiest mother alive. First Estee, now Lily."

"And I am the happiest man alive," Tyler said. "I will take good care of your daughter."

Mama and Dat laughed with delight.

Estee stood and grabbed Lily's hand and pulled her toward the stairs. "We'll be right back. I need to talk to Lily."

Reluctantly, Lily let herself be led up the stairs to their room. She didn't know what Estee planned to say, but Estee always spoke her mind, and right now, Lily didn't want to know what she thought.

Estee practically slammed the door before she whirled around and glared at Lily. "I can't believe you would do this." She kept her voice to a whisper, sounding all the harsher.

Lily took a hearty bite of her cookie. "Do what?" she attempted to ask with her mouth full.

"I saw how interested Tyler was, even before that whole mess with Aden, but I never thought you would encourage him. I want to kick myself for not saying something sooner." Estee threw up her hands. "Oh, Lily, how could you marry someone just to please Dat?"

Lily swallowed the large piece of cookie in her mouth. "It's not for Dat."

Estee's voice ripened into bitterness, even as she whispered, "Oh, really? Then are you marrying Tyler for his money? Because you certainly don't love him."

Lily folded her arms and looked away as her eyes began to sting. "What do you know about it?"

"Plenty." Estee began pacing the room, no doubt gearing up for her most impressive lecture ever. "I know that when I think of Floyd, I feel giddy and giggly and I want to be with him every minute. I know that when we're not together, I think about him with every breath I take. I love him. Can you say the same about Tyler?"

Lily ignored the ache in her chest. "He adores me. And I am fond of him. He is a godly man who will be good to me and give

401

me a good home and never let harm come to me. Dat and I both see his value. Love doesn't hit everybody like a speeding freight train. I don't have to rush my feelings for him. They'll come naturally, over time."

"Does Tyler know you don't love him?"

"I'm fond of him."

Estee pursed her lips and narrowed her eyes. "Tyler doesn't deserve this, Lily."

Lily was mere seconds away from tears. The ache in her chest spread to fill her body, sure to overflow with the least provocation. She walked to the window and stared into the pasture as if all her answers were out with the cows.

Estee followed her to the window, grabbed her shoulders, and forced Lily to look at her. "You kissed Aden. You love Aden. He's your Floyd, Lily. Will you trade a lifetime of happiness for Dat's approval and a nice, predictable husband?"

Lily couldn't hold back the floodgates any longer. The tears ran down her cheeks as Estee led her to the bed and they sat. Estee enfolded her in an embrace and nudged Lily's head to rest on her shoulder.

"I'm so confused, Estee. Aden is fun and exciting, but Dat says my interest was only a fascination. The night of my arrest, I saw how far I had fallen, how my feelings for

Aden had stolen my good judgment."

"You loved Aden enough to muster a little courage. Just because it ended badly doesn't mean you made the wrong decision."

"How do I know if I loved him or was just caught up in the excitement of it? I'm too young to be sure of such things. Can you blame me for taking hold of Dat's advice? He's been through this. He saw where Zeke's choices led. Dat's wisdom is the only thing I can be sure of."

"You can be sure of Aden's love and God's love."

"But I can't be sure of my own heart. The only times I get into trouble are when I'm incautious."

"Was getting arrested bad enough to throw away the rest of your life?"

Lily broke into full-blown sobs. "Don't say that, Estee. I'm doing the right thing, and the right thing isn't always the easy thing."

Estee sighed in resignation and smoothed a piece of hair from Lily's face. "Don't cry. This should be one of the happiest days of your life."

"It is," Lily lied. Maybe Estee would leave her alone.

Estee gave Lily one last squeeze and stood up. "You should flip some water on your face before we go downstairs. Tyler will want to see how deliriously happy you are."

Lily nodded and sniffed away the remaining tears.

Estee nudged Lily up and smoothed the covers of her bed. "You won't hear another word about this from me. You've made your bed. Now you can lie in it."

Chapter Twenty-Four

"Pilot, leave the squirrels alone."

Pilot quit barking up the tree, skipped through the shallow water, and planted himself obediently at Aden's side, as if he wouldn't dream of chasing squirrels. "If you want me to take you places, you've got to quit harassing the wildlife."

Aden patted Pilot's head and tromped along the edge of the stream looking for litter to collect in his big black garbage bag. He and Pilot didn't really constitute a cleaning crew, but an hour of litter control was better than nothing. He'd been working until every muscle ached to get Mammi and Dawdi ready for winter and for the time when he would no longer be on Huckleberry Hill. He worried about them. They weren't getting any younger, and winter was bound to be harsh. Frost had formed on the blades of grass in their front yard every morning this week. Soon there would be snow.

After he'd pushed himself hard all morning chopping wood, loading coal, milking, and pitching hay, Mammi had warned Aden he would work himself to death and ordered him to go somewhere outdoorsy and relax.

She didn't realize that Aden couldn't relax. If he sat still for more than a few seconds, his mind would inevitably wander to Lily and render him completely and utterly miserable. To keep himself from crumbling to dust, he worked himself to a stub.

So when Mammi refused to let him tote another bucket of coal, he'd borrowed Dawdi's buggy, driven down the hill, and located the nearest streambed he hadn't picked up yet. He hadn't found a body of water yet that wasn't littered with trash, and enough garbage cluttered the roads to keep him busy for several lifetimes.

He shrugged the collar of his coat around his neck. October was halfway over. Aden had served four weeks of his shunning "sentence." It hadn't been too bad, really, except for the fact that he'd forever lost the girl he loved and wouldn't be able to breathe properly for the rest of his life. Tyler still had a little time to spare for Aden, even though he spent most of his energy courting Lily. Most people went about their lives, ignoring Aden altogether or gifting him with unbearable pity. But Aden wanted all of it — every sideways glance, every click of the tongue, every disapproving look they heaped on him. He wanted full and complete justice. He deserved no less.

He heard someone tromp through the tall grass that grew near the stream and looked to see Floyd making his way to the water. Pilot lost all sense of propriety and jumped on Floyd, barking and licking Floyd's face like an old friend.

"Aden," Floyd called while trying to fend off Pilot's attack. "How good to see you!"

Aden exploded into a smile. Floyd was one of the few people who still treated him as if nothing had happened. "What are you doing here? Pilot, get down."

Floyd finally pushed himself free of Pilot and pointed in the direction of the road. "I was riding my bike from work and saw your buggy. Is everything okay?"

"Of course. I had an hour to spare, so I decided to do something useful."

"I will help. Estee and I filled three trash bags with junk at the pond. My back never gets tired."

"Thanks," Aden said, more than a little grateful. Floyd didn't have to give him the time of day, let alone a helping hand. "There are more garbage bags by that rock."

Floyd found a bag and wasted no time getting to work. "I know what to do if I find any cans. I've been trained by the best."

"Any garbage company would be proud to hire you."

Floyd picked up a muddy plastic water bottle and stuffed it into his bag. "How is the shunning going?" His cheeks turned an odd shade of pink. "Oh, I mean, that sounded bad. I didn't mean it to sound like, 'Hey, Aden, nice weather we're having. How's the shunning going?' I know it's serious, and you probably feel horrible about it."

"It's okay, Floyd. I don't feel horrible about the shunning. I'm really enjoying the instruction classes from the bishop."

Floyd shrugged. "I guess the only place it's horrible is at Eichers' house. David refuses to let anyone speak of the incident, and the mention of your name is strictly forbidden. I honestly don't think Lily will ever recover from the humiliation of being arrested, but Estee and I talk about you all the time."

Aden's chest tightened painfully. Lily still suffered. He should go to the bishop and ask for six more weeks of shunning.

Floyd turned a darker shade of red. "I mean, not that we gossip about you behind your back. We would never do that. She says you broke your nose."

"Jah. The bruises are mostly gone."

"Estee says Lily is ruined forever. Going with you was probably the first brave thing she's ever done, but it ended in disaster, and now she'll never even dare to sing loud in church."

Aden let the regret wash over him. "I'm sorry it happened. I have always admired Lily for her devotion to the church and her family. I hope I haven't ruined that."

Floyd shook his head and backpedaled once again. "Well, I didn't mean she is ruined. Estee used that word. I think Lily's as good a girl as ever."

"Me too."

Aden didn't want to talk about Lily. Fresh thoughts of her only served to widen the hole in his heart until it yawned bigger than the Grand Canyon. He searched desperately for a change of subject.

"Have the McCann boys tried to take your bike lately?"

"Every day."

"What do you do?"

Floyd smiled as if he were the smartest person in the world. "Right before I unlock my lock, I spit on both handlebars."

Aden raised an eyebrow. "You . . . you spit?"

"Even the McCanns think that's disgusting. They won't touch my bike after that, and I can ride it home."

"Okay."

"I don't mind touching my own spit. So far it's worked out. Although yesterday I heard Randy say something to his brother about wet wipes, so I might have to come up with something even more distasteful than that."

Aden stifled a grin. "Why don't you talk to a supervisor at the factory? The McCanns are adults, for goodness sake."

"Oh, they'll get over it. Randy's mom is sick, and he needs someone to take his frustration out on."

Aden curled up one corner of his mouth and chuckled. "You're a good man, Floyd. Estee is blessed to have you."

Floyd's face lit up like a propane lantern. "Here is a wonderful-gute piece of news. Estee and I are published, as of yesterday."

Aden would have been overjoyed if he didn't ache for a wedding of his own with Estee's sister, but still, he rejoiced at the news. "Oy anyhow, I am happy to hear it. When is the wedding?"

"Three weeks, November fifth. Estee and

Lily are planning a double wedding."

Lily?

As if he'd had the wind knocked out of him, Aden dropped his garbage bag and stumbled to a dry spot at the edge of the stream. Feeling dizzy, he sat down hard in the dirt and buried his face in his hands as grief flooded his entire being.

"Aden, are you okay?"

Why did he feel as if he'd been blindsided by an angry bull, when he'd been expecting it for weeks? Maybe deep down he'd been hoping that Lily couldn't discard him as easily as a candy wrapper. She hadn't even waited for Aden to leave Huckleberry Hill before getting serious with Tyler Yoder. He felt the sting of rejection as if she had slapped him in the face.

"Aden?"

Why was Floyd still here when Aden's heart had stopped beating? He wiped his hand across his mouth and didn't even try to steady his voice. "I think I've worked myself a little too hard today."

Floyd walked over, took a piece of gum from his pocket, and handed it to Aden. Aden didn't want to take it. He knew where Floyd's hands had been — specifically, gripping the handlebars of his bike. "Gum will help if it's vertigo," Floyd said. "It clears out your inner ear."

Aden took the gum and slipped it into his pocket. "Denki. I'm feeling better now."

Floyd sat next to Aden. "It's pretty cold out here. You might have to quit the rest of your cleanup projects until spring. You'll catch pneumonia or something."

Aden tried to breathe normally even though the pain would not release him. "So, Lily is published too?"

Floyd's face colored once again. "I shouldn't have told you that. I mean, jah, they are planning a double wedding, but Lily and Tyler are not going to announce it until Sunday. Don't tell anyone. Lily's dat won't be happy if I ruin the surprise."

"I'll try to keep it to myself."

Floyd smiled gratefully. "Denki, Aden. Sometimes my mouth says things before my brain catches up."

Aden thought he might drown with grief. "I'm very happy for all of you."

"Estee's dat is happy too. He whistles all the time and can't stop talking about his blessings." The corners of his lips quirked upward. "Tyler is going to be the favorite son-in-law. David praises Tyler all the time, as if Lily needs convincing of something she already knows."

"David knows what a gute husband you'll

be, Floyd."

Floyd glanced at Aden out of the corner of his eye. "I'm okay with it, really. Tyler has that dairy and all. I just work at the RV factory. Nothing special."

"You're special to Estee. That's more important than what her dat thinks."

"I guess so."

Floyd stood and offered Aden a hand. "Go home and eat some supper. You don't look so good. A thick piece of red meat will put some iron in your blood. You're pale as a sheet. Oh, no. You don't eat meat, do you? Sorry if that offended you."

"The mention of meat does not offend me."

Floyd furrowed his brow. "I don't care what you say. The bann is taking its toll on you. You've looked absolutely miserable since they shunned you."

"Isn't that the point?"

"They want you to repent, but I don't think misery helps anybody. I mean, not that you look terrible, like death walking around or anything. I didn't mean to say that. In fact, you look fine."

Floyd carried both garbage bags to Aden's buggy. "You'll come to the wedding, of course. We'll be sure to couple you up with the prettiest girl we can think of. How about

Erla Glick?"

Aden shrugged before climbing into the buggy.

He would not be attending the Eicher wedding. David Eicher need not worry about Aden harassing his family. He would make himself invisible to them. They would all like it better that way.

CHAPTER TWENTY-FIVE

"I've had just about enough of David Eicher," Mammi said as she dropped the letter into her lap.

Aden stood at the sink up to his elbows in dishwater. He had no idea what Mammi meant by that, and he didn't want to. The Eichers were none of his concern anymore. Or rather, he wished they were none of his concern. He thought about one particular Eicher every minute of every day.

"We ain't seen hide nor hair of David for a month, Banannie. How could you have enough of him?"

"My ears are still ringing from the set-down he gave us. Just because we're old doesn't mean we're deaf."

Would Aden ever remember that night without the stabbing pang of guilt? Even his grandparents had suffered the consequences. He scrubbed Mammi's frying pan vigorously.

The frying pan. He couldn't even do dishes without being reminded of Lily.

"I'm sorry about that, Mammi. I wish I would have been here so he could have yelled at me instead of you."

Mammi waved off his apology. "David Eicher can howl like the wind for all I care. I'm like the mountain. He can't budge me."

In the past four weeks, Aden hadn't ever been as grateful to anybody as he had been to his grandparents. They proved fiercely loyal, defending him against gossipy neighbors, cooking vegetarian meals, and saying uncomplimentary things about David Eicher whenever Aden felt especially blue. They even insisted on taking meals in the living room on the sofa so Aden didn't have to eat alone. That was their way around the no-eating-together-at-the-table rule.

Dawdi put down his paper, took off his glasses, and wiped them with his handkerchief. "Did David write you a letter, Annie?"

Mammi picked up the note in her lap and held it up for Dawdi to see. His glasses were off so he didn't see much. "I wrote a letter to Lily, and David replied to it. I expect he didn't even let her read it. I don't care if he has a shiny new mailbox. That doesn't give him the right to open other people's mail."

416

Aden's heart sank. "You wrote Lily a letter?"

Mammi couldn't face the painful truth. She still had her heart set on Lily for Aden's future companion in life. He'd given up explaining to her how hopeless it was.

Mammi never gave up hope.

Lily would probably be married with three babies before Mammi admitted defeat.

"We've got lots of huckleberry jam to sell this year for Christmas. I invited Lily to help me with the labels. David thinks we're some heathen group of people up here. He ain't seen a problem yet that he didn't overreact to."

Aden dried the shiny clean frying pan. "It's my fault, Mammi. When I'm gone, things will get better."

"Now, dear, don't you apologize for David Eicher's bad temper. And if that's why you want to go back to Ohio, there ain't no cause for it. David will come around when you and Lily marry."

"But, Banannie, do you really want to afflict Aden with such a father-in-law?"

"David Eicher ain't the worst I've seen. He'll soften when he sees the cover I knitted for his new mailbox."

Aden pulled the drain stopper from the sink and wiped his hands on the nearest

417

towel. He sat on the sofa next to Mammi's rocking chair. "Mammi, I want to tell you a secret, but you mustn't tell anyone until Sunday. Lily is engaged to Tyler Yoder."

Mammi looked genuinely puzzled. "What's she doing that for when she's going to marry you?"

Aden raked his fingers through his hair. Did he really believe this would do any good? "She's not going to marry me, Mammi." He took her hands in his and pinned her with a serious look. "Matching us up was a good idea, but some things don't work out." He felt horrible just saying the words.

Dawdi smiled sympathetically. "If you weren't leaving, we could couple you with Erla Glick. She's a nice little thing."

Mammi's jaw dropped to the floor and her eyes flamed with indignation. "Felty, how could you say such a thing? Aden is meant for Lily and no one else. I'm saving Erla Glick for somebody else."

"Who?"

Mammi folded her arms. "I'm not telling. I can only work on one match at a time. I leave the miracles to God."

Aden looked to Dawdi for help, but Dawdi shrugged his shoulders and looked up as if the ceiling held all the answers. He obviously knew from sixty years of experience not to argue with Mammi.

"Margaret Schrock is having a quilting bee at her house next week. Lily is bound to be there since she and Treva are such good friends. I think I'll invite myself."

Aden shook his head in resignation. No use trying to convince Mammi. Mammi and Dawdi were the only people in Bonduel who loved him. He wouldn't alienate them just because Mammi held on to a fantasy.

He would have liked to hold on to that fantasy himself.

"Do you have to go back to Ohio so soon?" Dawdi asked. "If you stay until January, you can help us collect sap from the sugar maples."

"I'm sorry, Dawdi, but I'm leaving in three weeks." Three days after they lifted the bann and the day of Lily's wedding. "But I've chopped enough wood to last through spring, and the coal is in the basement, and the potato cellar is full of potatoes and pumpkins. Moses will be here once a week too, and some of the other cousins."

"You've been busy as a bee," Dawdi said. "And that's just the work you done on our farm. You've been buzzing about doing all sorts of good works."

"Everybody went to the barn raising,

419

Dawdi."

"But not everybody helped with Enos Kanagy's fence."

Mammi patted his arm. "Then you'd better get busy with Lily. You don't have time to lollygag."

Aden gave Mammi his most affectionate smile even as he cried inside. His time for lollygagging had completely run out.

Treva watched as Lily's needle bobbed up and down through the fabric, securing the top of the quilt to the bottom with tiny, even stitches. Treva seldom attempted a stitch. She had pricked a finger or tangled her thread often enough that quilting held no pleasure for her. Instead, she contented herself sitting next to Lily, talking about kittens and thunderstorms while Lily quilted.

Treva could talk about kittens for hours. She loved animals, especially piglets, puppies, and kittens. She and Aden had that in common.

Lily sighed. If she had a penny for every time Aden crossed her mind during the day, she'd be a wealthy girl.

She didn't love Tyler — that much she could freely admit to herself. She'd practically confessed that fact to Estee the night she got engaged. But couldn't she at least turn her thoughts to her future groom once in a while? Tyler would be concerned at how little she thought of him. Would he cancel the wedding if he knew that she didn't return his affection? Why couldn't she muster more tenderness? Tyler was everything any girl in her right mind could want.

"You bleeding," Treva said.

Lily examined the small triangle of fabric she had been working on. A spot of blood marred the clean white shape. "Oh, dear. I didn't even notice."

Always prepared, Treva's mother Margaret handed Lily a bandage and a damp cloth. "It's not a true quilt unless there is a little blood on it."

"That's right," said Millie Burkholder, who sat opposite Lily and Treva. "Even with a thimble, there will always be a little blood."

Lily dabbed at the bloodstain with the damp cloth until it disappeared. "Look, Treva. All better."

Treva smiled and leaned her head on Lily's shoulder.

Someone knocked at the door and opened it before anyone had a chance to answer it. Lily's heart thumped on her rib cage as Anna Helmuth glided into the room.

The women sitting around the quilt

greeted Anna as if she were their long-lost cousin they hadn't seen in ages.

"Anna," Margaret said, "how nice of you to come such a long way for our quilting bee."

Anna's eyes twinkled and her cheeks, pinched by the cold outside, glowed rosy red. "I wouldn't have missed it for the world. My grandson Aden drove me over. I don't know what we'd do without him."

Lily's heartbeat pounded in her ears. Aden was outside in Anna's buggy, almost close enough to touch. Holding her breath, she sat with her needle halfway through the fabric and didn't move a muscle. If she sat perfectly still, the overwhelming longing in her chest was sure to pass.

Anna reached in her bag and handed Margaret a bottle of huckleberry jam. "This is for you. Lily helped me put it up."

"Denki," Margaret said. "Lily said you had a bumper crop this year."

"Lily and Aden were such a help. We never could have done it on our own."

Lily couldn't be comfortable. Every mention of Aden's name felt like a prick at her heart.

Anna plunged her hand into her bag again and retrieved a thimble. She deposited the bag in a corner, hung her coat on the stand,

and made a beeline for Lily's side of the quilt. Grinning with her entire face, Anna pulled a chair next to Lily and threaded a needle. "Oh, my, Lily dear. How we have missed you! Aden is so mopey, I think he's shrunk three inches from all the slouching."

"I'm . . . I've missed you too."

"Tell me about your wedding plans. Will you be visiting faraway relatives on your honeymoon trip?"

"We are going to La Crosse and Cashton."

"Are you excited?"

"Um, very excited."

"I saw Estee at the market. I expected her to float off the ground. She was like to burst with happiness."

In Lily's mind, Estee behaved like a true bride. She talked of nothing but Floyd and wedding plans. She'd taken way too much time making her dress because she'd redesigned and measured and picked until she felt satisfied. The family had eaten celery stuffing every night for a week because Estee wanted to get the recipe just right before the wedding.

Anna cut herself a length of thread and lowered her voice. "Estee doesn't stop smiling, but your frown is better suited to a funeral. Are you that unhappy?"

"I didn't realize I was frowning."

Anna started working on a burgundy square. "Do you know why the Amish don't arrange marriages?"

Lily jabbed the needle into the quilt. "Nae, I don't."

"Neither do I, but whoever decided against arranged marriages was very wise. Marriage is hard work. If you're not crazy in love with the boy before the wedding, afterward can be rough. I remember a spat Felty and I had three weeks after our wedding day. I was so angry, I refused to even look at him. He gave me a big hug and said, 'Annie, I'm mad as a hornet right now, but I love you, and that's all we got.' I hugged him back after that."

Lily couldn't speak. How did Anna know so much?

Lily thought she might disintegrate into a pile of dust with all the confusion swirling about her head. Could she marry Tyler when she didn't love him? Was she making the biggest mistake of her life? Her vision blurred, and she gave up on her needle altogether.

Anna lowered her voice further so no one but Lily could hear. "I know that Tyler is your dat's choice. Such a nice young man from a gute family, but Lily, if he isn't your choice, you won't be truly happy."

Treva patted Lily's hand. "She love Ayen."
An attack from both sides.

Anna's face lit up. "That's right, Treva," she whispered. "She loves Aden. But how long is she going to wait before she sets everything to rights?"

Anna's gaze pierced Lily's skull and rendered her speechless. Lily lowered her eyes to the quilt and tried to stitch in a straight line.

Anna slid her arm around Lily and gave her an affectionate squeeze. "Oh, Lily. You are a wonderful-gute girl. I know why Aden loves you so much." She stabbed her needle through the fabric and left it there. Rising to her feet, she said, "Margaret, this has been a lovely afternoon."

Margaret raised an eyebrow. "You're going?"

"Aden is waiting outside, and I must get home to fix Felty his supper. Please invite me again, and I promise to stay longer."

Lily felt as if she balanced on a cliff and one movement would send her tumbling to the rocky bottom. She thought of Aden, just outside, and became as stiff as a statue.

"Oh, okay," Margaret stuttered. "It was kind of you to come."

Anna shrugged off the compliment and shrugged on her coat. "My pleasure. I always enjoy seeing friends. Good-bye, Lily. I hope we'll see you very soon. Huckleberry Hill is not as sweet without you."

Anna blew out the door like a whirlwind, leaving all the quilters in her wake.

Lily stiffly fingered the thread Anna had left behind. Anna had come to the bee to make three stitches in the quilt and an impression on Lily.

She had accomplished both tasks.

Aden pressed the buttons on Moses's phone. Jamal answered in one ring.

"Hello?"

"Jamal, I got your message. What's the emergency?"

"The emergency is that you need to get a phone immediately, Aden. This primitive way of getting in touch with you is starting to get on my nerves."

"It doesn't seem that primitive to me."

Jamal huffed loudly. Aden could practically see his frustration over the phone. "Oh yeah? I need to talk to you, so I spend an hour trying to track down the number for your cousin's cheese factory. Then I call your cousin, who says he'll give you the message. Then I wait two days for you to return my call. You're still living in the nineteenth century. It drives me crazy."

"What's the emergency?"

"Trout Lake is my emergency. They're dumping stuff there again, and I've got proof. Amish farms surround that whole area. I need someone to testify. I need someone to picket the company, and you're my guy. I want you to put a face on the suffering of all the Amish people who don't have a voice in this fight. You've always generated a lot of sympathy. We can use you to shut them down."

Aden rubbed the back of his neck and prepared himself for the headache that was sure to come. "Jamal, I can't."

"Bring Lily along if you want."

"She's getting married next week." The words almost choked him.

"You're getting married? Congrats, man."

"She's not marrying me."

Silence on the other end. "Was it because of the puppy mill thing? None of us meant for it to go south like that."

"It's not because of the puppy mill, Jamal. She found a better man."

Jamal grunted.

"I'm taking a bus back to Ohio next week," Aden said.

"That's perfect. Just tell me when you'll be here, and I'll make sure the newspapers show up."

Aden took a deep breath and thought about all the people and wildlife affected by the dirty lake. He thought about what he wanted and about what God would want. Who would stop those polluters if not him?

Be still and know that I am God.

"Jamal, this is a great cause. My heart will be there with you every step of the way. But I won't help you."

More silence. Aden didn't usually possess the ability to shut Jamal up. "You're still mad at me."

"No, I'm not mad at you. It's my own fault Lily hates me." Aden was surprised that he was able to say it without his voice cracking. "But I've pledged my life to God and this is His job, not mine."

"But it's for the lake and your people."

"You can do this, Jamal. Nobody can move a group of ordinary citizens to action like you can. This is not my fight. I'm following Gelassenheit."

"I didn't sneeze."

"Gelassenheit — the yielding to a higher authority. I'm yielding my life to God."

"How long does this Gelassenheit thing last?"

"Forever."

Jamal's voice lost its energy. "So, that's it?"

"That's it."

"The guys will be really disappointed."

Aden smiled weakly. "They'll be okay."

"Maybe we'll cross paths when you come back to Ohio."

"I'd like that."

"I guess I'll go plan another strategy for the lake." Jamal sighed. "And, Aden?"

"Jah?"

"I'm real sorry about what happened with Lily."

"Me too."

If only that were enough to bring Lily back.

CHAPTER TWENTY-SIX

"Who would have thought we'd see a storm like this the day before the wedding?" Estee said. "The fourth of November. Who would have guessed? I hope all the relatives get into town okay."

"Most of the guests have already arrived, and the snow is supposed to stop later tonight," Lily said.

The snow fell in chunky tufts of cotton, heavy and thick, as Lily and Estee trudged up the country road in their snow boots.

Estee took Lily's arm as they crossed the slushy road. "Floyd's dat told me there would be snow. His knees ache right before a big storm." Estee giggled. "Floyd says it's just in time for my wedding present. I have a suspicion he's gone and bought the sleigh yet."

Lily wouldn't spoil the surprise. Floyd's new sleigh sat in the barn tucked neatly behind a wall of hay bales under a canvas tarp.

Estee's eyes twinkled with a thousand different delights. "Won't it be charming to ride off to our honeymoon visits in a sleigh? I'll have to remember to pack plenty of blankets because Floyd will forget." She squeezed Lily's arm. "He can remember my favorite kind of chocolate and the date of our first kiss, but he forgets to pack a lunch for work. Or if he remembers to pack a lunch, he forgets to eat it. Oh, Lily, he's so adorable. He's going to make the best father."

Less than twenty-four hours until the wedding. The last three weeks had flown away from her even though she had tried to hold fast to her precious time. She felt as if she were marching to her own execution rather than her nuptial day.

Nothing was right. None of this was right even though Dat couldn't stop smiling. The absurdity of her situation had become more apparent to Lily every day as she prepared for an event that held no joy for her. She had dutifully sewn herself a new dress and packed for her honeymoon trip and helped Tyler ready the dawdi house, but nothing was right.

She hadn't slept well for days. Since her

talk with Anna, the tension and anxiety had grown as one question ran through her head constantly: Should she go through with the wedding?

But since her engagement, she'd had the overwhelming feeling that it was too late to turn back.

Lily shook her head and tried to reassure herself before despair flattened her. Tyler was such a gute man. How could she not want to marry Tyler? Had she never heard of cold feet before? Every bride had doubts right before her wedding. Every bride panicked and wanted to run away at some point. Every bride had another boy who invaded her thoughts when she should be thinking about her groom.

"Floyd won't even let me see what he's done to the house. I bet he's put up curtains."

Well, every bride but Estee. She was so enamored with Floyd that they might as well be the only two people in the whole world.

With her arm still hooked with Lily's, Estee studied Lily's face. "I'm talking too much again. Tell me about your honeymoon plans. Are you going to La Crosse?"

"Jah. Tyler has an uncle there."

Estee didn't seem to expect any more

chitchat. They walked along the road in silence as white flakes continued to blanket the earth. Already the snow piled ankle-deep.

"Denki for coming to Mrs. Deforest's with me. I wanted to say good-bye one last time before she goes to that care center."

"Will she be to the wedding?"

"No. She leaves tomorrow morning, and her son refuses to delay her trip even a few more hours."

Mrs. Deforest lived on a good piece of land in Bonduel not twenty minutes from Lily's house. An ornamental iron fence with matching mailbox marked the south border of her property. Brown with rust, the fence stood almost four feet tall, and underneath the layer of new snow, yellow grass and dead leaves collected at the base of each post. Mrs. Deforest was too old to care for her property, and her son had no interest in upkeep.

A jumbo "For Sale" sign accosted Lily and Estee before they came in sight of the house. "What a shame," Estee said. "It's a nice little place. Mrs. Deforest used to plant geraniums in the front."

Some nice neighbor was shoveling Mrs. Deforest's sidewalk. Lily turned her face to the sky. They'd finish at one end and have to start again. The snow made down hard.

Lily saw a movement out of the corner of her eye and turned to see Pilot loping toward her.

A bolt of lightning couldn't have hit her more forcefully. She stumbled backward. Aden Helmuth was the neighbor shoveling Mrs. Deforest's sidewalk.

She couldn't breathe. Someone had sucked all the oxygen out of the surrounding air.

Estee tightened her grip on Lily's arm and plunged ahead before Lily had a chance to back away.

Pilot stopped at the edge of Mrs. Deforest's property and ventured no closer. He tilted his head and examined Lily as if she were a stranger and then took two steps back and whined pathetically.

She should have been pleased. At least that dog wouldn't get snow all over her dress.

"Aden," Estee called, with a cheerful lilt to her voice that only heightened Lily's panic.

Still hunkered over his shovel, Aden glanced their way and froze. Lily recognized a mixture of pain and embarrassment in his eyes as he slowly straightened to his full height. He was so tall. And so handsome.

Her gaze involuntarily flew to his lips, and she couldn't fight back the memory of his tender kisses or the way her heart raced when he enfolded her in his arms.

Why did she react like this? She'd seen him at gmay three times since the puppy mill disaster, but because of the bann, he always sat in front and stole away as soon as church ended.

Her heart was like to pound out of her chest. Was this still a childish fascination or something else?

They seemed to be the only two people in the world as Estee pulled Lily forward. His green eyes pierced hers as if he wanted to read her thoughts.

The connection broke when Estee swung open the creaky gate, and it screeched like a barn owl.

Aden held up a hand. "Wait. It's slippery."

After propping his shovel in the snow, he gingerly made his way down the sidewalk, put himself between them, and offered his arms. "You don't want to break your arm the day before your wedding," he said. He stared directly at Estee and ignored Lily completely.

Estee glanced at Lily and immediately latched onto Aden. "Denki. I didn't expect a snowstorm in early November."

Lily froze in confusion. She wanted to take Aden's arm more than she'd ever wanted anything in her entire life, but if she did, she might revive feelings she couldn't control.

Aden nodded at Estee and then lowered his gaze to the ground. "I am forbidden to speak to Lily or even be near her, but I think your fater would forgive me this one time." His voice trembled with emotion. "Maybe your dat will overlook my transgression since I am no longer under the bann."

Three days ago, Aden had given a kneeling confession and been reinstated into full fellowship, or so Estee had reported. Lily hadn't been there to witness it herself. She and Dat had agreed that it was a gute day to stay away from church.

"Lily?" Estee prompted.

Aden still averted his eyes as if to look at her might turn him to stone.

Some part of her registered that she would be very rude if she didn't take his offered arm, even if Dat were angry about it. She slipped her arm through his and couldn't help but feel the hard muscles beneath his coat. Of course he had strength. He'd lifted her from the water once as if she weighed no more than a feather.

They stepped carefully to the porch, with

Lily feeling increasingly grateful for Aden's arm. It would be too easy to slip on the icy sidewalk.

"I haven't salted it yet," Aden said apologetically, as if the falling snow and dangerous ice were somehow his fault.

He had cleared the steps. Lily grabbed the railing and pulled herself to the safety of the porch. Aden didn't let go until he made certain she and Estee were secure. "It will be salted by the time you come out," he assured them.

Lily dared a look into his face. He turned his head and studied the cracks in the sidewalk. She couldn't find her voice, even to thank him.

Thank goodness for Estee. "Denki, Aden. I'll make sure they save you a large helping of carrot pudding at our wedding. It always gets eaten first."

"I won't be to the wedding," Aden said. "I am going back to Sugarcreek tomorrow morning, Lord willing."

Lily should have been relieved. Of course she didn't want Aden at her wedding. Dat would not want him there either. But the disappointment almost choked her. Aden was leaving Huckleberry Hill? What about his grandparents? Did he care nothing for their well-being?

Estee frowned. "I wish you would stay. Floyd thinks you are the smartest man alive. And the roadsides have never been so clean."

"You'd better get inside and warm up," Aden said. "You don't want frostbite for the wedding."

Without a proper good-bye, he disappeared around the corner of the house with Pilot following close behind. At least that dog wouldn't be bothering Lily anymore. Without Pilot licking her all the time, her hand sanitizer supply would be good for months.

Mrs. Deforest answered the door gripping her walker with one hand. Her arms were thin and covered with age spots, and her face was a map of wrinkles against her salt-and-pepper gray hair. Lily hadn't seen her in over two years. She had aged significantly.

"Well, here's Estee come to see me off," she said in her gravelly voice, made rough from years of smoking. "It's 'bout time you come. That no-good son of mine says we're leaving tomorrow no matter how many good-byes ain't been said yet."

Estee had worked for Mrs. Deforest for almost five years. She didn't mind the old lady's cantankerous moods. Lily found her abrupt, but Estee understood her and said

Mrs. Deforest didn't mean harm to anybody.

She invited them in and glanced out the screen door. "I told him he didn't need to clear the sidewalk. I ain't going nowhere today. But he said there might be visitors."

Lily had to ask. "How . . . how do you know Aden Helmuth?"

Mrs. Deforest waved off Estee's assistance and motioned to the sofa. Estee and Lily sat and watched as Mrs. Deforest hobbled to her recliner and sat down with a grunt. "I'm taking the chair with me. I told Barnard I won't go without my chair. They feed you three meals a day and a snack." She shook her finger at Estee. "Though that hospital food won't be near as good as homemade Amish cooking. I might starve."

Maybe Mrs. Deforest hadn't heard the question or perhaps she'd forgotten it already. Lily didn't dare ask again. Besides, it was none of her business whose sidewalks Aden wanted to shovel.

A look of confusion crossed Mrs. Deforest's face before she nodded to herself. "Estee, go in that front bedroom and get your wedding present. It's on the dresser."

Estee obediently walked into the other room and came back with a gift wrapped in shiny white paper and tied with a baby blue

439

ribbon. "Thank you, Mrs. Deforest. You didn't have to get me a present."

"Well, I sure did. You've been with me for how many years, Estee?"

"Five."

Mrs. Deforest waved her hand in the air. "All this is going. Barnard sold it to an estate auction. Except my chair. And my horse. I told the young man to take my horse."

Now she had Lily's attention. "Aden?"

"I thought he was a hoodlum come to rob me. My imagination runs wild at night sometimes. He came to my door and said he noticed my skinny horse. Asked if he could feed her for me."

"Oh, that's nice," Estee said.

Mrs. Deforest leaned forward and lowered her voice. "His people think he's wicked for taking care of the animals, so I'm not to tell anybody. And don't you tell neither."

"Of course not," Estee said. "I don't think he's wicked."

Lily sat like a statue and barely heard another word as Estee and Mrs. Deforest talked about care centers and bad hospital food and Barnard Deforest, who wanted to sell the property and move to Miami.

Surely the Plain people didn't think Aden was wicked for taking care of animals or for cleaning up the pond so birds would have a place to nest, did they? They accepted Aden from the very first. They liked him and even sympathized with his tree story.

Lily's heart felt like a jagged stone. The community didn't have a problem with Aden's schemes. Aden had been shunned because her dat demanded it. His precious daughter, who'd rarely done a bad thing in her life, had been terrified and humiliated, and Aden had to pay.

". . . I hope your feelings aren't hurt, Lily," Mrs. Deforest said, as if she didn't care about Lily's feeling at all. "We're not that close, and you'll get plenty of other presents."

Lily tried to follow the thread of the conversation. Her mind barely registered what Mrs. Deforest had said. "Ach, no. Estee is the one who has taken care of you."

"Estee says you are quite anxious about leaving home. Some girls have trouble adjusting to marriage. I hope you're not one of them. A husband needs a sturdy wife, not a girl who whines like a kitten because she misses her mommy."

Estee didn't even glance at Lily. "Lily is more likely to miss our dat. They are very close."

"At least you Amish don't have phones.

You can't call your dat every day and complain about your husband."

"I won't ever complain about Floyd," Estee said. "He is nearly perfect."

Mrs. Deforest got a twinkle in her eye. "Any fool can see you're befuddled. I remember those days. I don't know what I ate for breakfast this morning, but I can clearly recall my wedding day. I tried on my wedding dress every day for a month before the wedding. Merlin wore his Navy uniform. When I walked down the aisle, he looked so handsome I thought I would burst." She sighed. "Those were happy days."

The space behind Lily's eyes throbbed with a dull ache. She didn't feel happy. She wasn't even content.

Estee stood. "We've got to be going, Mrs. Deforest. There is still lots and lots of celery to wash."

Mrs. Deforest made a great effort of standing up. "You'll write to me?"

"Of course."

"That's one thing I like about the Amish. Nobody writes an old-fashioned letter anymore. Barnard wants me to use email, but I don't even know how to turn on the computer."

"I will write you as often as you write me back," Estee said. She nodded to Lily, who

442

already had her coat and gloves on.

Another inch of new snow blanketed the sidewalk. Aden was nowhere to be seen. They walked carefully to the road where they could travel more easily by digging their boots into the snow.

With the wedding present tucked under her arm, Estee turned and looked at the house one last time. "Even though you don't approve, I'm glad Aden is taking Blossom. I feared her son would send that poor horse to the glue factory."

Lily stopped walking and stared at Estee. "What makes you think I don't approve? I care about the animals too."

"But you think he's wicked for barging in on other people's lives."

Lily was at a complete loss for words. "I . . . I don't think he's wicked."

Estee unleashed a laugh tinged with bitterness. "You could have fooled me. And everyone else in the district. You treat Aden like he is dirt under your fingernails."

"No, I don't. I shunned him like everybody else did."

Estee shoved her hand in her pocket and sighed. "I apologize. I promised I'd never mention Aden again. You better go home and tell Dat I spoke Aden's name. And while you're at it, if you have the guts, be sure to tell Dat that we saw Aden today and that I was friendly. Tell Dat how you did your best to ignore Aden even when he helped us across the ice. He won't be mad at you because nothing is ever your fault."

A tear slipped down Lily's cheek, and she hid it by wiping it away as if she were brushing an errant lock of hair from her face. "Estee, don't be mad."

Estee turned around. "I'm taking the long way home. Tell Mama I'll finish washing the celery when I get back."

Lily couldn't move. She wanted to brush off Estee's scolding but froze at the thought that she deserved every word Estee had thrown at her.

She remembered that horrible night, the look on Aden's face, and she cried out in pain as the truth hit her. Her sobs floated into the air and were caught by the drifting snow.

She wanted to crawl into a deep, black hole and never resurface. She had been cruel to Aden because she had been unable to see past her own humiliation, and he had felt so guilty about what had happened that he welcomed the shunning. He thought he deserved it. Tyler had said as much. He wanted to punish himself because of her suffering.

He knew how the arrest had traumatized her, and he hated himself for it.

Ashamed and embarrassed, she had laid the blame on the one person who would not fight back. To preserve her wounded pride and her father's affections, she had thrown Aden to the wolves.

What a fool she had been. Courage meant not knowing how things were going to turn out and taking the risk anyway, because the risk was worth the bad ending.

Aden thought she despised him, but who could dislike noble, brave, lovable Aden? He risked his life for dogs and didn't mind getting arrested to save horses and puppies. He had braided her hair and chained himself to a tree. He hated steel traps and bore a beautiful scar on his eyebrow.

And she loved him.

The feeling grew in her heart like a sunrise on a clear wintery day. She loved Aden Helmuth to her very bones.

But Dat had talked her out of loving him. He'd set his back against Aden and convinced Lily to do the same. She had obeyed him because she always obeyed him.

Reeling from the realization, Lily put one foot in front of the other in the direction of home.

This wasn't Dat's fault. She had talked

herself away from Aden because Dat had always been safe. She feared that if she didn't have his approval, she wouldn't have anything. Tears blurred her eyes until she could barely see where she stepped. She couldn't begin to fix the mess she'd created.

She didn't love Tyler, but since the day she'd talked to Anna, she'd been too terrified to admit that she couldn't marry him. Well, now she said it out loud. "I can't marry Tyler Yoder."

I want to marry for love.

The desire grew inside her until she felt like shouting.

I want to marry for love!

She wanted to get breathless when her husband walked through the door in the evening. She wanted his kisses to make her feel like she was flying. She wanted her husband to rock her babies and pray with her family. She wanted to believe the man she married was perfection before learning to love him for all his faults.

She wanted to marry for love. No other reason was good enough.

God had been trying to send her a message, and she finally found the courage to listen. How else could she explain Anna's strange quilting visit, Estee's lectures, or

Mrs. Deforest's wedding stories? She had felt God tugging at her for weeks.

She must cancel the wedding.

The idea made her ill.

What would all the relatives say? Everyone would be shocked. *She should have sorted out her feelings weeks ago,* they would say. Or *how cruel of her to string Tyler Yoder along like that.*

What about Tyler? His heart would be broken like glass against the pavement. She'd promised him things. He'd call her a liar.

Dat would invoke the memory of Onkel Zeke, ask her if she'd learned nothing from his mistakes. Then, when he saw he couldn't dissuade her, he'd rant and yell and kick her out of the house, refusing to speak to her ever again, just as he had done with Aden.

Aden.

She didn't care about anything else anymore.

Let Dat banish her from her own home. Let the people of the community, and especially Tyler, despise her forever. She would endure any embarrassment, any anger, any rejection for the chance of being with Aden.

If she didn't have Aden, she didn't have

anything.

Even as fear paralyzed her, Lily knew what she must do. She closed her eyes, thought of the man she couldn't live without, and mustered the courage for the most important undertaking of her life.

Aden ran as hard and as fast as he could through the unforgiving snow in no direction in particular. At first Pilot thought he was playing tag and loped merrily beside Aden with his tongue lolling to one side of his mouth.

But Aden soon outran even Pilot. He ran until his throat cried out in thirst and his legs burned with agonizing heat. He ran until he had no strength to stand. It didn't work. He could not run far enough to escape his love for Lily.

It made no sense to love her. She despised him. She was about to marry a better man than Aden. But that did nothing to subdue the ache that filled his soul at the thought of losing her.

Dawdi said to let God do His job. Aden had been trying to let go of what he couldn't control and go quietly about living a Christian life, trying to bless others but not to force them. He certainly couldn't force Lily to love him, no matter how badly he longed for her.

So why had God abandoned him?

The answer came as he stumbled to an ancient tree standing in the middle of a stranger's pasture. It wasn't God's job to see that Aden felt perfectly happy all the time. Everyone couldn't be happy all the time. If Aden were happy right now, it was a good guess that Lily's dat would be miserable.

One thing is needful. Choose that good part.

Rather, it was God's job to love His children. It was Aden's job to let that love carry him through the hard times as well as the good times.

For I am persuaded, that neither death, nor life, nor angels, nor principalities, nor powers, nor things present, nor things to come, nor height, nor depth, nor any other creature, shall separate us from the love of God, which is in Christ Jesus our Lord.

Well, he was certainly in the depths. Would God carry him through it?

Unable to support his legs any longer, he sat in the snow with his back against the trunk, buried his face in his hands, and wept.

CHAPTER TWENTY-SEVEN

Lily clutched her throat and swallowed hard. Since she'd left Mrs. Deforest's house, her heart had kept up a relentless pace, pounding against her rib cage. But as she had set her face toward home, her love for Aden burned in her bones, lending her determination amidst her growing distress.

But now, when the time had actually come to face Fater, she was so deliriously frightened that she wasn't altogether certain she wouldn't pass out.

Estee had been understandably cold to her during supper. Lily had been too terrified to speak. Even Dat, in all his excitement about the weddings, had sensed something amiss. He asked both girls three times if they felt well.

Mama had made all of Estee and Lily's favorites for supper, but Lily could barely force down two bites. Dat chuckled and said something about wedding-eve jitters. Lily could not give him a reply. He would find out soon enough.

She should have gone to Dat right after supper, but he had looked so ominous, lazily reading his paper in his brown recliner, that she stalled for time by helping Mama and Estee wash celery and bake pies. Even though she wasn't planning on getting married tomorrow, it was still Estee's big day. As desperate and terrified as she felt, Lily could not leave Estee celery-less.

Estee had gone off to bed while Mama put the finishing touches on the celery stuffing in the kitchen. Lily forced herself to walk into the living room. She loved Aden. She wasn't going to marry Tyler. She must tell Fater now.

Her eyes never strayed from her dat's face as she tiptoed into the living room and stood by his chair. She didn't think her heart could pound any harder. Was this what a heart attack felt like?

"Dat?"

"Hmm?"

"May I speak with you?" Lily cringed. She sounded timid and unsure. Dat would never be convinced of her resolve.

Dat peered over the rims of his reading glasses. "What is it?" He furrowed his brow. "You look pale."

Maybe she didn't have to tell her dat. He would find out when she didn't show up for her wedding in the morning.

Lily's fear made her lose control of her limbs, and she trembled like a match flame in the wind. It was no use. She couldn't speak without crying, and she *must* speak, so she let the tears flow. If she had to concentrate on keeping her emotions in check, she would lose her nerve. No matter what, she had to get this out.

Dat's expression flooded with sympathy, and he stood and took her into his arms. "There, there," he said gently, patting her on the back. "Don't cry. Tomorrow is your wedding day."

"Oh, Dat. You're going to be very disappointed in me."

He nudged her away from him and clicked his tongue. "How could you ever disappoint me when you try so hard to do right?"

His reassurance gave her hope. Maybe Dat would understand how sincerely she wanted to do the right thing.

He touched the tip of her nose. "You are fretting over nothing. Estee told me about what happened with that boy at Mrs. Deforest's today. I'm proud of the way you behaved. Tomorrow we will be rid of him for good."

Lily deflated slightly before thinking of Aden, squaring her shoulders, and wiping her eyes. "Dat, there is something I must tell you, and I have never been so certain of the rightness of any decision."

"Of course. You could not ask for a better husband than Tyler."

Her heart pounded in her throat, but she stood her ground. "I'm not going to get married tomorrow."

"What?"

"I made a terrible mistake when I agreed to marry Tyler. I don't love him. I can't marry him."

Dat snorted and sat down in his chair as if the discussion were over. "Every bride gets cold feet before her wedding. You will be fine."

"I know it is almost too late, Dat. It was wrong of me to wait so long. But this is not the jitters. I can't marry tomorrow. I just can't."

Dat leaned back in his chair and cleared his throat. "I worried this would happen. You get so nervous, and the thought of being married and sharing everything with a husband can be upsetting. Have you spoken to your mother about all the women things?"

Lily felt her face get hot. "It's not about

453

that, Dat. I don't want to marry Tyler. Ever."

He narrowed his eyes. "You're serious."

She almost wept with relief. "Yes. I am going to break off the engagement."

Dat's frown sank deeper into his face. "What will Tyler say?"

She looked at the floor. "I don't know," she whispered, not even wanting to think of the hurt she would cause.

Dat stood and paced purposefully around the room. "I've got to think. Let's think for a minute. We could talk to Tyler. He loves you. It would certainly upset the apple cart, but he wouldn't mind postponing the wedding until January so you feel comfortable."

Lily raised her voice so Dat could hear her over his own thoughts. "Dat! I love someone else."

He stopped pacing and glared at her, his eyes wide. She had never spoken to him like that. "Love someone else?"

"I'm sorry, Dat."

A fire ignited in Dat's eyes, and his lips twisted in disgust. "He doesn't love you."

His words stung more than he could have imagined. "You don't know that."

"A boy like Aden Helmuth only loves himself."

Lily blinked back more tears. "I can't pretend anymore. I can't discard his love like an old shoe. He's a part of me, Dat."

"Don't be dramatic."

Mama rushed into the room. "What is the matter?"

"Lily says she's in love with Aden Helmuth." Lily recognized the surprise in her dat's voice. She had never defied him before.

"But what about the wedding?"

"It's off," Lily said.

Dat slapped his hand against the wall. Both Mama and Lily jumped. "No, it's not. I expect better from you, Lily. Better than what I got from Zeke. And so I'm doing what my dat should have done the day Zeke took up with those new friends. If you walk away from Tyler Yoder, you will never be allowed in my home again."

"David, you don't mean that," Mama said.

"Yes, I do. To keep her from making the worst decision of her life." He pointed a finger at Lily. "You are blinded by this infatuation for that boy. I understand boys like him."

Lily bawled in frustration and misery. "You know nothing about Aden. He is good and brave and would just as soon cut off his arm as hurt anyone."

"Go back to that boy, and you'll regret it. And my heart will break to see you live with that regret when I could have prevented it.

455

And I *will* prevent it."

Great sobs racked her body. She would lose her family if she called off the wedding.

But she would lose everything if she didn't have Aden.

"So, Lily. What is it going to be? It's mighty cold out there tonight."

Mama gasped but didn't speak.

Still whimpering, but with more determination than ever, Lily pulled her coat from the closet, put it on, and turned to face her parents. "I'm sorry, Dat, but I love Aden better than my own soul."

"Then get out of my house."

She shuffled out the door without closing it behind her. Was this courage? Her heart beat so wildly it felt more like fear. But she didn't turn back.

"David," she heard her mother say, "we can't send her out into the night like that."

Her dat's voice sounded soft, comforting. "Give her some time to think about it. She'll be back."

Chapter Twenty-Eight

The propane lantern hissed to life, casting eerie shadows into every corner of the barn. Lily's hand trembled as she blew out the match. She hoped her fingers wouldn't be numb with cold before she could figure out how to hook up Floyd's sleigh.

Dust motes and strands of hay swirled into the air as Lily flung the tarp off the sleigh, a brand new two-seater with blue vinyl upholstery and shiny black runners. She ignored the twinge of guilt as she guided Sandy from the stall. She had no choice but to steal Estee's wedding present. She must go to Tyler's, and the roads were heavy with layers of snow. She hadn't dared ride in the saddle for years, so it had to be the sleigh. Besides, Floyd's displeasure was the least of her worries tonight.

Sniffling away her still-falling tears, Lily held Sandy's reins and examined the sleigh. She considered waking Estee to help her hitch it up. She would go with Lily to Tyler's if Lily asked her to.

But she decided against that. She had to do this on her own. For Aden.

Urgency made her clumsy. Would Dat come out and discover her before she had a chance to escape? She fumbled with the buckles and stumbled over the runners as she hitched Sandy to the sleigh, which to her relief was much like hitching the horse to the buggy.

With some effort, she maneuvered the horse and sleigh out of the barn without knocking over any hay bales. The snow made down harder now, in chunks of ice that pelted her face as she guided the horse up the lane. She wished for a pair of goggles and hoped she could find her way to Tyler's house even if she couldn't see.

The sleigh glided across the snow. Lily didn't know if the feeling of exhilaration or terror was stronger. It went so fast, she felt as if she were flying. She made a mental note to ask Floyd's forgiveness and then thank him profusely. A buggy would have gotten stuck in the driveway.

The cold had numbed her face by the time she saw the shadowy outlines of Tyler's house and silos against the dark sky. Lights burned inside. It might be late, but it seemed someone was up.

Lily stopped the horse in the snowy lane, jumped out of the sleigh, and tromped breathlessly to Tyler's porch. How could she bear to do this?

Saying a prayer for courage, she rapped on the door. She wanted to be sure to be heard.

Tyler's mother answered, and the sound of rowdy laughter attacked Lily's ears. Of course. Relatives were here for the wedding tomorrow. A small propane lantern hung from a hook on the wall, dimly lighting the entry. Tyler's mother smiled in delight before studying Lily's face. Obviously troubled by what she saw, she lost her smile and a worry line appeared between her eyebrows. "Lily? I did not expect to see you tonight. Is everything all right?"

Breathless, Lily grabbed Tyler's mother's wrist, partly to keep herself from falling over. Her knees felt like rubber. "Please, may I talk to Tyler?"

His mother hesitated for a moment as the puzzlement on her face gave way to concern. "I will get him."

Thankfully, the entryway in Tyler's house was nothing but a landing. The kitchen and living room were up the stairs in front of Lily, and the bedrooms were down. The

459

laughter came from upstairs. It sounded like they had a houseful of visitors, but Lily couldn't see any of them and they couldn't see her. Praise the Lord for small blessings. She would be able to avoid the awkward silence and curious looks from Tyler's relatives. The bride showing up at the groom's house with eyes red from crying would not bode well the night before the wedding.

Lily stood in wretched silence as the yelling and laughing continued. "One, two, three . . ."

They must have been playing a game. The counting stopped, and the laughing got louder.

Tyler appeared at the top step, smiling at whatever silliness went on in the kitchen. He saw who his visitor was and froze halfway down the stairs. His smile faded and apprehension immediately leaped into his eyes. Her heart sank to her toes. This was going to hurt both of them.

Hurt very badly.

He stood there staring at her, as if he didn't know what to do next, as if taking one more step down those stairs would ruin everything.

Lily had no control over her trembling. "Tyler, is there somewhere we can talk?"

With worry saturating his features, he

swallowed hard and nodded. Pointing down the stairs, he motioned for Lily to lead the way. "The cellar," he said. "Turn right."

The laughter faded as they descended, and the sound of their shoes clunking against the wooden steps thundered in Lily's ears. And of course, the pounding of her heart created a cacophony inside her head.

They reached the cellar, and Tyler lit a lantern on a post. He scooted a barrel near the lantern and invited her to sit. Lily shook her head. If she sat still, she might explode. Tyler stayed standing as well. He wasn't one to relax if he felt he needed to keep his wits about him.

Even with her coat on, Lily shivered. Tyler thought of everything. He couldn't very well be alone with her in one of the bedrooms on the night before the wedding. The only other private place in the house was the dark cellar with cold cement walls and low, oppressive ceilings.

Even in the basement, they could hear the muted counting upstairs followed by up-roarious laughter.

Tyler glanced up the stairs. "My uncles and cousins from Albany. They're having a push-up contest." He smiled weakly, but there was no joy in it.

461

He fell silent, and they stared at each other as the unspoken words between them lodged in Lily's throat.

She hadn't been able to come up with one comforting thing, not one thing to say to Tyler that might soften the blow. The brutal truth served plain and ungarnished would be poison to him, but Lily could see no other way.

Tyler turned his back on her, placed his hand on the wall above his head, and leaned against it. Bowing his head, he let out a long, slow breath. "Something is wrong, isn't it?"

"Jah."

His voice shook with emotion. "Are you calling it off?"

"Jah," she whispered, so softly that she almost didn't hear herself.

"Oy anyhow, you're brave."

She didn't miss the astonishment in his voice. Her heart beat wildly. Not very brave. Fear and uncertainty were an icy hand around her throat.

He still had his back to her, maybe so she wouldn't see what was on his face. "I'm sorry, Lily. I knew you weren't ready. I think . . . I wanted to marry you so bad. It hurt so much when I thought of you not being in my life."

Lily closed her eyes and pushed down the tears that threatened to spill onto the cold cement floor. "Don't apologize. I encouraged you. I wanted you to ask me."

He lifted his head and looked at her. "Jah, you did. I know you did."

"Because you are the best kind of man."

He shook his head. "I know you think of me that way, and I have always been humbled by your opinion. It's why I dared to even hope you might say yes." He relinquished his wall and gently clasped her upper arms. "But you don't love me."

She couldn't meet his gaze, not with that fire burning in his eyes. "No."

He dropped his hands and shoved his fingers through his hair. "Then it doesn't matter how many times I've read the Bible or how often I help my mamm with the dishes or how much your fater likes me. I cannot be your husband if I am not the best man for you." The intensity in his gaze could have melted a meadow of ice. "There are other men out there, Lily, gute men who get beat up by life because they think with their hearts instead of their heads. Gute men who always try to do the right thing even when it's messy or turns out bad. Men who love big, hairy dogs."

Lily's legs wobbled, and she sat down hard

on the barrel.

He took her hand and enfolded it in both of his. "It's my own fault because I wanted to believe you loved me. I ignored the way you look at Aden, like every delight in the world lives in his face." The corner of Tyler's mouth quirked upward. "He's not even that handsome."

"Yes, he is."

"Well, don't tell me about it. I'm sick of Aden Helmuth already."

Relieved laughter escaped Lily's lips.

Tyler knit his brows in concern. "Was your dat angry?"

Lily's heart resumed galloping. "He has thrown me out of the house."

She saw a fierce emotion in Tyler's face she'd never seen before. "How could he treat his daughter that way?"

"He hoped his harshness would force me to reconsider. He says I am blind to Aden's faults."

"Aden's only fault is caring too much." His lips twitched. "I can't believe I'm defending him when he's ruined all my happiness."

Lily didn't know whether to laugh or weep.

Tyler directed a steely gaze up the stairs. "I will go to your fater. He will know how I feel about what he has done."

"Nae. You have no argument with him. I have never opposed him before, and he did not know what to do. But he needs to see that I am strong enough to do what I feel is right. I won't have you fighting my battles for me."

Tyler frowned. "It took a lot of courage to tell your fater. And me. I'm proud of you."

"I am anything but brave. I thought I might faint."

"That's what courage is. If it weren't scary, it would take no bravery to see it through."

A warm glow filled Lily's chest. She wished she had a sister for Tyler. He deserved an angel to be his wife.

Another blast of laughter sounded from upstairs. Lily lowered her eyes and studied her hands. "I suppose we should tell your family."

"Why spoil their evening just yet?" He took her hand and pulled her up the steps. "There is an errand we need to run."

"Where are we going?" she said, as they climbed.

"To Huckleberry Hill, because Aden's got the stupid idea that he's leaving tomorrow. I think you should talk him out of it."

Lily's heart soared to the sky. She threw

her arms around Tyler's neck and squeezed with all the joy of affectionate friendship. He truly was the best of men. Him and Aden. "Why would you do that for me?"

Sadness flitted across Tyler's face. "I want you to be happy."

A tear escaped her eye even as she grinned.

"But don't act too happy," Tyler said wryly. "I'm still heartbroken over losing you. Can you muster a little respect for my feelings?"

Lily kissed him soundly on the cheek. "I have more respect for you than ever."

CHAPTER TWENTY-NINE

Aden lay staring at the ceiling even though it was too dark to actually see the ceiling. He didn't fight the insomnia. Since the puppy mill, he felt blessed if he got three or four solid hours a night.

Tomorrow all hope of happiness would die for him. Lily would get married, and Aden would go home. He wondered if Mamm had moved one of his little brothers into his old room yet. Or maybe she had turned it into a quilting space where she could spread her fabric all over his bed and design squares to her heart's content. Maybe Mamm and Dat wouldn't want him back. He'd given them enough to worry about when he lived there.

Because of the pain, he'd trained himself to put Lily out of his mind, to accept a sort of numbness about his daily life so he wouldn't walk around in perpetual despair. But tonight, Aden surrendered and pictured

Lily as he had seen her earlier today, her cheeks rosy with the cold, the brilliance of the snow reflecting in her eyes. This would be the last time he let himself dream about her. If such thoughts seized him back in Ohio, he'd drive himself crazy.

A loud tap on his window startled him, and he bolted upright, suddenly alert. Another insistent tap got him to his feet. Aden lifted the blinds and peeked into the dark night. Would he be able to see who harassed him?

Someone held a flashlight beneath his chin and shined it onto his own face. From the odd angle of the light, it took Aden a few seconds to realize Tyler Yoder was the one haunting his house.

The sight of Tyler assaulted him with a fresh wave of longing. What did Tyler want, tonight of all nights? Didn't he have better things to do than come and remind Aden of his loss?

"Come out," was Tyler's muffled plea.

Come out? *It's freezing cold in the middle of the night, and I'm leaving for Ohio tomorrow. I'm not in the mood to say good-bye or to wish you well on your wedding day or whatever it is you're expecting from me.* Had he come all this way in the middle of the night in the freezing cold to gloat?

Aden was tempted to crawl back into bed and let Tyler freeze.

Instead, he fumbled around in the dark for his clothes and tried not to make any noise when he tromped down the hall in his clunky boots. Mammi and Dawdi needed their sleep even if Tyler didn't think Aden did.

Pilot and Sparky sprawled on the rag rug in front of the sofa, but Pilot lifted his head and twitched an ear when Aden passed. "Go back to sleep, Pilot."

Pilot rose and stepped lightly across the kitchen floor to stand by Aden. Aden patted him on the head. "Not a bad idea, boy. You can protect me from predators."

Aden lit a lantern before stepping out onto the porch. He'd rather not converse while Tyler pointed that flashlight in his face.

Tyler stood in the middle of the yard, but the flashlight had disappeared. At the edges of the lantern's light, Aden could see a dark horse and a sleigh standing in the lane. The snow, which had been falling all day, drifted lazily to the ground as if ready to give up falling altogether. Aden clomped down the steps and crunched through the snow. Pilot contented himself on the porch, sitting on his haunches, peering at Aden and Tyler like a curious scholar.

The lantern illuminated Tyler's features. He wore his normal somber expression, but Aden could tell by the hard line of his mouth and the intensity of his gaze that he wasn't happy.

Aden wanted to growl. What did Tyler have to be unhappy about? He was about to marry Lily Eicher, the most wonderful girl in the world.

"Could you put the lantern down?" Tyler said.

Reaching back, Aden suppressed his confusion and set the lantern on the porch next to Pilot.

Tyler nodded, stepped closer, and without warning, punched Aden squarely in the mouth.

Aden stumbled backward and fell to the ground out of sheer surprise. Tyler's fist struck hard, as if packed with every bit of anger Tyler had ever buried. Aden groaned as the taste of salty blood filled his mouth and his ears rang with the blow. He really should have stayed in bed. Aden glanced at his sorry excuse for a guard dog who sat on the porch, oblivious to the fact that someone had attacked his master. He'd get no help from Pilot.

The pain of losing Lily left no room for anger, not even for Tyler Yoder. If Tyler felt the need to hit him, Aden must have deserved it.

Still frowning fiercely, Tyler reached out his hand. Aden hesitated to take it. Did Tyler want to help him up so he could hit him again?

He reluctantly took the proffered hand, stood with a grunt, and rubbed his tender jaw. "What was that for?"

"So that tomorrow you won't feel so bad about ruining my life. I want you to remember that I fought back. It will help soothe your guilty conscience."

"What do I have to feel guilty about?"

That was a stupid question. He had a lot to feel guilty about: Lily's arrest, Eicher's mailbox, loving Tyler's fiancée. A long list.

Tyler pulled a handkerchief from his pocket and handed it to Aden. "Your lip's bleeding."

"No kidding."

"I'm going in the house so I don't freeze to death," Tyler said as he walked up the porch steps. Pilot didn't move a muscle, not even to growl.

This visit got stranger and stranger. "You came all this way to sock me in the mouth and take over my house?"

Tyler turned back, and one corner of his mouth curled slightly. "Did I break a tooth?

471

I hope I broke a tooth."

Aden was about to follow his crazy friend up the steps and demand some answers when a glint of light appeared from around the corner of the house. Someone walked his way holding the shining flashlight.

She stepped into the light of the lantern, and Aden held his breath. Was this what it felt like to see a vision?

His surprise was nothing compared to the sharp yearning he experienced when he laid eyes on her. How could he bear to let her go, this bright, beautiful girl who never left his thoughts and held his heart in her hands? His love burned like a forest fire, irrational, fierce, and completely out of control.

Pilot thawed instantaneously and jumped off the porch. Lily held up her hand. "Stay, Pilot. Stay there."

Pilot whined and wagged his tail, but he sat down in the snow and came no closer.

She'd been crying. Even in the dim light of the lantern, Aden could see the red, swollen eyes and the weariness in her expression. Her violent trembling tempted Aden to wrap her in an embrace.

He couldn't help himself. He reached out and tenderly grasped her arms. "What's wrong? Did Tyler do something to upset you?"

"Aden, I'm so sorry. I've been unforgivably unkind to you."

He let his hands fall to his side. Was this some sort of pre-wedding ritual? Tyler and Lily visiting all the people they'd offended and making apologies before the big day? Didn't they know such a gesture only made him feel like dirt?

Hurt flashed in her eyes. "Am I too late?"

He cleared his throat and tried to appear apathetic. She couldn't know how her presence stabbed through his heart. "You don't need to apologize for anything, Lily. Ever."

Her expression brimmed with tenderness, and she seemed to gravitate closer to him. Or did Aden involuntarily gravitate closer to her? He didn't know, but he found his face within inches of hers.

"You're hurt," she said, retrieving a handkerchief from her coat pocket. Aden didn't dare move a muscle as she reached up and dabbed at his lip, maddeningly brushing her fingers against his jaw, sending his pulse racing. He clenched his fists in an attempt to gain some control. Didn't she understand the torture he experienced just being near her?

Slowly, deliberately, she rose to her tippy-toes and brushed her lips across his. He thought his heart might escape his chest and gallop down the road. He stood perfectly still in case any movement from him would make her come to her senses, because she had certainly lost them.

She pulled away from him and searched his face for something. He didn't know what. "Is there any possibility you could love me?" she said, in a whisper soft voice.

He must not have heard her correctly. In bewilderment, he pointed to the house. "Do you . . . do you know that Tyler is in there?"

"I called it off with Tyler."

Aden's head reeled like the time Mahlon Byler beaned him with a softball. "You . . . you mean you . . . are you getting married tomorrow?"

"Nae."

Aden didn't think he'd ever heard a sweeter word in his life. If he were a bird, he could have soared to the sun. Weeks of the deepest despair gave way to happiness so exquisite it almost blinded him. It certainly took his breath away.

She visibly trembled again. "Tyler is heartbroken, I stole Floyd's sleigh, and my dat kicked me out of the house, but I finally found someone I'm willing to risk everything for." She placed a hand on his chest.

"It's you, Aden."

Not caring whom he woke, Aden whooped at the top of his lungs, picked Lily up, and whirled her around. Pilot lost all control. He barked cheerfully and leaped like a rabbit in the snow-covered yard.

Throaty laughter burst from Lily's lips, and her smile set his heart ablaze. Aden laughed at the sheer delight of it all. He spun her until he got dizzy, then set her on her feet and kissed her as if he had every right to. She melted into his arms, and he lifted her off her feet again to bring her closer to his heart.

After a few blissful seconds that could have filled eternity, she pulled away from him. He made sure she stood firmly on the ground when he let go. "So, you forgive me?" she said.

He chuckled before he slid his arms around her and kissed her tenderly. She wrapped her fingers around his suspenders and pulled herself closer.

He was so happy, he thought he might burst if he didn't voice what he carried in his heart. With his lips within inches of hers, he said, "I love you, Lily."

She sighed as if to release whatever emotions she'd bottled up. Tears brimmed in her eyes before overflowing. She giggled.

"You don't know how I have longed to hear you say those words."

He kissed her again and tasted not only her sweet lips, but her salty tears as well.

Oh, how he loved her!

Kissing Lily always sent him reeling, so he didn't know how he finally managed to make some sense of everything she'd said. He stiffened as her earlier words came back and indignation seized him. "Your dat kicked you out?"

She lowered her eyes. "He was frantic. And desperate. I've always been so easily persuaded. He thought he could change my mind."

Aden wished he could make the pain go away by holding her close. "My darling, adorable Lily. I can only imagine how you felt and what horrible things your dat must have said." Horrible things about Aden, no doubt.

"I was shaking and ill and so terrified I was like to pass out. But I promise, from now on, you will not regret loving me. You'll see I've changed."

He brushed his thumb across her bottom lip. She fell silent. "Don't change a thing. I fell in love with the girl who scolded me every time I waded knee-deep into a puddle of water and sprouted that adorably anxious pout when I wouldn't heed her. I fell in love with the girl who wouldn't stop worrying about me and commanded my dog better than I ever could. You are my treasure, Lily. I would not have you any different."

She curled her lips. "All right. If you take care of the puppies and the horses and the ponds, I will take care of you."

They stood holding each other until Lily started to shiver. "What am I thinking, keeping you out in the cold like this? This would be more romantic inside where it's warm."

Lily laughed and traced her fingers along his jawline. "I came so close to losing you. I don't want to let you go even long enough to walk into the house."

"I'll hold tight."

Lily frowned suddenly and slumped her shoulders. "Tyler's in there."

Aden's happiness deflated a bit. "Oh, jah, I forgot." They couldn't go inside. Aden didn't want to rub it in, but he didn't think it would be possible to keep a smile from his face.

"He drove me over here. He didn't have one bitter word for me, and I have treated him so poorly." Lily closed her eyes and shook her head. "It is a wonder either of you can stand to be near me."

"Not a wonder at all. You are worth every

risk, you know." He emphasized his sincerity with a swift kiss. "I'm glad Tyler hit me. I don't feel so guilty about stealing his fiancée."

Aden took Lily's hand in his. There could never be a better fit. He tugged her to the house with Pilot trotting close behind. Aden snatched up the lantern before opening the door.

Pilot barged into the room ahead of them. The floor lantern had been lit, and Tyler sat on the sofa with Mammi and Dawdi on either side of him. Mammi clutched one of Tyler's hands in hers and her eyes twinkled with delight and sympathy. She wore her petal-pink nightgown with that strange puffy nightcap that looked like a purple cat had made a bed on the top of her head. Dawdi wore an undershirt with his trousers and suspenders, and his horseshoe beard stuck out from his face like the roots of a tree. Tyler looked as if he had swallowed a toad. Tyler and his grandparents must have been having a very awkward time of it.

Pilot loped to the sofa and propped his paws on Tyler's lap as if Tyler were his best friend.

"Pilot, get down," Lily commanded.

Tyler stood, offered an arm to each of the grandparents, and pulled them up.

Mammi beckoned for Aden to come closer. Unable to bear the thought of letting go of Lily's hand, he took her along with him, and Mammi's arms went around them both.

"Tyler told us all about it," Mammi said. "I knew how it would be." She patted Lily on the cheek. "I kept telling Felty and Aden, but neither of them would believe me. Men don't understand these things."

Mammi went to the kitchen and shoved two logs into the cookstove. "I've got cocoa. Would anyone like cocoa? Aden's dat sent me a can of Mint Chocolate Swirl."

"Mammi, Lily's dat threw her out of the house. Can she sleep here tonight?"

Mammi clicked her tongue. "Poor David. He's dug his heels in real deep. That mailbox cover I knitted must not have helped at all."

"I'm afraid he fed it to the goat," Lily said.

Mammi poured some milk into a pan. "You are welcome to stay as long as you want. There is a small room at the end of the hall."

Aden wouldn't hear of it. "She can sleep in my room, and I will sleep in the barn." Sleeping in the same house as Lily would drive him to the edge of madness.

Lily shook her head. "Too cold. I am happy to have the small room."

A momentous idea popped into Aden's head and wouldn't leave. He lost his breath just thinking about it. He faced Lily and took both of her hands. "Lily, will you marry me?"

Her eyes danced with a thousand bright fires. She stood on tiptoe and kissed him on the lips, in front of Mammi and Dawdi and her former fiancé. She *had* changed.

Aden's heart beat the unfamiliar cadence of perfect bliss. "Is that a yes?"

"If I could say yes a million times, I would."

Aden cleared his throat and plunged into deep waters. "What I mean is, will you marry me tomorrow?"

Tyler shook his head and groaned. "This day just gets better and better."

Lily trembled even as she smiled. "Tomorrow? Aden, do you really think we could?"

Dawdi smoothed his beard into a more uniform shape. "Lily's family will already be there. They're expecting a wedding. The food is ready. It'll just be a different groom."

Lily furrowed her brow. "The wedding's at my house. What if Dat won't let us inside?"

"Then we can marry on your porch."

Tyler interlaced his fingers and leaned his elbows on his knees. "Your dat doesn't have

480

a say in who you marry. It's the bishop who has to approve."

It went against every wedding convention they knew, but Aden could tell Lily wanted to be talked into it.

"But what about your family, Aden? Will they be okay to miss it?"

"Most of my aunts and uncles and cousins live in Bonduel. It won't be hard to spread the word," Aden said. What would Mamm and Dat say? All Aden knew was that he wanted to marry Lily so badly, he was willing to suffer his mother's wrath.

Mammi waved her hand in Aden's direction. "Aden's mamm will write me a ten-page letter, which I will be expected to read, but then she'll get over it. She has five other unmarried children. She can attend their weddings."

Aden took Lily's hand and kissed it. "If you're even the least bit uneasy, we will wait. I only want you to be happy."

"I think it sounds lovely," Mammi said.

Lily began to cry again. "I am happy. I wouldn't have believed this much happiness possible in an entire lifetime. The thought of facing all those people is terrifying, but I promised you I'd be brave. Yes, I will marry you tomorrow."

With every passing moment, Aden didn't

think he could be any happier. But knowing that Lily would truly be his in a matter of hours, he thought his heart would burst. He wrapped his arms around his fiancée. Mammi and Dawdi refused to be left out. Soon the four of them were tangled up in a toasty bear hug.

Mammi giggled as the nightcap slipped off her head. "That hat never liked to behave."

Aden stole a glance at Tyler, who looked positively miserable. A twinge of guilt tugged at him. He touched the split in his lip. At least Tyler had gotten his last licks in.

"Your lip looks bad. Does it hurt?" Tyler said, almost hopefully.

Aden grinned. "You're always putting other people's feelings before your own."

"Glad I could be of help."

Aden huffed out a breath as he considered things more carefully. He pulled from the group hug with a grimace. "We can't get married tomorrow."

"Why not?" Mammi and Lily said in unison.

"It wouldn't be right to do that to Tyler. Tyler's feelings are more important than our wishes. He is the person who has been hurt the most by this."

"You're right," Lily said, compassion

flooding her voice. "We should wait until Tyler gives the okay. It would be like pouring salt into a wound."

"I'm sitting over here," Tyler said. "You don't have to talk about me like I'm not in the room."

Aden and Lily glanced at each other, walked to the sofa, and sat on either side of Tyler.

"Don't look at me like I'm a little boy who lost his puppy," Tyler said.

"You don't like dogs," Aden said.

Tyler's lips twitched as if he were trying not to smile. Then he chuckled. "Well, quit feeling sorry for me. I'm going to look like a fool no matter when you two marry. Besides, it's Aden I feel sorry for. He has to face Lily's dat tomorrow." Tyler leaned back and propped his hands behind his head. "I hope I'm there to see it."

Aden raised his eyebrow. "So you can gloat?"

"Yep."

Lily didn't look so cheerful. "I must face my fater tomorrow too."

"You won't have to say a word," Aden insisted. "I'll do all the explaining."

"I'm the one who should talk to Lily's dat," Tyler said.

"Nae. She will be my wife. I will face her

fater like a man, and he will come to respect me, Lord willing."

Lily reached across Tyler and placed a hand on Aden's knee. "I won't allow either of you to shield me from my fater's anger."

Aden felt such tenderness for her that he thought he might melt. She had nothing to fear from her fater. Aden would protect her with everything he had in him.

Tyler sighed and stood up. "Come on, Aden. It's not getting any warmer or any earlier. Felty, can we take your horse?"

Aden and Lily rose from the sofa. "Where are we going?" Aden asked.

Tyler grabbed his coat where he had draped it over one of the kitchen chairs. "You've got to clear this mess with the bishop, and the bishop will no doubt like to hear from the ex-groom who happens to be his son." Tyler zipped his coat. "And you're sleeping at my house."

"I can bed down in the barn. I don't mind."

"It would be bad for the groom to freeze the night before his wedding. We're filled to the rafters with people, but we'll be able to find you a place to sleep."

Aden couldn't hope to repay Tyler's kindness in a thousand lifetimes. "I can't believe you're helping us like this."

Tyler opened the door and let in a wave of chilly air. "Neither can I. I should see a doctor."

Aden gave Lily one last kiss. "If there is any problem with Tyler's dat, I will come back. Otherwise, ride the sleigh to your house in the morning, and I will see you at the wedding."

Her lips quirked in amusement. "I'll be there. Don't chicken out."

Aden looked at Tyler. "What time is my wedding tomorrow?"

Tyler growled in exasperation. "Eleven."

"Don't be late," Mammi said. "You want to make a good impression on your new in-laws."

Aden laughed. "I would hate to start off on the wrong foot. Stay here, Pilot," he said before he followed Tyler out and shut the door behind him.

He and Tyler crunched through the snow. Aden saddled Dawdi's horse while Tyler unhitched Lily's horse from the sleigh and stabled her. Aden led the horse from the barn and motioned for Tyler to mount first. "You really are a good man, Tyler. I'd feel a whole lot better if you beat the tar out of me."

Tyler formed his lips into a wry grin. "Don't tempt me. It's been a long night."

■ ■ ■ ■

"I really don't understand what is going on here," the bishop said.

Tyler shoved his fingers through his hair. "It's pretty simple, Dat. Aden and I are making a swap. He wants to marry Lily tomorrow, and I don't."

The bishop shook his head. "I *really* don't understand what is going on here."

Near midnight, Aden, Tyler, and the bishop sat in a circle of milking stools in the cold, musty barn. Relatives crammed every room of Yoder's house, and the barn proved the only place that afforded any privacy, unless the cows that moved quietly in the dark shadows were listening in.

"Lily doesn't love me, Dat. She wants to marry Aden instead."

The bishop eyed Aden suspiciously. "So he stole Lily from you? I can't approve of that. It is a serious offense to court another man's fiancée."

Tyler patted his fater's leg. "Aden didn't do anything wrong, Dat. Lily's fater preferred me."

"But she encouraged you. She agreed to marry you. What kind of a girl would do that to a young man?"

Tyler stood and paced out his agitation. "I won't deny she made mistakes, especially since both Aden and I had to suffer for them. But, Dat, she set all to rights before it was truly too late."

The bishop stood and placed his hands on Tyler's shoulders. "This surely must hurt you."

A spark of sadness ignited on Tyler's face. "I feel rotten, Dat. But I want to be loved by my fiancée, not just my fiancée's fater."

In resignation, the bishop sat and scratched the beard at his chin. "Your mother will not be happy."

Tyler glanced at Aden. "Keep her away from Aden until after the wedding."

The bishop nodded. "For four or five years after the wedding."

Aden didn't laugh. The bishop was not joking. Aden thought of his own mother. She would be quite annoyed at missing Aden's wedding. He might have to stay away from *her* for four or five years.

The bishop sat down and slapped his hands on his thighs. "Okay, Aden. Let's talk about your wedding."

"First," Aden said, "can I use your phone?"

"Jah," Tyler said.

The Yoders, like many Amish families with

businesses, had a telephone in their barn. Aden quickly stepped into the small office and dialed his favorite phone number. "Hello? Jamal . . . Yes, I know what time it is, but I saved your life once, and I need your help."

CHAPTER THIRTY

Lily decided to try the front door first. If she couldn't get in that way, she'd go to the back and try to get Estee's attention by throwing pebbles at her window.

Dread wrestled with complete joy inside her. Most likely, Dat would order her off his property and leave her no choice but to sneak into her own wedding with the rest of the guests. But there was also a chance that he would take pity on her and at least let her warm herself by the wood stove before she made her vows.

Her vows. Today she would marry Aden Helmuth. She could not even form the words in her mind to describe her utter happiness. This was how a bride should feel on her wedding day, as if she were the only person in the whole world who ever loved. It was impossible that Estee could love Floyd anywhere near as much as Lily loved Aden.

Three unhitched buggies stood side by side in the lane in front of Lily's house. Many of the relatives would have arrived early to help in the food preparation; some were close enough to come in buggies, others would have been dropped off by drivers.

Sandy pulled the sleigh to the barn where Lily unhitched it and repositioned the tarp. Had anyone noticed it was missing?

She ambled to the porch and didn't know whether to walk into the house as if she belonged or knock like a visitor. She felt like a stranger to her former life.

Her knock was barely a tap, but then she remembered that she determined to be brave. She gave five sharp raps on the door, loudly enough for all the relatives inside to hear. Her heart echoed the beat.

Dat opened the door as if he had been waiting for her. He furrowed his brow, a mixture of anger and concern flickering in his eyes.

She must look a sight. Her cheeks were surely bright red from the sleigh ride. She hadn't slept a wink last night, and the dark circles under her eyes might evoke some sympathy. But she also knew that her affection for Aden would glow through her very skin and make her eyes seem extra lively. What would Dat see?

He didn't invite her in to her own house. "Do you know how worried we were? I never thought my Lily would do such a thing." The lines on his face had deepened overnight. She felt sorry for him. Of course he would have worried when she hadn't come back last night.

"I'm sorry, Dat, but I didn't know what else to do."

"Did you think on your sins?"

"Jah." She had thought on her sins, but not the ones Dat wanted her to think on. She had hurt both Tyler and Aden badly. Those sins she would not soon forget.

"And are you getting married today or not?"

Lily took a deep breath. Her answer would no doubt get her kicked out of the house forever. "Jah, Dat, I am."

Dat's smile knocked the wind out of her, especially since she was about to deflate all his hopes.

"But —"

Estee bounded down the steps like a herd of sheep. "Lily," she squealed, catapulting herself into Lily's arms. "You're back!"

Lily gave her sister a cursory hug and nudged her away. "Dat, I must tell you —"

Estee pulled her into the house and practically dragged her up the stairs. "Plenty of

491

time for that. It's only two hours until the service starts, and we've got to wash your hair."

Dat looked ten years younger than he had a minute ago. "Go, Lily. We will talk later."

Despite the guilt that niggled at the edge of her thoughts, Lily let Estee pull her upstairs without another word. She hadn't actually lied to Fater, and she really did want a bath.

Estee yanked her into their room and shut the door. Her smile disappeared as if it had only been there for Dat's benefit. "What is going on? Dat told me you'd gone to sleep over at the cousins', but I heard every word of that fight last night." She frowned. "I'm sorry about being so nasty yesterday. If that fight was my fault . . ."

Lily hugged Estee and held on for dear life. "Oh, Estee, I'm so happy. I feel like I'm going to burst into laughter every moment."

"Where did you go last night?"

"First I went to Tyler's."

Estee's face fell even further. "You've decided to go through with it?"

"I couldn't do it, Estee. I don't love him."

Estee pulled away, her eyes popping with astonishment. "You're not going to marry Tyler?"

Lily nodded. Thinking of Tyler brought a

lump to her throat.

"Oh, poor Tyler. What did he say?"

"You know Tyler. He doesn't have a mean bone in his body."

Estee sank to the bed, unable to bear all this information standing on her feet. "It's a gute thing I am getting married today, or Dat would have had to send all the relatives home without a wedding."

Lily's heart sped up. "Not quite."

"Not quite?"

"Aden asked me to marry him, and it seemed practical to do it when all the family would be here."

Could Estee's eyes get any wider? "You're marrying Aden today?"

Lily couldn't contain her widest smile. "Jah."

Estee leaped from the bed and screamed loudly enough to wake sleepers in China. She clapped her arms around Lily, and they jumped up and down together, squealing and giggling.

Mama came flying into the room. "Is everything all right?"

Lily and Estee stopped the racket. Mama clicked her tongue and tugged Lily into a warm embrace. "We didn't think you'd be gone so long. Dat never would have thrown you out if he thought for one minute that you wouldn't return immediately."

"It's okay, Mama. I have never been better."

Mama patted Lily's cheek. "Oh, my dear girl, Dat told me. You won't regret your decision. Such a fine young man." She patted Estee's cheek with her other hand. "Two weddings today. My cup runneth over."

Lily enfolded her mama in a solid embrace and savored the smell of her hair and skin against her cheek. After today, her mamm might not want to see her.

"You two had better get ready. I still have two salads to make."

Lily swallowed hard. She would have to break the news to her parents soon, before the service. She pictured Aden's face in her mind and tried to muster more courage. Thinking of Aden sent little pulses of delight surging through her body. It was all so sudden, so reckless, but she had never felt more sure of anything. Oh, she would burst!

Mama closed the door behind her.

"Oh no," Estee said quietly.

"I know." Lily reached for the doorknob. "I really should go tell them now. They're so happy."

"No, wait. We need to wash your hair, and it's got to have time to dry. Aden deserves a freshly scrubbed bride." Their eyes met, and

Estee squeaked in delight. "Oh, Lily, he is so good-looking." She raised her hand as if to stop all protest. "I know that appearance doesn't matter. It certainly doesn't matter to me, but it can't hurt to have a husband who's pleasant to look at. And Aden is as gute as he is handsome. Maybe more so. After me, you are the most blessed girl alive."

"Oh, Estee. I'm so happy."

Once again, the door burst open. Floyd stood at the threshold with his hat in his hand and a frantic look in his eyes. "I'm sorry to bother you. David said I could come up here even though I didn't want to come up here. I mean, I wanted to see you but didn't know if I should see you before the wedding. I don't mean to interrupt." He strode quickly into the room and took both of Estee's hands. "Your wedding present is gone."

"What do you mean?" Estee asked.

"Disappeared. I hid it in the barn, and this morning I came to fetch it and it was gone."

Lily grimaced. "I stole it last night."

Floyd looked as if he hadn't even noticed Lily in the room before. "You stole it?"

"I'm sorry, Floyd. It was an emergency."

Floyd couldn't quite grasp what she told

him. "You shouldn't steal other people's things."

"I brought it back. It's in the barn, safe and sound."

Floyd thought about that for a minute before jerking to attention and rushing out the door. Estee lifted an eyebrow in puzzlement and stared at Lily. Floyd ran back into the room. "You look very pretty today, Estee," he said, before disappearing once again.

"You're really going to like your present," Lily said.

They laughed until Estee wiped the smile off her face and propped her hands on her hips. "If we don't wash your hair immediately, you will make your vows in a soggy kapp."

"I'm all yours," Lily said.

An hour later, Lily descended the stairs with a damp bun ready to be kicked out of the house once again. She wore the royal blue dress she had sewn for her wedding and a crisp white apron. The kitchen teemed with aunts and cousins slicing bread and frosting cakes and cutting vegetables.

Aunt Lisa looked up from where she sat at the table counting paper plates. "What a beautiful bride you are."

Lily forced a smile and barely paid heed to the compliments and good wishes of her relatives. She must find Dat this minute.

Mama supervised the whipping cream for the pies with Aunt Arie. "Mama, where is Dat?"

Mama licked a dollop of whipped cream off her finger. "It needs more sugar, Arie."

"Mama, I need to talk to Dat."

Mama's eyes sparkled merrily. Lily hoped it would still be a happy day for her, even if only one of her daughters married an acceptable young man. "Tyler is here. He asked to speak to your father. They went to the toolshed where they could have a little privacy."

Lily didn't know whether to be irritated or grateful. She had told Tyler she would be brave enough to talk to Dat herself, but the way her knees shook, it might be nice to have an ally.

She weaved around the cooks, threw on her coat, and slipped out the back door. The toolshed sat to the side of the house, set off from the road with its back against the pasture. Lily breathed a sigh of relief when she burst out of the house and saw Dat and Tyler ambling toward the shed. She wasn't too late.

Tyler carried himself solemnly, as if attending a funeral. Dat would not have been able to guess that anything was amiss by the expression on Tyler's face.

Lily caught up with them. "I need to talk to you, Dat," she said breathlessly. Tyler barely looked at her, and her heart ached. She hadn't expected an affectionate greeting, but it pained her to see how deeply Tyler grieved.

Or maybe something else had gone wrong. Had the bishop refused to give his permission for a substitute wedding?

Dat narrowed his eyes but tried to keep up the pretense of cheerfulness. The last thing he would want to do was alarm Tyler. "Lily, go back inside," he said through his clenched, but smiling, teeth.

Tyler pressed his lips together, took Lily's hand, and pulled her toward the shed door. "Come in with us, Lily."

Dat couldn't very well protest. He opened the door and stopped short. Aden stood inside the shed, hat in hand, shoulders pulled back, ramrod straight. The top of his head nearly touched the low ceiling. His expression spoke of his steely determination, as it had on the day he ran into the woods after that bear. Lily had never seen a more breathtaking sight in her life.

His eyes darted toward Lily before he

returned his gaze to her father. "Tyler," he said, "I'll not have Lily hear something that might distress her."

"I wanted to come," Lily said, never taking her eyes from Aden's face. She stood like a starving woman looking at a banquet. How had she ever convinced herself that she was indifferent to Aden Helmuth?

He turned to her now, and his expression flooded with tenderness. Warmth spread through her like a mug of hot chocolate. With marshmallows.

Dat scowled. "What is he doing here?"

Aden stood taller, if that were possible. "I've come to ask permission to marry your daughter."

Sucking in his breath, Dat's head snapped in Lily's direction. "What have you done?"

Lily managed to withstand his scowl, even though her hands shook. "Please, Dat. I want you to understand. I love Aden." She glanced at Tyler. He didn't even wince.

Dat softened his expression slightly. "I am disappointed in you, Lily. You have always been a sensible girl, but in the last few months, I don't recognize you." He pointed to Aden. "This is his doing."

Lily lowered her gaze to the floor. She couldn't bear the look of sorrow in her dat's eyes. "It breaks my heart to disappoint you."

Dat turned all his attention to her. "When you were just a teeny girl, you were my buddy. Remember how you milked the cows with me while Estee helped Mama in the kitchen? I always protected you, kept you from muddy puddles and busy streets. I've never stopped trying to keep you safe."

"I know, Dat."

"You have those scars on your arm because of disobedience. Have you learned nothing? Can you trust me now when I tell you to turn your back on this boy no matter how much it hurts or how much you think you love him?"

Lily glanced at Aden. He studied her face with intense concern, as if she might dissolve if he didn't keep an eye on her. Did he worry that Dat might be able to sway her? Did he expect her to be weak?

She walked past her father and took Aden's hand. The muscles in Aden's jaw relaxed as he lifted her hand and pressed it against his chest. She could feel his steady heartbeat. "Did you know, Dat, that I have never heard an unkind word come out of Aden's mouth? He stood between me and a bear with no thought for his own safety. When we got arrested, his only concern was for me, even though he was the one with a broken nose."

Aden let go of her hand and slipped his arm around her shoulders. She fit nicely, tucked under his arm. Dat pursed his lips and flared his nostrils.

"You need not worry about your daughter's safety," Aden said. "I will see that no harm comes to her ever."

The sound of his voice, clear and determined, sent a ribbon of warmth up Lily's spine.

"That's a fine promise, coming from the boy who led her to jail."

Lily looked into Aden's face and gave him a faint smile. "Aden has asked me to marry him, and we are going to be married today. Here. With Estee and Floyd," she added, in case Dat didn't catch on.

The surprise on Dat's face didn't last long. Anger followed close behind. He balled his hands into fists as his neck turned bright red. "Not in my house, you won't," he sputtered. "You will marry Tyler or I will wash my hands of you."

"I don't want to marry her," Tyler interjected.

Dat turned as if he were the bottle in a Spin the Bottle game. He knit his brows together. He didn't have a leg to stand on if Tyler backed out. "Jah, you do."

"I've changed my mind. I wouldn't marry

Lily today even if she wanted me to, which she doesn't." He glanced at Lily, and the corner of his mouth curled slightly. Lily breathed out all the tension she'd bottled up.

Tyler put a hand on Dat's shoulder. "David, would you want to marry a girl who doesn't love you?"

"Love grows with time," Dat countered, but Tyler had knocked the wind out of him.

Tyler shook his head and frowned. "Aden is a gute man. You raised Lily well. Trust her judgment." He held Dat's gaze for a few seconds before turning to Aden and Lily. "You'd better go. It's almost time."

Aden grabbed Lily's hand.

Tyler gave Dat's shoulder one last pat. "A fuss at the wedding wouldn't do anybody any good."

Tyler marched out of the shed, and Aden and Lily followed close behind. Dat didn't move.

Lily looked toward the house. Women in blue, green, and purple dresses and men in dark hats and suspenders flocked to the yard. A row of buggies sat side by side on the road with a few cars and a van in the mix.

Tyler regarded the gathering crowd. "They're in for a surprise."

502

Aden kept a tight hold on Lily's hand. "There aren't enough words in the whole world to thank you, Tyler."

Tyler smirked. "Your lip is swollen and your nose is crooked. Why would anyone want to marry you?"

"I've been asking myself that all morning."

Tyler growled. "I'm really trying to hate you, Aden Helmuth, but I can't. I like you too much."

Lily sidled closer to Aden. "I'm sorry you got hurt, Tyler."

"I'm not. Stuff like this keeps me humble." Tyler swiped his hand across his forehead and let the air out of his lungs. "My uncles and aunts should be here by now."

"They're coming?" Aden asked.

"They've come all this way for a wedding. Might as well enjoy the food yet."

Aden laughed. "And glare at the groom."

"None of my family will glare at you. Except my mamm. She might give you a dirty look."

"I won't be offended."

"I know you won't. You think you deserve it." Tyler tromped to the front yard without looking back.

Dat marched past them on his way to the house. He didn't say anything, but he

503

looked as formidable as a gathering storm. With great effort, Lily subdued the powerful ache that filled every corner of her body.

She didn't fool Aden. He pulled her close to the house where curious eyes would be less likely to see them. "Oh, Lily, I'm so sorry."

The compassion in his voice unraveled her composure, and she let several tears slip down her cheeks. She sighed as he wrapped his strong arms around her, the best balm she could ask for.

"I feel like a big chunk has been ripped out of my heart," she said, nearly unintelligible between sobs. "He used to love me so much."

"He still loves you." Aden rested his chin on the top of her head and gently stroked her arm. "We don't have to marry today. You can go back home, and I will work to gain your father's approval. I could put up another mailbox."

Lily giggled through her tears. "Jah. That worked out so well."

He cleared his throat as if his next words might choke him. "Then if you want, I'll go away. I only want you to be happy."

She abruptly pulled out of his grasp. "You'll do no such thing. I don't have a life if not with you, even if it's in Ohio."

He smiled with relief and folded her into his arms. "What would you say if I bought Mrs. Deforest's old house? She offered to sell it to me yesterday. We'd be close enough to your family to mend some fences, I think."

Lily buried her face in his chest. "I . . . I would really like that."

He let her cry for a minute before nudging her chin with his finger. When she tilted her head up, he brought his lips down on hers and kissed her until she thought she might float to the sky. How did he do that?

He pulled away and took a step back. "I don't know how I could stand another day without you."

They neither of them saw him before it was too late. Pilot tore around the corner of the house, took a flying leap, and toppled Aden to the ground.

Clearly surprised, Aden threw his arms around Pilot's neck and let Pilot lick his cheek, his chin, his ear. When he'd had enough dog slobber, Aden tried to push Pilot off his chest. Having the time of his life toying with Aden, Pilot wouldn't budge. "Pilot, you rascal. Get off me." Aden looked at Lily, his eyes pleading. "Can you please get this dog under control?"

Lily giggled and folded her arms. "He's

505

your dog. You should have trained him better."

Aden groaned in exasperation. "I deserve that. Pilot's flattened you a few times." Aden struggled to his feet while Pilot did his best to thwart him. "Stupid dog," Aden said, "to trample a man on his wedding day." Aden brushed the dirt and grass from his trousers. The wet spots from landing in the snow would have to dry on their own. "I'm still reeling from that kiss. Pilot has never been able to knock me down before."

His eyes twinkled, and he leaned in for another kiss.

She held up a hand to stop him. "You've got dog germs all over your face."

His countenance fell. "Do you have lip sanitizer?"

"Here." Always prepared for an emergency, Lily pulled a package of wet wipes out of her coat pocket. Aden bent over and held his gaze on her as she tenderly cleaned his face, finishing with his lips, which to her knowledge hadn't touched dog saliva at all. But unable to resist that smiling mouth, she wiped it anyway just before giving him a kiss.

"Okay," he said in a loud, authoritative voice as they walked around to the front yard. "I'm marrying you right now. Does

Estee mind if we go first?"

They heard the creaking, scraping sound of a very sick vehicle before they saw it. A faded-yellow school bus lumbered up the road, wobbling and tilting to one side as its axles groaned and complained with every inch. The bus stopped in the middle of the road. Whoever drove didn't even bother to pull it to the side out of the way of oncoming traffic. The driver killed the engine, or it died of old age. Lily wasn't sure which.

The door swung open, and Jamal hopped out of the ancient bus, grinning as if he had parted the Red Sea.

With Lily determined to keep up, Aden sprinted to Jamal and hugged him as if to squeeze all the air out of his lungs.

"Jamal, I can't believe it!"

Jamal gave Aden a friendly slug. "You owe me, brother. Do you have any idea the hoops I had to jump through to find this bus last night? At midnight? And then, of course, none of your relatives have phones. That would have been too convenient."

Lily watched in amazement as one by one people emerged from the bus as if they'd just gotten off a roller coaster. They took stock of their surroundings and headed toward the house.

"I called about ten friends to round up

your family so I could get them here in time," Jamal said. "Your cousin Freeman's family wouldn't leave their house because they thought Dylan was a kidnapper."

Aden raised his scarred eyebrow. "You sent Dylan to pick up my cousins?"

"I know, I know, the tattoos and three nose rings make Amish people suspicious, but I didn't think they'd refuse to come."

An older man with thick glasses and a snowy white beard passed arm in arm with an equally elderly woman. She waved to Aden. "Hullo, Aden."

"Hullo, Aunt Hannah." Aden patted Jamal on the back. "I can't believe you're here."

"It took us all night, even though I broke every speed limit between here and Sugarcreek. I didn't want your family to miss it."

"What did my mamm say?"

"She didn't sleep on the bus, that's for sure. That woman could talk Snoop Lion under the table. She bawled me out for three hours and then spent the rest of the trip telling me what she planned to do to you. I'd steer clear of her if I were you."

"Aden?" a woman called from the direction of the bus.

"Too late," Aden said.

Two people who could only be Aden's parents stepped off the bus, walking as if

508

they hadn't used their legs for days. Aden's mamm was a small, wiry woman with dark eyes, a thin face, and a smattering of freckles across her nose. Just like Aden.

Aden's dat stood only a few inches shorter than Aden, with the same green eyes and square jaw. Lily could see the family resemblance with Felty too. Grandfather, father, and son all had a strong brow and intelligent eyes.

Jamal made a beeline for the house. "Don't let her see me."

Lily took a step back as Aden's mamm and dat hobbled closer. Aden's dat smiled affectionately, if wearily, and gave his son a stiff hug. His mamm frowned, reached up, and took Aden's face in her hands. He bent over as she stood on her tiptoes and pecked him on the cheek.

Aden's smile was so wide that the corners of his mouth almost touched his ears. "Mamm, I'm so glad you made it."

His mamm planted her hands on her hips and stared Aden down as if he were a pesky fly to swat. "You're *glad*? I got ten minutes' notice, young man. Ten minutes to pack my bags and get on that bus or I would miss my son's wedding. I was informed that my son, who never writes, was marrying a girl I've never met ten hours' drive from Sugarcreek. Have you no more consideration than that for your parents?" She jabbed a finger in the direction of the bus as her voice rose in pitch. "And that Jamal fellow is, hands down, the worst driver I have ever seen. He steers with his knee."

Aden twisted his mouth sheepishly. "I really wanted you to be here."

Aden's mamm didn't seem to draw a breath, even when she paused to let him answer. "No, if you'd really wanted us to be here, you would have hinted that you'd met a girl in one of your letters. Oh, I forgot. You only wrote us once to tell us you'd been arrested. Such a pleasant note for a mother to receive. If you'd really wanted us here, you would have told us you were engaged weeks ago and actually informed us of the date. You deserve a spanking, young man."

Aden wrapped his arms around his mamm and smiled. "Yes, I do, Mamm. I really do." She seemed to soften in his embrace. Lily smiled to herself. Who could resist Aden's innocent charm?

"I love you, Mamm," Aden said. "Don't ever forget that."

"I love you too, you big knucklehead." She cuffed him lightly on the back of the head.

"Ouch!" Aden rubbed the base of his skull even though his mamm hadn't given him more than a tap.

"I better be the first to hear about any new grandbabies, or there's more where that came from."

Another group of relatives disembarked from the bus. "Gute day for a wedding," someone called.

Aden waved and smiled. "Hello, Onkel Manny."

"And you can forget about a gift," Aden's mamm said. "They didn't have anything suitable at the gas station where we stopped to go to the bathroom."

Lily liked Aden's mamm instantly. It was easy to tell that she was all bluster and no bite. "I'm sorry," said Lily. "This is all my fault."

Aden's mamm turned her attention to Lily. "It's never the woman's fault, dear. Aden knows that."

Aden and his dat nodded to each other, as if they'd had this conversation dozens of times.

Aden's mamm bloomed into an affection-ate smile. "Are you the bride?"

Butterflies started making a fuss in Lily's stomach. Not butterflies — more like a herd of buffaloes. She was about to officially meet Aden's parents. "Jah. I am Lily Eicher."

"I am Frieda, Aden's mamm. To own the truth, Jamal couldn't say enough about you, Lily." Frieda shielded her mouth with her hand in case anybody tried to listen in. "That boy can talk the hind legs off a goat. But don't get him talking while he drives. He doesn't look at the road."

Lily giggled. "It's not safe to be in a car with him. Do you have another way home?"

Frieda took Lily by the arms and stared into her eyes as if she were trying to read her mind. "Lily Eicher, do you love my son?"

A thrill shot through her just thinking about it, and unbidden tears sprang to her eyes. "Jah, more than anything and with all my heart. I am so grateful he chose me. God is good."

Frieda kept her eyes locked on Lily. "Are you willing to put up with his nonsense?"

Aden rubbed the side of his face. "Mamm, I'm not going to get arrested ever again."

"Don't interrupt us, Aden. You have no say in this."

Lily wrapped her hands around Frieda's arms. "I'd chain myself to a tree for your son."

Frieda broke eye contact and glared at Aden. "Aden, you didn't!"

"Mamm, Lily has never chained herself to a tree."

Frieda nodded and smirked. "I'm glad to know she has more sense than that."

Those pesky tears managed to escape. "My heart's desire is Aden's happiness."

Frieda's eyes began to dance. "Will you see to it that he keeps himself out of trouble?"

"Of course."

To Lily's surprise, Frieda tugged her into a fierce embrace. "I told Emmon it would take a remarkable girl to see into Aden's heart. I'm so glad my son found you."

Out of the corner of her eye, Lily saw her mamm emerge from the house and march down the porch steps. Lily's throat dropped to her toes. What would Aden's parents think?

"Lily," said her mother, in a stern voice that Lily had probably only heard a handful of times in her life. "Tell me this instant what is going on."

Frieda turned to Mama with wide eyes. "You didn't know about this wedding either?"

Mama put her hands on her hips. "No, I certainly did not."

Aden's mamm propped her hands on her hips as well and glared at her son. "Aden, this is outrageous. What do you have to say for yourself?"

Aden grinned stupidly and shrugged.

"You must be Lily's mother," Frieda said.

Mama eyed Frieda suspiciously and nodded.

"I am Frieda Helmuth, and I am shocked, *shocked* by these goings-on. I hope you don't take this the wrong way, but I am almost glad that you didn't know about the wedding. I hate being the only one left in the dark."

Mama frowned. "This is wrong, Lily. You don't know what you're getting into."

"Mama, please try to understand. I love Aden." She sidled next to him and took his hand in full view of everyone. His warmth spread through her.

"But what about all the relatives?"

Frowning intently at Aden, Frieda hooked her arm around Mama's elbow and pulled her toward the house. "Cum. We must figure out a way to feed all these people you didn't expect. Have you got pickles? Everybody likes pickles."

Aden squeezed Lily's hand. "They'll work it out. My mamm has a way of making everything turn around all right."

"This is a lot of people to feed," Aden's dat said.

Lily twisted her mouth into an uncomfortable grimace. "My mama expected a wedding. She didn't expect Aden."

Aden's dat's forehead sprouted furrows. "Oh, my."

"There was a different groom," Aden added.

"Oh, my."

"Aden did nothing wrong. It's all my fault," Lily said.

"It's never the woman's fault," Aden's dat said.

He and Aden burst into brief laughter, and then Aden's dat stopped laughing as if someone had put a cork in his mouth. "Your mamm will have strong words for you when she finds out."

Aden groaned. "Do you think I could avoid her until I'm married? She won't be quite so mad when she knows she can't undo what's been done."

"Maybe I'll see if I can soften the blow." His dat hurried to the house.

Relatives and friends and complete strangers passed them on the way to the house. They waved and smiled and shared their congratulations. Pilot tried to greet everyone and scared more than one small child, until Felty appeared and grabbed him by the collar, tied him to a leash, and hooked the leash to a fence post.

Felty winked at Lily as he walked toward the house. Anna must have already gone inside. "I found Arizona," he said.

"Was it lost?"

"The license plate. It's on that rickety yellow bus over there. It wonders me who brought a school bus all the way from Arizona."

In the midst of the crowd, Aden turned and caressed Lily's cheek with his fingers. "My dearest, sweetest Lily, are you happy?"

"Happier than I could ever imagine."

He smiled with his whole face. "Then let's go make it permanent."

The Eicher home was packed in every nook and cranny with enough guests for three weddings. A temporary extension had been erected to the side of the house that sheltered two hundred people snugly. Another two hundred crammed into the Eichers' living room, hallways, and kitchen. Some of the youths sat outside on the porch, even though it was chilly, while others sat on the stairs and peered between the spindles of the banister. Anna found herself crowded to the edge of one of the women's rows sitting next to Felty who was squished on the end of one of the men's rows.

"Isn't this lovely, Felty?" Anna said. "We've never sat together in church before."

"You'll have to make sure I stay awake, Banannie. With all the goings-on last night, I don't think I got but four hours of sleep."

Anna sighed. "Wasn't it wondrous?"

"Do you think David Eicher will scowl through the entire service?" Felty said, straining to see David's face.

"Of course, dear. But look at how happy Aden is. Everyone should be that happy. We made a very good match."

"Praise the Lord. But let's not match anyone else. I've lost too much sleep."

"Don't worry, dear. I'll make sure you stay awake long enough to see your grandson married. Wouldn't it be wonderful gute if we could make someone else that happy?"

"Nobody needs any help from us, Annie Banannie."

"Look, Felty. Tyler Yoder's whole family came. What a nice bunch of people."

"That or they're planning on ambushing Aden right after the service."

"Now, Felty." Anna patted Felty's arm. "Tyler is such a fine young man. It pains me to see him so unhappy." Anna lowered her voice, in case the three hundred people sitting within earshot took interest in her conversation. "He would do very well for our great-granddaughter Beth."

"Beth? Don't even think about it, Annie. She told me herself she doesn't want to marry again. That first husband of hers was a pill."

"It's not Christian to speak ill of the dead, Felty. Besides, all the more reason to match her with a gute boy who will fill her life with love instead of bitterness."

Felty might have thrown his hands in the air in surrender if not that they were pinned by Enos Kanagy on one side and Anna on the other. "Don't say I didn't warn you. You'll get nowhere with Beth."

"Hush, Felty. I'm already set on bringing Beth and Tyler together. Wild horses couldn't convince me otherwise."

"Believe me, Annie. I already know."

Lily fidgeted on the bench through three songs, two sermons, and two prayers. Even though her dat's glare bored a hole through her head, she felt like a bird about to take flight. Aden had never looked so handsome, and church had never seemed so long.

Estee alternated between mooning at Floyd and studying Lily with concern. Lily squeezed Estee's hand reassuringly. Even with Dat's displeasure, it was the best day of her life.

Almost envious of her sister's good fortune to go first, Lily watched as Estee and Floyd stood facing each other before the bishop and took their vows. Floyd shook so violently that he seemed to be tapping his foot to a silent rhythm.

The bishop hadn't seen fit to enlighten the congregation about the change in grooms. News spread like influenza in an Amish community, even without cell phones and email, but there were still a few gasps and puzzled expressions when Aden Helmuth stood to receive Tyler Yoder's bride.

Lily couldn't take her eyes off Aden. How could she even begin to contain the overflowing love in her heart? She felt like a cherry tree bent to the ground, laden with plump, red fruit. The windows of heaven had truly opened, and there was not room enough to receive her blessings.

The bishop had nearly finished when Pilot, using someone's shoulders as a springboard, leaped over the boys sitting on the porch and through the open front door. Some of the women squealed, and more than one man stood to see if he could shoo Pilot out of the house. Lily even heard a little laughter mixed in. Pilot created quite a kerfuffle as he planted his paws on Aden's nice blue shirt and licked Aden's face.

Lily used her sternest tone. "Pilot, get down."

Pilot sank to all fours, whined pathetically at Lily, and planted himself by her side. He watched with silent curiosity and excellent manners as the bishop, without missing a word, finished the wedding vows and announced that Lily and Aden were now married.

You don't know what you're getting into, her mama had warned.

But Lily *did* know.

Lord willing, she would live a long life with the man she adored, the man she had risked everything for, the man with the slobbery, aggravating, adorable dog.

A life full of love, rejoicing, and gallons of hand sanitizer.